PRINCE OF LEGEND

Thanks to the stratagems of Bohemund de Hauteville, leader of the Apulian Normans, the Crusade has taken the city of Antioch, and just in time. Once the besiegers, Bohemund and his men are about to become besieged – a huge Turkish-led army, commanded by the fearsome General Kerbogha, is fast approaching. Provisions are needed to support not only the army, but also thousands of camp followers and pilgrims. But the surrounding countryside is near barren and the storerooms of Antioch much depleted. It soon becomes obvious that the Crusaders cannot hold out long without falling prey to starvation.

PRINCE OF LEGEND

PRINCE OF LEGEND

by

Jack Ludlow

Magna Large Print Books
Long Preston, North Yorkshire,
BD23 4ND, England.

British Library Cataloguing in Publication Data.

Ludlow, Jack
    Prince of legend.

    A catalogue record of this book is
    available from the British Library

    ISBN   978-0-7505-3936-4

First published in Great Britain by Allison & Busby in 2013

Copyright © 2013 by David Donachie
(writing as Jack Ludlow)

Cover illustration © Collaboration JS by arrangement with
Arcangel Images

Published in Large Print 2015 by arrangement with
Allison & Busby Limited

Magna Large Print is an imprint of Library Magna Books Ltd.

Printed and bound in Great Britain by
T.J. (International) Ltd., Cornwall, PL28 8RW

To Bob Sykes
who coached Junior Rugby with me for a decade:
all those cold wet Sundays were worth it, Robert!

PROLOGUE

Bohemund de Hauteville, Count of Taranto and leader of the Apulian Normans, stood on the narrow glacis before the massive and forbidding fortress that dominated the skyline. The citadel of Antioch had been the lynchpin of the city during the eight-month siege and a position from which Yaghi Siyan, the Turkish governor, had co-ordinated every act of the tenacious defence.

Designed for a twin purpose, it formed part of the mighty outer walls of the city but also served as a place to which the garrison could retreat if the mass of Antiochene citizens, Armenian Christians, broke out in revolt. The citadel was a stronghold with its own water cistern and storerooms that they could hold until the time came to reassert control.

Tancred of Lecce, Bohemund's nephew, stood with him, both Crusaders covered from head to foot in the blood of the numberless victims they had slaughtered in a night of bloody mayhem that had brought the siege of the city to an end. It had been a sore trial of a contest, in which they had experienced both the abundance of food as well as near starvation, summer heat and winter chill, and fought battles against the near impenetrable walls as well as far to the east in open country, this to drive off two attempts at relief by the Seljuk Turks. Now, finally, the crusading army were inside, if not completely in control.

That last point was one of some importance and it did not merely apply to the Turks: prior to the fall, Bohemund had engaged in a battle of wills with his fellow crusading magnates as to who should have possession of Antioch when it fell, he insisting the law of conquest must apply – that whosoever could first breech the walls then raise their standard above the city, by long custom, should have possession of it.

A proposition originally and vehemently denied, especially by Counts Raymond of Toulouse and Hugh of Vermandois, it had only been acceded to when the position of the besiegers became so desperate that any means of achieving a result, in what was a rapidly deteriorating outlook, must be accepted.

A call went up to the new Turkish leader, who stood on the barbican that protected the gate, the demand simple: that he should open that portal and surrender. Shams ad-Daulah, eldest son of the now deceased governor, spoke neither the Frankish tongue nor Latin and Greek, so these words had to be translated into his own tongue, this carried out by the fellow who had aided Bohemund in the capture of the city.

A Muslim convert called Firuz, he had commanded one of the towers on the southern wall with a body of his fellow Armenians, initially with as much zeal as any of his Turkish contemporaries, only to find his efforts not appreciated by Yaghi Siyan, who had, to keep him loyal, stripped him of his possessions, an act that had rebounded spectacularly. Firuz had conspired with Bohemund and allowed his tower to be used as the point of entry.

'You know who I am?'

'Who could fail to recognise mighty Bohemund?' the Greek-speaking interpreter replied, following his master's lead.

There was truth in that; given his height and build, massive even for one of Norman blood, as well as his flaxen-coloured hair, not to mention his fame, he could be identified easily even at a distance. Bohemund stood head and shoulders above his peers, wherever they came from, even those from his father's Normandy birthplace. Tancred, his mother a de Hauteville and of towering height himself, still conceded half a hand to his uncle.

'On yonder high battlement you will see my banner.'

The pointed finger was hardly necessary; the huge red flag, with its diagonal bar showing the blue and white chequer of the de Hauteville family, flew stiff in a strong breeze and was easily visible from anywhere on the wide expanse of the River Orontes plain, lit as it was by the blazing morning sun.

'We have possession of the city and we have the body of your father, who failed to make good his escape. If you wish that to be respected, and if you wish yourself to live, grant us possession of this fortress and march out with all honour.'

Two heads came close and composed the reply, which occasioned much discussion before the interpreter spoke once more. 'My Lord esteems his father still, but says if he is dead, then his

13

body is of no account, for his soul will surely be welcomed into paradise.'

'Where your master shall join him,' Bohemund responded.

This got a furious reaction from Shams ad-Daulah when translated, which his interpreter sought to pass on by a form of shouting strangely devoid of a similar level of passion.

'Idle boast, Christian, you have got inside the walls of our city, but My Lord holds this citadel. Allah be praised, it is written that you will die here, for an army of the faithful is coming that will crush you like a fly.'

That had Tancred swiftly crossing himself, that being no idle boast: a Turkish relief force, led by a general with a fearsome reputation called Kerbogha, famed across Asia Minor for both the application of terror and military success, was marching towards Antioch, leading an army of such staggering reported numbers that made the notion of meeting them in open battle seem suicidal, given the crusading army was now a much reduced force, fully half the number it had been when they set out from Constantinople.

The Atabeg of Mosul, Kerbogha had, with the active support of the Sultan in Baghdad, united the many disparate elements of the interior, Turkish, Arab and Persian tribes that normally fought each other, melding them into a body large enough to annihilate these troublesome western invaders.

It was the approach of these forces that had prompted swift action from the Frankish princes in both pressing home the siege and accepting the law of conquest, for they feared to be crushed between the anvil of Yaghi Siyan's stout defence of his city and the approaching host. Yet it was telling, and a testament to the strength of Antioch, that only internal betrayal had provided the key to its fall.

In essence, when it came to Kerbogha, the Crusaders were a victim of their own success: brought east by a plea from Pope Urban to aid Greek Byzantium in its century-old conflict with the Seljuk Turks, the true task was to proceed on to Palestine and free from the control of Islam the Holy Places of Christendom, visited each year by Christians in their thousands and from which came, regularly, tales of those pilgrims being maltreated – robbed, women molested, both they and their menfolk sometimes killed.

The fury engendered by such tales had come in the wake of yet another entreaty from the Emperor Alexius Comnenus – there had been dozens over the previous decades – claiming that the faith in the east, the Greek Orthodox Church, was in danger of annihilation from these Turkish infidels. Byzantium had gained much from the arrival from Europe of a truly formidable host, the cream of Europe's fighting men, Alexius Comnenus directing them first to invest that which he saw as the greatest threat to Constantinople, the formidable city of Nicaea.

Turkish held and only three days' march from Constantinople, Nicaea was a vital bastion that threatened the very heart of an empire that had failed to recapture it in three attempts and had little hand in taking on this occasion. Thanks to the efforts of the Crusader Host, the imperial banner now flew from its battlements, which in turn secured the safety of the imperial capital.

From there the Crusade moved south: originally seen as an irritant when Nicaea succumbed, they had impinged more and more upon the Sultan's concerns the further they progressed, winning battles and taking possession of populous regional centres without a fight, stinging him especially hard when one of their number, Baldwin of Boulogne, acting independently of the Crusade and keen to line his own purse, had invested and captured the important city of Edessa on the far side of the River Euphrates.

Yet the main body had come to worry the Sultan more: they had swept aside one attempt to check them at the Battle of Dorylaeum, then, with seeming impunity, had marched across Anatolia and Armenia to invest mighty Antioch, once the third greatest city in the Roman Empire, and this had provoked a spirited reaction. Both the sons of the Sultan had separately tried to relieve Antioch – they hated each other too much to combine – and had been fought off and forced to flee. What was coming now was of a different order of magnitude.

Safety lay with the walls and that had now been achieved, yet if going from months of investing Antioch to possession of the city was change enough, to also turn from besieger to being besieged was singular. To simultaneously be both was the strangest state of all for they must contain this citadel and its garrison, a bane throughout the months of siege, standing, as it did, on such an

16

elevated mountain top location as to give it a clear sight of any preparations being made for an assault on gates or walls.

Likewise, any gathering and movement of mobile forces on the Antiochene Plain had to take place in plain view, allowing the late Yaghi Siyan to send out his mounted archers to counter any threat, or to merely ensure that the gates or section of the walls the besiegers were aiming to attack were both closed and well defended. This made worse what was an already gruelling task, for the defences of Antioch were legendary in their construction.

No pilgrim knight, on the return journey from Jerusalem, failed to mention to his avid home listeners how formidable they were. Sat at the base of two mountains and with the River Orontes on Antioch's western flank, the walls were held to be impregnable. Not only did they restrict the attacker on the riverside, constricting the area in which a besieger could operate, but the high and multi-towered walls rose up the steep mountainsides in a way that made them impossible to overcome; the citadel, if it did not enjoy these advantages to the same degree, was nevertheless a redoubtable fortress in its own right.

'There is no taking this place but by ladders,' said Tancred, in response to the retort by Shams ad-Daulah, the way that was said testimony to how hard such an assault would be.

The response from his uncle was equally grim in tone. 'Yet take it we must.'

The truth of Tancred's assertion was self-evident: the walls were high, the garrison that

17

had escaped into the fort from the lower city likely to be numerous and aware their sole options were surrender or death. From the gate before which they stood ran a winding path that led down into the teeming city and that would need to be held at all costs, while the single piece of flat ground before it was the one on which both these knights stood, the rest being surrounded by screed-covered inclines which would not allow for the application of any other form of siege equipment.

Bohemund's response that it must be taken was just as apposite: the main threat was not from within the walls of the citadel but before the main defences of the city, yet there was no doubt Shams ad-Daulah would essay out to do battle if he were allowed, which meant a split in the forces opposing him.

Those two difficulties were confounded by the fact that Antioch was not in a good state of supply. Eight months of diminishing provisions – slowly the besiegers had increased their stranglehold on the city gates – had left it short of food. In eight months the Crusaders had near stripped the locality bare and with Kerbogha approaching fast there was little time for the Crusaders to forage, of necessity far and wide, and make good that combined dearth.

'Then let us hope for another betrayal, nephew, that there is someone within the walls that wants so badly to live that he will deny his faith.'

Bohemund turned to engage the Armenian who had facilitated his entry, a man who spoke good Greek. 'Firuz, put your best efforts to making contact with someone, anyone inside.'

'Lord Bohemund!'

That call forced him to face an approaching messenger, clearly intent on delivering a communication of some import judging by the speed of his approach and his concerned expression, as well as his sweaty demeanour.

'Count Raymond of Toulouse has taken possession of the Bridge Gate and his standard flies above it.'

Bohemund uttered a hissed curse, for if anyone had stood in the way of his claim of conquest it was the aforesaid Raymond. He looked beyond him to see the truth of the words spoken, for the gate was visible from where he stood, as was every feature of the huge city. Then he turned once more to gaze up at the solid and impressive walls of the citadel. Softly he addressed Tancred, who would also know the importance of that information.

'Not all our fights, it seems, will be here in the coming weeks.'

CHAPTER ONE

The bright red standard with the gilded Occitan cross, the flag of the Count of Toulouse, fluttered from the Bridge Gate barbican to taunt Bohemund the closer he approached. The most powerful, as well as the wealthiest of the crusading princes, this Provençal magnate had never been happy with the application of the right of conquest, for the fear it would not fall to him. He had chosen well if he intended to dispute possession of the city with the leader of the Apulian Normans as well as the banner high above the city that proclaimed it as a fief for Bohemund.

Outside the Bridge Gate lay the only crossing of the River Orontes, while over that arched stone bridge ran the roads that led north and south as well as to the coast and the port of St Simeon. These were all the points from which any supplies could come to what was now becoming a Crusader garrison and one Toulouse could choke off from resupply if he so chose.

As of this moment the Bridge Gate, like the rest of the entries to Antioch, was wide open: knights who had spent months outside Antioch – Provençal, Normans, Apulians and Lotharingians in their thousands – were busy moving all their possessions into the city and behind them would come their foot-slogging *milities*, then those who provided support for an army on campaign: camp wives, sutlers, farriers, armourers, harness and saddle makers, as well as the drovers who looked after food on the hoof, people without which no host could hope to survive in the field.

Last to enter would be the mass of non-combatant religious pilgrims who had increasingly swelled the numbers travelling to Palestine in the wake of the fighting men, all intent on finding remission for past sins as promised to them by Pope Urban. Useless mouths, who nevertheless demanded to be fed, they could not be left outside: Kerbogha would simply massacre them.

To observe the army, as it trickled through the gates, was to cast an eye over a much diminished force, for it was no longer the all-powerful entity that had crossed the Bosphorus from Constantinople the previous year; siege warfare, battles in the field, disease, loss of faith in the crusading ideal leading to desertion had plagued them prior to Antioch.

The long siege had only multiplied every one of those difficulties tenfold and nowhere was that more obvious than in their lack of horses. The main advantage for western knights in combat lay in their ability to impose their will by a shock charge when mounted, the foot soldiers used more as an aid to that than a body able to affect the outcome of a battle on their own.

Now that force of knights could barely muster one horse for every tenth lance and in terms of quality they could not compare with the kind of mounts with which they had set out from home; too many of those had died on the way. The Normans, in particular, whether from the rain-washed north or sun-baked Southern Italy, were reckoned the most fearsome warriors in the known world but that reputation rested on animals they no longer possessed, the sturdy destriers as fearless as the men who rode them.

No contingent, when they had set out, had been any better supplied when it came to horses trained for battle. Now, even with careful husbandry – Bohemund had sent his herds away when they were not required to places with pasture – they were as near to deficiency as any of the others.

As he approached the Bridge Gate the thought

of fighting for possession had to be put aside, regardless of the tactics employed; the Crusade was a delicate construct, led by men who were too proud to allow anyone to hold sway over their actions. But the one purpose they all shared and one that they had sworn the most solemn oaths to progress was that an army must march on to Jerusalem to make it once more a Christian city.

That any of the princes should allow their pride to overcome their faith, that any of their men should fall to fighting and killing each other rather than the infidel, was held to be anathema and a certain route to perdition. The only result of such an action would be the complete collapse of the enterprise, with a massive amount of opprobrium being heaped on those who had broken their vows.

Trial by single combat as a means of settling disputes was also out of the question, yet by his action Toulouse had taken the harmony and cohesion which had sustained the Crusade so far, albeit often strained, dangerously close to breaking, so close that one inadvertent incident, the kind of unforeseen accident committed by any man high or low in a passion, could fatally fracture it.

On the way down from the citadel Bohemund had heard of the other places seized by Toulouse, the Governor's Palace being one, but such things were baubles compared to the Bridge Gate, which was a strategic asset of huge significance.

'I hope we Apulians still hold the St Paul's Gate?' Bohemund asked, looking at that bright red Toulouse banner atop the barbican. 'Otherwise I feel a squeezing hand upon my groin.'

'It seems,' Tancred responded bitterly, 'that our Count Raymond spent more time securing this gate than in seeking out and disposing of our enemies in the city. Perhaps if he and his knights had attended to that we might have the citadel too.'

The mention of the fortress had Bohemund turning round and craning his neck; above the city flew not only his standard but also the green crescent banner of Yaghi Siyan, which had fluttered throughout the siege and was now the insignia of Shams ad-Daulah. It was as if both were mocking him, telling him that for all he desired possession of the city he still had a long hard fight on his hands to make it so.

'Come, Tancred, we smell of death and blood. Let us bathe and change before we face our foes.'

'Is Toulouse now a foe?'

Bohemund pointed at the man's fluttering standard above his head. 'By such an act as this he may have rendered himself so.'

No meeting of the Council of Princes, the body set up to coordinate the joint efforts of the Papal Crusade, could be convened before the man who called it into being had said a Mass for victory. In the city of Antioch there was only one location where such a celebration could take place, for it was here that St Peter had founded his first church, carved out of a cave in the side of one of the twin peaks that dominated the city and thus one of the holiest places in Christendom.

For a religion that venerated Jesus as a prophet

to rank with Muhammad, it was saddening that the Turks had recently used it as a latrine but that was soon remedied by willing pilgrim hands and the application of vinegar. With blazing candles illuminating the interior and much plain chant from the attendant monks, the papal legate, Adémar de Monteil, Bishop of Puy, had led his dukes and counts into the sacred space.

Raymond of Toulouse was there, carrying his fifty years well, tall and florid of face, never willing to catch the eye of the Count of Taranto, not easy in any case since Bohemund was forced to bend his head in such a low enclosure due to his remarkable height. Equally guarded in such a place, where God could see into their innermost thoughts and tot up their sins, came Count Hugh of Vermandois, brother of the King of France: slim, handsome, blue eyes, golden-haired and with an arrogance to go with a lack of military ability hidden from everyone but himself.

Two Roberts followed: the Duke of Normandy, second son of William the Conqueror, and alongside him the Count of Flanders, his brother-in-law – another relative of that contingent, Stephen of Blois, had abandoned the siege and retired further north to the safety of Alexandretta. Each magnate held their own thoughts masked, aware that following their devotions matters would be brought to the fore that would require them to take a position for what was rapidly turning into a choice of faction.

Only Godfrey de Bouillon, the barrel-chested Duke of Lower Lorraine, seemed unaffected by what was to come, his much battered face alight with devotion. Pious and without any personal ambition other than to reach and take Jerusalem from the infidel, his round face shone with the sheer delight of being in such a hallowed cave. On entering, Godfrey fell to his knees and allowed his head to touch the floor in obeisance to the memory of Christ's leading disciple.

At the tiny rock altar, Adémar began his Latin Mass in the company of the much abused and venerable John the Oxite, previously Patriarch of Antioch until removed by the Turks. Outside in the still bloodstained streets – the bodies of the Turkish slain had been tossed into a deep pit or the River Orontes, which would carry them out to sea – men and women, both Roman and Armenian in their Christianity, many of whom had converted to Islam to survive, knelt and prayed in unison with a cleric most of them could not understand, happy to be alive and able to take from the passing priests of both branches of the faith the absolution for their transgressions which was being freely distributed.

'Antioch belongs to the Emperor Alexius Comnenus, as many here confirmed by sacred oath and for which I gave my bounden word, which no man is at liberty to break.'

'That is not disputed.'

Bishop Adémar, as he uttered that reply, gave Raymond of Toulouse, who had made such a forthright statement, the kind of look that implied he should calm himself, for the way he had spoken lacked the necessary level of diplomacy when dealing with men of equal rank. Once the

25

possessor of an unlined and rosy countenance –
the kind of well-fed, youthful and contented face
too often the condition of high clerics – time and
the cares of the Crusade, not least the need to
keep happy this assembly of proud magnates,
had played upon Adémar till he had now begun
to look like an old man.

'It would be foolish, My Lord Bishop,' Hugh of
Vermandois interjected, 'not to acknowledge that
there is ambition in that direction.'

Robert of Normandy responded to that with a
slice of wicked wit; if he was ever at war with his
brother the King of England for possession of his
lands, then his other enemy on his eastern border
was France, so bearding the royal sibling Vermandois, a man devoid of irony, was a game he enjoyed.

'We all accept that you have aspirations for
Antioch, Count Hugh.'

A wise man would have shucked that aside;
Vermandois was a dolt. 'I do not mean myself
and you know it.'

'Our Lord Bishop may have an insight into the
souls of men,' Robert intoned sonorously, 'God
has not granted me that ability.'

'We are all ambitious in the cause of God,'
Adémar snapped, impatiently falling back on an
unassailable reminder of their purpose to kill off
the secret smiles caused by the Frenchman's
stupidity. 'Which is why we are where we are.'

He then gave Normandy a bit of a glare that extended to his equally amused brother-in-law of
Flanders: he knew there were more telling disputes in this chamber, the one-time palace of the

26

Turkish Governor, than the bearding of the arrogant Vermandois. The question that troubled him and one he was determined to keep from open disclosure was who would side with whom between the two emerging protagonists seeking to clarify the situation of Antioch, Bohemund and Raymond.

By the right of conquest, previously agreed, the Count of Taranto had a valid claim to the city, albeit he was bound by oath, sworn on the bones of martyrs in front of the Emperor Alexius in the imperial palace, to hold it for Byzantium. Yet Bohemund and his late father, as well as his numerous de Hauteville uncles, had fought that polity and a succession of emperors all their lives, first in South Italy, now under their control and then in the lands of Romania, which in the previous decade the Apulians had twice invaded.

Should he be given sole possession would Bohemund keep to his word and hand Antioch back to his old enemy Alexius Comnenus, who should, at this very moment, be marching with all his might to their aid? Would a man like Bohemund even hold it for Byzantium with the Emperor as his acknowledged suzerain? If he did not, he would not only break his own oath but the given undertaking of everyone present.

'I would suggest,' Bohemund said, 'that such a discussion, given what we face, is a distraction.'

'Better discussed now than left to fester on an altar of greed,' Raymond responded, making no attempt to soften his tone.

'My Lords!'

That loud interruption focused all eyes on

Godfrey de Bouillon, a man respected by all present for there could be no accusation of ambition related to him, if you excluded the recapture of Jerusalem.

'The army of this Kerbogha is on its way to us and we have yet to have news that Byzantium is likewise marching, and even if it is, Kerbogha will get here long before the Emperor. How we deal with such a threat carries more weight than talk of personal ambition, in whosoever breast it may reside. What hopes and stratagems do we have to deal with – that should be paramount.'

'Quite,' Adémar concurred. 'Let us put aside all discussion of the possession of Antioch...'

'We have yet to discuss it at all!' Raymond cried.

'And we will in time, My Lord,' the Bishop replied with unaccustomed firmness, he and Toulouse being close. 'But we face a threat to our very existence, and with that we must take issue first.'

Vermandois was quick to respond. 'We must hold the walls with the same spirit as those we have just overcome.'

Godfrey de Bouillon was quick to pounce on that. 'Then I suggest, Count Hugh, that you withdraw your men stationed at the Iron Bridge to help man them.'

'They are there for a purpose, as is my banner.'

That induced an uncomfortable silence; the standard and the man to whom it belonged were well separated, for he had not assumed personal command at the Iron Bridge but devolved it to an inferior captain. Crossing that viaduct provided

28

the main route an army must take to invest the city – the Crusaders had done so eight months previously, finding it undefended by Yaghi Siyan.

Now French knights and *milities* in some numbers had garrisoned it. No one but Vermandois saw what he had done as a sensible move, suspecting he had only made it to assert his independence and to have the fleur-de-lis flying over something.

'If what we are told of his numbers is accurate,' Godfrey continued, 'to meet this Kerbogha in the open would not serve. That we have agreed and I cannot see that the Iron Bridge falls outside that.'

That got what was an almost childlike pout from the royal brat. 'The bridge is fortified and the river flows too strong for easy fording above and below. I have no doubt my men will hold it long enough to delay Kerbogha.'

'How far off is he?' Adémar asked, which deflected any more discussion, it being the business of Vermandois alone how he disposed of his lances. He had never been inclined to heed the advice of others better qualified in warfare, for he would not admit to the notion. To press him would only have him dig in his heels.

'Days away,' Robert of Flanders replied, for it was his scouts who were out to the east and had provided the latest intelligence. 'He stopped to invest Edessa, but raised it after only a week to come on to Antioch, which does not much aid us.'

That had everyone looking at Godfrey de Bouillon again: Baldwin, who held Edessa, was his wayward brother and a man over whom hung certain questions, one his actions in leaving the Crusade without warning and another regarding a massacre of a body of Norman knights outside Tarsus the previous year. If the Duke of Lower Lorraine was seen as something of a saint, then Baldwin of Boulogne, or as he now preferred to be called, of Edessa, was the obverse side of the family coin.

Bohemund spoke speedily to spare the blushes of a fellow magnate he esteemed; of all men he knew that no one could be held accountable for their relatives, given he had troublesome de Hauteville cousins in abundance, as well as a half-brother he loathed.

'Abandoning a siege of Edessa can only have come about because of the news sent to him from here. Yaghi Siyan must have intimated Antioch was in such grave danger of falling that for Kerbogha to delay outside Edessa would be to risk the city.'

'A look at the grain stores confirms his concerns were well founded.'

That interjection came from the Duke of Normandy, in times past, albeit decades, the de Hauteville family suzerain, one to whom Bohemund responded with no hint of servility; what had pertained in the old homelands did not do so here.

'Then we had best get foraging to seek to get those storerooms filled again, for without food we will not hold the Atabeg of Mosul at bay for the time we need, which is to allow Byzantium to affect the issue.'

Adémar was quick to concur – anything to

delay discussion of Antiochene possession, the solution to which, he thought, rested with the personal presence of Alexius Comnenus. Once he was here and with soldiers to support him, the Emperor could decide if he wanted an old enemy in control of such an important fief, or someone in whom he could repose more trust.

'We must send messengers to tell the Emperor Alexius that Antioch is ours and to make all speed with every man he can muster. Combined, we will outnumber this Kerbogha and drive him back from whence he came.'

As he spoke the words Adémar could not avoid a look at Bohemund, to see how such a notion, the idea of Alexius being present in person, was being received; all he observed was bland indifference.

'Kerbogha must thread the bulk of his army across the Iron Bridge, is that not so?'

Tancred received an affirmative reply to that. The so-called Iron Bridge, which spanned the River Orontes north of Antioch, in reality made of arched stone, had tall, fortified towers at either end and lay a shade over two leagues distant to the north of the city. How it had come by its designation as 'iron' was a mystery no one had bothered to seek to solve.

'Then why does Duke Godfrey so vehemently disagree with Count Hugh that we should deny him that crossing, or at the very least impose a check on his advance? Time, after all, is our ally.'

Not wishing to give an immediate reply, Bohemund cast an eye over the shoulder to look at the

31

convoy of wagons they were escorting, supplies they were fetching from a pair of Genoese ships that had berthed the day before at the nearby port of St Simeon, bringing with them a welcome cargo. What they carried looked impressive: dozens of ox-drawn and fully laden carts, the contents of the ships' holds, impressive until you counted the mouths such a cargo must feed.

Provisions had to be found for twenty thousand fighting men, both knights and *milities*, many weakened by various disorders brought on by siege warfare and needing to be brought back to full health and strength, as well as the same number of camp followers and pilgrims, so it would scarce last for a week. A clearing of his throat from Tancred brought his mind back to his nephew's question.

'The men Vermandois has placed there can hold the Iron Bridge for a time, but eventually they will have to seek to retire or die where they stand, and flight on foot will bring about that same fate. The Turks, on their fast ponies, will fill their backs with their arrows.'

'Then give them mounts.'

'We require that we use every horse we have left for foraging, Tancred. Give the bridge guard mounts and they will fight on them, after which they would be blown, not able to outrun their too numerous enemies, so the horses will either die also or fall into enemy hands. Kerbogha, given his strength, will take Iron Bridge, so all Vermandois will do is put a minimal check on the Turks and at great loss to our cause in terms of fighting men. He would be best to admit we lack the power to keep the Atabeg from the city and, as of this moment, don't have much chance of keeping him outside without the Emperor comes to our aid.'

'Do I sense you doubt that he will?' Tancred asked in disbelief.

'Let's just say I have dealt with Byzantium all of my life and at no time have I ever reposed faith that they will hold to their given promise. The lack of any word of his approach troubles me. At the very least he might be too far off to affect what we face.'

'Then what hope do we have?'

'Hope that when Kerbogha spies the walls of Antioch and sees we are on the parapets, he decides it is too tough to assault and too strong to starve out.'

'He will know within an hour of his arrival how low we are on the means to feed ourselves. A goodly number of the Armenians who claim to have reconverted to Christianity are still Islamic at heart. Those who are not will be in terror of his revenge and eager to ingratiate themselves with information, lest he seeks to slit their throats.'

'True, but when you ask me what will happen in the coming days, which I think you are about to do, I will remind you many times of what I have said before and that is I cannot see into the future.'

Now it was Tancred's turn to smile. 'There are those who say you can, Uncle, have indeed insisted you had your eye on Antioch before we even sailed from Brindisi.'

There was a degree of irritation in the response. 'Then they are fools and I hope and pray that description does not include you.'

'It would be revealing to see into the mind of Raymond of Toulouse, to find out if he shares such desires.'

'I sense you are trying to provoke me, Tancred, so that you may be allowed to see into my mind. Antioch is mine by agreement among my peers, to hold until Alexius arrives, at which time I will claim it with him as suzerain and that is all you will find should you succeed, along with thoughts and concerns as to how we are going to keep Kerbogha at bay till then. Perhaps, if you could see into the mind of Toulouse, you would come across the same disquiet.'

They were now passing La Mahomerie, the siege fort the Crusaders had built on the plain before the Bridge Gate, improving with heavy timbers the site of an abandoned mosque. Robert of Flanders now held that and it had been decided it should be defended and denied to Kerbogha, albeit with a plan for safe abandonment. There had been another exterior siege fort, Malregard, which Bohemund had constructed on the hillside above what had come to be called the St Paul's Gate, outside which the Apulians had been encamped.

It was a spot he had specifically chosen at the beginning of the siege, for the gate had obvious advantages. It was the northernmost entrance to the city and the only place with a wide and flat approach in ground that meant that a section of the walls could be closely invested in strength. Thus, if a breakthrough was to be achieved, it offered the most likely place where the walls could be overcome. Yet it had disadvantages too;

it suffered from being exposed to attacks from the steep hillside of Mount Staurin, the slightly lower peak that dominated the north of Antioch, which lay to its left.

Malregard had been built to counter that threat, but now being indefensible from within the walls it had been set alight and burnt to cinders, likewise the bridge of boats put together by Godfrey de Bouillon had been broken up to deny it to the enemy. That, a pontoon of lashed barges, had given good if hazardous service in crossing the Orontes to provide support for those camped on the exposed sliver of the eastern bank and likely to be outnumbered by a sudden attack.

For all his concerns Bohemund knew that Kerbogha would suffer from the same difficulties that had faced the Crusaders on coming to Antioch: those steep walls that ran up the side of and around the mountains north and south of the city were impervious to assault, as much for the loose screed that covered the ground as the sheer degree of the slope itself.

On the east bank of the Orontes the spit of land between the western wall and the river was too narrow to safely camp men in any number and this left them vulnerable to sorties from within, as the Latins had found many times to their cost. That same stretch of water cut off any main body of fighters from the men who must invest the southernmost entry to Antioch, named by the Crusaders as the gate of St George, while to get across in force, lacking a pontoon of boats, required a long detour south to the next proper bridge.

Past La Mahomerie, the convoy was in plain sight of the Bridge Gate and that bright red and gold Occitan banner. If the Apulians were bringing welcome supplies, there was no air of gratitude in the men designated to guard it: they were surly, no doubt taking their cue from their lord and master. Just before he went under the barbican and through the gates Bohemund, still thinking on what was coming, looked up to the one huge advantage gifted to Kerbogha that had not been granted to the Crusade.

Any lookout from the high citadel could tell him where the walls of Antioch were well manned or weak. Men could be brought in from the rear through the mountains, less steep on their eastern flank, for part of that citadel formed the outer defence of the high part of the city and it had an exterior gate. From within they could debouch in strength which meant that would have to be contained, thus diminishing the numbers that could man the other points of danger; holding the city was going to be much harder for the Crusaders than it had been for the Turks.

If cogitating on this troubled Bohemund, or even Tancred – seventeen years the younger and much less experienced than his uncle – it would not have brought on dread; they were men born to fight and that brought with it the ever-present possibility of death. If God willed that Antioch was the place where they gave up life so be it, but that would not be sold cheaply by men who valued that their deeds be recounted to a listening world, long after they were gone, as the acts of paragons.

CHAPTER TWO

Nearly every available horse was being used in foraging, yet good sense dictated that a small body of cavalry be kept by each of the city gates ready to sortie out in case of need – not to necessarily do battle but to put a check on any sudden appearance by any advance party of Turks.

That duly came to pass: a body of some two hundred mounted archers was spotted to the south of the city and their presence, if left unchallenged, might cut off the Crusaders from the fertile Ruj Valley, one place where if food was not plentiful – the locals had taken to hiding it in cellars and pits – such locations could at least be tortured out of them.

Thus the horns blew and everyone not occupied rushed to the walls to watch their champions ride out to drive off the infidel. In command on the St George's Gate was Roger de Barneville, one of Bohemund's most experienced captains, a man of high reputation and one the Apulian leaders trusted to show good sense. That seemed initially to be well placed, for his furious charge, along with fifteen other knights, had the more lightly armed Turks, in their hundreds, wheel away and retire in seeming panic.

De Barneville should have then called a halt; close to Antioch he could count on support, the further off he rode the less effective that could be

37

until, at distance, it became impossible to provide succour. Still in plain but faint view from the battlements, the Turks, who had sensed this, wheeled to attack and on faster, smaller mounts they soon closed with their pursuit. Those watching saw their men enveloped by numbers that would have taken many more lances to contain.

That Roger and his men would fight valiantly was never in doubt; he was famous for his valour throughout the whole host, but the next sight was of those fifteen knights in full retreat, seeking sanctuary as a hail of arrows followed in their wake. Roger's banner marked him out as the man in command and that attracted the most attention, which at least allowed half of his men to escape unscathed or with wounds so light as to not threaten their lives.

He was pierced several times, his horse too, and that slowed him enough to make the rest of the arrow flights, fired at very close quarters, deadly enough to negate the protection afforded by his chain mail. In slow and unfolding horror those watching saw him slide sideways on his saddle, his mount slowing, until both were overtaken. Knocked to the ground the still living but grievously wounded knight was hauled closer to the walls by the triumphant Turks who threw him to his knees and, to a wail from those watching, promptly cut off his head before sticking it on his own captured lance.

An even greater blow followed quickly: that Turkish party was naught but a precursor of a multitude yet to arrive, and as Godfrey de Bouillon had predicted and Bohemund had seconded, the party of men Vermandois had left to hold the Iron Bridge could not do so against such overwhelming numbers.

Their fate, to be massacred, was no secret: the local Armenians passed on to the Crusaders everything that happened in the countryside. Only the man in command had survived to occupy the oft-flooded dungeon, no doubt to be offered for a ransom that would not be forthcoming.

Yet having crossed the river Kerbogha halted and began to form up his camp.

'Why does he not come on?'

Bohemund asked this as he stood looking out from one of the towers of the St Paul's Gate, which faced the direction by which the Atabeg must march, really a question to himself rather than any of his nearby knights. He had expected to see Kerbogha's banners closing in on the city walls, yet there was no sign of anything other than more light forces skirmishing ahead of the main body, many swirling around the La Maho-merie siege fort, though not actually attacking.

'Perhaps he fears us,' suggested Robert of Salerno with a braying laugh, making an inappropriate jest for what was a very serious situation.

He was a man much given to what he called his humour and others saw as mockery, which many put down to his bloodline. Robert was the grandson of Gisulf, the one-time prince of the wealthy city state of Salerno. He had been a tyrannical fool, a military incompetent and an endemic conspirator until Bohemund's father, Robert de Hauteville, the first Duke of Apulia and the prince's brother-in-law, had unceremoniously deposed him.

The possession of Salerno had devolved to the man who had a claim to be Robert's heir, Roger *Borsa*, the present Duke of Apulia, a man with whom Bohemund was in permanent dispute, given he was his father's firstborn and had only been deprived of his inheritance by a marital annulment made for the sole purpose of political gain, an act which had rendered both Bohemund and his sister Emma illegitimate.

If Bohemund hankered after what his father had bequeathed, Robert must wish for his part of that estate. At one time wary of the youngster and still vigilant given his love of risk, this scion of Salerno had become second only to Tancred in terms of trust. If he did harbour any resentment as to how his inheritance had been stolen from him by the de Hauteville family he kept it well hidden, never ever raising with Bohemund the actions of his sire.

'I think it is more he has another plan, Robert, but still...'

That musing was left unfinished for it set off a train of contemplation in the Count of Taranto's mind on which action could be based: the thought that before he attacked the main walls Kerbogha would employ access to the citadel to both strengthen the garrison as well as to use it as a sally port, if only to split the defence, the other obvious conclusion being little could be done to hinder that.

The Crusaders could not fight outside the walls on the eastern slopes of the mountains to destroy any men seeking to reinforce the citadel: the only gate from which to issue onto that ground in numbers, and one through which they would have to retire if faced with overwhelming force, was at the end of a narrow gorge which the Turks could take control of with ease. To sortie out was to risk being trapped, so it came down to the finding of a method of containment.

'Robert, gather up any able-bodied citizens and take them up to your cousin outside the citadel. Tancred must build some kind of wall across the path down to the city and quickly, far enough off from the fortress to be safe from archery but close enough to stop anyone emerging from the gate having all the advantage, for they will be attacking downhill. A wall will break their charge.'

'We could demolish the nearest mosque and use the stones from that.'

Sensing another jest Bohemund replied with good humour. 'If you do, Robert, demolish a church as well, otherwise we will have every Muslim left inside Antioch seeking our downfall.'

'They do that already.'

'If they do in their hearts, let us not provide a means to excite their passions so they are tempted to riot.'

It took little time to find out the entire disposition and make-up of the Turkish host; many of the Armenians crowding into the city were only too willing to tell them. Thus the various tribes, faiths and sects were identified and added to that was a true figure of their number, which even if it turned out to be half of what had been rumoured was still in the order of fifty thousand and frightening, yet it was the mere fact of the combination that caused the greatest alarm.

It had always been known to the Crusaders that success depended on the factions of Islam maintaining their mutual distrust. The most powerful of the two main groups, and they truly loathed each other, were the Abbasids of Asia Minor and much of Persia, who had as their titular head the Sultan of Baghdad.

Opposition to them came from the Fatimids of Egypt, led from distant Cairo, yet even inside those polities rivalries were rife. The authority of the Abbasid Sultan of Baghdad appeared to be weak – few seemed to obey his directives or gather to fight for his cause – and that had done much to aid the penetration of the Crusade; how this Kerbogha had managed to get these fractious elements to put aside their differences mattered less than that they were now camped as a body not far from Antioch.

The one hope the besieged had, that such a massive host would fall apart or could not be supplied, was dashed early; Kerbogha was a good general who knew the value of keeping his army contented and fed. When it came to cohesion he was so feared for his cruelties throughout the land that dread provided glue where loyalty did not, just as such terror as he projected went far to explain how he had achieved his combination of force.

Added to that and for the same reason, food was being brought in from far and wide, much of it by those who had previously supplied the

Crusade, given that to even show reluctance – and most would have preferred Kerbogha gone – was enough to bring on his murderous wrath.

The Atabeg set up his main camp a whole league away from the northern walls, this being a disposition all of the Crusade leaders struggled to comprehend when success surely depended on pressing the siege close. Not that such a distance allowed them much freedom of movement; to cross the short distance from the Bridge Gate to La Mahomerie siege fort still required careful observation, and that was ten times more hazardous when sending men to the port of St Simeon, where some ships, unaware of the changed circumstances in Antioch, continued to arrive.

Most of their cargoes ended up stacked on shore for the lack of the means to get them safely to the city. Before either excursion could be attempted it was necessary to see what forces of the enemy were close by enough to interfere, while those holding La Mahomerie were in no doubt that an attack would soon be launched in enough strength to take it from them and cut the route to the coast completely.

High up behind the city the men Tancred had set to constructing a wall toiled away in the tremendous daytime heat, the means to build supplied by an endless stream of reluctant and dragooned citizens, often bearing up the steep hill the stones of their own destroyed dwellings, churches and mosques having been left alone for fear of disturbance.

Running across the face of the hillside all the

way to the point where it adjoined the outer curtain wall, there was no mortar to fix the pieces in place; it was drystone at best and flimsy because of that, so much so that, even with buttresses, it might well collapse from the weight of attackers pushing against it.

If days went by without activity, they did not pass without increasing anxiety. Despite strict control of the food supply and a diet ill-equipped to feed the fighting men – the pilgrims and citizens were left to fend for themselves – the storerooms were emptying at a rate that indicated they would struggle to hold out for weeks.

A month, without relief, was impossible, so much time was spent with an eye to the northern horizon for some sight of the armies of Byzantium, though messages getting through – smugglers by trade knew how to circumvent any restrictions by either cunning or bribery – brought no news of any such prospect, which left the besieged nothing to do but wait; all the dice were in the hands of the Turks.

The expected attack of La Mahomerie came first, a furious assault that those not in the siege fort could only watch helplessly from the battlements. The Turks surged around, probing hard and sometimes seeming about to overwhelm the defence. With a courage born of desperation the men led by Robert of Flanders somehow managed to drive them back till the pile of bodies on the perimeter rose to make it increasingly hard for those following to exchange blows and inflict injury.

If the first day was difficult it did not ease in those that followed. Overnight the Turks came to remove their dead and as soon as the light was strong enough the attack was renewed with the same ferocity. It was inevitable that Robert's men, however stalwart they were, must suffer wounds and losses, added to which the sheer physical effort of maintaining the fight without any chance of being reinforced was debilitating in itself.

That he held out for four days was a feat of brilliance but unsupported it could not go on. As darkness fell on the fourth night, having once more been in combat all day, Robert dipped his banner three times, the signal that he was about to abandon the siege fort and retire through the Bridge Gate. A strong body of Provençal knights had to stand by to provide assistance and they waited until the Turks came for the bodies of their freshly fallen comrades, who by religious decree had to be buried within a day.

Emerging in near silence they slaughtered the gatherers, allowing Robert of Flanders to evacuate his remaining men – those who had died remained within, their souls commended to God – and to set the wooden structure alight, it going up like a torch given the inside of the walls had been soaked from barrels of oil kept for the purpose.

That it burnt bright enough to illuminate the slaughter so recently carried out was not a thing to bring cheer: if holding the siege fort had put a check on the enemy it was not much of one, and for all the Turkish losses they were in affordable

45

numbers. Likewise, if the road to the coast was not actually cut to individuals, nothing more could be brought in from there, even by donkey.

With little left to distract him, Kerbogha finally began to act. He fed men up the eastern slopes of the mountains to crowd into the citadel, which naturally brought crusading reinforcements from Flanders and Normandy to the temporary wall. That it had taken him days to do so surprised Bohemund, but the possible answer to that curious behaviour came when he saw Shams ad-Daulah's banner being lowered.

The flag of the Atabeg of Mosul soon replaced it. Clearly there had been negotiations: Kerbogha was not prepared to aid the man who held the citadel until he was sure that when Antioch fell his right to it would not be disputed.

'It seems, Tancred, that I am not the only lord who is wishing for possession of the title of Prince of Antioch.'

Delivered with wry humour, it was a dig at his nephew, who had acclaimed him as that when they had only just breached the walls, it being the designation of the last satrap to hold it for Byzantium. The reply was swift and with no mirth in it at all, for at that very moment the gates of the citadel swung open and with wild cries, trumpets and thumping drums, a whole horde of fighters, Turks by their dress, began to emerge and deploy for an assault.

'Then let us hope that those who wish to deny you that put as much effort into stopping Kerbogha.'

On command the knights present couched and

46

lowered their lances to set up a frieze of points at the rim of the wall onto which the lead attackers must be impaled. Whatever words of faith had inspired them before the attack required more to sustain them and it was clear that the sight of those sharp metal lances brought a palpable amount of hesitation, yet the Turks were doughty fighters and had proved it many times and not just against this Crusade.

Over a century they had fought and repeatedly defeated Byzantium and the Arabs in their progress west to take and hold the lands they had conquered. So they came on, either through love of battle, a belief in Allah, fear of shame, perhaps Kerbogha, or the sheer pressure of those at their backs, swinging their swords to lop off the lance points while their fellows fired arrows over their heads to disrupt the defence.

Some attackers died from those falling short, others were impaled, this while Bohemund, Tancred, the two noble Roberts and their defenders held their shields over their heads as protection from the falling bolts, where that failed their chain mail deflecting arrows that were losing their velocity. Within a blink it was sword against sword, axe against spear and bloody combat to hold and deny the attackers the way down into the city.

Kerbogha had numbers in abundance; if his losses were high they were a price he was willing to pay for success, no doubt with promises of paradise for those who succumbed and gold for the survivors. That first charge was not repeated in weight, though the assault, if it ebbed and flowed, never let up throughout the whole of the day, the main action taking place across a small depression where the Turks sought to dislodge the defenders from the place where their two points of defence adjoined – the permanent city curtain wall and the drystone and makeshift one.

The women camp followers were as vital as the knights who held the line, fetching water to them in the short pauses between combat to ease throats that had become parched at the very prospect of a fight, the chanting priests encouraging them to pray to God for strength less so. Arms ached from the swinging of great broadswords and heavy axes, but it was tribute to the Norman way of training, applied in both the homeland and Apulia, that men sustained their ability to keep fighting, killing and maiming.

These were men who, when they were not fighting, practised daily to do so. Time spent in the sand-filled manège day after day and hour upon hour, in mock play of what they were now doing for a purpose, allowed them to keep going when lesser mortals would have succumbed from sheer exhaustion.

Bohemund's standard flew above his head; along the line to one side fluttered the similar device of Tancred and beyond that those of Normandy and Flanders, while to the other flank, stiff on the breeze, flew the pennant of Robert of Salerno. If he was not a full-blooded Norman – neither was Tancred truly that with his Lombard father – he, like all the Italians who served as knights with the men from the far north, had been induced entirely into their ways.

Danger threatened when, as had been feared, the sheer pressure of Turkish bodies pressing against it led to the collapse of a section of the drystone wall. Bohemund, alerted to the crisis, immediately disengaged and called to the knights behind him who made up a reserve to join in response – if a man fell they were needed to move into and maintain the line. Together they headed towards the breach, which had become a melee of intermingled fighters: paramount was the need to restore the perimeter, and scant consideration had to be given to those engaged.

With his bulk and massive strength the Count of Taranto drove into the crowd, slashing right and left and never stopping to consider he might maim or kill his own, the men he had brought forming a wedge behind him, able by driving hard to push back the Turks and to kill so many that their bodies filled the breech in the wall. To get to the line of defenders obliged the attackers to now cross a barrier of blood, gore, severed limbs and twitching remains.

Whoever had command, perhaps Kerbogha himself, ordered the horns blown and the Turks retreated, to leave a line of Crusaders too weary to even think of pursuit, thus allowing the enemy to filter back through the inner gate untroubled. Much as he wanted to sink to his knees, as had many of his lances, Bohemund and his fellow magnates had to stay visible, had to raise their swords and emit the first sound of a hoarse cheer, that slowly taken up by the others, to what was far from an outright victory but was enough to tell their enemies that they were of good heart.

Yet they only had to look around to observe the number of their confrères who had either fallen or were groaning and grievously wounded to assess what had occurred: if they had driven off the Turks it had not been without cost.

'If he attacks the walls at the same time as he sorties out from the citadel we will be on a set of sharp horns, my friends.'

No one at the meeting of the Council of Princes wanted to disagree with Godfrey de Bouillon for the very simple reason he was right. He and Toulouse had held the western walls overlooking the river, but in much diminished strength for such a task, the necessity of holding the higher ground being paramount. Yet if no one responded, all must be wondering at the lack of what they feared: Kerbogha had the strength to do as he wished as well as a clear view of the Crusaders' lack of means. He could attack in two places at once.

Robert of Normandy, '*Curthose*' by soubriquet because of a pair of short legs, spoke up next. 'We cannot just let him act as he wishes.'

'I cannot see how we can stop him.'

Hugh of Vermandois said that with an accompanying look that sought confirmation; what he got was indifference, his view on anything discounted almost by default.

'We have all agreed we cannot fight outside the walls,' Bishop Adémar reminded them, 'but can we not raid a little to disrupt them?'

Bohemund was amused by that; early in the Crusade Adémar had been keen to emphasise that

50

he was a mere cleric, not a military man in any sense, and that he was ever willing to bow to the superior knowledge of his knightly confrères. Yet he had bought a mailed hauberk in Constantinople and had been seen to read the historical Greek chronicles of Herodotus and Xenophon to glean insight into how battles were fought in Asia Minor.

Increasingly, at Nicaea, he had advanced his own theories until, after the city fell, a chance came for the Bishop to show his mettle. At the Battle of Dorylaeum he had led a party of knights with great gusto and had come to see himself after that, albeit with discretion when he spoke, as the tactical equal of any of these men who had led armies. It was a mark of the respect in which he was held that none now disputed it; even if he had got above himself Adémar had a clever mind and a clear sight of necessities.

'Surely,' the Bishop continued, 'the way to counter Kerbogha at the citadel is to attack the men encamped to the rear of the mountains?'

'Who are,' Vermandois cried, seeking to latch on to the Bishop's popularity, 'more numerous than those actually in the citadel.'

Even stating the obvious got the Frenchman scant attention; at one time Vermandois had been advised by his brother's constable, he an experienced and well-regarded soldier trusted by the King of France to keep the enthusiasms of his younger sibling in check. That poor fellow had been slain in a most shameful manner, having been sent to secretly negotiate with a group Turks seemingly willing to surrender one of the gates, in a meeting set up by Count Hugh, who declined to go himself. All Vermandois got back was the poor fellow's severed head fired from a catapult.

Yet his outburst concentrated minds: the citadel might be formidable but it was not large. It could not possibly hold the number of men necessary for the assault Kerbogha had launched, indeed he had only used a proportion of his available strength so far, almost exclusively Turks, and to march such a host to and fro from the main camp each day was folly. On the rear slopes behind the citadel, visible from the towers held by the Crusaders, lay a satellite camp of some seeming permanence; the enemy were there to stay or at least until Antioch fell.

'We could launch a night raid,' Adémar suggested. 'After all, we have a postern gate nearby that would serve very well by which to exit.'

'Such an act is not without risk,' Bohemund responded, as he contemplated the pros and cons.

Toulouse was quick to speak and sharply. 'What is not?'

His reaction being brought on by rivalry – anything the Apulian said had to be countered by Provence – obliged Adémar to concur with both Toulouse and Bohemund, talking in a way that debarred interruption like Solomon applying his famous wisdom. If it irritated Bohemund it infuriated the man with whom the Bishop of Puy had set out on Crusade: Toulouse fairly spat at the cleric.

'If the Apulians fear to set foot outside the walls the men of Provence do not!'

The response from Bohemund was delivered in

an even tone and quietly, but lost nothing by that; he would hold to his vows if he could, but there arose times, and this was one of them, when it was required that anyone who insulted him did so at some peril.

'Have a care, My Lord, about whom you choose to affront.'

'No slur was intended,' cried Adémar, a remark that flew in the face of the obvious. 'But if we could send out a strong party, perhaps a hundred men, we might impose a check on the devil of Mosul.'

'I will provide fifty,' Vermandois said, glaring at Bohemund until that was returned in full measure, which had him look away; such a giant was not a man to challenge.

'And I the rest,' exclaimed Toulouse.

'Good,' Bohemund added, 'then I need provide no one.'

On a night with little moon, with a heat haze to obscure what light came from the stars, getting out onto the escarpment and doing murder was not hard, the surprise being the way Kerbogha's soldiers panicked and fled as soon as the Crusaders got amongst them. For every one that died a hundred ran away, using the down slope of the mountains to speed their departure and leaving their entire camp to be looted.

There was much to plunder: weapons, private possessions, especially those of the commanders, whose tents yielded objects of value. Most of all there was abundant food, some of it ready to eat, for hungry men too much of a temptation. It was hard to carry that off, but in their enthusiasm to pillage and gorge, the men in command, French and Provençal captains, did not think to set a piquet to ensure that those who had fled did not return.

Likewise it did not occur to them that the darkness, which had aided their enterprise, was just as likely to favour the enemy. Had they been given warning of the Turkish approach they might have safely departed, and heavily laden. As it was, the Turks arrived in great numbers and suddenly, so that the panic was reversed: now it was the Crusaders who had to flee, some foolishly seeking to carry with them what they had looted, which slowed their retreat.

Yet that was not the main source of the debacle that followed: the cause was the postern gate by which they had exited. It was narrow, as such entrances have to be, only of a width enough to allow one man passage through at a time, so that the first few were lucky, the rest less so and those at the rear doomed to be slaughtered. In the balance of those slain on both sides, made public at another council meeting, it was moot as to which host had suffered most.

The following morning, as if sending a hard message, the enemy again essayed out from the citadel to do battle and the same men who had fought the previous day were once more desperately engaged. Adémar, who had taken the reverse on his plan badly, was at the same time saying a special Mass for the souls of those who had been lost.

CHAPTER THREE

The attack from the citadel was repeated over four long days, always by the doughty Turks, sapping strength in both numbers and the ability to keep fighting, so much so that morale plummeted to a point where it began to affect men who claimed to be immune. Escape from besieged Antioch had been, if a dribble, a constant even before the Turks actually arrived, with individual *milities* lowering themselves from the walls at night to make a run for open country or St Simeon, for the nearby small port was unaccountably still not in Turkish hands: such desertions, if not approved, could be ignored.

The depth of creeping despair really struck home when a twenty-strong party of influential knights chose to defect: these were trusted men, cohort leaders from every contingent, including William of Grandmesnil, a relative by marriage and a seemingly dependable captain of Bohemund. It was scant comfort that the act of such a numerous group seemed to activate the normally somnolent Turks.

Alerted by their numbers the enemy pursued them to St Simeon, where, as later reported, they did great slaughter in the town while also setting fire to any ships that had not been quick enough to clear the harbour, the smoke from those still burning vessels visible from the walls at dawn.

How many knights got away was unclear; more obvious was the envy generated by the notion that they might have succeeded and survived.

The whole siege was in crisis and this could only make matters worse; if such high-born fellows and indomitable fighters could desert it could only be because they knew the outcome to be decided. Antioch would fall and every Latin, from lowly pilgrim to great nobleman, determined to abide by their faith was likely a dead man.

A rumour swept through the city that even the magnates themselves were about to flee and leave the common folk to face the wrath of Kerbogha. A public display of fortitude had to be arranged, at which each leader swore in turn, in a solemn oath administered by a weary-looking Adémar, not to desert the crusading cause.

The Bishop, once so smooth of countenance that no wrinkle troubled his brow, did not now look well: if the clerical lack of vigour could be explained by the military circumstances, he was finding religion just as debilitating. Hunger amongst the deeply religious pilgrims by nature brought on visions of either an approaching apocalypse or divine salvation. Many of them were simple folk who had come to Asia in droves to seek deliverance and they represented every walk of life in the chequered board that was the Latin Christian heartland.

Some, a very few, had been prosperous merchants, much reduced now, the majority everything from guild tradesmen to shopkeepers, housewives, landless peasants and, it had to be admitted, a strong contingent of the dregs and feckless of European society, albeit they had one thing in common: they had been led to seek salvation by non-sanctified preachers who promised them not only the remission of sins granted by the Pope, but had raised that to a guarantee of entry to heaven upon death, once they had breached the walls of the Holy City.

If there was rivalry amongst the magnates, called upon to swear their attachment to the cause till death or victory, they could not be outdone by the vicious jealousies that animated the various self-appointed divines. Clerical hierarchy, namely Adémar as the papal legate, could at least keep proper churchmen, the priests, deacons and abbots who had accompanied the great lords, in check. Not so the numerous unconsecrated preachers, who claimed to derive their authority directly from God and would have challenged Pope Urban himself to gainsay their rights.

The most noted of these charismatics was Peter the Hermit: he had set out for Palestine before a single warrior lance had pledged service, leading the first contingent of pilgrims from France and Germany to Constantinople. Twenty thousand strong, they had caused mayhem on the way given, if Peter had spiritual influence, he had no secular control at all.

The People's Crusade, which it had come to be called, had plundered and looted their way through Bavaria, Bohemia and Hungary, robbing the locals of food and wine, sometimes committing murder and rapine on their fellow Christians while visiting much worse on any Jews they had encountered; they, being deemed Christ killers, had been ritually slaughtered and their synagogues torched, often with the believers inside.

Entering Byzantine territory had not tempered their abuses: imperial troops had been obliged to engage in pitched battles to contain their depredations and that had not lessened when, strongly shepherded, they came to the capital city of the Roman Empire. One of their lesser crimes was to strip the lead off church roofs to pay for not only food but also the more dubious pleasures of the bazaar. Worse, they robbed the locals at will and were a real danger to the womenfolk.

Fearing riot – the citizens of Constantinople wished to take revenge for the pilgrims desecrations – the Emperor Alexius had shipped them over the Bosphorus to a less-than-salubrious town called Civetot, where he had kept them supplied with food in the hope that they would rest still and content until the fighting Crusaders arrived. He added a strong warning that not to do so would rouse the warlike Turks of nearby Nicaea.

That had been a mistake soon made to appear like folly; those who could walk ravaged the lands near Civetot, caring not for the religion of those they robbed, be they Muslim or Christian, Turk or Greek. Those with horses, knights who had attached themselves to the People's Crusade, plundered further afield, one party penetrating deep into the littoral to take a small fortress called Xerigordos with the intention of holding it as a fief.

The very thing Alexius feared came to pass: stung by such an act the massively strong Turks of Nicaea set out to deal with these Latin vermin.

Xerigordos was soon recaptured and the Crusaders either had their throats cut or were forced to convert to Islam. On hearing this news the rest of the People's Crusade, or at least those who could bear a weapon and were certain God was on their side, set out in an unruly and impossible-to-control multitude to gain revenge by taking Nicaea.

What they got instead was a massacre in open battle, mounted Turkish archers making mincemeat out of their so-called host. That was followed by the sack of Civetot itself, now defenceless, in which the Turks of Nicaea butchered every living and mature man and woman. The same fate befell any child they could find and all the bodies were piled in a great mound of rotting flesh. Only the young and comely of both sexes survived: they were led off to do carnal servitude in the brothels of Asia Minor.

Peter had not been in Civetot when the Turks descended – he had been in the capital seeking extra supplies of food and wine from the Emperor – so despite this near total loss and subsequent transgressions, such as a recent attempt to desert the bogged-down siege of Antioch and travel back to Constantinople, he was still highly respected by the pilgrims who had come along afterwards, brought by his reputation – a steady stream to be again now numbered in thousands.

His attempted flight had been kept from the armed host as well as the pilgrims for fear of its effect on morale, while his own belief in his divine mission as well as his powers of oratory had not been in any way diminished; he still preached as if he had a direct connection to the Almighty and seemed to have little difficulty in erasing from his mind any guilt for what had gone before.

Yet Peter was not alone in his hubris and in an atmosphere of heightened superstition it was not hard for such people to prey on the minds of those who believed in an all-seeing God and were in fear of a horrible death at the hands of the infidel – even worse was the notion of forced conversion – so that when such preachers called to their flocks that they should scourge themselves of sin it fell on willing ears.

People who were emaciated with hunger engaged madly in fasts lasting days to purify their souls, while flagellation and bodily mortification for the same purpose was common. All this was happening as many of the same men were fighting, for religious fervour was not confined to the non-combatants.

One preacher, by the name of Stephen, swore that he had seen a vision of Christ and the Virgin Mary, with an admonishment that the Crusaders should purify their souls by a five-day fast, and his claim was backed up by some of the attendant clerics, Adémar not amongst them. That might have scotched the whole thing but the personal confessor of the highly credulous Raymond of Toulouse chose to believe Stephen and that was enough for his claims to be taken as serious.

Stephen added to his certainties by claiming the appearance of a bright and streaking light in the sky, larger than those that normally filled the summer nights of Syria, was the body of Christ himself come to underline his message of victory and absolution. The meteor came down in a flaming ball of increasingly crimson fire, to crash into the distant mountains, which heartened the defence and, judging by the wailing from without the walls, unnerved the equally superstitious Turks.

If the believers thought to wake to find their enemies gone, they were sorely disappointed; in truth it was worse, for they were finally in the process of undertaking the dispositions that had been anticipated when they first arrived.

'Kerbogha does not, it seems, believe in divine portents.'

Bohemund was watching the massed ranks of the approaching host, again Kerbogha's best Turkish troops, deploy for the first time outside the western and northern sections of the defence. Like the Crusaders they targeted the Bridge and St Paul's Gates, really the only segments they could get to and hope to be effective, thousands of men with siege ladders and the clear intention to press home an assault. Aware that his uncle was more cynical of visions than he, Tancred crossed himself before replying.

'It matters if his men do.'

The response was harsh. 'Look hard at them, Tancred, and tell me if you see a fear that divine fire is about to descend upon them?'

'As long as our people are of good heart, as long as we believe.'

Bohemund, from his vantage point outside the citadel, looked along the walls, the rear parapet in plain view, noting how thinly they were defended. That would alter as the attack was pressed home, men would coalesce at the points of maximum danger and if they were not too numerous they should prevail. If there were a great many he would have to thin his own ranks to provide support and hope that having decided to change his tactics Kerbogha did not launch a simultaneous assault to those of the proceeding days.

'Place less faith in visions and more in your sword arm, nephew.'

'You pray to God before every fight, I have heard you!'

'I pray that should I fall my soul will gain entry to heaven, not that Christ in person should come to my aid in battle.'

'Even when, as now, we need such a divine intervention?'

'What we need is the army of Alexius to press upon Kerbogha's rear.'

'Perhaps that is the meaning of the vision?'

'Citadel gates are opening,' came the call.

This killed off Bohemund's reply, which would have been that the need for divine portents did not bring about compliance; if Alexius was even on the way there was no proof of it, and besides, there was no time to speculate on such matters. What he had feared, an attack in many places at once, was about to happen.

'We are in for a hard day, Tancred. You take what comfort you need from what you believe and allow me to take my own.'

That assessment turned out to be an understatement: when dusk fell no one, certainly not Bohemund, could have told a listener how they had survived such a relentless assault, lasting as it did throughout the daylight hours. Everywhere the Crusaders fought they had lost ground and been obliged to recover it. Sections of the western wall had been taken by the enemy, including the barbican above the Bridge Gate, and in the very short breaks in his own action Bohemund had been able to see the Provençal knights take it back again, which, if he did not admire their leader, laid low and too ill he claimed to take part, did not in any way diminish respect for his men.

Godfrey de Bouillon struggled just as hard at the St Paul's Gate, where Kerbogha had concentrated his main strength. There, only the narrowness of the area of assault – he was constrained between the River Orontes and the steep slope of Mount Staurin – held him in check, but it was a close run as several times he got substantial bodies of fighting men onto the parapet, where they engaged hand-to-hand with the Lotharingians in a fight that came down to knives, clubs and sometimes nothing but fists or gouging.

Matters were just as desperate outside the citadel and they turned critical when the Turks came close to taking one of the towers along the eastern wall, which would have outflanked the Apulians and rendered their drystone edifice untenable, their efforts scotched single-handedly by one knight who held his ground against stupendous odds until reinforced. Dusk fell on a besieged city full of spent men but they had held and that was all that mattered, even if they knew the morning would bring a renewal of the same.

Yet it did not come and some hoped that because Kerbogha had suffered great loss in his assault he was weakening in his resolve, a hope that was not long in being dashed as wiser heads prevailed. The Atabeg of Mosul knew very well the state of the besieged Crusaders; he had tested them as good sense dictated he must and then made a tactical judgement. Over the next days it became obvious he had decided that to throw bodies at the walls to seek to overcome them was a waste: time and hunger would do for him that which main force would not.

To sit in passive acceptance was neither natural nor wise and Godfrey of Bouillon was most determined to act; two days later, just before dawn, he led five hundred knights out of the St Paul's Gate to attack the Turkish encampment, first overcoming and slaughtering the small body Kerbogha had kept close to the walls. Emboldened by that and the passion such success aroused in his men, he carried on towards the main camp only to discover that his enemy had taken precautions against just such a sortie. Godfrey and his men walked into a trap and it was only sheer bloody-mindedness that allowed a good half of them to escape, over two hundred left behind as dead, which imposed a salutary lesson to all.

'It is madness to exit from any of the gates and in numbers,' Tancred insisted when his uncle related the discussion he had just engaged in at the council. 'Better to go out in small groups and spread terror.'

'Do you intend to attempt that?' Bohemund enquired, as he considered the notion.

'If you will permit it, Uncle.'

'I have noticed you often call me that when you want something.'

'I mean it as a mark of respect,' Tancred protested, until he realised Bohemund was smiling.

'You second me in command of our Apulians, nephew, and I know you chafe at the restraint.'

'I do not deny it. When I was sent away on my own and took Mamistra as my fief, I confess I took pleasure in not having anyone to question my decisions.'

That caused Bohemund's face to cloud over; it was during that expedition, to clear the passes on the shortest route to Antioch, that, despite Tancred's successes, his uncle had lost a hundred and fifty lances to a massacre in which Baldwin of Boulogne might be implicated. Yet he did not dwell on it for long.

Baldwin was in far-off Edessa and nothing could be done about him or his deeds now. Nor did he think on the reason such an expedition had been sent out: those passes known to now be free of defence would allow the Byzantines to use them as a fast route to join with the Crusade outside Antioch. That meant if Alexius was coming he should be here by now.

'I would want you to feel free to act on your own.' Seeing the doubt that induced, Bohemund added, 'Have I not said many times that the day will come when you will need to seek your own future?'

Now it was Tancred's turn to be amused and that came with a grin and a sweeping glance at the walls of Antioch. 'A proposition hard to realise now.'

'Act as you see fit, nephew, and that is a command.'

Watching him depart as he went to make his arrangements, Bohemund could allow himself to feel a sense of contentment; his sister's boy had been with him for so many years he was more like a son than a nephew, though there was no thought to dispute the designation with Tancred's father, a Lombard who had been a faithful servant and fighting knight to his own sire.

Such musings turned almost without effort to the image of Robert, the mighty Duke of Apulia, known throughout Christendom as the *Guiscard*, which meant cunning to those who admired his guile and the very reverse, more than weasel-like, to the many who hated and feared him. Even the latter could not doubt his abilities, which were the stuff of legend and that only marginally outshone those of his elder siblings.

Robert de Hauteville came from a family of twelve brothers and two sisters, the offspring of his nephew's namesake, who had, with two wives, sired a remarkable brood on what was a small demesne in the north-western part of Normandy known as the Contentin. Old Tancred, now long dead, had been a doughty soldier himself and, if far from wealthy, had raised his sons, all tall and as stoutly formed as their giant of a father, equipping them to be that too.

Tancred the Elder had hoped this would be in the service of the then ruler of Normandy, only to find that, having wed as his first bride the illegitimate daughter of Richard, the reigning Duke's father, such a connection worked not for but against his heirs. Duke Robert the First, known as 'the devil' for the suspicion that he had murdered his brother, was a man who lacked a legitimate heir of his own.

His only son, William, at one time called the Bastard of Falaise, now known to Christendom as the Conqueror, had been sired out of wedlock, and his father had quite obviously feared a de Hauteville bloodline of puissant fighters and outstanding physical presence, who might claim precedence by a superior bloodline.

To constrain them as well as any perceived ambitions for the dukedom he had refused them service as close knights to his body and thus any hope of moving from relative poverty to a position of some wealth and possible influence.

With all chance of advancement gone – ducal disfavour made that unattainable across the whole of Normandy – the two most senior of Tancred's sons, William and Drogo, had set out for Italy to make their way as mercenaries with nothing but their swords, lances and their fighting prowess, following in the wake of many who had departed Normandy before them.

In the eldest son, William, the world had discovered not only a fighter who well deserved the soubriquet 'Iron Arm', but also a soldier with a quite remarkable tactical brain and no shortage of guile when it came to dealing with the one-time ruling Lombards of Apulia, his fellow Norman freebooters who fought their battles, as well as the Byzantines who now lorded it over them.

William had set the family on its way in Southern Italy, sidestepping his mercenary confrères as well as the slippery Lombards, trouncing the Byzantines in numerous battles, being followed in turn by Drogo and Humphrey, the brothers next in age. Humphrey had humbled the papacy as well as their Byzantines allies at the Battle of Civitate to consolidate and extend the family power in South Italy.

Succession by maturity had been set aside when Humphrey died and Bohemund's father had leapt over, by acclamation, two of the other brothers to assume the leadership of the family and the forces they had created. In a life of constant warfare, devious manoeuvring and greed for possessions the *Guiscard* had made Apulia secure by his conquest of the coastal cities of Brindisi, Bari and Otranto.

Far from content and aided by the youngest of his brothers, Roger, he next conquered Calabria, then led an expedition across the Straits of Messina to take control of Sicily from the Saracens. Robert de Hauteville, like William Iron Arm, had risen from penury to become, by papal investiture, the Duke of Apulia, Calabria and Sicily as well as the most famous soldier in Christendom.

No such ruminations were possible for Bohemund without a reflection on how he had been robbed of his inheritance. For reasons of political necessity, though it was disguised as being required by the sin of consanguinity, Robert had, with the connivance of a well-bribed pope, put aside his first wife to marry Sichelgaita, a Lombard princess and sister of Prince Gisulf of Salerno. She had produced two sons as well as several daughters, the eldest of whom had, through the manoeuvring of his formidable mother, inherited all the ducal titles.

Bohemund immediately went to war with his half-brother Roger, known as *Borsa*, and he would have taken what he saw to be rightfully his if *Borsa*'s namesake uncle, who held the title of Great Count of Sicily and was every bit a match as a soldier for any of his siblings, had not stepped in to prevent it. If Roger of Sicily had also ensured *Borsa* likewise never enjoyed the whip hand it was small compensation; the Great Count held them in balance and Bohemund suspected he did so, not as he claimed for any vow he had made to his elder brother, but for some long-term aim of his own.

Many, Bohemund knew, suspected he had come on Crusade to repair that paternal fault, to gain in Asia Minor what he had been denied in Italy, and if pushed, he would have been hard-pressed to tell if that were true or false. Certainly he chafed to be denied his titles but more he had come here to get away from the endless need to fight with and sometimes serve under his half-sibling, this to preserve intact the whole inheritance – *Borsa* was a weak creature, a poor general and a man who placed more credence in priests than common sense, which made just being in his presence a trial.

Perhaps a more telling truth was that Bohemund was like most of his race – his mother had been a full-blood Norman – a man who lived to fight and conquer, made restless by the lack of it. From that he might accrue the rewards that his bloodline indicated to him he deserved, but what would come of this adventure, as he had told Tancred many times, he did not know, for the future was to him, as to all men, a mystery.

Yet chance was ever on the wing and it might be that here in Syria he might find that which he sought, an undisputed destiny and a fame all of his own to match or even surpass his famous sire.

CHAPTER FOUR

The men Tancred led, a dozen in number, let themselves down rope ladders in Stygian darkness onto the steep part of the slopes of Mount Staurin, those being hauled out of sight as soon as they were on the ground. Lightly clad, eschewing mail, they moved with slow deliberation downhill towards the fires of the forward Turkish camp, re-established after Godfrey of Bouillon's debacle.

There was no attempt to kill on the scale the Lotharingians had attempted; the aim was to spread alarm. So the party stayed well clear of the men on guard and out of the arc of those flickering flames that stood central to the camp, choosing a tent where the sounds of deep slumber were obvious through the canvas.

The killing was silent, even to the point of the removal of the heads and, the deed done, they retired and called for their ladders to be relowered so they could re-enter the city. The whole affair had not lasted less than three glasses of sand and the half a dozen Turkish heads sat on Bohemund's table were a welcome sight. Tancred's enthusiasm would have been infectious to a less experienced soldier; for all that, his uncle made his pleasure more obvious than any reservations.

'This way we spread terror. Let our enemies wake up each morning, whatever camp they occupy, to find six or more of their number decapitated and with no knowledge of how it had occurred. If we cannot fight them in open battle let us make slumber a risk.'

'You have done well, Tancred, but have a care if you attempt to repeat this. What works once will not always allow for a second attempt.'

'I am not fool enough to strike twice in the same place, Uncle.'

'Wise,' Bohemund responded, though he looked down to avoid Tancred's eye. How could he say to his young and passionate nephew that at this rate of attrition he would still be killing Turks at the coming of the second millennium? 'But next time leave the heads and bring back their victuals, which is a more pressing need.'

There was food, if not in abundance, but it was in the hands of those who wished to profit from ownership, and not just smugglers. The citizens of Antioch, or at least a good body of them, were as shrewd and rapacious as folk anywhere, sharpened by having already gone through one siege.

They knew how to hide what they had so it could not be stolen or sequestered by whoever held the city at a time of siege – livestock was kept in straw-lined cellars to avoid their bleating and

71

crowing being overheard, wheat was stored in the rafters until desperation made the prices that could be extracted from the tired and famished fighting men rise to the right level.

Any Crusader who had managed to come upon and keep hold of some coin in the march from Nicaea was obliged to part with it now and for very little in return. Knights started by drinking the blood of their horses for sustenance, then when they became too weak to be of use in battle they killed them and consumed their carcasses, ignoring the effect on the loss of the ability to fight.

A dead oxen caused high excitement as the owner sought to sell it bit by bit, while the sight of a scrawny and ill-fed chicken being auctioned was enough to start a near riot so that the successful bidder was obliged to make a fast escape to keep what he had bought. Every member of the Council of Princes ate better, for they had the funds to do so, but they were also distributing a dole to their men, small payments that should have been enough to buy food, yet seemed to purchase less and less each day.

Toulouse was the wealthiest of the magnates, for fertile Provence, a rich region even before the Romans arrived, had for years made his coffers groan with gold and the silver coins still known by the Roman name of *solidi*.

If he used it to provide sustenance to his Provençal lances, he was also employing it to suborn men from the other contingents – Franks, Apulians, Normans and Lotharingians – urging them to desert to his banner so as to strengthen his hand in the council, sure his increasing numbers would eventually hold sway on any decisions made.

Bohemund worked hard to hold his men to him; he had managed to get some of his revenues from Apulia shipped over to St Simeon to bolster the fortune in treasure – literally a room full of gold, silver and jewels – he had received from the Emperor Alexius, his one-time enemy, in a bid to buy his loyalty.

Likewise every other prince had disbursed what Byzantine largesse they had been gifted and what they had in coin. Yet even with such subventions, hunger could not be staved off, any more than could Kerbogha be turned into a chimera, and if the acts of Toulouse caused resentment nought could be done to counter that either.

The pilgrims, many of whom had no money at all and received none from on high, were chewing old leather belts and making soup from grass and weeds – some were said to be eating their shoes – and being deeply devout and close to starvation, visions were becoming even more rife. Every act and every untoward noise was a portent, positive or the reverse, prophecies laden with either glorious deliverance and entry into heaven as martyrs or to a collective descent into flaming hell, there to burn for their transgressions, their pride and their heresies.

Many came to believe there was no salvation at all without divine intervention and that within days. Less superstitious minds still hoped for Byzantine aid, though with a decreasing level of expectation, for no news came of any approaching host.

There was nothing grand about any of the knights, ten in number, who stepped ashore at Alexandretta; their clothes were ragged and every one had days of facial growth, untidy and salt-streaked, evidence that the means to shave had not been available for the several days which must have been spent at sea.

That was the impression created when they were still afloat and it was not improved on closer inspection, for there were traces of dried blood, mixed with filth, on every one of their garments and not a few were carrying wounds, added to which they looked half-starved, standing in sharp contrast to the man who greeted them as they stepped onto the jetty.

'Grandmesnil, is it you? And do I see Hugh of Liverot under all that hair? Bernard of Maine?'

Count Stephen of Blois was not only dressed in fine and clean garments, both his smooth face and ample body showed that no shortage of food had attended him for some time; indeed he was sleek to the point of causing resentment to men who, racked with hunger, had been obliged to scrape down the walls of Antioch in the dead of a cloudy and moonless night.

That achieved they had then to creep, many times on their belly, through lines of Turks to get to the rear of their camp before they could stand upright and try for a swifter progress. Blois rattled off several more names in greeting, for these were well-known captains he was addressing.

'It is us as named, My Lord,' William croaked, speaking for all.

'Come from Antioch?'

'Where else?'

The blood seemed to drain from the well-fed face. 'Has it fallen to the Turk?'

'No.'

William made that reply before he realised that an opportunity had been missed, for if it had not fallen what was he doing here? Blois clearly knew that it had been taken by the Crusade, just as he seemed well aware that it was now besieged and that would imply he was also aware of by whom and in what strength.

He recalled that Count Stephen had abandoned the siege while the army of the Crusade was still outside the walls, had fled the hunger, indeed near famine, of the winter and taken his three hundred lances with him. When it came to desertion the escaped knights could hold their heads up in the presence of this particular magnate. Added to that, William had the wit to employ an immediate excuse.

'The situation is grave...'

'It was far from ever good, William,' Stephen interrupted, his voice sombre as he continued, having about it a speed of expression that robbed the words that followed of any verisimilitude. 'I had intended to rejoin you all not long past, but then that devil Kerbogha got across my route to Antioch. I have spent much time trying to think of a way to get through his host without I lose every one of my men and my own life with it.'

About to tell a falsehood himself, it seemed clear to Grandmesnil that Blois was engaged in just that; he had never had any intention of a return to the siege of Antioch and it was apparent not just in the haste of his justification, it was also in the way he would not look the man he was addressing in the eye, instead half turning, as if by glancing south for a second he could underline the risks he had declined to run.

Grandmesnil put as much force as he could into his reply. 'I have come at the request of your fellow lords to seek out the Emperor Alexius and his army so that they may know how our confrères are faring and ask that he hurries to their assistance.'

If Blois had any inclination to believe that, the reaction of the rest of the unkempt knights would have disabused him; long stubble and unkempt hair did nothing to obscure the look of surprise in their salt-crusted eyes, albeit that disappeared almost as quickly as it had materialised. Such a fleeting set of expressions cheered the Count of Blois; to be lied to is acceptable when one is also engaged in a high degree of dissimulation.

'We cannot stand here when you are clearly in need of sustenance.' A twitching nose also indicated that some clean water to wash would not go amiss. 'Come, I will have a feast prepared and we shall search you out some decent garments. Then, with wine in hand and food in your belly, you can tell me of your adventures.'

This Grandmesnil was only too happy to relate, though first he had to describe the dire state of both the defences and the defenders of Antioch. Much was made of the daring of he and his companions, as well as the sterling aid they received in their flight from those hopefuls they left behind, added to what it took to avoid detection close to the walls. First had been the sheer difficulty of escape, for they needed to lower not just themselves but flat boards on which to float across the Orontes and they were soaked by the time they made the opposite bank. But soon he was on to their subsequent travails.

Their mistake had been to stick to the St Simeon road once they had got clear of the main Turkish lines, for the enemy had posted a piquet on that, probably more to stop and rob smugglers than to catch fleeing Latins; after all, the fewer who remained the better. The men manning the post, alerted by such a large number of knights, possibly saw not flight, which they might have ignored, but an attack.

They ignited a pre-prepared alarm beacon and set up enough of a hue before they expired on Crusader swords to set in chain a strong pursuit, luckily on foot and not mounted, otherwise Grandmesnil and his hard-running compatriots would never have got to St Simeon ahead of them.

There was no attempt to halt that pursuit, no attempt to stand and fight; their enemies were too numerous. As soon as they made the berthing jetty their only concern was to choose the best ship, one that was at single anchor, waiting for dawn to set sail. An axe saw to the anchor cable but even that was not a solution.

The Turks took to boats to seek to stop them, leading to a long and bloody fight over the bulwarks and on the ship's deck as it drifted out to sea, a contest that accounted for many of the wounds they now carried. In all, eight of their number had either been killed or had injuries so severe that they succumbed over the following days to be, like those already expired, buried at sea.

It was natural that the talk turned back to the situation at Antioch just as it was natural that William of Grandmesnil, left by his fellow escapees as their spokesman – he was, after all, sat on the right hand of the Count of Blois, who had his comely looking Armenian mistress on his left – should paint a picture of the situation being close to hopeless, albeit that could change with the arrival of the Emperor.

There was no attempt to in any way embarrass his host, to hint that he might have seen it as his duty to come to their aid, though Blois continued to insist with every opportunity that was presented to him that he should try; both men were happy in their falsehoods.

'The Emperor must be told what the true situation is,' the Count insisted.

'Which we could do if we had any notion of where he is, My Lord.'

'We owe it to our fellows to find him, do we not?'

There was both sense and comfort in that, which led to ready agreement; to head north and find the Byzantine army was to be active without much in the way of risk. Stephen was quick to procure a ship by which the two, and they alone, should proceed by sea, heading for the last known place where imperial troops had been reported to be active under John Comnenus, the Emperor's nephew, who commanded the imperial fleet.

A landing at Tarsus brought more solid information: Alexius himself was in command and
camped to the north at Philomelium and to there
they proceeded as fast as they could on horseback.
Sighting the huge tented encampment, thousands
of men spread over the fertile plain and having
identified themselves to the guards, they were
ushered into the splendid pavilion of the man who
was addressed in the style, by those who served
him, as the reigning Roman Emperor.

To a pair who had been riding for most of the
day and were subsequently coated with dust, the
magnificence of the imperial accommodation
was doubly impressive: Alexius even had along a
dais on which he could place a throne-like chair
so as to be above anyone whom he addressed. As
in his palace, high officials, courtiers, as well as
his huge axe-wielding Varangian guards surrounded the Emperor, while the decor matched
anything to be found in a more solid structure.

Thick carpets lay one over the other on the
ground, while military standards lined the silken
sides. The light from the numerous oil lamps, as
well as the sun, which streamed through the
canvas roof, sent beams of glitter flashing off the
kind of gold and silver objects with which Imperial Constantinople surrounded itself; it was
display, of course, and impressive enough to cow
anyone who came upon it as a friend. More importantly it would astound the representative of
an enemy come to parley.

Yet it was not all Byzantium; there were Franks
in attendance too, men who had come east to

join the Crusade and, it seemed, expected to do so in the company of the imperial host, among them Guy de Hauteville, Duke of Amalfi, half-brother to Bohemund and a man well known to William of Grandmesnil. If he was greeted with nothing but eye contact – protocol denied any other way – it was as a friend. The two arrivals having made their obeisance with deep bows, Alexius immediately enquired as to from where they had come.

'I from Alexandretta, Highness,' replied Blois, adding to an immediately raised and quizzical eyebrow, 'where I was recovering from a long and debilitating illness.'

'Cared for by three hundred lances, I am told,' Alexius replied, though he was careful to add to that there had also been mendicant monks to bring the Lord of Blois back to full health.

The eyes of Count Stephen flicked towards Tacitus then, the half-breed general with the golden nose Alexius had sent south with the Crusade to ensure imperial interests were served; such information very likely came from him. However it was imparted or gilded it told Blois that the Emperor knew what had been happening around Antioch, while the temptation to refer to the fact that Tacitus and his men had also left the siege at much the same time had to be resisted. He would have done so under orders from the man on the throne.

'And you, Grandmesnil?' Alexius asked.

A falsehood now so well honed by repetition came out without hesitation, William looking the Emperor right in the eye, both to give credence

80

to what he was saying and to seek to discern if he was being believed. That was a waste of time with a man like Alexius Comnenus, so well trained, as he had to be, in masking his feelings.

'And how do you see their prospects in Antioch now?'

Such a question demanded a response larded with both gravity and sorrow, both of which Grandmesnil managed in abundance, lent more of both by the speaker's belief than it was true.

'Your Eminence, I cannot see how they are still holding the walls against the might of the army of Kerbogha. I say this not from any lack of valour on the part of my confrères, but merely from the belief that they are in want of the means of sustenance to keep on fighting. Most of their mounts have either died or are so weak they are useless. When I left there was nothing in the grain stores but an echo, and as for meat, none was to be had even for those like my Lord of Blois, with purses deep enough to meet the demands of the hoarders and smugglers.'

Stephen stiffened at the reference to his having a deep purse, which got Grandmesnil a glare, one that was ignored. Here in the imperial presence and its very obvious magnificence William could sense opportunity; in that, Blois would not be a companion but a potential rival, a difference he underlined as he continued, for it was necessary to raise his own standing and to diminish that of his fellow messenger.

'Had my confrères been as well fed as I found to be the lances attending Count Stephen, I would say they could hold till the moon fell from the sky but with no food and the Turks holding the citadel...'

'I was seeking to join them, Highness,' Blois protested, his face showing he was well aware of what Grandmesnil was seeking to do. 'But with Turks in their many thousands between Antioch and me, what could I do rather than engage in useless sacrifice? Better to hold Alexandretta for both the Crusade and the empire than that!'

Stephen was about to go on, indeed to protest too much, but a held-up imperial hand stopped him and that was followed by silence, no one daring to speak and disrupt the imperial ruminations. Neither man could see into the mind of the Emperor Alexius, nor be privy to his thinking. Perhaps Bohemund alone amongst the Latin magnates would have been able to perceive the train of his thoughts, for he had lived cheek by jowl with Byzantium all his life and had an insight in to the manner of its deliberations.

He might have sensed that paramount to Alexius Comnenus was the security of the Byzantine Empire and with that the continuance of both his rule and that of his family, for in truth Alexius had usurped the title from his predecessor and it was scant comfort to the darker nights of his soul that Nikephoros, the man in question, had taken the diadem dishonestly himself from a previous incumbent. It was thus not a wholly secure inheritance for the son to whom Alexius was determined it would devolve.

The Eastern Roman Empire had always had to fight on its borders but it had, in Asia Minor, been in retreat for many centuries, a shadow of the power it was in the days of the Emperors Constantine and Julian. First they had, in the seventh and subsequent centuries after the birth of Christ, lost ground to the Arabs emerging from the desert fastness, inspired by the teachings of the Prophet Muhammad.

In more recent times it had been the Seljuk Turks who had prospered at imperial cost. They too had taken much land and treasure, to the point where they had sat no more than three days' march from his capital. The arrival of a massive Frankish army had changed that: they had pushed the Turks as far back south as Antioch.

Working to take advantage of their successes his armies and fleets had taken full possession of lands through which the Crusaders had only passed, giving him possession of rich towns and cities that had not flown an imperial banner for decades, as well as great swathes of fertile land. The question now was simple: should he rush to the aid of the Crusaders or should he show caution?

At the forefront of his ruminations lay memory of the Battle of Manzikert in which, twenty-seven years previously, the Byzantine army had been destroyed by the Turks, a defeat so complete that the then emperor had been taken as a captive, while most of those he led were slaughtered like cattle.

The force that Kerbogha had assembled was every bit as powerful as that which had been met at Manzikert and if the Franks were in trouble at Antioch, indeed from what had been hinted at by Grandmesnil it may have already fallen, was it wise for him to seek to uphold an already lost cause and risk battle on his own?

Added to that was the fact of mistrust: if Alexius was grateful for the success of the Crusade, he had been just as keen, having seen them as both a blessing and a plague, to hurry them on their way, for he knew that there was as much avarice as faith in their higher ranks and the man he trusted least of all was Bohemund of Taranto.

Despite the pledges all the magnates had made, no man was immune to temptation when presented with the prospect of untold riches – one only had to examine the actions of Baldwin of Boulogne to see that – and that was why he had sent Tacitus and a token force of soldiers with the Crusade, to ensure that should they take back one-time Byzantine possessions, they were handed over to imperial control.

Tacitus had been withdrawn because of doubts that the Franks would ever take Antioch; now, even if they had, it seemed the situation was even more dire. Kerbogha would not be lenient if he took them as prisoners and having spilt their blood his next aim would be to do the same to the imperial forces coming to their aid.

His army was strong, but not so much so that they would outnumber the Turks. In such a situation he could lose everything he had gained since the Crusaders crossed the Bosphorus, including Nicaea; worse, he could lose even more and might find Kerbogha at the very gates of Constantinople itself.

'I am bound to ask you both,' the Emperor asked finally, 'for an assessment of what could be achieved for us all by an immediate and forced march south?'

The 'us all' was cunning; the imperial mind was that of a man who had to live in a court seething with intrigue, where emperors without number had been deposed in palace coups by poison or the knife. Alexius was better placed to guess at the thinking and motivation of both Blois and Grandmesnil than any other man present. He was asking them if they would march themselves to the aid of their confrères, albeit within his army.

'I fear,' Grandmesnil replied, when Blois declined to do so, 'that we might find we are too late.'

'William!'

That outburst came from Guy of Amalfi and his cry received a gasp of amazement from the rest of the assembled Byzantines; no man spoke without invitation in the imperial presence. Yet Guy was a de Hauteville, his father had been Robert *Guiscard*, and if his brother the reigning Duke of Apulia was a weakling who made men wonder at his blood, Guy was not. Despite black looks he would not be silenced.

'How can you even think to abandon Bohemund, your liege lord, not to mention my cousin Tancred and the men you yourself led?'

'Do you think I take any joy in saying such things? I told you, when I left they had no horses, no food and no way of breaking out and that was two weeks past.'

'You say you came to seek aid for them, now you are telling us that is no longer the case.'

If it was not an outright accusation of cowardice there was enough in Guy's look to imply that it was just that.

85

'I asked the question,' Alexius barked. 'The answer he gives me, if it is truthful, provides me no more pleasure than it does to Grandmesnil.'

By sinking his head to his chest, Alexius commanded silence, which even Guy of Amalfi had to respect. The deep thoughts did not last long; the conclusion he reached then being delivered with suitable solemnity.

'Prepare to break camp. We march north!'

CHAPTER FIVE

In the time since Grandmesnil had deserted matters had not improved and that did not apply just to the need to fight or a lack of supplies. It seemed every day someone was having a vision of angels descending from heaven to their aid or the earth opening to take them into the arms of Satan and his eternal fires. Not to be outdone by the revelations of others, a Provençal peasant called Peter Bartholomew, no preacher but one who chose to clothe himself in monkish attire, claimed his own experiences and related stories so startling he was obliged to appear before Bishop Adémar and his natural lord, a recumbent and ailing Raymond of Toulouse.

Bartholomew recounted how, over several months and on many occasions, apparitions had appeared to him that seemed to wake him from his slumbers, yet did not. Two ethereal presences surrounded by a glowing orb of light had come to him, one a bearded, elderly man who looked like a benign biblical prophet, the second young, dark and silent yet with a cast to his penetrating blue eyes that spoke of his divinity.

'They are, I believe, the spirits of St Andrew, who speaks to me, and of Christ our Saviour himself, who does not.'

'You do realise,' Adémar pointed out, 'that to make such a claim, if it is false, will lay you open to a charge of sacrilege?'

'Like every other person come on this journey, Your Grace, I left home and dedicated my life to God. If it his wish that I surrender my being, then who am I to raise a question?'

'You say this has happened more than once?'

Addressed by Raymond, Bartholomew immediately dropped to one knee and threw back the cowl that had covered his head, for he had grown up hearing of the mighty deeds of the Count of Toulouse and now, only ever having seen him from afar, he was in that illustrious presence.

'Yes, My Lord, first when we crossed Anatolia on that desperate march through the desert in which we nearly died of thirst, and many times since.'

'In Antioch?' demanded Adémar, with a sharpness born of too much exposure to visions.

'Not just here, My Lord Bishop, in many places as I went foraging for food to support our cause, but always at night and yes, once here, when we were first encamped outside the walls.'

'You say the older man spoke?' Raymond asked, hauling himself upright. 'What did he say?'

'That a piece of the Holy Lance, which pierced

the very body of Christ on the crucifix, lay within the confines of St Peter's original cave church. On that last visitation I was told to go to the spot where it was buried by the hand of St Peter himself so that I would recognise the place when the city fell and be able to recover it should the need for divine inspiration arise.'

Adémar had a carapace of seeming interest in such situations – he had dealt with many religious fanatics in his time – which masked any scepticism. Yet this claim was stretching that to the limit and what followed from this peasant did nothing to make easy holding his incredulity at bay, not that his expression dented Bartholomew's certainty.

'I was instructed to go to St Peter's Church and stand over the place of burial.'

'You entered Antioch while we had it still besieged?' Raymond demanded.

His tone demonstrated wonder as well as an acceptance and that had Adémar questioning the seriousness of his ailment. Perhaps it was of greater threat than he had hitherto supposed for it might be affecting his mind, which had always been too superstitious for the Bishop's liking, while his body, especially his florid, well-fed face, seemed to show few ill effects.

'I did so in spirit, My Lord, not in person, clad in the very garment in which I now stand before you, which with a celestial touch made me invisible to the infidels who held the city. Such was my transcendence that the walls proved no barrier to my progress, so great is the power of God.'

88

'You speak well for a peasant, do you not?' Adémar scoffed, seeking to knock a man he thought a charlatan off his stride, only to receive a confident response.

'I speak as my saint has instructed me, for I could not, humble and lacking in schooling as I am, conjure up such words.'

Count Raymond's eyes were now alight, either with fever or faith, Adémar could not tell. 'You say you could take us to the place where the Holy Lance is buried?'

'My Lord, that is why I have come to you, for with that lance no Christian knight could be defeated in battle against an infidel and no man is more deserving to hold such a relic in his fighting hand as you, who, if men could see right, would have command of the whole host that will lead us to Jerusalem.'

About to respond with agreement, Raymond hesitated, no doubt from the presence of the papal legate, who was *de facto* in that position. That the Count of Toulouse felt he should have the leadership of the Crusade had been a barely disguised fact ever since he had arrived in Constantinople, the only man he was prepared to bow the knee to being the Emperor Alexius himself, who had hinted he would lead the enterprise personally but had signally failed to make good on his vague undertaking.

'You waited a long time to reveal this,' Adémar added. 'Why?'

'Before this day I hesitated out of fear and doubted even my own experience, but I was again visited last night and by an angry saint, so I am

89

commanded by him and God to bring to your attention the means to strike down the force that threatens our endeavour. Even if I face a burning at the stake for speaking out, I cannot remain silent.'

'This is nonsense,' Adémar expostulated, waving an arm to dismiss Bartholomew.

'That, My Lord Bishop is easy to establish,' Raymond insisted, with a look of cunning that Adémar had never taken to. 'Let our fellow here take us to the spot where he claims the Holy Lance is buried. If he speaks the truth we will find it, if not...'

'Fire for my body and damnation for my soul,' Bartholomew intoned, his eyes closed.

A search for such a holy relic, as close to the body and blood of Christ as it was possible to get, could not be kept secret and nothing so inspired faith as anything which had a connection to the Crucifixion – the bones of a martyr were as nothing by comparison and there were several of those being borne to Palestine by the Crusaders.

Adémar himself had a piece of the True Cross in his baggage, which he had bought from the Emperor Alexius. It was not the notion that a piece of the Holy Lance might exist that made him a sceptic, more the timing and claimed placement of Bartholomew's disclosure; it was too convenient.

The reaction of the other magnates varied as Bartholomew reprised his vision, on the insistence and in the presence of Raymond, to the Council of Princes. Bohemund and Robert of

Normandy were vocally dubious as to the truth of the assertion, Vermandois not willing to sway one way or the other, while Godfrey de Bouillon was sure, if it could be found, it would, as it was claimed, lead them to victory.

Robert of Flanders, a man in love with relics and the owner of many, was excited by the notion but none came to see the need to exhume the lance more than the Count of Toulouse who claimed the right, as Bartholomew's lord and master, to oversee the endeavour; his fervour knew no bounds, yet that turned to frustration as two days of digging produced no positive result.

Six men had hacked at the floor of the cave, through the compacted earth of a millennium of worship to the softer ground below, spades wielded with decreasing gusto as they sunk ever lower to a depth where their heads were hidden from view. All this went on while sporadic fighting took place in every quarter of the defence as Kerbogha worked, not to overcome the walls but to keep his enemies on their mettle and exhausted. Peter Bartholomew stood over the dig, eyes closed and praying to the heavens, though never in doubt and hope, more in certainty that his vision was real.

Raymond, somewhat recovered in health on the prospect of the find, came to visit often, for to him the discovery of such an object had become of paramount concern, many observing this as a sign of his loss of faith and the need that it be restored by a divine revelation.

It was not long before his confidence in Bartholomew began to waver, which produced a flood of questions, the most telling being: what hands, those who had buried the Holy Lance, would dig so deep? The peasant seer pointed out that it had needed to survive many occupations of Antioch, even the reversal of Christianity and the return to paganism forced by the Byzantine Emperor Julian, followed by the arrival and occupation of Islam.

Those who had interred it knew the dangers that would be faced by such a holy object over a thousand years, knew that the lance had a purpose and the day of that need would come just as spiritual guidance would be required to exhume it. They would not burrow a shallow hiding place, but one so deep that only a person of true faith and divine resolve could find it.

'Then I suggest you do so, Bartholomew,' Raymond growled finally, his sombre tone of voice made more ethereal by being echoed off the walls of the cave church. 'For if it is a lie I will not be alone in wishing to flay the skin from your back and see your entrails in your hands before we set light to the faggots around your body.'

'Give me the means, My Lord, and I will expose it myself.'

'You men cease digging and help this miscreant down.' Raymond then fixed his Provençal peasant with a basilisk stare. 'Dig well, Peter Bartholomew, for what remains of you should you fail will aid us in refilling this.'

The diggers needed a ladder now to allow them both into the hole and out. Gathering his monkish garment around him Bartholomew disdained any aid as he clambered down into the small area lit by a single guttering oil lamp, taking up one of the spades left and beginning to slash at the earth with fury. The clang as he hit rock reverberated up and out to fill the chamber, which had Raymond's diggers looking at a lord who would not return their stare, he too busy in contemplation of the problems of being made to look like a credulous fool.

Judging by the sound now coming from below, Bartholomew had taken up a pick, also left below, and was hacking at the rock, which tempted one of those standing above to snigger, that dying as the Count gave him a black look, which seemed to deepen with each blow of that instrument, now a rhythmic ringing that might have passed for a church bell, given the mountains on which Antioch had been built were made of near indestructible stone.

'Hallelujah!'

That cry had all pressing forward, lanterns in hand, to gaze down at the dirt-blackened face of Peter Bartholomew gazing up, his eyes seeming to glow and in his hand an object too indistinct to identify.

'God be praised!' was his next cry, before he sunk to his knees so that the sounds of his loud and thankful prayers now rose up to the waiting ears.

'What have you found?' Raymond demanded.

The response was slow in coming; Bartholomew was too busy thanking God. 'That which I was sent to discover, My Lord.'

The temptation to blaspheme with impatience had to be curbed. 'Get up here and at once.'

Bartholomew's ascent was slow and what appeared before him, held aloft in one hand, did not look in any way divine: was it even metal, for time and burial had dimmed its shine with rust and grime? What became apparent when examined more closely, as Bartholomew held it out for inspection, was its shape, it being very like the partial tip of a Roman *pilum*, a finger width at the base and reducing to the point, the very form of a weapon that truly might have been carried by a legionary on the Mount of Calvary.

'Where is the shaft?' Raymond demanded, only to be met with a look of disdain, with a manner to match, by a man now confident of his safety.

'Who would bury that, and if they did, would the timber not rot?'

If Raymond missed the tone of voice, as well as the lack of acknowledgment to his title, the others present did not and one spoke up to tell Bartholomew of whom he was addressing, only to be reminded, and with discourtesy, that the man he was talking to was blessed by God and to mind his manners.

'Pass it here.'

The pointed metal shard, a hand and a half in length, was passed to Raymond who took it gingerly, as if expecting the contact to scorch his flesh. Instead it was cold, as it should be, which sent a look of doubt across his face, noted by the man who had found it and responded to swiftly.

'Do not expect it to glow or burn your skin, My Lord, the force it carries is in the flesh of whom it once pierced. Underneath that dirt and rust – who can tell? – may still lie the dried blood of Jesus.'

94

Raymond recoiled at that and he was not alone; those who had been digging previously stood back in near horror at being perhaps so close to such a liquid, even if dried. These were men who believed that when shriven by a priest what they received in the Eucharist was the very blood of Christ transformed; to be in the presence of reality was overpowering.

The noise from the mouth of the cave church began to grow, for there had been believers as well as doubters gathered there throughout, diminishing in numbers as time went by, it was true, but never so few that one or two were not keeping vigil. Bartholomew's cry of hallelujah had echoed out of that hole in the ground, bounced off the walls of the tiny cave church, flying out to those waiting ears.

Those lacking faith crossed themselves but the greater effect was on the devout: their wailing and gnashing of ecstasy had brought many more running to see what they hoped would be a sure sign of their deliverance. The man who carried it out into daylight and a now milling crowd was not the man who found it, though the dirt-covered Bartholomew was close on his heels.

It was Raymond of Toulouse, eyes alight and gait steady, who held it aloft to the gathering throng and he who paraded it through the streets, where likewise all who observed it, be they knight, fighting foot soldier, camp follower, pilgrim or Armenian Christian, fell to their knees and sent up a keening sound of worship that was, in truth, mass entreaty.

It was no surprise, then, that the work of Peter

Bartholomew in actually disinterring the relic was overborne by the spreading fame of the man who had possession and was eager to show it off. The relic was hailed wherever Raymond went, for he never subsequently moved without it – rumour had it that he took it to his bed with him that first night – and it was not long, those who shared his rank thought, before he seemed to confuse worship of the Holy Lance with praise for his own person.

With the whole city in a spasm of religious fervour, Peter Bartholomew called for the sinners to fast yet more vigorously and to give up to God alms that would be used to aid their deliverance, and thousands complied, it being noted that such coins as were gifted ended up with Raymond of Toulouse to swell his coffers to such an extent that he was soon far ahead of his peers in wealth and therefore influence.

'I wonder,' Bohemund opined, 'if anyone thought to search this Bartholomew before he entered St Peter's Church?' That Tancred doubted the wisdom of such an enquiry was plain to see; his faith had always been stronger. 'Examine the tale, nephew, and ask yourself if it is not a miracle too far?'

'Miracles happen, Uncle.'

'So I do believe, even if I have never witnessed one. But the convenience of this troubles me.'

'Do you intend to question and deny it?'

'No. Adémar, I suspect, thinks as I do, Robert of Normandy also, but if anyone is going to doubt it is a true relic let it be a consecrated bishop.'

'Is he not a Provençal bishop?'

That got a meaningful shrug, for Adémar and Toulouse came from the same part of Christendom. 'If he is careful not to cause Raymond offence, for the sake of harmony, that is an attribute he applies to us all. He will not show partiality.'

'Adémar dare not say it is false when all of Christian Antioch thinks it genuine.'

'Not all, Tancred, but that is less important than that he stops anyone from using it to guide our actions. Let the ones who hold it to be a true point of the Holy Lance take what comfort they need from it being in their midst. But it will not feed them nor will it drive off Kerbogha and his thousands.'

'My Lords,' Raymond said to the assembly of his peers, this accompanied by an arch look of triumph, 'who can not welcome the prospect of divine intervention?'

That brought a murmur of 'Amens', which faded somewhat as the Count of Taranto spoke out to repeat what he had said to Tancred about the shortage of food and the very powerful enemy encamped nearby, as well as the fact that no word had come of Byzantine aid.

'If we remain within Antioch we will either die from hunger or be so weak as to be unable to resist.' Pausing to await the comments of others, none came; he had spoken the unvarnished truth and all knew it. 'Such is the dearth of food that we are talking of days before we will be obliged to throw ourselves on the mercy of Kerbogha, which I suspect will not be in large supply.'

'Even a Turk likes ransom,' Vermandois insisted.

'True, Count Hugh, but while we may be sold back to our subjects, those we lead will not, and who knows, he may cut our throats as quick as he slices theirs. I look around me and ask who is inclined to trust in his greed?'

'Not I,' Robert of Normandy stated, emphatically.

Raymond, who had with him the Holy Lance, held his relic out for all to see. 'Let us seek terms. If this divine object cannot feed us or drive our enemies away, perhaps that is not the message it brings.'

'You think,' Adémar responded, 'that it will aid us in negotiation?'

'I am bound to ask why we have not tried before to talk to the Atabeg?'

Godfrey of Bouillon responded to that by showing a rare flash of exasperation. 'You know very well, My Lord, that it is common in siege for those outside the walls to demand we cease to resist. Kerbogha has not followed that custom; in short, he has not come to us with terms.'

'Then we must go to him,' Raymond insisted, 'with an offer to allow us to depart Antioch as a host. Does he want the city or our blood?'

'I would say our heads on pikes would satisfy him,' Bohemund replied.

'I say it is worth an attempt.'

Bohemund was adamant. 'While I think that will be worse than useless.'

Florid-faced Toulouse went a deeper shade of

scarlet but he got no chance to speak, for Adémar exercised his right to do so as the man who acted as the representative of the Pope. If few believed what Raymond proposed to be the case, it led to a long and heated discussion in which his view finally held sway, for in truth it was folly to keep fighting in a hopeless situation if the mere surrender of the city might spare them.

The first suggestion, that Adémar should go as envoy, was squashed by Godfrey of Bouillon, who required much circumlocution to tell his peers that the Bishop was too valuable to be made a hostage to fortune without bringing the cleric to the blush. In truth, he held the ground between them, which might turn to open conflict were he no longer alive.

Yet no one else would put themselves forward, Godfrey, Raymond and Bohemund included, for what was being spoken of was abject surrender and none amongst these magnates could face being the bearer of such a communication, an act which would stay with their name till the Second Coming. In the end it was decided that Peter the Hermit was a suitable messenger.

'Will he agree?' asked Vermandois.

Adémar spoke then in a manner rare for him; he was close to spitting, given the trouble such preachers had caused him ever since he had first encountered them. Peter was a particular bane: months before, when food had been short, and sensing the siege of Antioch to be failing, he had sought to flee back to the safety of Constantinople, only to be pursued, captured and brought back.

'After his attempt at flight he will do what he is told, if for no other reason than to redeem himself. He has learnt Greek since he came to the east, if he has learnt little else. Let him put that to our use.'

Peter was called to the Bishop, as ever looking like a biblical prophet with his long snowy hair and beard, as well as the look of mysticism he had in his eyes, to be reminded of his disgraceful transgression and how he had not been as severely punished as he should have been for deserting people who he had claimed as his flock.

He would be given an interpreter, a fellow called Firuz, who had been suggested by Count Bohemund, and he would go to Kerbogha's camp. That such a command provoked terror in the old man's soul was obvious, yet he knew his sin was not forgiven but in remission and that Adémar had the power to apply whatever sanction he chose.

The prospect of being burnt as a traitor to the Crusade, which had been hinted at by Adémar and was felt, it seemed, to be a just fate by the higher lords, was greater than any fear of the Atabeg and with heavy tread he prepared, next morning, to exit one of the smaller gates with a truce flag, dressed in robes of white, to make his way towards the camp of a man he thought near to the devil.

Firuz stood with Peter. Prior to surrendering his tower to the Apulians and facilitating the capture of the city, he had been a Muslim convert but was now once more a Christian. The Armenian was less fearful than the preacher: he was a military man and had that carapace of indifference to death that attended his chosen profession. Living and dying was in the hands of powers greater than he, but he had a task to perform, one outlined by Bohemund.

So far, Kerbogha had employed mainly Turks to invest and attack the city – it was they who had issued from the citadel and only once had he tested the walls with mixed contingents. The men he had left in the nearby camps, easy to distinguish because of their attire, had been of the same single and clearly dependable race. To rate the quality and spirit of the rest of the enemy host, those yet to be committed to battle, had been denied to the Crusaders, so Firuz was to examine with great care the main Islamic lines and report back what he observed about their make-up, strength and confidence.

CHAPTER SIX

Just getting the Hermit and Firuz out of the Bridge Gate took much negotiation, indeed permission had to be sought from Kerbogha himself to allow them passage, consent brought back by a richly dressed rider leading what was clearly a strong escort. So with a final sign of the cross the pair slipped through the postern gate and crossed the arched stone bridge to the other side of the River Orontes.

The main Turkish encampment was just south

of the western end of the Iron Bridge and as soon as they were sighted, what was a seemingly somnolent area of tents and cooking fires came to life; men leapt to their feet and hurried to see this apparition in his flowing robes, others exited their canvas to come and stare at Peter and his plainly clad companion, their escort slowing so they could be clearly seen and derided.

'Keep your head high,' Firuz commanded, as Peter let it sink on his chest rather than meet an enemy look. 'Do not show fear if you want to live.'

The eyes of the Armenian were darting around, doing what he had been asked, seeking to drink in what he could of the dispositions of Kerbogha's host as well as their true numbers, for the messages that had come into Antioch over the weeks since the arrival of this army had thrown up variations that were either low and designed to reassure, or fantastical and aimed at inducing terror.

Some estimate of the true figure could be discerned from the time it took to get from the edge of the camp to the centre, where sat the huge black pavilion of Kerbogha. Here were camped his own personal retainers, those on guard duty well armed, alert and wearing mail, leading Firuz to wonder if they were set there to protect their lord from his own host rather than display.

Once outside the main flap they were forced to wait in the broiling sun, offered nothing to drink or even spoken to by those entering and exiting with their leader's commands. They also had to wait when the entire host was called to prayer, Peter at last allowed to close his eyes, in truth joining in the devotions to pray for his corporeal body not his soul.

When they were called to go inside that was carried out in silence, merely a sharp nod by a man who pulled aside the flap designed to keep out the dust, while inside the passageway there were bowls of burning incense to kill off the latrine smell which attended the gathering of every host. Through another flap they entered the main area, lit by numerous oil lamps that sent out shadows that seemed to exaggerate the hard features of the Turkish commander.

Kerbogha had a visage that went with his reputation: long, oiled hair swept back to expose a narrow, much lined brow, heavy eyebrows atop black orbs that rarely blinked, hooked nose over full lips that arced down at the corners and a prominent chin covered with a well-trimmed beard, all set off by his dark skin. Hunched forward it was still possible to see he was a man of some strength, for he wore a short, sleeveless tunic that exposed his muscular arms while his calves were likewise huge. When he spoke his voice seemed to be coming from the soles of his soft leather boots.

'He asks why we have come,' Firuz said.

It was a tremulous voice that replied; Peter was in dread of his imagined fate and if it was not the one he had faced in Antioch, it promised to be even worse. 'You can tell him.'

'You must speak, Peter,' Firuz hissed. 'It must seem to come from you, and choose your words with care for there will be Greek speakers in this tent. Also, look him in the eye and reply with firmness. Imagine you are preaching to your flock and that God is using you as his instrument.'

It was not immediate; Peter seemed to want to fill his body with air before he opened his mouth and steadied his nerves. When words did come out, they made him. sound more demanding than good sense allowed.

'I am Peter the Hermit and I come from the mighty Council of Princes of the Holy Crusade.'

Firuz translated that in a softer tone and with a higher degree of tact, the council being noble not mighty, not that it mattered for another whispered the true words in Kerbogha's ear.

'I have come to seek by what terms you will allow us pass out of Antioch and make our way back to our far-off homes?'

Firuz added to that, 'In peace.'

The Atabeg actually began to laugh, it starting with a chuckle then turning into a bellow of amusement, soon taken up by all his attendants. Peter and Firuz watched as his head went back and his body rocked in his curule chair, so hard that the front legs were lifted from the floor. Then it died out, like a candle being extinguished, to be replaced by a glare that had Peter take an alarmed step backwards, only stopped from going further by the restraining arm of Firuz.

'Did you come in peace?' Kerbogha demanded, not waiting for a reply, leaving Firuz talking simultaneously and quietly while the Atabeg ranted about Crusaders, Franks, the Christian faith – Latin and Orthodox – as well as the crimes of all of those and the mercy of Islam, spittle bursting from those thick, dark lips to spray the carpeted ground between them until he concluded and sat back with the words, 'You came to kill, it is fitting, therefore, that you should die.'

It took some nudging to get Peter to deliver the offer as it had been given to him by the council: that the Crusaders and the pilgrims would abandon any attempt to get to Palestine and march instead to the north, leaving behind their arms and what few mounts they still possessed as well as any treasure they still had from their previous actions. Nor would they stop, not even at Constantinople.

'It is also my duty,' Firuz translated, 'to remind you that we are not alone in making war on your faith. We act in concert with the mighty Emperor Alexius of Byzantium who is at this very moment marching to our aid.'

An idea put forward by Vermandois, for once his suggestion had not been ignored – that it was wasted became obvious after another bout of loud mirth.

'Your mighty emperor is now marching back to his capital, burning everything in his wake, crops, shelter, slaughtering animals to stop me from pursuing and destroying him. That is because he thinks you lost, which proves that for a Christian he is no fool.'

Peter, shocked at such news, had to be nudged to say, 'Our offer stands.'

The Atabeg made a pretence of thinking on it, only to slowly shake his head and start speaking again, the low and calm of his voice lending more effect to his words than if he had shouted them, Firuz matching the tone.

'No messenger, go back to your mighty council and tell them they are as sheep and their offer a bleat. Perhaps they will, like that beast, succumb and be roasted on my fires. Or maybe they will die from lack of pasture.'

That last notion seemed to amuse Kerbogha; it chilled the men at whom it was aimed.

'My host will pray you to come out and fight, but Allah does not always grant a wish to the faithful. So you will expire from a lack of food, and when your knights can no longer stand and do battle I will walk into Antioch at my pleasure.'

Kerbogha fell silent for a moment, which had all eyes on him for it was plain he had not finished. If it was merely for effect it worked.

'I offer you this, for it is not fitting that I should fail to be merciful. Leave the city and your clothing, banners, weapons and armour, come out naked and I promise you will all die quickly, rather than the slow death you now face. And because Allah is merciful he will take to his bosom anyone who turns to the Prophet and the true faith.'

Peter opened his mouth to speak but the sharp command to take both he and Firuz back to Antioch cut right across the attempt. As they left the pavilion Firuz whispered that Peter should walk slowly and look sad, an admonition that was in fact unnecessary, for the older man was near to stumbling and tears ran down his cheeks.

Clearly he feared what was coming, which made a fellow who had converted twice wonder at why a preacher who claimed to be so holy and had spent his life spreading the gospel and underlining the route to salvation was so frightened to

106

meet his maker?

It took time enough to assemble the council and that allowed Bohemund to question Firuz about what he had observed. The Armenian was truthful: the host was great, well armed and seemed in good spirits, with no sign of dissension amongst the various groupings. Antioch being a trading city was a magnet to merchants from all over the interior, so Firuz had, by what they wore on their heads and the colouring of their garments, been able to identify the different clans and sub-faiths that made up Kerbogha's army, not without a sense of wonder that such grouping, famed for their internecine conflicts, could ever come together. In his opinion this was only made possible by the evil reputation of their general.

'Tell me everything, from the moment you entered the camp to the time you left.'

That took a while, with Bohemund listening and saying not a word, until a call came to say that the council was assembled and his presence was required. The air he adopted when he entered the chamber, of seeming confidence, stood in stark contrast to the looks of gloom by which he was greeted and he maintained that as the message Peter had been given was relayed in all its barbarous clarity.

'Do you think it true about the Emperor?' Vermandois asked, in a manner that spoke of near despair.

'I cannot see,' Normandy replied, 'why Kerbogha would lie, and, if there was threat from the north, would he still be in his full strength where he is camped?'

Robert of Flanders pitched in. 'Sense would dictate he moves to meet that threat if it exists. It takes little of his forces to keep us bottled up.'

'Then we must do what he least expects,' said Bohemund softly.

'What do you suggest, Count Bohemund?' Adémar asked.

'We must fight him and beat him, but on terms of our choosing.'

'Easily advanced,' Vermandois scoffed, 'but how do you think that can be achieved?'

'Surely if the Holy Lance has a purpose, it is to aid us in that!'

The reactions to those words were mixed, but Raymond of Toulouse was openly irritated – Bohemund's scepticism about the relic and how it was discovered had not remained a secret for the very simple reason he had made no attempt that it should.

Godfrey of Bouillon spoke next. 'Whatever the Holy Lance brings to our cause, Count Bohemund has the right of it. We stay here within the walls and starve like curs or we die like men in battle.'

'Outside the walls,' Bohemund insisted.

This was said with a grateful look at Godfrey, whose views carried weight. That there was mutual regard was true; Bohemund, with the aid of Tancred, had, a year past, saved Godfrey's life when he was about to be killed by a bear that had already savaged him severely. Yet he would not grant an opinion based on gratitude just for the sake of that; if Godfrey spoke it was with honesty.

'We can barely muster a hundred fit horses,' Raymond protested.

'And if we had ten thousand I would not employ them. To go to Kerbogha would be fatal, for that allows him to choose the field of battle, something my forebears taught me was always a flawed notion. Let us choose where we fight, let us make him come to us and let us fight on foot as we did at Dorylaeum.'

'Which you would have lost without we came to your relief.'

'We held for a day and would have held for another,' Normandy barked, for no knight liked his deeds to be belittled and the Normans had held off a Turkish force that massively outnumbered them. 'The enemy you and your companions chased from the field was one we had much diminished.'

In truth it had been nip and tuck: Bohemund and Duke Robert, riding ahead from Nicaea with a third of the crusading host to ease the problem of supply, had been caught unawares by a force of Turks, led by the Sultan of Rüm. Bold action by the Duke and Bohemund, leading their own familia knights, had blunted the initial assault, but it was only sheer bloody-mindedness and ability that had got them out from the men who eventually surrounded them.

Their actions gave Tancred time to get the rest of the host, pilgrims included, into a place the Normans could defend. Retiring into a nearby marsh, with a soft crust of ground that would negate the Turkish cavalry, they had been forced to fight on foot until relief came, which it did when Raymond, Godfrey, Flanders and the Bishop of Puy arrived to chase their attackers away. That had ended in a rout for the Sultan and the capture of much booty.

'There is still hope that Kerbogha was lying,' Count Hugh insisted, as if Normandy had not spoken. 'Alexius might bring the might of Byzantium to our aid.'

Adémar cut off any scoffing by saying quickly to Vermandois that it was a very tenuous thing to hope for and gave ground when Bohemund took up the discussion again.

'The promises of Alexius Comnenus are worthless – all he has ever been concerned with is the integrity of his empire.'

Nor did he stop at that, for it was time to tell the truth, however unpalatable it was to listen to. How many times had Bohemund been tempted to tell them this, to show how little trust they should place in the word of a Byzantine emperor, whoever he was and regardless of his winning manner? He could speak his mind instead, acting in a manner that he had been obliged to curb since their first council.

They had been dazzled by Byzantine magnificence and saw virtue where there was corruption and deceit, this driven home by a harsh assessment of the Emperor's motives. If the Crusade aided him, taking back the old Byzantine possessions from the Seljuk Turks and handing them over to him, such offerings would be gratefully received. If, however, they died in the attempt, that was a loss with which Alexius could live, for in doing so they must diminish those who could

110

threaten him, quite apart from the fact that they might themselves represent a future menace.

'I fear,' Adémar responded, 'and it gives me no joy to admit it, that you may speak the truth.'

'Mark it, My Lord Bishop, as no lie, for if it was not so, why is Alexius no threat to Kerbogha?'

The weary-looking cleric cast a glance around the assembly, as if seeking someone to refute what Bohemund had said, but not even Raymond was prepared to challenge a man who knew Byzantium too well. Having waited for what seemed an age, Adémar finally set things in motion again.

'Do you have a way of proceeding to suggest, Count Bohemund?' That got a sharp nod. 'Then perhaps it would be a notion to outline your thinking to all present.'

Which he proceeded to do, and if it was bold as a plan it was also, if it failed, a route to certain annihilation. Many times it had to be restated that such a fate awaited them regardless of how they acted, and after much discussion it was agreed that to die by wasting away was not a fitting death for men of such stature, while those of lesser rank would follow either from the same feeling or because they had enough belief in God or relics like that which Raymond displayed to them.

'Let them see the Holy Lance before the battle,' Bohemund suggested, for if he was cynical him-self he knew that others were not. 'And let them kiss it if they so desire.'

Toulouse reacted as if the smelly mob was being invited to plant their lips on him.

'But let us put my plan in execution and place

our faith in our abilities.'

Put to the vote it was agreed, then came the vexed question of who was to lead, that immediately countered by the suggestion from Raymond that they should, as they had in the past, command their own contingents.

'No!' Bohemund maintained and not with much tact. 'Such a battle requires one leader, one general, for a divided command will not serve.'

'And no doubt, Count Bohemund, you see yourself in that position?'

'I have a plan, Count Raymond, do you?'

That would have descended into unseemly wrangling if Godfrey de Bouillon had not spoken out forcefully. 'I will say, without equivocation, that I will not assent to take my men into this battle under anyone else but Count Bohemund!'

'He saved your life once, Duke Godfrey,' Toulouse scoffed, 'do not be so sure he will do so again.'

The reply was stinging and would have seen a sword drawn if it had come from anyone else.

'I have often wondered if you are capable of being a fool, Count Raymond, now I know it to be so. You are a puissant lord, a famous knight, but do you think the Turks whisper in terror of you in the dark of the night? I know they do not fear my name any more than did Alexius Comnenus. He feared Bohemund de Hauteville, not anyone else of our number and I think our enemies know best of him and his deeds to be likewise affected. It is his banner that will draw their gaze, therefore let the man who has brought us to this conclusion and has at least a plan have

112

the command.'

'For the very good other reason,' Robert of Normandy cut in, 'that amongst us he is by any measure the best and most experienced general.'

'You would serve under a man who owes you fealty?'

'Better that than die under one in whom I repose no faith.'

That was like a slap to Toulouse, really the only other contender, and he was angry. Yet he was no fool despite what Godfrey had said and to put it to a vote was to lose. Flanders would go with his brother-in-law of Normandy, which only left Vermandois to back the Provençal case to the leadership, Adémar only having a casting vote if it was required. With a sharp nod and still holding his relic, he left the room.

'Then,' Adémar said, 'it is needful that we say a Mass for our hopes.'

When it came to a choice of where to fight a battle, Bohemund had always been aware he was not gifted with much choice. Without horses he could not attack an enemy camped so far off from Antioch and, as he had said, would not have done so even if he was well supplied with mounts – that left the actual point of contact too open to chance. On foot he dare not stray too far from the security of the city walls, so all that was left was to use those as an anchor.

His aim was to deploy in such a way that would invite Kerbogha to attack him, but just to get what was left of the crusading army out through the Bridge Gate was hard enough and, despite his feelings, that seemed to require a strong body should be left behind to mask the citadel, thus weakening what could be put in the field and that he declined to do. The notion that it be left unguarded alarmed more than the men he led: Toulouse, who scoffed at any suggestion the Count of Taranto put forward, was vocal in his scorn.

'They could take the city while we are outside!'

'If we are beaten Kerbogha will take Antioch anyway, Count Raymond, and I am putting my faith in the fact that we will tempt our Atabeg with a morsel he cannot resist.'

Sensing the need to explain further Bohemund stood closer to the table on which lay the map of Antioch and its surroundings.

'Kerbogha wants to destroy us, wants to say to all of his peers that the men who defeated every army sent against it was brought low by him.'

'You can see into his mind?'

'Perhaps,' the Duke of Normandy interjected, to put Raymond in his place 'my confrère can see into more than one.'

'It does no harm,' Adémar suggested, emollient as ever, 'to test notions of what might be. Even as a mere cleric I know that.'

Godfrey of Bouillon laughed out loud. 'If God had many mere clerics like you, My Lord Bishop, then all of Islam would quake and Kerbogha would up sticks and flee back to Mosul.'

If the Bishop of Puy-en-Velay was flattered, he hid it behind a display of becoming modesty, but Godfrey's sally had spread amusement and done more to lighten the atmosphere than all the

114

priestly soothing, which allowed Bohemund to continue.

'I suggest we tempt him with that destruction and hope that seeing us outside the walls he will do nothing to require us to withdraw, which an attack from the citadel will most surely require. I am guessing...'

That word got an indrawn breath from Vermandois and Toulouse which Bohemund ignored: what was the point of explaining to men who knew as well as he did that war was a game of chance and this was no different? All any general could do was make a plan and hope that he could maintain his, while throwing his opponents off their own.

'I believe he will order those in and to the rear of the citadel to do nothing to take the shine off his anticipated glory. Those men are commanded by Shams ad-Daulah even if he fights under Kerbogha's banner. The last thing our Atabeg will want is possession of the city gifted to him by the son of the last governor.'

'And if you are mistaken?' Toulouse demanded.

Bohemund declined to respond directly to that meaningless question and instead spoke to them all.

'Do I need to remind you of how desperate our situation is, My Lords? We either fight on what terms we can manage or we march out with naked, shrunken bellies and halters round our necks within days, to have our blood turn the Orontes red. I tell you, if we cannot engage as a body of maximum strength, I will march out alone with my Apulians and you can watch the slaughter

115

from the walls and get an early sight of your own fate.'

'Finish outlining your plan, Count Bohemund,' Adémar replied, his voice strong and commanding for once. 'And by my faith let us all attend to it.'

CHAPTER SEVEN

Bohemund's first act was to seek to seal the city, which was difficult, and to keep his preparations from common discussion, which was even harder. If Kerbogha got wind of his intentions he could easily move to counter them and render any exit from the city impossible. That imposed a time constraint as well: to keep matters covert would not last long. Luckily, all the fighting men had weapons that were ready for use; indeed they expected to employ them every day, so they could be left in ignorance until just before the action.

What they lacked was satisfied bellies, but no more so than the small number of mounts he could muster, who were near to being skeletal. His first act, tactfully including the council in the decision, was to make a quick distribution of the available food to both, not enough to remedy weeks of shortage, but one massively more than that to which they had been recently accustomed, which acted upon their spirits as well as their stomachs.

Ever since the departure of William of Grand-mesnil and his deserting knights, the walls had been more carefully patrolled as a matter of course, with a system of token checks, on the old Roman model, by section leaders, they visiting each sentry at irregular intervals to ensure those guarding them were both awake and alert, while a captain made flying visits and kept everyone on their toes.

They had added instructions to alert the Turks to any flight by an individual. As a sanction that was made effective by the way the enemy reacted, waiting till daylight and allowing those still inside to watch the skin being stripped off the screaming victims they had intercepted, for, despite every precaution, some still tried.

Every fellow magnate was allotted a role, and despite his earlier demand for sole control it was clear to the Count of Taranto that men would fight better for their liege lord than any other commander; all he asked was that his peers stick to his initial plan and act positively to any instructions he subsequently issued.

It was just as important that the men leading individual companies were made aware of what was required and they were gathered the evening before the plan was to be executed to be made privy to the outline. Looking at them in guttering candlelight Bohemund could see in their eyes what was in every heart including his own: this as an enterprise was likely to be terminal.

If Vermandois was a military ignoramus he was a fiery one, always seeking to initiate a wild charge even when circumstances demanded

117

caution, convinced that in times to come chroniclers of bravery and knightly good conduct would sing of his sterling deeds. One of the attributes of good generalship is the ability to use those gifts possessed by any man you command, even if they are limited. Thus Count Hugh was given the task of driving the Turks away from the Bridge Gate to allow the rest of the crusading host to deploy, for he had the recklessness such a mission required.

Given all of the horses as well as every single man who could use a bow, either mounted or on foot, Bohemund had them crowd behind the barred gate in darkness and in silence so as not to alert the citadel. Behind this body of men the streets and squares were filling up with all the other fighting contingents, every one on foot, all silent and commending their souls to heaven, while the pilgrims prayed for them in the churches and the local Armenians hid and trembled in their cellars.

Somehow Vermandois had got hold of a sleek white horse, albeit also with prominent ribs – he had probably sold the last of his plate to acquire such a beast – and he had upon his surcoat not the Crusader cross but the multi fleur-de-lis device of Clovis, founder of the French Kingdom and his claimed ancestor. His eyes at the final conference, before he donned his helmet, had shone with the prospect of the glory he was sure he was bound to achieve.

Bohemund, who would give the order to attack, looking at him by the light of a single torch in the deep doorway of the palace of the Patriarch of

Antioch, wondered if, in his quest for that laurel, he might lead his contingent to an ignominious death. The temptation to speak, to ask Count Hugh to calm himself, was put aside for it would have been pointless; all he could do was follow him to the head of his troops.

The first daylight to touch anything visible lit the huge green flag that flew high above the citadel, hanging limp in the calm of a windless morning. That would begin to lightly flutter as the sun rose over the mountains to the east, its heat stirring the first breeze of the day, while down below it was still in shadow and that was where advantage lay. There would be enough time to commence an attack and enough light, Bohemund had calculated, to press it home before the citadel could sound a trumpet to alert those camped close to the city walls.

Several large Apulian Normans leant their back against the huge wooden gate as the great baulk of timber that barred it was quietly lifted off its cleats. Others stood to each side holding ropes that had been attached to the timbers so that when the two halves were opened it would happen at a speed that would allow for an immediate charge by the horsemen.

Surprise was essential, the timing acute and both had been carefully calculated to gain them the maximum advantage. The Turkish encampments would have just bestirred and they would be deploying for dawn themselves, always the time to protect against sudden attack. Yet light was essential too: Vermandois and his men had to see their targets and the enemy had to observe what was approaching and the speed at which it was closing to be induced, the man in command hoped, to panic.

Bohemund watched as the sun turned the sky from silver to a hint of burnished gold, throwing the shadow of the citadel itself over the higher part of the city. There were two cohorts of Provençal knights up there holding the drystone wall, a couple of hundred men, all that could be spared to mask the fortress – and they should have been led by their liege lord.

Raymond, either through a recurrence of genuine illness or pique, had taken once more to his cot and left one of his vassals to command his men, which was poor behaviour, especially since Bishop Adémar, not in full vigour himself, had decided he too must lead a contingent and fight.

'May God commend your efforts, Count Hugh,' Bohemund said quietly, before issuing a louder command that had the gates swung open.

Vermandois let out a piercing yell and spurred his horse as soon as a gap appeared, those behind doing likewise, and the mounted men streamed through the gate to clatter over the arched stone of the bridge, quickly followed by the foot-bound archers. The Turks had a small piquet on the far side, which was ridden over in seconds, and the advance party was out on the open plain to the west of the river, firing arrows at men only halfway through their dawn deployment.

That they were so engaged worked in the Crusaders' favour, for being loosely bunched they became easier targets for arrows fired by foot-bound knights, many of whom lacked full competence in the use of a bow and arrow. Fortunately the enemy was short on the discipline that comes from being properly formed, so the archers' inexperience was not exposed.

Just as effective were Vermandois and his mounted fighters, who having emptied their quills proceeded to ride into the enemy ranks with their swords doing great damage, if not by killing, in forcing into flight any body of Muslims that sought to form a defence, they hampered by the fact that much of the forces deployed before the walls could not come to their aid.

It was no mystery to any of the Crusade leaders that Kerbogha's men suffered from the same constraints that had troubled them during their siege: the deep River Orontes forced those seeking to invest the walls into a dispersed separation in which mutual support was slow to gather, and Bohemund had built this factor into his plan. He needed time to get his entire force deployed and they would have to fight to achieve the position he knew was a minimum, an unbroken line that arced with its back to the Bridge Gate so it could not be outflanked from the north.

Yet it was not a simple affair: to get fifteen thousand men out of one gate was bound to cause crowding and confusion and it was thankful that Vermandois had the sense to split his force, driving the greater part of the Muslim force back toward Kerbogha's main encampment while allowing the rest to flee south, the smaller body now cut off from a quick retreat and any support by the river. Not that Vermandois could hold, he lacked the numbers, and it was only the arrival of

121

the leading ranks of his northern French knights on foot that gave a tenuous stability to his line.

Men were streaming untidily out and over the arch of the stone bridge, their captains using the flat of their sword blades to try to get them into some form of order. Above their heads the walls were lined with priests in deep prayer, calling to God for aid, while higher still, not in full daylight, a huge black flag with no device flew from the citadel tower, obviously a sign to Kerbogha that the Crusaders had set in motion an attack: to those of a superstitious bent it was of a shade that spoke of imminent death.

Bohemund got out on the Antioch plain on the heels of Vermandois to set up a command post on the small mount that had once housed the siege fort of La Mahomerie. His banner was soon aloft at his back and his eyes straining north to see how quickly Kerbogha would come, worrying that he would do so before he could get what was at present a rabble into place.

The plan was, at this moment, in the balance without that should happen, for the close besiegers, still all Turks by their dress, having been swept from their prepared positions had not panicked and fled but had begun to regroup. They were showing a stiffening resistance which, given their numbers, would soon turn into a dangerous attack difficult to contain.

The northern French were fully engaged and now it was the Lotharingians debouching through the gate, led by an ebullient Godfrey de Bouillon, who went by Bohemund with a cry that 'By God it was good to see grass again, even if it stinks of

Turkish shit', before turning to berate his men to make haste.

Half a glass of sand must have gone by before the next contingent, the two Roberts of Normandy and Flanders, began to lead out their warriors, followed by Bishop Adémar at the head of the remaining Provençals, in full chain mail and under his blue banner with the device of the Virgin Mary, each party going to the right of those who had preceded it to form a continuous line.

Last out were the Apulians, led by Tancred, who had been held back just in case an attack developed from the citadel and overwhelmed the men set to prevent them interfering in the battle. That would have led to fighting in the streets of the lower town, for the Apulians could not have got up to save the Provençals from annihilation, but better that than those outside should find their own gates closed against them. Tancred's men gathered around Bohemund's banner to act as a reserve that could be rushed to plug any gap in the defence.

With the sun full up the Latin forces were fully engaged against those who had been deployed against the walls and doing no more than what had been asked of them, that they hold their ground. When the main part of Kerbogha's huge force came it was going to be hard, but contain them they must and that needed solid defensive cohesion, not ambition.

The sun rose higher and higher, the heat intensifying until the ground began to shimmer, while before him the line of Crusaders waved in both directions as some advanced and others fell back slightly, both positions reversed over time yet never enough to be a threat to either side.

Of the main Muslim host there was no sign, no telltale cloud of dust that was the mark of a great army on the march, and that held until every faction of the men of Antioch were in place, as well as the supplies of water and the means to deliver them, without which, on a late June day, they would not last. The first part of Bohemund's plan had succeeded, but where was Kerbogha?

That black banner above the citadel had sent hundreds of horns blowing throughout the main enemy camp as the various contingents got ready to march and soon, rippling with anticipation, they were lined up to do so. That no order came was a surprise and all eyes were aimed across the huge encampment to where flew the standard of their general, wondering when he would give the command to advance and crush these feeble nonbelievers. Inside the pavilion it was the same; the senior officers watched Kerbogha and wondered what was going through his mind, for he had said little.

Aware that all eyes were upon him Kerbogha showed no sign of anxiety. Before him was a map that told him what position the Crusaders had taken up, whose banner flew in what was obviously the command position, and runners brought him information that suggested they were out in total, that they were being held, yet were maintaining themselves an unbroken line; no threatening advance but no hint of a retreat.

Standing orders to those who masked the St George's Gate already had them hurrying south to the lower bridge that crossed the Orontes and they would come upon the rear of the Latins, while boats had been provided for the men camped outside the St Paul's Gate and along the inland riverbank so they could reinforce the men who, originally driven back, had been camped opposite the Bridge Gate. The latter, with more men coming to their aid, would not falter, so he had time to think on the best way to react, for if an immediate frontal advance was the most obvious, it was not the sole option.

'I sense,' he said finally, without lifting his head, 'that you are eager to rush into battle.'

That got a low murmur of agreement.

'I have years on all of you, and experience too. We are in no peril, my good fellows.' The call to prayer began to echo through the camp, and that made Kerbogha smile, for the imams would show no concern for anything other than the souls of their flock. 'Let us say our prayers and then we may have guidance as to how to react.'

In truth the Atabeg of Mosul had concerns, even if they were slight, given the relative numbers: his force was a heterogeneous one, made up of so many tribes and different religious affiliations, albeit they were all Muslims. He had caution about exposing them too quickly to battle. On the way to Antioch he had besieged Edessa and what he had seen there did not fill him with confidence as to how they would perform, added to which this was a host that had never engaged in open combat, an arena so much

125

more open to malign chance than a siege. It was why he had used his Turks as the main weapon – they were fierce warriors by nature and could be relied on to fight well.

Would the Crusaders, upon sight of the whole host moving up, merely fade back behind their walls? Would they hold out against the forces already engaged and at this very moment being substantially reinforced? It was paramount to Kerbogha that this battle, even if it was forced upon him, should be the last fight over Antioch and wholly successful, added to which if there was any reputation to be gained from its fall, then it should be his and his alone, hence his standing instruction to the citadel and Shams ad-Daulah, repeated by messenger, to stay within their walls.

'My intention,' he said, once prayers were over, 'is to keep the Latins outside the walls and fighting. Our men are holding and will find it possible to continue to do so as their losses are replaced from the other side of the Orontes. We will march, but let some sand run through the glass before we do, for on sight of us our enemies will merely fade away and we will once more face their walls. I want them too weary to retreat with any speed, and even if they try I have issued orders so that they will find they have to fight just to get back to the gate.'

'Victory will come anyway, My Lord Kerbogha,' cried one of his senior commanders, a Persian and a reluctant ally. 'They are starving and our men may die to no purpose.'

The face closed up, what had been a narrow forehead near to disappearing: Kerbogha was not a man who liked his actions or decisions to be questioned. 'You may die for want of respect.'

That was threat enough to silence the speaker and more than enough to make cautious the others present. Kerbogha's black eyes swept the room and all dropped their heads enough to avoid contact with his glare. There was no need for him to speak: they would obey his commands whenever he chose to issue them.

'Keep the host at readiness and I will give the order to march when I think the time is right.'

Standing on his slight mound, with the baking sun making both his helmet and his mail hard to bear, Bohemund was lost in confusion and racking his brain to think if there was some way Kerbogha could outmanoeuvre him. The Atabeg had to stay this side of the Orontes; he could not get at the Crusaders by any other means and if he tried a long flank march to the west it would take him time and could not be kept from being observed. In that event Bohemund would swing his line to face it, an option open to him in an interior position. As long as he held the Bridge Gate he held the ability to withdraw at will, not that he would order that unless the battle was well and truly lost.

Several times he had been obliged to send forward Tancred at the head of a strong party of Apulians to straighten a deep kink in the Christian line, and on one occasion he had withdrawn some of Vermandois' men and replaced them to give them some respite, they having been fighting the longest. It was a mark of their ability and morale

127

that they took this amiss and were keen to resume their place as soon as a lull in the fighting made this possible.

And pauses there were; for all their martial prowess, and the Turks could hold their head for valour with any Christian, no man could keep fighting at full tilt for several hours under a hot sun. Respite came when an enemy fell back to regroup, a slight suspension but enough to take on a drink of water, to mop the streaming sweat from their brows, to look their opponents in the eye before one or the other rushed forward to re-engage.

Yet such breathers happened in parts of the line not the whole, so the air was never free of the clash of weapons and the cries of men, either to give force to their efforts or to react to a painful blow, added to that endless loud pleas to saints or the paladins of the Muslim religion for succour and strength.

A careful eye was kept on the various banners, for it was important that they held steady. If the army of which Bohemund had been given temporary command was fighting for its life and its faith, it was those fellow magnates of his who could inspire their efforts by both their personal example and the ability they had to encourage by word and deed.

'Lord Bohemund, the Turks from the St George's Gate have crossed the river over the southern bridge and are coming up on our rear.'

That got a nod; one of the lesser gates and the furthest south, the numbers there had not been great, some five hundred men who could not defeat the Crusaders but could, by their actions and if their timing was right, cause serious problems, for they were as a body mounted on swift ponies. He looked over to the group of mounted French knights, part of those who had first exited the Bridge Gate under Vermandois, standing by their horses, holding their heads tight so they could not graze or drink too much: a horse with a full belly was of no use in a fight.

'Who has Count Hugh left in command over there?'

'Reinhard of Toul,' Tancred replied, 'in the service of France. Shall I call him to you?'

'No,' Bohemund replied with a smile, 'it is only fitting I go to him. Keep your eye on our front, Tancred and act to provide support as you see fit.'

Reinhard pulled himself to his full height when Bohemund approached, for here was a fighter of legend. The Count of Taranto was a man with whom he had enjoyed little contact and he knew, because he had heard it spoken, of his liege lord's less than sterling view of the Apulian, but since he did not much admire Count Hugh he discounted his opinion. Looking up and blinking at the sky – there was no choice with such a giant – he nodded as his instructions were relayed, based on the notion that Kerbogha would have given the commander at the southernmost gate certain instructions in the event of a full-blooded sortie from within the walls.

'They will not attack us unless we are so pressed they have little fear of taking on a superior force. But if matters become critical they will try to cut off what they see as our line of retreat.'

'Little do they know it is not one we will choose to take.'

Bohemund smiled at Reinhard then; here was a knight with no illusions about their fate should they fail and one who intended to die in battle, not as a slave.

'They must be stopped before they can get close enough to affect matters, and if we lose every horse and every man in achieving that then that is a price that must be paid. We cannot have mounted men attacking our rear, even in small numbers, while we are fully engaged and in a struggle for survival to the front, for they will wreak havoc.'

To a knight of much experience that required no further explanation: it was not numbers that mattered but the effect such a sight would have on those struggling to hold the line against Kerbogha's host. Men would be bound to turn away from their primary duty to fend off an attack by a man on horseback, especially archers, and that would give a chance for the Turks to break through any gap created in the front line.

'These mounts are not fit for the kind of fight I must engage in, My Lord. One charge and they will be spent. And then there are the numbers – we are too few.'

'I will detach some *milities* to go with you, Reinhard; let the foot soldiers take the bulk of the action and reserve your cavalry till the last. And know this, as much as I do myself, you hold the fate of all of our confrères in your hands. If you fail to stop those coming up from the south and they interfere when we face the whole might of

Kerbogha, we cannot hold.'

'It would not wound my pride if you were to give the command to another.'

Bohemund knew that was not fear: Reinhard was telling him he would happily serve under a knight more senior and of greater experience than himself. The widening of the smile was as reassuring as the words.

'We are all captains today, Reinhard, or even generals. You will do as well as anyone, of that I am sure.'

'Thank you, My Lord.'

That got him a slap on the shoulder. 'Make the King of France proud so that, even if he is not present, he will hear of your valour and praise you.'

CHAPTER EIGHT

Reinhard moved with little haste, more interested in keeping his formation in order and free from fatigue than covering ground. The men he was about to face were not going to engage in an immediate assault, their aim was to get into a good position for a later attack; indeed, when they were sighted, even if they were in superior numbers, they ceased to come on. This being far enough off from the southern walls of Antioch served the purpose of the Crusader army well, albeit the Turks were in sight of the citadel and any instruction Kerbogha chose to relay from its towers.

The Crusader had two options: to go on the defensive himself or to attack. Bohemund, even if it was more by chance than knowledge, had chosen well, for in Reinhard of Toul he had appointed a leader able to take all of the pertaining factors into account, able to reason that his men, over a long period without supply and given their diminished state at the beginning of the battle, not to mention their inferior numbers, were not in a fit condition for a long drawn-out action; as time went by their inherent weaknesses against a well-fed enemy would tell.

Another reason to act quickly was that it would be unexpected: normal tactics dictated that Reinhard should stay on the defensive; as long as he stopped the Turks from getting to the battle area his job was done and in the ordinary course of events they would seek to overcome him to get into the fight at a time of their own choosing. The state of his men, and more importantly his mounts, would be no mystery to a Turkish commander who oversaw the interdiction of the St George's Gate, by far the most porous of the five entrances and exits from the city.

Smugglers plied their trade at great risk and ameliorated that not only by bribery but also by being conduits of information to both sides; they would tell the Crusaders the numbers and spirit of the besieging Turks once inside and do the reverse on their egress, which had to include the lack of such things as food and fit horses. If there was a degree of supposition in Reinhard's thinking that was what any commander was obliged to rely on; certainty was never available in battle.

Another positive trait was him seeing the need to explain to those who would carry out his orders why they were being asked to act in that way; better men risking their lives should know the reason than hesitate in wonder once engaged. In battle you seek to see into the mind of your opposite number, to anticipate his thinking, and by doing so lead him to conclusions which he will see as rational when they are in fact false.

Tactical outline over, Reinhard lined up his *milities* in several ranks, so that they formed a rough square, and set them to advance with his cavalry bringing up the rear, but so slowly and wearily that the gap between the two bodies grew perceptibly wider.

A good commander, once he has made and explained his dispositions, prays that they are correct and only seeks to alter them, not by the gnawing worry that they might be wrong, but only when aware of the certainty that they are flawed. This led to an extended period of anxious watchfulness in the hope that the enemy, once they did move, would do so as had been hoped. Reinhard breathed easier when he saw them begin to deploy for an obvious attack, for if they had not he would have been obliged, lacking the force to press home upon them, to retreat to his starting position.

Mounted archers – one of, if not the main Turkish assault weapon – were deadly in open country and this was where Reinhard and his men found themselves, for they had declined to use the one flank partially protected by the River Orontes. The Turks held back on an immediate attack, instead riding around in a flurry of circles as if threatening rather than with intent, this because the opening gap between the Crusaders' horse and foot looked to be playing into their hands, the divergence beginning to increase enough to allow them to assault the *milities* with impunity from all sides.

The blowing of a distant horn, coming from a small group under a green banner, obviously the commander, set the mounted archers into a fast canter, their mounts controlled by knees alone, both hands occupied with their bows, in a display of horsemanship which would have been admirable if it had not also been deadly.

Against such an attack the *milities* had only their shields and their helmets and these were rendered near to useless by the proximity of their assailants as they loosed off their deadly darts. Men were dropping in increasing numbers and the temptation to take aim at their less well-protected backs brought the bulk of the mounted archers into the ground between the *milities* and Reinhard.

In their enthusiasm for killing and maiming, the Turks were firing off their arrows with no discrimination, seeking to do with quantity what would have been better served by careful aim, and in acting so they presented Reinhard with the opportunity for which he had prayed and calculated. As soon as he saw the first fellow turn back towards his own side for want of anything in his quill, he called upon his men to advance, kicking into a fast canter his supposedly weary horses.

His primary aim was to induce confusion in his

enemy, a lack of certainty about how to act, and Reinhard achieved that for there was no immediate response from his opposite number, now, in any case, partially hidden by a cloud of dust kicked up by his own men. Lacking clear orders they were unsure as to how they should react to this sudden alteration to the state of the battle, these Latin horsemen, who had looked to be spent before they started, coming on at pace with lowered and deadly lances; this had not been anticipated.

The *milities* suddenly broke ranks and spread out to get between the bulk of the mounted archers and safety, albeit they left behind a ground covered in writhing bodies. At a rush the lead elements got to the riverbank and took up a kneeling position with extended pikes to bar passage, which obliged their enemies, if they wanted to get away, to ride across their front. At the back of that first line the rest had turned to face south so as to hold at bay any Turks seeking to assist their comrades.

'Choose your target!'

Reinhard's yelled command immediately broke up the advancing line as each lance point was aimed at an individual Turk, now widely dispersed, those with arrows firing them off uselessly at men in full chain mail, others with empty quills drawing swords that only had one blow with which to stop the gleaming metal point heading for their vital trunk. Several arrows hit the horses, which slowed their progress if it did not entirely stop them, but within a blink the Turks began to go down to Crusader lance points, that soon followed by cleaving broadswords.

Lightly armed, the Muslims were no match for European knights in this kind of combat and when the *milities*, knives in hand, joined the fray to drag them to the ground and either pierce their breasts or cut their throats, the outcome of this part of the action was decided. With loud shouting the knights began to clear a path through their own *milities* to get to the rest of the Turks, now milling about in confusion between the fight and their leader.

The sight of heavily armed knights emerging from the dust-filled throng, even if they were struggling to keep their mounts in motion, sent the enemy riding off in panic and that communicated itself to their now visible commander, who sounded the horn as he abandoned both the field and those of his men who could not get clear. It was not necessary for Reinhard to call a halt to his men; sheer equine fatigue did that for him. Now, still outnumbered, he had to prepare for a counter-attack.

It did not come: the ground to the south was filled with riders carrying flaming torches and the tinder-dry, still-maturing fields of wheat began to smoke, soon turning into an inferno as the Turkish commander set light to the crops, obviously to cover his retreat; there would be no more fighting on this field and that occasioned a ragged cheer as everyone came to realise they had scored an outright victory.

For all the joy of success a look at the cost was sobering. His foot soldiers had suffered terribly and the fact that such a thing had been necessary did not make it easy to bear. He ordered that once the enemy dead had been stripped – there were none left wounded – their ponies should be gathered up and along with his own horses be used to carry the Crusader dead back to Antioch.

'For these men, who might by their sacrifice have saved us all, deserve a proper Mass, a decent burial and a memorial to their memory.'

Even with most of his attention on what was happening to his front, Bohemund had spent much time anxiously glancing to the south to seek some indication of how Reinhard and his men were faring. When he espied the first sign of their return, such was their outline it was hard to tell if they were coming back in despair or triumph.

Only when he was in plain sight did Reinhard mount his own horse to close with the Apulian banner and report his victory. For all the elation this produced, it was not much more than a skirmish and such good news had to be set against the whole, which was still in a state of flux.

That the Crusaders were winning on balance was obvious; they were able to advance where the Turks could not, indeed it had become part of his task to stop them doing so, lest by moving forward they break the cohesion of the whole, for still there was no sign of Kerbogha. As a command such restraint was becoming more and more difficult to impose, so much so that Bohemund feared that one of his peers would be presented with such an opportunity that no words of his would cause them to avoid exploiting it.

'The black banner, Uncle,' Tancred called. 'It is waving.'

It was obviously a message, but what it implied and its import was impossible to fathom. Was Shams ad-Daulah asking for permission to take part, or was it a sign to Kerbogha that his line was wavering and he should make haste?

What he could not see was the reaction in Kerbogha's camp, where that flag had also been marked. From presenting an image of the relaxed and omniscient commander, the Atabeg of Mosul was suddenly presented with the possibility that his men fighting at Antioch might not hold for as long as he had hoped. That had him order the trumpets sounded for an immediate move.

To get such a huge host in motion, even when they had been waiting an age for the order, was not simple and, given haste was now important, nor was it possible to stop the contingents from getting mixed up in the eagerness for individual glory. The shouting that ensued, the blaring of horns and trumpets, did nothing to help; nor did the determination of Kerbogha and his close aides to get to the front of the army help either, for their rough attitude, as well as their willingness to ride over anyone unfortunate enough to fall beneath their rushing hooves, produced loud cursing.

Bohemund had placed Firuz, who had keen eyes, on the northern battlements of Antioch, so he knew within very little time that Kerbogha was on the move, yet he was surprised later when the message was sent to him that the force moving south seemed to be in some kind of disorder.

Close questioning produced no more than that information was an impression rather than a fact: what Firuz could see was limited, but by seeking to differentiate the various designs of headgear or the colours of cloaks, he was sure they were mixed up rather than in separate bodies.

It was when seeking to assess the meaning of this information that Vermandois succumbed to too much temptation. He advanced so far that he left a gap on his left into which the nearest Turks poured, forcing his neighbour Godfrey de Bouillon to turn his Lotharingians to face a flank assault.

Tancred noted it as quickly as Bohemund and did not wait for any command from his uncle; with a yell he led the entire Apulian contingent forward to restore the line, which occasioned much hand-to-hand combat with Turks encouraged by their rare opportunity.

Bohemund had to resist the temptation to join Tancred; he was in overall command, which could not in this arena be properly exercised in the battle line, but he had much to think on. If what had happened with Vermandois reoccurred with the whole of Kerbogha's host on this plain, the chance to repair the breach would be impossible. Yet it would also be impracticable to seek to avoid such engagement for it could decide the outcome of the contest. Why the Atabeg had delayed he did not know and it made no sense, but he was coming now and at a time when the Crusaders had been fighting for over half a day.

The men the Count of Taranto was tasked to

lead, even if he had sought to rotate them with his own reserve, were bound to be tired and that, if they were caught in an unrelenting battle, would soon turn to the kind of exhaustion that made continued resistance impracticable and positively guaranteed errors of judgement, which left only two options and to retire back into Antioch was the least attractive.

Observing that Tancred had repaired the breach made by the folly of Vermandois and that he had also managed to pull the Frenchman and his knights back into a solid line, Bohemund reasoned that the point of crisis had been reached.

To make a decision which could prove fatal is the lot of any commander, and in the making of it a whole mass of factors intrude in a fashion that precludes the kind of clear thinking of which chroniclers of battles later write. It is as much a feeling as knowledge, a tingling of the extremities that says to delay is the worst of all possible options, that the time is right to strike and to do so hard, for the Turks before him were weakened and their reinforcements had failed to yet deploy.

Leaving his mound, with his personal knights around him, Bohemund made his way to the far left of the line to speak first to an exhausted Bishop Adémar, now wearing garments stained with enough blood to hide any decoration or hint at Christian piety. Having issued his instruction he moved on to the right, stopping by each of his peers to tell them what he intended, sensing doubt from Normandy, but acquiescence; the same from Flanders, getting just a nod from both de Bouillon and Tancred. Vermandois he took station alongside, for he was a man who required close control, before commanding the horns to sound the advance.

There was no sort of rush; the tactic was one step at a time along the entire line, take on your enemy individually, force him onto his back foot by the ferocity of your assault, then press forward in such a way as to make him take a full step to the rear. That achieved, stand your ground for the counter-assault, then, when that tires, repeat the manoeuvre, all of which was done with shouted orders from every one of the leaders to mark their banners.

There comes a time, having achieved such a success more than once, that fear starts to appear in the eyes of your enemies, not least because this cannot be continued without those forced into retreat beginning to fall either to wounds or death; the Turks, for all their valour, knew they were unable to match on an individual basis the fighting ability and weapon reach of European knights and now that was being relentlessly driven home.

Soon the ability of those in reserve, there to fill the gaps, falters and openings appear as they are too slow to fill in. The first true break, a wide opening, came in front of Godfrey of Bouillon, who looked along the line to the towering figure of Bohemund and yelled of his success.

This had the Count of Taranto, who had already been required to step over six dead bodies, redoubling the strength of his blows, and they were mighty, for of all the magnates he was the most potent as well as the freshest. His one step at a time became two as the enemy melted before his assault, this matched by those at his side, Vermandois included, for if he was a fool he was also a fighter; very soon it was three and four as the Turkish line began to crumble.

'Blow the horns,' he yelled, having no idea where now stood those who would do so, but he knew from the reaction of those lining the walls, and their hysterical cheering, that the critical time had come. The priests on the battlements were no longer praying for deliverance, they were shrieking encouragement, waving their crosses to excite and advance with as much vigour as the knights below swung their swords and axes.

The final break was, as ever, sudden, a collective awareness along the whole Turkish line that if they sought to hold they would die. It only took so very few to seek to save themselves for that to multiply and induce panic in even the most stalwart followers of the Prophet. For all the promises of paradise, life becomes more important than faith and that brought for Bohemund the next difficulty: with the enemy breaking before them, how could he control the next phase of the battle?

In truth he could not, and soon, his voice hoarse from yelling, he gave up even trying; the Turks were running, heading up the roadway that led back to the Iron Bridge, enclosed and narrowed by orchards, the men they had so cruelly tormented in wild pursuit. At the head of that chase Bohemund saw what happened when they clashed with the forward elements of Kerbogha's host, not least the man himself, busy trying to rally his best and fleeing troops.

His cries were ignored and soon the retreating soldiers were in amongst those coming up to do battle, spreading the thought of defeat by their mere flight. The leading elements of the main host soon turned and fled into the trees, to further infect those at their rear, which turned the whole of the Atabeg's army into more of a rabble as they sought safety.

For many that was a false hope, they were cut down by Crusader weapons to litter the roadway and fields of fruit trees, while to the rear others, who had failed to make the road, were being forced into the River Orontes, a few to swim to the opposite bank, many more to drown.

To run near a full league is not possible in chain mail and it is far from easy without it, unless panic aids your efforts, the advent of which brought death to many of Kerbogha's captains, this while their charges now fled in any direction that they thought safe. By the time Bohemund and his fellow magnates reached the main encampment there was not an enemy in sight, from the general himself to the man employed to wipe his arse.

But it was not deserted: it was full of the defenders of Antioch, looting with gusto and not just the valuable objects. There was food in such quantity as had not been seen for an age and, less honourably, the women the host had abandoned suffered as women do in such situations, ravaged before being killed by men suffused with bloodlust.

Some Apulian knights had secured Kerbogha's black pavilion, very obvious by his flying standard, and Bohemund, first to the flap, stood aside to let Adémar enter ahead of him, as the papal legate and titular Crusade leader. Even a man who had seen the inside of the Vatican and the palaces of Constantinople stopped, so impressed was he by what he saw. No different to other rich men, the Atabeg of Mosul was a man who travelled with his wealth and there it was for each and every man to help himself if they so desired.

'Set up a place of collection,' Adémar instructed. 'All valuables, all food to be brought to one point for even distribution by rank.'

If the men with him agreed to this they did so with hidden humour: the Bishop had as much chance of getting all the plunder into one surrendered place as he had of flying to Jerusalem. Yet it mattered not: judging by what was in this one pavilion, not least in the chests of gold and silver that Kerbogha had been obliged to abandon, there was enough for all.

When the Crusader army fell back on Antioch, with the light of the day fading away to darkness, they left behind not a single object, not even a tent. Kerbogha's great encampment had become an empty and barren field and, as a bonus, the only survivor of the men Vermandois had lost at the Iron Bridge – filthy, albeit verminous – had been released from his dungeon.

If Raymond of Toulouse had really been sick, he had mustered enough strength when told of the victory to get himself up to the citadel and demand that they haul down Kerbogha's banner and replace it with his own, prior to being invited

144

to formally surrender the following day. Thus when dawn came the sight of the Occidental flag was plain for all to see, not least to the man who had commanded the triumph of what was already being called the Great Battle of Antioch.

Not long after daylight a furious Bohemund was once more stood with his nephew and Firuz on the narrow bit of flat ground before the citadel where he had first and uselessly called for its surrender, seeking to control his anger at the sight of Raymond's banner. The man Firuz was obliged to address was not Shams ad-Daulah, who had obviously abandoned his post.

Outside the main walls, to the rear, the camp that had been there was as deserted and barren as the one they had left the night before; the men who had rested there had, like the rest of Kerbogha's host, taken flight and the place had been stripped bare of everything of value. Yet a token force had been left to hold the citadel and had no doubt been encouraged to martyr themselves for the sake of the safety of their leader.

'Bohemund, Count of Taranto,' Firuz shouted, 'stands before you and asks how that flag you fly comes to be where his should be?'

'That is not the flag of Bohemund?'

'Ask him what kind of fool he is?' Bohemund spat when that was translated.

Firuz, thinking that unwise, merely advised him of the truth, to then be told by the man left in command that had they known it would never have been raised, for they had seen from these very walls to whom the victory had been granted on the Antioch Plain.

'A lie, of course,' Firuz suggested, as the Occidental Cross was hurriedly lowered, 'but a harsh one for which to punish them.'

'Then tell him the terms are simple, Firuz. He and his men can march unmolested out of the rear gate of the fortress and head east to safety. They may take their weapons but nothing else and they must leave open these gates before us. I give my word not to enter until they are gone.'

Such a message took time to translate but the garrison had no choice but to accept: the citadel might be formidable but it could not hold out for ever without support and that was not going to come at any time in the foreseeable future; to stay was to die. So the answer came back as agreement and it must have been anticipated because the citadel was abandoned before a glass of sand had run through the neck of the timepiece and Bohemund, with his nephew and Robert of Salerno at his heels, marched in.

'Robert,' Bohemund said, handing Robert his banner, 'for the honour of Apulia, set this flying from the staff that is now bare.'

'Shall I go down and tell Raymond to take his flag off the Bridge Gate too?' asked Tancred. 'He cannot dispute Antioch with you now.'

'Let it fly there, nephew, for it signifies nothing.'

CHAPTER NINE

Raymond was not a man to give up lightly; not only did he hang on to the Bridge Gate and keep his standard flying, he moved quickly to seize the site of the ruined fort of La Mahomerie, the very point from which Bohemund had directed his battle. Thus he controlled the roads to both St Simeon and Alexandretta, which once more meant any supplies thereof.

The banner of the de Hautevilles might fly from the citadel and the battlements of Antioch but the Count of Toulouse was still not prepared to acknowledge Bohemund as the man who held title and that was followed by a display of avarice that staggered many, given his lack of effort: he claimed, and got from Adémar, his full share of the spoils from Kerbogha's pavilion to fill coffers already bulging from the alms committed to the Holy Lance.

With the roads now open to the north, news filtered through of the way Alexius Comnenus had deserted them, putting his own safety and survival above the very notion of their existence, retiring all the way to Nicaea and abandoning, indeed scorching, everything the Crusaders had achieved in a year of brutal campaigning. It was telling that while most of his peers despaired of this, and Bohemund actively condemned it, Raymond found ready excuses for the Emperor's behaviour.

'He thought us lost, sensed that to come to our rescue would see his destruction as well as that of the Eastern Christian Empire, was fearful of another Manzikert where the imperial army was destroyed. Surely we must allow that such an outcome would not be welcome to anyone who professes faith in Christ the Redeemer.'

'What I see,' Bohemund responded, 'is a man who cares more for his city and his title than he does for his God, his religion or those committed to his aid.'

'It does not show him in a good light, I grant you,' wheezed Adémar, who was looking to be in a poor state, unlike Toulouse, who for all his claims of a recurring malady appeared remarkably robust, his face ruddy and his eyes flashing. 'But who amongst us has not made errors?'

'Your compassion is admirable, Bishop,' Godfrey de Bouillon suggested, to a round of nodded agreement.

'Compassion is one thing,' Raymond asserted with real force, 'the rights of the Emperor are another. We are obliged to hand possession of the city over to his control and I will not countenance that we should act in any other way.'

'So you do not feel betrayed?'

'You made an oath to Alexius,' Toulouse barked at Bohemund, before looking around at the others. 'As did you all, only I declined. Is it irony or bad faith that causes it to fall to me to remind you of what you swore on the holy relics?'

'I have said it once and I repeat it,' Bohemund insisted. 'Alexius swore on the same relics to

148

support us. He has broken his oath and I contend it was one he never intended to keep, which releases us all from whatever commitment we made to him.'

'Can you say,' Vermandois asked, 'that he never intended to keep it?'

'I can say my family have been fighting Byzantium for decades and never once has their word been worth acceptance.'

'I do not see that the word of your de Hauteville forbears was any more truthful.'

'While I am sure, Count Raymond, that the lands around your domains will teem with those who feel your word is meaningless.'

'My Lords!' Adémar called, seeking to half rise from his chair and immediately sinking back.

'Power,' Bohemund added, 'attracts such accusations to us all.'

If it was not an apology for insulting Toulouse it was enough to stay him from widening the breach to the point Adémar feared – open conflict between the knights of Apulia and those of Provence – and given that, he was content to let the Count of Taranto continue.

'Recall how we were greeted as saviours in Constantinople?'

That produced wry smiles, if not from Toulouse, from everyone else; they had been greeted as threatening interlopers and hurried across the Bosphorus for fear they might attack the capital city.

'We all have reasoned that the Emperor got more for his request for aid against the Turks than he had bargained for, a host so great he came to dread us as much as he feared them. Who amongst us did not expect Alexius to take the field in person and lead us?'

'His duties precluded it,' Toulouse protested.

'Not his duties, Count Raymond, his policy! Alexius was content to use us to beat his long-time enemies but never to trust us, which is why we had his general Tacitus along with us to ensure that whatever fief we took reverted immediately to an imperial possession. He had no faith we would do so unbidden.'

'Which seems,' Raymond sneered, 'given the discussion we are now engaged in, to be a wise precaution.'

'I expected him outside Nicaea,' Normandy growled.

'And I,' added Flanders. 'Yet he never moved from his camp while we laid siege. I cannot see why he failed to join with us, even just to show the numbers the defenders must face.'

Alexius had left the capital but had gone no further than a camp two days' march from Nicaea. The whole siege and capture of the city was left to the Crusaders, apart from a token force of two thousand men under the aforementioned Tacitus who, in any event, took no part in the fighting. Yet when Nicaea surrendered it was Tacitus and his Byzantines who marched into the city and raised the yellow and black imperial banner.

'He kept his distance in case we failed, my friends, and if we had he would have made offers of peace to the city and the Sultan of Rüm, perhaps even offered him gold as a payment for

150

allowing us to dare besiege his city.'

'You cannot say that with certainty.'

'While I wonder, Count Hugh, why it needs saying at all. Alexius has not been part of our progress at any time. He has lagged behind, securing what fiefs were at one time Byzantine, many not held since centuries past, leaving us to march on and face whatever the Turks decide to put in our path.'

Bohemund paused then, enough to even let Count Raymond object, but he could not gainsay it.

'When news came of his flight back to Constantinople I asked the man who brought the message if Alexius had fought any major battles before that and the answer was no. He used his fleet to secure the coast and then proceeded with a caution designed more to achieve the surrender of any towns he passed than to join us and fight off our shared enemy. So we are the stalking horse, the prey who, if we beat the infidel, he will pat on the head and dazzle us with a tiny part of his treasure. If we fail, he will not even stoop to bury our bones. Yet be assured we will see Alexius now, when we have secured a city so prized as Antioch without the spilling of a drop of Byzantine blood.'

'And much of our own,' Godfrey de Bouillon commented, though there was no force in the response; it was given more in sorrow than any anger.

'Yet he will demand we hand it over to him.'

'An oath is an oath.'

'It is, Count Raymond, until it is broken. I say here and publicly that the Emperor Alexius has broken his word by failing to support us here and

151

has thus freed me of mine to him and Byzantium, which I suggest applies to all who likewise made their pledge.'

Raymond must have sensed that the mood of the meeting was again not in his favour, so he played what had to be a last card – for all decisions, it had been agreed at the outset, had to be unanimous. 'While I insist that the Emperor be asked what it is he wishes for the city.'

'An envoy must go to him,' cried Vermandois.

Raymond was quick to jump on that and he replied in a sonorous tone that was at odds with his widely known opinion of the scatterbrained, glory-seeking Frenchman.

'Count Hugh, I can think of no man better qualified to undertake such a mission than yourself.'

'I am humbled,' Vermandois responded, though with a manner very much not that: he could not hide the notion that such a mission might add lustre to a reputation he already held to be glowing. 'But I will only accede if it is the opinion of the whole council.'

'Count Bohemund?' Adémar asked, having got nodded assent from the others.

That made the man questioned smile but he too gave silent agreement; Alexius could be asked till he was blue what he wanted of Antioch – without he led an army to back up his wishes they were so much air.

Raymond had thrown delay into the discussion: with that nothing was decided and Bohemund could hold what he had and time was an ally. Yet it was not agreement, nor the peace that Adémar had set out to achieve; Raymond of Toulouse and

Bohemund were as far apart as ever, perhaps even more so, and it was with a weary and false expression that he brought the discussion to an end.

'Good. Count Hugh, I beg you to make ready to go to the Emperor and seek his instructions. Until then, we must put our minds to what progress we can make to Jerusalem.'

That left another more vital point hanging in the air and one that also acted in Bohemund's favour: no military leader with an ounce of sense would progress south to the Holy City unless he knew Antioch, on his line of communication and his main source of supply, was secure, and to be that someone of ability had to hold it safe.

Not that such a matter was the sole concern of the council: it was still high summer with the hottest month of the year yet to arrive. Having experienced such temperatures the previous year, not one of the leaders saw sense in repeating the horror of what had so very nearly been a death march across the barren, waterless and deliberately scorched lands of Anatolia.

'But surely the Holy City awaits,' Adémar insisted, 'and after we have humbled Kerbogha what infidel will stand in our way?'

'General Summer will kill us, not the Turks or the Arabs,' Normandy responded. 'Let us wait till the weather cools and the stocks of food will be high in the country we pass through. Then we can move swiftly, in such a way and at such speed I would not be surprised to see Jerusalem surrender as soon as they sight our banners from the Temple Mount.'

That was gilding the lily; their enemies had rarely melted away before them and were unlikely to do so now, but the point left unsaid was the army was not ready for an immediate advance: from brave knights to the lowest *milities* all had suffered privation, desperate battle and an abiding fear of damnation and death, which had only just been lifted. To seek to march them on immediately and in searing heat would be folly.

'Let us recover our strength and our purpose,' Duke Robert continued, looking round to ensure he was speaking for all, 'and let us have time to send word to our homes of our success and to seek men to make up for our losses.'

'That could take months,' Adémar protested.

Raymond intervened then, though no one was certain of his motives. Was it to allow time for Alexius to come and take control of Antioch, or was it because he genuinely agreed with what had been said? In the calm months of summer, speedy sailing vessels could get to Provence and back to bring him men and money, though Apulia was even closer, so Bohemund would not be weakened by it.

'Let it be so, Bishop Adémar. July and August are a furnace and September perhaps still too hot.'

'October is reputed scarce better,' added Flanders.

'Let it be November, then.' Given it was Godfrey de Bouillon who stated this, it had added weight; he was a hard man with whom to argue when it came to Jerusalem. 'Then the temperature will be clement, to which we men of the north are more accustomed.'

Seeing the gloom on Adémar's face, a man who could only advise, not command, Godfrey added with heartfelt enthusiasm, 'And fear not, Your Grace: before the feast of Christmastide is upon us, you will say Mass in the Holy City.'

Adémar rubbed a weary hand across a heavily creased brow; where now that so flawless countenance which he had brought from his Provençal home? Even if he had donned armour and fought alongside these magnates, they were the men who knew about soldiering. For all his disappointment and the fact that he lacked energy there was real passion in his voice when he announced his agreement.

'I will not delay past the first day of November, even if I have to go on alone.'

Busy fighting off Kerbogha, the Crusaders had not given any time to the restoration of the Christian faith; they had that now and every church that had been converted into a mosque was reconsecrated. Yet even within that lay dispute: the Patriarch and the local priests, men who had survived a double siege, much persecution and two times the amount of hunger, were adherents of the Greek Creed.

Those who had come with the Crusade were firmly Latin and wished that the places of worship, having been freed by Roman Christians, should celebrate their liturgy in that rite and that the man appointed Bishop of Antioch should be one of their own.

'Which I most heartily support, Your Grace.'

155

'While I cannot agree, Count Bohemund,' came the reply from a somewhat restored bishop, and it was not without a barely disguised waspish tone at odds with his habitual diplomacy, 'when Pope Urban appointed me to this post it was with the express instruction to take back from the infidel those lands and places of worship once Christian. In what we have conquered that means the Orthodox rite and I gave my word to the Emperor Alexius that I would fulfil my task as it was given to me.'

'I have in mind to meet the wishes of the flock you lead.'

'While I have in mind the wish to meet the dictates of my conscience.'

As usual, much was not being said: Adémar suspected that Bohemund wanted a Latin bishop for his own advantage; it was part of his ambition to have Antioch as his possession. A Byzantine cleric would owe allegiance to and take his instructions from Constantinople and he would also resist any attempt to turn the population towards Rome. If Alexius Comnenus did appear and demand the city be turned over to him, a Greek Patriarch and a rigidly Orthodox flock would make holding out against him much more difficult.

The Bishop also knew he was on safe ground: this was a matter in which no layman could interfere, however strong his reputation or his determination. Pope Urban was keen to mend the schism that had split the two branches of the faith these last forty years and throughout the reign of half a dozen of his predecessors, arguments on the true interpretation of the Holy Trinity and the status of the Bishop of Rome as head of the Christian faith.

These deeply theological questions were also muddied by disagreements over priestly celibacy: Rome insisted upon it and was driving it forward in the lands where it held sway, while Constantinople denied the need and held that priests should live as did their flock. Added to that was a matter as arcane as the correct form of bread to be used in the Mass. Such divergences, Pope Urban knew, would not be overcome by aggressive attempts to bring the Creed of Rome to Asia Minor.

Applying papal policy, for once Bishop Adémar could be adamant and had Bohemund observed the cleric once he had departed in disappointment he would have wondered at the quiet smile the divine allowed himself, perhaps one that would have been tempered if he could have seen into the Count of Taranto's mind: Bohemund was a man accustomed to setbacks and he was also, given his de Hauteville bloodline, very adept at thinking of ways round them.

It was hard to be sure what it was that turned most of his fellow magnates against Raymond of Toulouse, but turn they did, each one hauling down the banners of the sections of the city they had occupied and allowing the Apulians to raise that of their Count, a sure sign that they were willing to cede to him the title to Antioch.

Was it that he had not fought alongside them in the battle? Or was it that, with the deepest chests of money in his possession, he was still seeking –

and often succeeding – to seduce their knights from their primary allegiance to them and have them move over to serve under his banner?

The Duke of Normandy was furious and made no attempt to hide it when any of his knights succumbed to Provençal blandishments and money, while the saintly Godfrey de Bouillon took the view that who served whom mattered less than that all turned up outside the walls of Jerusalem to deliver the city into the hands of the True Faith. Most success was achieved with the now leaderless French, Vermandois having set out for Constantinople, yet even the Apulians were not immune, especially those of deep religious feeling.

At the centre of Raymond's influence lay the Holy Lance, of which he maintained sole possession, and now he was using it to allude to a success in which he had taken no part. The Great Battle of Antioch had been such an overwhelming victory against such stupendous odds that no one of faith could seriously doubt that it had been brought about by divine intervention and that was easy to attribute to the discovery of the lance.

As he had before, wherever he went, Raymond was keen to display the relic, and simpler minds than those of his peers easily forgot that he had been abed during the event he was seeking to exploit with his shard of rusty metal. Aiding him in this he had Peter Bartholomew, no longer a mere peasant with visions but seen as an oracle, in fine garments, with a line of contact through the saints to Christ himself.

His one-time humble gait and diffident manner had been transformed into strutting arrogance and he had taken to preaching from outside the citadel, the hillsides below him black with those eager to hear his every word, in what the likes of Adémar saw, and this troubled him greatly, as a parody of the Sermon on the Mount.

Faced with this the Bishop hurriedly brought forward, and in the face of opposition from such seemingly disparate voices as Bohemund of Taranto and Peter Bartholomew, the re-enthronement of the Patriarch of Antioch. John the Oxite had held the office previously, until removed by the Turkish governor at the beginning of the Crusader siege, and he had suffered much during the subsequent weeks, often hung from the walls by his feet to be humiliated as a method of infuriating the besiegers, who could not but feel sympathy for an old and venerable man.

That he was an already installed bishop made the ceremony a demonstration more than a true investiture; Adémar was determined that any notion of forcing the Latin Mass on the Armenian population should be laid to rest for good and in that he was able to show just how strong was the faith among the Antiochenes themselves. They had been denied much to celebrate over so many years that they turned out en masse – thousands of men, women and children, even those still at the breast – to celebrate the placing of John the Oxite back on his patriarchal throne.

Looking at him, old, white-haired and scarce able to move in his heavy episcopal garments,

Bohemund was not alone in thinking that age and ill-treatment by the Turks had left him frail. As the prayers and chants rose around him the old man, blinking and seeming confused, gave the appearance of one not long for this life, which indicated that the argument would soon be revisited and that he would be wise to prepare his ground.

Naturally, it was incumbent upon the Crusaders to tell the Pontiff of the success in taking Antioch, which Adémar did in a long and fawning epistle in which as much ink was expended praising Urban's acumen and his titles as was used to describing how the city had fallen and the great battle by which victory had finally been achieved.

His real purpose in the main part of his submission was concerned, even if it was not stated, with the increasingly febrile relationship between Bohemund and Raymond that ended in a plea that Pope Urban come to Antioch himself and lead the onward journey to, as well as the capture of, Jerusalem.

Perhaps because of his increasing frailty, possibly because he could not see the import or the potential consequences, he allowed Bohemund to add a rider regarding the behaviour of Alexius Comnenus, which alluded more to his failures than any support he had provided in the previous two years, which was at the very least ungracious and at worst a betrayal. So strongly worded was this addendum and so powerfully did it condemn the Emperor as well as the Eastern Church of which he was secular head, that it was tantamount to identifying Byzantium as an enemy of equal potency to the Turks.

Bohemund was looking to his own advantage, so he sought to drive home that the hopes held by Rome were misplaced. The forty-year schism between the western and eastern branches of Christendom would never be healed and nor would the Pope ever be acclaimed as the fount of Christian doctrine. Constantinople would never accept celibacy or give way on the form of bread used in the Eucharist. There was no genuine desire on the part of Constantinople to move to reconciliation on such matters, yet the possibility would be dangled before the Papacy as a means of extracting military support. Alexius Comnenus was playing Rome for a dupe, this to help bolster his own power and to secure the Empire for his heirs.

The reference to his Uncle Roger and what he had achieved in Sicily was a subtle reminder of how the Great Count had furthered the cause of Roman Catholicism in that one-time Saracen-ruled island – and had it not been Greek prior to that? Had Count Roger not also pushed back the Orthodox divines and replaced them with priests who celebrated Mass as it should be, in the Roman rite? Had he not endowed and built monasteries to rival anything that pre-existed with the Basilian monks who looked east for spiritual guidance?

His father Robert *Guiscard* had done the same in Apulia and Calabria, even while at loggerheads, indeed at war, with the fiery Pope Gregory VII, installing Latin bishops and enforcing the celibacy so desired by the Vatican. He, Bohe-

161

mund de Hauteville, was as committed to the same policy and would pursue it wherever he had the means to do so.

CHAPTER TEN

'These people,' Bohemund insisted, 'are no longer there to be plundered by us. Just as we cannot starve, neither can they.'

If food had ceased to be scarce it had not become so plentiful that it could both feed the local Armenians as well as the warriors and pilgrims of the Crusade. Now that Antioch and the whole of Northern Syria was effectively in Latin hands, the people they had previously exploited to survive had been transformed into a future source of tax revenue and so a responsibility for which they had to care, notwithstanding that who would benefit was still in dispute.

Shortage imposed the burden of payment for expensive supplies brought in from distant territories, while any early local harvesting had been severely curtailed by both the presence and needs of Kerbogha and his host. After such an extended period of military occupation by two armies, the whole region was suffering.

In the first months the Crusaders had quickly consumed the kind of surplus that grew over years of peaceful agriculture, then thanks to their own self-indulgence they had lived, or was it survived, a winter of dearth that had not spared the people who lived there. Fertile the Antiochene plain might be but to keep the army fed prior to the harvest would impose too much of a burden, and to forage in the old manner – to take what they wanted without payment – was no longer fitting.

'What do you suggest, Count Bohemund?' Raymond asked, his smile one of scorn. 'That we all move away and leave you behind?'

'No. I think that our good Bishop, with enough men, can hold Antioch and control both the city and the immediate countryside with a few hundred lances, for there is no threat to speak of. For the rest, we should disperse and maintain our forces in lands that have suffered less deprivation, which will also go some way to asserting our right to rule over the littoral.'

'Which,' Godfrey de Bouillon added in a deeply serious tone, 'will also help to keep our lances from mischief.'

To the pious Duke of Lower Lorraine that meant temptations of the flesh as much as anything else – he was strong against debauchery and forceful in imposing piety – yet it was a sound notion without those activities: if they were not going to march on to Jerusalem for near to four months, then to leave their men idle in the region was asking for trouble, an inactive army being an unmanageable one.

The longer they were not employed in fighting the more harm they would do and not just by waywardness. Morale would plummet, internationality rivalry would increase and what were now minor grievances would grow in the telling to become a collective difficulty.

'I am happy to accept my part of the Count of Taranto's proposition,' said Adémar.

'My nephew, Tancred, had some success in Cilicia and holds title to the city of Mamistra. Good sense dictates, given that the Emperor has abandoned and scorched the region to the north of his possessions, that such an area be made secure for us all, not just my own flesh and blood.'

If Bohemund's expression was one of bland unconcern, that fooled no one. The intentions of Alexius Comnenus were unknown: yes, he had retired to Nicaea but that was bound to be before he heard the news that Antioch had been secured. This would not be long in reaching his ears, with Vermandois, accompanied by the Lord of Hainault, well on the way to conveying information of their astounding victory.

What would he then do, march south at once to stake his claim to what they had captured? If he did, Bohemund would be in a strong position to both take control of events and either prevent further progress or negotiate; he could block the narrow pass known as the Cilician Gates and, if he lacked the strength to hold it, extract from the Emperor personal concessions to allow him through so that the Byzantines would avoid a lengthy circular detour.

'Count Raymond, you controlled the Ruj Valley before we besieged Antioch and in that region you have interests which you might see the need to enforce.'

'I see many things that need to be enforced, Count Bohemund.'

'The pity being, My Lord, that what a man

wants he does not always get, even if he feels he has a special blessing from God.'

That was a reference to the way Raymond was exploiting the Holy Lance to his own ends, the effect of which, among the superstitious elements of the soldiery, would be diminished by dispersal.

'I could take the road to Edessa,' Godfrey interjected quickly.

This was done as much to prevent the insults flying as to agree the wisdom of a move to the north-east, yet he too was being disingenuous. His younger brother held Edessa and his power and influence had grown by first defying a siege by Kerbogha, added to his tightening grip of the surroundings, for if Baldwin was a man of doubtful morals – many said none – he was a good fighter, had a sharp brain and he knew how to exploit a thriving region; if there was luck in his prosperity there was also ability. For the Crusade, Godfrey moving into his lands would secure the whole north-eastern flank.

The discussion was not brief, it could not be with so many competing interests, made more telling by the mutual dislike of Raymond and Bohemund, but eventually it was resolved. Robert of Flanders would join with Raymond, taking with him the bulk of his brother-in-law's Normans. The Duke himself would stay with the small garrison and aid Adémar in the administration of a city much ravaged by recent events, albeit the Apulians would garrison the citadel and Toulouse would continue to hold those parts of the city and outside he had seized after Bohemund's victory. Thus the lines of their dispute remained unresolved.

To get away from Antioch and the rest of the crusading army, riding north into a country unravaged by war, where food was plentiful for a sizeable but not massive force, was in itself a blessing. It was not just the magnates who had quarrels: petty many of them might be amongst knights, but they were prevalent and would fester if the men were not kept apart. Shared blood did not soothe Norman rivalry and the men from Apulia were wont to tease their northern brethren about being backward, the Lombard levies of foot soldiers assuming airs with both.

The high-and-mighty French hated any who bordered on their lands, for they had been fighting them all their days, and were quick to condescend to everyone, Normans, Angevins, Provençals and the Lotharingians, while no contingent could ever be content that others had fought as hard in the Great Battle of Antioch as they. Naturally, each wanted to lay claim to the victory and sometimes it went as far as accusations of some folk being shy of a real contest.

This slight was mostly aimed at the Apulians who had formed their leader's reserve; with their fiery blood that was not an accusation to be taken lying down. Distance was the best remedy to prevent a war of words descending to a contest with weapons and that went higher than the ordinary lance; several captains had nearly come to a contest, the tale of one such being related to Bohemund now.

'It started as a jest,' Tancred exclaimed. 'But it did not stay that way and Reinhard of Toul has come to be near insufferable since he did your bidding. I was sore tempted to beat my sword about his swollen head.'

'Then may the good Lord send him a reverse to dent his pride,' Bohemund replied in a soothing tone, well aware that his nephew was upset, having fought as hard as anyone in that desperate battle and with many a cut and bruise to prove it. 'There is nothing like it to bring a man down to earth. The Greek word is "hubris", as I know to my cost.'

No man likes to recall his failures and Bohemund was no exception, but the word left him no option. He lapsed into silence with his nephew who, knowing him well, was sure he had fallen, as he did sometimes, to reviewing every one of his reverses, some of them imposed on him by his own uncle, Roger of Sicily, which if they had never been bloody routs had been disappointments. More often the occasion of uncomfortable parley, they had led to him having to give up lands he had conquered.

Worse in memory were those occasions when Alexius Comnenus had bested him in the previous decade, during the two Apulian invasions of Byzantine territory set in motion by his father. If Alexius had never driven the Apulians from his soil by military ability, the Emperor, with his bottomless chests of gold, had managed to fend off his enemies. Twice gold was sent to the Duke of Apulia's contentious subjects to encourage them to rebel, thus forcing the *Guiscard* to depart the campaign to control his own rebellious barons.

On the second invasion Bohemund had been left

in command and had pushed forward through Macedonia and on to the borders of Thessaly, inflicting several defeats on the Byzantines. Yet the deeper he forced his way into the lands of Romania the greater his problems became: supply, losses to fighting and disease, not to mention the odd desertion from a host that was fighting for personal gain, not loyalty to the cause of the de Hautevilles.

In the end that was how Alexius vanquished his enemies: the Apulian captains, weary of campaigning for a whole year without much in the way of plunder and while their leader was absent from the camp seeking reinforcements, accepted bribes to abandon the campaign and go home.

Bohemund had never made any secret to Tancred that he thought of Alexius as an enemy with whom he had a score to settle, a man who had dented the lustre of a reputation of which he was proud. Although not a victim of vanity, it could not be anything but pleasing to know that your fame as a warrior had spread well beyond the confines of Southern Italy. Maybe it was something to do with his outstanding physical dimensions as well as his fighting skill, but the name of Bohemund of Taranto was spoken of with awe across Christendom.

'Do you intend to fight him again?'

'Who?' Bohemund asked, though he could hardly fail to be aware of what Tancred was driving at.

'Or is the task to get from Alexius more than he wants to give? Title to Antioch, for instance.'

'Do you never tire of probing?'

'No,' came the reply, 'and if you wonder at it, I am curious to know how far you will go to secure possession of the city. And I would be obliged if you did not, as you usually do, take defence in an unknown future or our shared blood.'

Being close-mouthed, never showing your hand unless it was absolutely necessary, was a de Hauteville trait, which some called deceitful – usually those who were the losers in any dispute with the family. Yet it had even been termed that by those who had loyally supported and fought with them. Bohemund's father had often given the impression of not knowing his own mind on the very good grounds that if you appeared to be confused, that surely must apply to your enemy, while all those who supported you had to do was follow your directives.

'Am I being challenged?'

'I think I have the right, if not to challenge, to seek to be informed.'

The time was long past when Bohemund could reply to that with severity. Tancred was grown to full and puissant manhood now, was a fine and competent commander of men who had stature; he had fought too many battles, both with his uncle and independently, to just be dismissed. At the heart of his enquiry was his own future: if his uncle was planning to stay in Antioch, whatever his status and regardless of who was suzerain, what did that mean for a nephew needing to make his own way in the world?

'The truth?'

'Nothing less would please me.'

That led to another silence and a backward

look at the long line of mounted men and *milities* in their wake. Bohemund dismounted – it was time to walk the horses to ease fatigue and his lances did likewise – so it was at a steady walking gait that the reply finally came.

'I will seek to hold Antioch under my own title...'

'It is not just Alexius who will dispute that.'

'No.' There was no need to name Raymond. 'But that is my aim.'

'And if the Emperor denies it?'

'Toulouse must be dealt with first, but even with what he holds, not having the citadel puts me in a better position than he.'

Tancred listened as his uncle outlined, in what was for him an uncharacteristically detailed way, both the problems and advantages of the prevailing situation in terms of supply, the possibility of having to fight Raymond's Provençal knights for possession of the Bridge Gate and Mahomerie – to be avoided unless impossible – and most importantly the value of time.

'Toulouse has alienated all my peers by his high-handedness and I think even Adémar is sick of his pretensions with the Holy Lance.'

'You do not mention Jerusalem,' Tancred said in a deliberate way; he felt he was being fobbed off with discussion about matters of which he already knew.

Getting his innermost feelings out of Bohemund was like drawing blood from a stone; it went against his whole nature to be utterly open and it took some time and a certain amount of rumination to conclude that only a straight answer would satisfy.

'You must have realised by now, Tancred, that Jerusalem holds no attraction for me. I would want it to be wrested from Islam for the glory of our faith but...'

'Without your efforts?'

'We spoke of this before, nephew, do you not recall, and I advanced the notion that there would be as much dispute over the title to Jerusalem as we are now having regarding Antioch.'

'And you favour de Bouillon, I know.'

'I do, for the very good reason that he has only the restoration of Christianity as his purpose. There are no other ambitions to distract him.'

'Raymond will claim it, despite your partiality for Godfrey, and he will use the Holy Lance to further his cause.'

'You mean the Holy Fraud,' Bohemund replied bitterly, 'and if that offends you, I do not care.'

'Fraud or real, the mass of our charges believe in it.'

That got a snapped response. 'Without knowing the truth of how it was found!'

'Jerusalem?'

'Let others have the glory of rescuing the Holy City. I will be content to guard their rear and give what assistance I can. You once asked me if I had Antioch marked as a prize before we ever set out from home. The answer is no, but I did tell you that I had no intention to do for Alexius or Byzantium that which they could not do on their own. Antioch is the richest prize in this part of the world and one Alexius forfeited by failing to come to our aid when he had sworn to do so.'

'And if he comes now?'

'Then he had best do so with his sword raised.'

'And do you think that will happen?'

Bohemund slowly shook his head. 'In time, per-haps, but not soon. Would a man who could not take Nicaea, only three days' march from his capital, and in fear of losing everything, undertake a three month advance into what could be enemy territory just to get to the walls of the most for-midable fortress in the whole of Asia Minor when it is held by me?'

'He need not march, Uncle, he could come by sea. Byzantium still has a fleet even if it is much diminished.'

That brought forth a smile. 'So might I,' to be followed by an enigmatic silence, this time accom-panied by a sly smile, until Tancred had to finally ask how that could be?

'I have sent offers of trading concessions to both Pisa and Genoa, both of whom are a night-mare for Byzantium. Their fleets are larger, their vessels are better, their fighting ability proven and they stand to make fortunes from trading through Antioch, a city under the Turks that was denied to them. With naval support from such city states Alexius will not dare to seek to get to Syria by sea, for he risks destruction on water just as he fears he might also do on land. Likewise he will not be able to supply his army by sea and we both know that a land march through Cilicia without that has many difficulties. And what will the Turks do then, with Constantinople bereft of defenders?'

'And in all this, Uncle, what do you have in

mind for me?'

'The true purpose of your probing.'

'I will not deny it and neither will I seek to excuse it.'

'There is no need why you should, Tancred, you are my nephew and as close to me as would be a son. You may demand of me things that others cannot and if I can give of them, I shall.'

'And if I seek the freedom to act for myself?'

Bohemund replied with real feeling. 'That, of all things, is the easiest to grant. Did I not say you would need at some time to strike out on your own?'

'Not as easy to do as to say! Every command I have held, bar one, has been under your banner and leading your lances.'

'Some of our Apulians will follow you.'

'How many?'

Bohemund laughed. 'If you are intent on Jerusalem, that should guarantee those with the most sins to repent, and besides that you have the men from your own fiefs of Lecce and Monterone.'

'Will you release some of your men to my banner?'

'I will allow that you may seek to detach them to your service and I think that will suffice, but I will not go so far as to diminish myself to further your ambitions if it does not.'

'But—'

'Be satisfied with that, Tancred,' Bohemund interrupted softly, 'for I can offer you no more.'

The weeks following were spent in taking control of the lands of Southern Cilicia, which involved cowing some fortified towns and making alliances with others, not least those held by Armenians. Wealthy and important Tarsus, which had been taken and garrisoned by Baldwin of Boulogne, now became an Apulian fief, the men the new master of Edessa had left behind sent east to tell him of his loss, with a message that the city was a price to be paid for the massacre of Bohemund's men outside these very walls.

If taking a string of towns created a buffer for Bohemund it was not one he could expect to impede the army of Byzantium if it did come this way; to do that would require that he be present and in force, but it did help to secure his northern flank, enough to provide ample warning of any difficulties.

The mountain passes that narrowed the road from Constantinople were the key, the Cilician Gates and, further south, the Belen Pass; those he could hold with less men than had sufficed at Thermopylae, which would, if Alexius knew of his presence and wished to avoid him, force a long march through the Anti-Taurus Mountains to the east.

'If he is coming,' Bohemund said, standing atop a high peak of the Taurus Mountains and looking north to the lands of Anatolia, 'he will be marching by now.'

Alexius Comnenus was, in fact, residing in his Imperial Palace of Blachernae, as yet unaware of what had happened at Antioch. When he thought of the Crusade, which he did in between the travails of running the empire, he saw that it had been of benefit to him in the reduction of the closest threat to his capital city – he held Nicaea again, which acted as a serious buffer to anyone wishing to attack Constantinople – while it had made safer the hinterlands beyond by driving back the Turks so they had to concentrate on defeating the Latins and not making further incursions into imperial lands.

Sure they had perished he had, as was his duty as a Roman Emperor and secular head of the Orthodox Christian Church, ordered that Masses be said for their souls – this also helped to appease those who had come east too late to join their confrères in the annihilation, like Bohemund's half-brother, Guy of Amalfi, now on his way back to Italy.

Yet with a complicated and difficult empire to run it was not at the forefront of his thinking until it was brought into sharp focus by the arrival at the city gates of a dishevelled Count Hugh of Vermandois, quickly shown into the imperial presence and Alexius sat on his throne.

'My Lord of Hainault and I were attacked on the way here, robbed and left without horses, which delayed our bringing to you the news from Antioch.'

'And where is Hainault?' Alexius asked in Latin, which Vermandois had used, unwilling to hear that these two men might be the only survivors of an action which he did not think of without a twinge of guilt. If he had been given no choice but to leave the Crusade in dire straits it had not been a comfortable decision to make.

'Dead, Your Eminence, from wounds he took

fighting off our assailants. That too delayed me as I sought to care for him.'

Alexius signalled that Vermandois, whose voice was hoarse, be given something to drink, which was brought to him and greedily consumed. 'I fear the news you have for me, but I beg you not to be hasty. What has occurred is only a measure of God's will...'

'Such a victory can be nothing else!' Vermandois exclaimed, cutting right across Alexius, which would have got him a glare had the words he used not shocked his listener. 'Praise be to God.'

Count Hugh began to babble, speaking so quickly that the Emperor, despite his knowledge of Latin, struggled both to keep up and make sense of what was being said. How could it be that the Crusaders had beaten Kerbogha's mighty host? Was this man before him suffering from too much exposure to the sun? By calming Vermandois down and posing a series of sharp questions he came to realise the truth and it was not news that pleased him, even if those he thought perished were in the main still alive.

Antioch was held by the Crusade, which might have been good; Bohemund held the citadel, which was not, especially when Count Hugh, albeit reluctantly, admitted that the Count of Taranto had felt abandoned, indeed betrayed. The fact that all the lords had felt so was glossed over, for Count Hugh was no partisan of the Apulian leader, even if he had given him an opportunity to add lustre to his name, one he was keen to not only relate but to massively embellish.

'You do not tell me that your Crusader lords

176

are eager that I should claim my rights to Antioch?'

'Count Raymond of Toulouse has defended those most assiduously, as do I, which is why I came to inform you that the city is now secure.'

'But not, it seems, Count Bohemund?'

'I fear he has ambitions of his own.'

'Count Hugh, you are weary and in need of rest, not to mention a more fitting set of clothes. I beg you retire to a chamber I shall provide for you to bathe and take sustenance. Then, later, we will speak more of this and you can describe in detail to me this Battle of Antioch and how the crusading army, under your command, achieved your victory.'

When Vermandois had left, Alexius remained in a contemplative state on his throne, yet none of the courtiers observing him could doubt the train of his thoughts, for if they had not, being Greeks, initially understood Count Hugh, the import of his words had soon been made plain.

Antioch was in the hands of the Crusade, the vital citadel held by a man he knew to be an enemy and in abandoning them to their fate he had given that adversary an excuse to repudiate his vows. He would hear tell of the battle and the surprising victory and would nod sagely when Vermandois told him of his astounding generalship, not a word of which he would believe, for if Count Hugh did not know of his limitations, Alexius, a fine commander himself, did.

Perhaps those waiting for their emperor to speak did not quite comprehend the meaning of what had been said, but Alexius had no doubts whatsoever: if he wanted to have control of Antioch it would not be achieved by demanding or even pleading that it be handed over. If he wished to press his claim he could only do so by the threat of force.

CHAPTER ELEVEN

The relative ease of life in Cilicia and Northern Syria, making treaties, securing and garrisoning towns only too willing to open their gates, was interrupted when news came of the plague that had struck the region of Antioch, first cleaving through the port of St Simeon, killing a large party of newly arrived German knights come to join the Crusade, soon to spread up the road to the city itself.

If the lowly died in droves it was not a malaise to spare the mighty, for one of the victims was Adémar de Monteil, Bishop of Puy and that presaged a possible crisis, given Robert, Duke of Normandy, had moved his troops out of the city, which left the Apulian garrison of the citadel isolated and at risk of falling to disease.

Returning south, Bohemund, regardless of his concerns, had to be cautious in his progress, holding back – he later discovered his fellow magnates had adopted the same ploy – till the deadly fever had run its course and no more deaths were being reported from its effects.

That allowed them to re-enter Antioch and

resume what was bound to be a more troubled negotiation regarding the next phase of the campaign, given the man who had held the peace between the factions was no longer present. It also allowed these princes to consider what had changed regarding their circumstances and assess what that implied for the future.

If the Apulians had indulged in a peaceful attempt to control the territories to the north the same could not be said of Raymond of Toulouse. In company with Robert of Flanders he had attacked the Muslim town of Albara, an ancient settlement, now fortified, surrounded by the near intact remains of both the Greeks and Romans who had occupied it in times past.

There, it transpired, he did great slaughter, sparing no one who was unwilling to convert to Christianity, his boast that he and Robert had shed the blood of many thousands and had also provided the slave markets of Antioch with so many souls of every age and sex that prices had collapsed.

Godfrey de Bouillon returned to the city with his numbers enhanced by the support from his brother Baldwin of Edessa, yet nothing had changed in his demeanour: he still hankered after the relief of Jerusalem with as much fervour as he had demonstrated previously and there remained about him that air of patent honesty which made him trusted whenever he chose to speak.

There was little doubt that the loss of the papal legate complicated matters. After a Mass was said for Adémar's soul, they assembled once more in the old Governor's Palace, the obvious need being unchanged: for an acknowledged leader to take control of the march to Jerusalem. Raymond was still by far the man with the most strength in terms of men and money and might have secured that had he not been so previously high-handed and now so boastful of his exploits in taking Albara after a short and bloody siege, as well as crowing of the massacre he had inflicted after his victory.

The town he had garrisoned, but more than that he had installed that which Bohemund had sought for Antioch: a Latin bishop who, if he had been consecrated by the Greek Orthodox Patriarch of Antioch, John the Oxite, nevertheless made it plain that he owed his allegiance to Rome. Every mosque in Albara was converted to become a place of Christian worship, which allowed Raymond to show himself as a representative of the true faith, which would sit well with the Pope should matters regarding leadership remain unresolved.

He was once more parading the Holy Lance around Antioch to raise his standing amongst the faithful, and was again employing bribery to seduce lances and long-serving captains away from his peers, this while he made no attempt to hide his supposition that the command was his by right; never men to willingly bow the knee they would not accede to presumption where even persuasion would have struggled.

Bohemund would not have stood against him if the debate had been open: the notion of getting the man who blocked his control of Antioch marching away with the light of salvation in his eyes was a tempting one. Yet he could not make his position plain for fear of being too direct regarding his own ambitions, not that they were in any way secret. But what might be known in such an arena as the Council of Princes could not be baldly stated: it was enough for the other princes that he did not put himself forward for them to know his mind.

If no one was prepared to accede to Toulouse he was unwilling to acknowledge the only other candidate, Godfrey of Bouillon, and in amongst all this Antioch was still a running sore that both main protagonists realised could only be settled by that which was anathema to men supposedly crusading on behalf of the Holy Cross.

To the despair of the many pilgrims, whose numbers were now swollen by new and doubly eager arrivals transported to St Simeon, the date set for the march to Jerusalem slipped by: with no leader there could be no Crusade, while again, and for the same reasons as previously – the burden of supply for a large army as well as the risk of some incident sparking fighting between the Apulians and Provençals – the various armed contingents were obliged to disperse.

Once more the Count of Taranto moved north, but stopped short of going all the way back to Cilicia, the situation being too febrile. Yet he maintained about him a seeming air of confidence. No one who knew him, especially Tancred, who was closest of all, could be sure whether it was genuine or contrived.

'Matters will resolve themselves. Even if still divided, my fellow princes cannot just delay and allow things to fester. They must move south or disperse back to their homes.'

Tancred slowly shook his head; the real point did not have to be stated: time was on Bohemund's side, and if his nephew was of the opinion it was a less than gallant way to behave, he kept that to himself – he was still dependant on his uncle as his liege lord and that would remain the case until the purpose of the Crusade was re-established.

'That they will never do, Uncle – return home having failed, I mean. To do so would gain them nothing but the kind of ridicule heaped on Count Hugh.'

That made Bohemund laugh so loud his horse shied beneath him. With shipping now plying regularly to and from Europe, news had swiftly been borne to Syria of the way Vermandois had been greeted when he returned to France, which he had chosen to do from Constantinople rather than rejoin the Crusade. News of the victory at Antioch had preceded him, as had the name of the true victor, which led to his claims of personal leadership being treated as what they were, downright falsehoods.

Far from being cheered, as he had anticipated, Vermandois had been howled at by the mob as a coward, a liar and a deserter of the Cross. Denied the expected crowns of laurel, his surcoat was instead, it was reported, regularly decorated with clods of horseshit whenever he attempted to ride out, so much so that he never did so without a strong escort of personal retainers. If not clods of ordure, scorn was a fate that had also befallen

Stephen of Blois, likewise back in his domains. If any of the other magnates even contemplated such a course, the way these two men had been received as inglorious failures was enough to kill off such a notion.

'Prepare the men to move at once!' For a man so normally confident in his demeanour, regardless of circumstance, Bohemund was clearly agitated and was obliged, as his nephew looked at him hard, to add his reasons. 'Raymond has outwitted us.'

Further explanation had to wait until they were saddled and moving south as fast as their mounts could bear; sure he could leave matters to sort themselves out – that time was his friend – had led Bohemund to underestimate Raymond of Toulouse, who had proved he was not lacking in the kind of cunning for which the de Hautevilles were famed.

Aware that he could not take control of the walls of Antioch, and most assuredly not the citadel, while being utterly determined to deny control to the Count of Apulia, he had decided to secure for himself those regions essential for the supply of food to the city. The Ruj Valley, where he was already in control, was very much that, but only a part of the agricultural belt that fed such a major urban centre.

Antioch needed all that could be harvested from many different areas to keep healthy both the citizenry and any garrison, not to mention, as of now, the mass of newly arrived pilgrims waiting for the military elements of the Crusade to proceed south. Raymond had moved his lances from Albara, with a horde of Holy Lance-adoring pilgrims, on to a hugely fertile plateau called the Jabal as-Summaq.

This was an area the Crusaders, with Bohemund as joint commander with Robert of Flanders, had sought to exploit during their own siege when matters of supply became critical, only to suffer a major reverse, the mounted lances forced to abandon every cart they had with them, as well as the mass of food they had gathered over several weeks and the drovers who controlled their teams of oxen.

Worse had been the need to desert the *milities* who had accompanied the cavalry to carry out the work of gathering those supplies, which often amounted to exhorting them painfully from the farmers who had hidden food they needed to survive. Caught in open country and taken totally unawares by a Turkish army marching to the relief of Antioch, faced with archers on horseback in overwhelming numbers who they could not outrun, under leaders who lacked the mounted forces required to impose a check on the enemy, it became a bloody massacre.

After the fall of Antioch a knight called Raymond Pilet had detached himself from the Crusade, much in the manner earlier adopted by Baldwin of Edessa, and set off for the same purpose as that reprobate – namely to line his pockets and capture a fief that he could hold as his own. In that he had failed miserably, losing most of his lances and barely surviving the adventure. A fertile plateau it may be but Jabal as-

Summaq was, for the Crusaders, also something of a graveyard.

That still rendered a tempting prospect for someone as powerful as Toulouse: no map was required to see that if his Provençal lances kept possession of the Bridge Gate at Antioch and thus access to the coast, then add to that the whole arc of territory that covered the southern approaches and thus deny Bohemund any of its produce, he could make holding the city without his acquiescence close to untenable.

'I saw his gaze as being on Jerusalem but I should have realised that when he massacred and enslaved all those Muslims in Albara it was for a reason.'

If both Tancred and Bohemund had wondered at that bloodthirsty act, they had not been alone. It had been a tenet of the Crusade, for the very sound reason that it made tactical sense, not to make war on the non-combatant Muslim population outside the need to forage, which often involved inherent cruelties.

But outright butchery was different: enemy soldiers were routinely killed and often made to suffer before they died, that being a reciprocal part of fighting a determined enemy who rarely spared a Christian who fell into their hands. Raymond had, at Albara, broken that convention and it could only have been to spread terror.

'And now he is moving to besiege Ma'arrat an-Numan, where that terror will prove to be a powerful weapon. It may fall to him for fear of what resistance might mean.'

The city stood on the road between Aleppo and

Damascus as well as crossing an old and well-used trading route to the interior and was a wealthy centre of commerce with a mixed Muslim Armenian population. It was reputed to have strong walls, but if mighty Antioch had failed to keep out the Crusaders, then Ma'arrat an-Numan, a much less formidable fortress, would struggle to do so.

Taken, it would finish off the arc of possession that Raymond was seeking to the south of Antioch, giving him a solid line of both land and supply routes from the coast deep into the interior. Given its strategic importance, Bohemund could no more grant him the sole right to that city than Raymond of Toulouse would give him clear title to his own claims.

The country through which they marched, for all its fruitfulness, showed the ravages already of a passing army, with much of the place stripped of food, and given it was now November there was not going to be time for that to be replenished before the next harvest. A peasantry who had suffered before was called upon to feed another transient force of rapacious soldiers, that rendered doubly vicious by what had been extracted from them already, for no delay could be allowed lest the Apulians arrive too late and they must, when they made their goal, to have any security, do so with food of their own.

Throughout the march they came across bands of pilgrims, some on their way from Antioch intent on joining with the man and the holy relic they saw as holding the key to their future. Other pilgrims, and more numerous, began to appear when

186

they got closer to Ma'arrat an-Numan, ragged-looking figures seeking food, for when it came to sustenance the fighting men outside the city were a priority, which left the non-combatants to very much fend for themselves. No succour could be given these unfortunates regardless of their lamentations; the Apulians ignored their pleas with the same disregard as would the men with whom they had set out.

If it was relief to find that Raymond and his army were still camped outside the walls, it was equally obvious that the arrival of this new force was unwelcome and not just by the men in command. Knights and lances who fought for plunder, faced with a prosperous city they fully expected to capture, saw the addition of more lances and *milities* as a possible dilution of what they might gain from the eventual sack, so it came as no surprise they were greeted with a rate of catcalls, insults and demands that they be gone.

Against that, the forces of Raymond and Robert of Flanders, who had come with him, were making little headway against the Muslim part of the population, determined to resist for the very good reason that they were only too aware of the cost of failure. In terms of professional soldiers what they faced was apparently small, a few dozen at best, who formed the governor's personal retainers, which should have made the siege a formality, but the opposite was the case.

The city, it seemed, was strong in the desire to resist. Having been offered terms of surrender and turned them down there was no other fate awaiting the Muslim inhabitants of Ma'arrat an-

Numan than the ravages of a successful siege. If the lesson of Albara had failed to get them to open their gates, it still had an effect; it made the citizenry that formed the bulk of those opposing them doubly tenacious in defence. Raymond's terror had worked against, not for him.

Raymond refused to even talk to Bohemund, indeed he did not even exit from his pavilion when his banners appeared and his horns were blown, so it fell to a reluctant Robert of Flanders to explain the situation. The first assaults, made with hastily constructed ladders, had failed, added to which, with the numbers available, it had been impossible to close off Ma'arrat an-Numan from the surrounding hinterland, which obviated the possibility of starving them out.

Bohemund made the point that with his Apulians engaged the situation was now altered, though there were other concerns that he was quick to broach. 'How well supplied are you, Robert?'

The lack of eye contact that question produced was answer in itself; it took no great genius to see that if the country the Apulians had marched through to get here was practically bare of supply, and the pilgrims who had flocked to follow Raymond and his Holy Lance were scrabbling for food, then the likelihood existed of such a situation being spread in all directions to the whole plateau, and that would not only be due to the extra numbers the area now needed to support.

The siege would not have come as a surprise to the inhabitants of Ma'arrat an-Numan. With

Albara in Crusader hands their city stood to be next; they would have been active in filling their storerooms, and sense dictated they would have also destroyed much of that which they could not transport into the city so as to deny sustenance to their approaching enemy.

It took little time for a besieging army, even just trailing with it the normal level of camp followers, to take what was shortage of provender to a situation where it became dearth. The addition of thousands of pilgrims made that many times worse, a situation that had arisen outside Antioch the previous year where the Crusade, both fighters and non-combatants, had come close to actual starvation.

'I have no appetite for a repeat of that,' Bohemund said, using the pun to lighten his point, given he was reminding a man who had shared that foul period with him of what they had suffered, 'which is what we might face if we spend the whole winter engaged in this siege.'

'Then,' Robert replied, making no attempt to hide his irritation, 'a man would be entitled to wonder at your being here.'

'He would if he did not already know.'

Such a sharp comment made the Count of Flanders uncomfortable, which Bohemund took as a positive sign: if he had hitched his star to Raymond of Toulouse it was not without his being able to discern his motives, which were no more chivalrous than those of the Count of Taranto. Yet he was still inclined to be distant, there being, for instance, no indication of any plan that Raymond might have or where the

Apulians could position themselves to be the most effective as an addition to the siege, leaving Bohemund to make his own dispositions based on what he could observe.

If being entirely cut off disheartened the inhabitants of Ma'arrat an-Numan it was not immediately obvious; more for the sake of prestige than any real hope of success Bohemund, himself employing hastily constructed ladders, opened an assault against the walls opposite where he had pitched his pavilion, only to be swiftly repulsed; his men were good fighters and they were brave, but they were not what they needed to be, Gods of antiquity with wings to fly.

The whole city, its walls broken into sections with towers, was surrounded by a deep ditch, a dry moat, which made getting any climbing equipment to the walls so slow as to render the attempt doubly hazardous, extending the time that the attackers were exposed to all the usual tools of defence: archery in the approach and retreat, boiling oil and cast-down rocks when actually close enough to the masonry to raise their ladders. Not one of them made it more than a halfway ascent, so it made sense to quickly call the attack off, it being a probe that looked likely to be too expensive.

Having made that demonstration and shown he was here for a purpose, Bohemund expected that Raymond would be obliged to soften his stand and call him to a conference to coordinate any future tactics; he waited in vain and his own pride would not allow that he abase himself by making an open approach.

Even Robert of Flanders seemed inclined to do no more than exchange the minimum of words needed to retain some element of contact and he certainly made no attempt to pass on what the Count of Toulouse might be thinking and contemplating, not that there was any activity to speak of; it was as if by ignoring them he could wish the Apulians away.

'Perhaps when our bellies are swollen with hunger it will dent his arrogance,' Bohemund ranted, loud enough to be overheard by many, as he rode through the Provençal lines, paying no heed to the glares he received, this to give Raymond a chance to relent. 'Or maybe he seeks the shame of having us all retire with our honour besmirched.'

'I doubt he can hear you, Uncle, his pavilion is too far off.'

'He will hear me by proxy, Tancred, for my words will be reported to his ears before we are out of sight of that damned Occitan banner.'

'And they will serve to moderate his behaviour?'

The irony in that question was not hidden; Tancred was sure that his uncle was allowing the behaviour of Raymond to cloud his judgement about what was militarily necessary, which was a rare thing and stood to demonstrate how the dispute over Antioch had got under the normally impenetrable de Hauteville skin. The reply, when it came, was a deep and unpleasant growl.

'I await what you are sure to tell me, that you have a better notion of how to shake the dolt into action.'

'If I had, would I be permitted to act upon it?'

191

'What do you mean?'

'Simply this, that your own pride is so injured that you may see me talking to Raymond as a betrayal.'

Tancred waited for a reply, but in vain; all he got was a broody silence, which encouraged him to think he had penetrated Bohemund's anger enough to engage his mind to think in those areas that were of more import: to augment that he reprised the need for haste, due to potential hunger as well as the fanaticism of citizen defenders.

'Their hope is that hunger will drive us away.' Still there was no response. 'And perhaps that is what Raymond wishes also, that we Apulians will be obliged to retire to Antioch for the sake of our bellies, for we have with us only that which we scourged on the way.'

'As long as Toulouse is here, so are we.'

'Which is as I expected, but Raymond will not act without he is pushed to do so and you lack the means to make him.'

The tone softened; Bohemund's brain was working. 'What are you suggesting?'

'That I try to shift him?'

'How?'

'By creating the fear you might beat him to breaching the walls by your superior knowledge of siege warfare. After all, you got into Antioch before he did and for that he has never forgiven you. If he has troubled dreams they will be made up of such an anxiety.'

For the first time in days Bohemund was able to laugh. 'By the saints, Tancred, you have your grandfather's cunning.'

CHAPTER TWELVE

Subtlety was required to deal with Raymond of Toulouse, but Tancred was also aware of the lack of time which, given it was not a secret, became a weapon not an impediment. If Ma'arrat an-Numan could not compare with other places they had besieged, the defences had enough about them, as well as bodies to man them, to provide an obstacle that could keep the combined forces at bay for many weeks, too long for any sense of comfort.

Bohemund's conclusion, after another day of Provençal inactivity, was stark and at total odds with his previous angry contention after they had ridden through the Provençal camp. It was brought on by an examination of his own level of supply and stood as testimony to the tactical flexibility that made him a first-rate commander of men.

'As soon as I deem it impossible to take this place in the time we have I will depart and ahead of Raymond and his pilgrims. What is left in the countryside between here and Antioch is too sparse to feed us all.'

'What if it then falls to him alone?'

'It won't!'

Bohemund insisted this was the case with such doggedness that his nephew did not bother to seek an explanation, given a possible answer as to how Ma'arrat could be taken had occurred to him.

'So, nephew, what is your plan?'

'I have no notion, as yet,' Tancred lied, 'but I am sure something will occur.'

That got him a hard look; devious himself Bohemund was ever on guard for the same trait in others and perhaps Tancred had been too breezy in his response. To the young man on the receiving end, being less than open was justified both by his de Hauteville blood, as well as the number of times his uncle had been less than frank with him. Then, added to that, was the notion his idea might not work.

To approach Raymond directly would be useless and that also applied to making any move to contact those Apulian knights who had been bribed by the Count of Toulouse to desert his uncle's banner. Instead, Tancred approached a Provençal knight called Bardel, with whom he had formed a bond. For all the various contingents usually did battle in contained units there had been many times where they had combined to forage together, and in that friendships had been shaped that transcended territorial boundaries and the enmities of the higher nobles.

Knowing Bardel, and sure he would be welcome, enabled Tancred to enter the lines of Raymond's lances where, round a blazing fire, lay within them the seeds of his idea. These must, he was certain, feed back to their liege lord, for men like Bardel would have an appreciation of the parlous nature of the enterprise. They could calculate as well as anyone the dwindling level of supplies, just as they would see the low quantity of the same being fetched in by foraging parties that were forced to travel in a wider and wider arc, as well as in greater numbers, to secure anything at all. Given the time of year, that included growing supplies of wood to provide warmth in the increasingly cold nights, which sapped the will, as well as the dispiriting days when the skies clouded over and the rains that made fertile this high plateau fell to drench men with only canvas to provide shelter. Bardel was quick to allude to the way such conditions led to increasing sickness.

'And that weakens us more than the need to forage when it comes to the fighting.'

If it was both obvious and a commonplace it did not diminish its significance, every siege faced the same dilemma: the more men a leader detached to forage, which tended to increase in direct proportion to the length of the endeavour, the less he could commit to battle. The longer a siege lasted in poor weather – and it was getting worse here as winter came upon them – the more men were exposed to agues and fevers, and there was always the risk of the more deadly plagues that could sweep through and decimate an army in a matter of days.

A log cast onto the fire around which they were sat sent up a shower of sparks into the cold, damp air and one of Bardel's cohort, shivering for effect, aired a complaint that got many a nod.

'May the Good Lord forgive me for saying so, but I would welcome a bit of that baking heat we had in summer.'

'I heard you curse that, my friend,' Bardel laughed, 'as heartily as you now curse the cold.'

'My prayers fell on stony ground then, Bardel, but we need the sun to shine on us now, when we can bear it.'

'They say it snows deep here sometimes,' interjected another to increase feelings of gloom, present anyway under a grey sky.

The moaning went the rounds, but that was not anything to remark upon: soldiers, when not fighting, always grumbled, cursing heat if it was hot as heartily as they damned the misery of being cold and the food they were given whatever the weather.

Only talk of plunder could render them cheerful, the dream that one day they would uncover a treasure so great and on their own that they could look forward to a life of ease and comfort. This tended to be in a manor house of their own choosing, with a plump, willing and fecund wife, fertile land and villeins to plough it, with a church and a priest endowed by them within the confines of their demesne, where Masses would be said daily for his soul to secure entry to heaven.

As the talk moved on it was natural to speculate on what of value might lie within Ma'arrat an-Numan, a city full of rich merchants at the crossroads of two major trade routes, and this in turn led, as it was bound to do, on to the prospects of ever getting inside. This was commonly held to be sparse, given they had tried and been so resoundingly repulsed by folk who were not proper soldiers, but mere citizens, which disheartened them even more.

'Perhaps the mighty Bohemund, now that he has joined us, has a way to get us over yonder walls?'

The tone of that comment, made from beyond the flames, was not friendly; indeed, it was downright acerbic. If Bardel and Tancred, in the time they had spent in each other's company, had formed a bond of companionship, that did not apply to everyone present. Several members of Bardel's cohort had looked distinctly piqued when he invited Tancred, wandering around inside their encampment, to warm his hams and drink some hot wine.

'Perhaps,' opined another, 'he can tell us why we are outside Ma'arrat at all?'

The remark set up a murmur of agreement, showing that the sentiment was shared, while further interjections made it clear where the complaint lay. These men had come on Crusade to free Jerusalem from Islam, albeit they expected to prosper both on the way and once they arrived. Ma'arrat an-Numan was not in the direction of that goal, so why were they here if it was not for lordly pride? It was a grievance that had surfaced at Antioch when progress south was delayed by the infighting of Bohemund and Raymond, yet it seemed to be of a deeper hue on this high windswept plateau.

Listening carefully and taking no part, lest his view be seen as tarnished by his bloodline, Tancred heard many a curse directed at his uncle – they were eager to damn the Count of Taranto for his ambition and inflexibility – but more telling was the way Raymond's own lances were prepared to castigate him too, and wonder if his head had been turned by the discovery of the Holy Lance.

Men like Bardel did not lack for piety and were strong in their Christian faith: if they saw the spiritual value of the relic and were prepared to openly ascribe the victory outside the walls of Antioch to its influence, they failed to see why it was not now leading them to their stated destination.

The way their liege lord tended to posture with the holy relic, always carrying it with him and eager to show it to the pilgrims, who would fall to their knees at the sight of such a marvel, patently fed his pride, of which the Count of Toulouse had never been in short supply. For all he kept his silence it was a grievance that Tancred shared and for the same reasons: he too was frustrated at the way the dispute had tempered the true purpose of the Crusade, which had his loyalty to his uncle at loggerheads with his faith.

He only spoke again when that complaint had run its course. 'My uncle had a notion that with so few real soldiers the way to overcome the walls is with a siege tower.'

That was received with nods, for it made some sense, such a weapon being difficult to defend against even for trained fighters, until a sour voice pointed out, again to general approval, that they were naught but lances and lacked the skills to construct one.

'He is minded to send back to Antioch for the English carpenters who are still there to have them build it.'

'Waiting, like us, to fulfil their vow,' came the sharp response from the other side of the flames. 'They want to employ their skill outside Jerusalem, not here.'

'Here would be better as of now,' Bardel countered. 'They might aid us in getting over yonder walls.'

'The English devils work for pay, not faith,' called another.

'Worse than Normans, they are!'

'The only thing worse than a Norman,' Bardel shouted angrily, 'is a man who ignores the law of hospitality.'

'How would you have them behave, friend?' Tancred enquired, for the barb about Normans was aimed at him, even if he was the son of a Lombard. 'Such men must eat, and since no lord will feed them and they cannot fight, how are they to live?'

'Let them spend your uncle's gold, perhaps when they have left his coffers bare it will dent his pride.'

'And what if they do, by building him a siege tower?' Tancred asked. 'Who then will have the plundering of Ma'arrat?'

That brought silence: any tower built for Apulians would not be gifted as a weapon to the Provençals, which set up another bout of murmuring, though this time it had a deeper and more irate tone that made Tancred think of a disturbed beehive. They had so recently been talking about what they could each gain if Ma'arrat fell; his claim had got them to consider the unpalatable fact that they might secure nothing.

'My friends,' he called, getting to his feet, 'I thank you for the hot wine and the talk.'

Standing at the same time, Bardel clasped Tancred's hand. 'Drop by as you please, for you are ever welcome.'

The sound then emitted from some of the others gave a lie to his words.

'And I invite you to join us in our lines, perhaps in the manège we have set up by the Aleppo road.'

'Do you Normans never cease to test each other?'

'No, Bardel, and in truth, if it hones our skills it also eases the boredom. You would be well to take up my offer, for I fear you will be sitting round your fires for so long your skills will rust along with your weapons.'

The message came to Bohemund the next day, given to him as he and his knights emerged from their daily session of practice, each still heaving from their exertions. There had been fighting on foot with sword and shield in the manège, but no lance work; as yet the Apulians had been unable to replace their fighting destriers, horses trained to be fearless in battle in the very same kind of sand-filled enclosure in which they had just been exercising their combat skills.

Even if they could have found mounts of the right kind, a breed common in Normandy and now Apulia, while being unknown in Asia Minor, they took years to train to the pitch where they would be steady in battle. Such horses had been sent for and at great expense, the beginnings of a breeding herd, but until they arrived, mated, foaled and their offspring then grew to full strength, it would be several years before they could be employed. Not that such a thing mattered here: you could not ride any horse into battle in a siege.

'Raymond has sent messengers back to Antioch, nephew, to fetch the English carpenters, as well as a large sum of money to ensure they come in haste, which is something you did not discover in your meanderings.'

Tancred was careful not to smirk; if he was not surprised at the speed with which his lie about Bohemund doing the same had reached the pavilion of the Count of Toulouse, the way it had been acted upon was astonishing.

'He will have them build a siege tower.'

'It is a clever notion, Tancred, but not one that favours us if it comes to pass.'

Feeling slighted, Tancred was sharp. 'Yet it is not a course you would have adopted.'

'I have sent to Apulia for destriers, which you know very well, just as you can guess from that I lack the depth of Raymond's purse. Added to that, these carpenters are Anglo-Saxons, even if they came at the behest of King William Rufus. How much more would I have to disburse to get them to work for a Norman who is not their overlord?'

'Of which I was aware, and others were not, when I threw the stone onto the water.'

'You?'

There was no need to respond, the truth was in

201

the expression of Tancred's face, nor was there any requirement to outline the fact that Raymond would no more permit the Apulians to use any siege tower he built, always assuming he could do so, than would be gifted if the positions were inverted; it would be reserved for his own men.

'So now, Uncle, we must put our minds to how we might take advantage of a weapon of which we will be given no use.'

'I have a feeling you have thought of that too.'

'I have.'

'Let me see if I can guess. Raymond, if he has a siege tower, will draw the defence to the part of the walls at which he sets it...'

'Leaving gaps elsewhere that we will be able to exploit. I have talked to those who tried the assault before we arrived and failed to overcome the walls.'

'As did we, nephew.'

'Even if they lost many of their confrères in the attempt, I was told the defenders seemed not so numerous that they can cover every part of their walls at the same time.'

'Yet you have in mind to repeat their failure?' Bohemund responded.

'I had in mind to do so with a set of sturdy frames, not single ladders.'

That got a slow nod; if it was a rare tactic it was one that had been known to work against a stretched defence. A long climbing frame allowed the attackers to spread out, as well as to ascend in numbers, the effect of that being to also extend the defence. As a tactic singly employed it was less than perfect, but if the Provençals drew the best of the defenders, the small knot of the governor's retainers, it might get the Apulians over the walls and onto the parapet before Raymond's men could debouch from their siege tower.

'I daresay Toulouse had already sent out cutting parties to find suitable timber; I suggest, Uncle, we would be advised to do the same.'

The haste with which those Anglo-Saxon carpenters came from Antioch testified to the fact that Raymond had dug deep into his purse, for they were known to be an avaricious bunch who demanded and received high fees and they had not been idle in a recently captured city in which much required to be rebuilt, not least those mosques reconsecrated as Christian churches, places where their skill at carving was in high demand.

Like all men of their trade – only cathedral-building stonemasons were worse – they had arrogance too, which came from the knowledge that for all their fighting ability the mail-clad knights often required their skills to overcome a stout defence. Antioch had tempered that somewhat, there being only one small section of wall at which a siege tower could be used, so they had been employed in fortress building, bastions that shut access to the gates of a city near impossible to assault.

Ma'arrat an-Numan was not simple either because no tower could get close to the walls due to that deep ditch, added to which, aware of the shortage of time, Raymond was asking for a rough-hewn edifice, not some smooth example of the carpenter's art. If they were disgruntled to be rushed they were even happier to be well paid and they demanded to be properly fed, which caused resentment in an encampment where food was now being rationed. No fool, Raymond was disbursing his money in stages to ensure he had oversight of their work, while always present in person demanding haste.

The Apulians were busy too, though eager to keep their heavy frames out of sight, buried, once constructed, under piles of brushwood. Any Provençal knight approaching their lines would see the ladders they had built of a standard size and weight, which led to amusement as they contemplated these rivals for plunder enduring the same fate as had been visited on them. Not that their liege lord of Toulouse, or his captains, gifted them much time to gloat, for a roadway had to be made and the dry moat had to be filled in.

The place chosen was adjacent to one of the towers, which, if it told the defenders precisely where the attack would come and by what means – they could hardly avoid observing what was being constructed just out of the range of their archery – also served as a sign of the determination of the attackers to overcome them. The Muslim garrison dare not essay out to disrupt the effort: standing by was a strong force of knights to kill anyone who tried.

Just like the construction of the siege tower, the filling in of the dry moat had to be done with haste: there was no time to construct a bombardment screen as well, so Raymond's men were obliged to cram it by running towards the wall with a shield over their head and a large stone in their one free hand, that cast at the base of the wall before they could beat a hasty retreat. It was a run for safety that some did not make, either felled by a rock themselves or caught by the burning pitch and oil the defenders cast down on their heads.

'At least with what they are casting down,' Bohemund said, his tone mordant, 'the infidel are contributing to their own downfall.'

Rocks on their own did not suffice to create a crossing over which the wheels of a siege tower could move forward. Once the ditch was filled to a certain point it had to be topped by a combination of pebbles and earth. Day after day the Apulians watched as their Provençal counterparts risked being killed or maimed to make good that pathway, sometimes seeing their efforts washed away by rain, while all the time the siege tower rose behind them, until after ten days the Count of Toulouse pronounced himself satisfied and proper preparations could be made for an assault.

Bohemund sent a message to Raymond offering to act in concert with his men and to attack any point of the walls he chose to allot to them. The reply that came back was uncivil in the extreme: he would prefer Bohemund's men to stand and observe, but since he could not stop them if they wished to make an assault, it was a matter of indifference to him where they chose to do so.

205

'I have had many occasion to regret that we are on Crusade, Tancred, and this is just another one of them. In any other place, on any other purpose and at any time, Raymond and I would have settled this dispute by a contest of arms. Bishop Adémar kept us from that while he was alive.'

'And now his spirit does the same.'

'Partly. But who could so throw their reputation to the wolves by engaging in battle with a fellow Crusader?'

Tempted to say that his uncle was equally at fault, Tancred, as he had done these many months, held his tongue. All around him were the sounds of men making ready for battle, swords being honed on stone wheels, mail and the straps that held it tight being checked, as well as the murmured prayers of those who would do battle in the morning, going into action immediately after they had been shriven by the accompanying priests.

It was at these times that men wondered at being in such a place at such a time, thought fondly of home and hearth, perhaps of wives and children, which was a rosy glow not tempered by the knowledge of reality. In their lives they rarely sat by a home-built fire, for they were a caste of warriors who made their way in the world by fighting, not by tending sheep, cattle or hauling a plough along behind the fat arse of an ox.

They would attend and say Mass in the knowledge, while indifferent to the fact, that death might await them. Each man would swallow the Eucharist and the wine, which represented the body and blood of Jesus Christ, and commend his soul to God before setting out to kill any fellow man with whom he fought, and once the battle was over, to then take, in the form of anything of value, what he could from those who survived.

CHAPTER THIRTEEN

Raymond was slow to start, letting dawn, the normal hour for an assault, pass by before he gave the order to form up, that extended by several more turns of sand passing through the narrow neck of glass. It was near to noontime before the first horn blew and the tower began to move, a red-backed flag with its golden Occitan cross fluttering in the stiff morning breeze. Not that it was very obvious the sun was at its zenith, hidden as it was in a grey and cloudy sky that looked to threaten rain.

Many of the stones that now filled that dry moat had come from the roadway that led to the western curtain wall – it would be madness to try to take one of the many towers, naturally higher in construction, so the siege tower was rolled slowly forward with a relative ease that decreased the closer it came to the masonry. There the pathway narrowed considerably: in the killing zone it had been harder to make it so wide and so smooth and the continued forward motion on less than perfect ground now made the structure rock to and fro and from side to side in what looked, from a distance, to be an alarming degree.

The men who suffered most from the movement were the archers on the very top level, there to engage in an exchange with their counterparts of the walls, who started firing flaming bolts as soon as it came in extreme range, aimed at setting the less solid parts of the tower alight, especially the brushwood screens that lined each level. With Raymond's bowman was a gigantic huntsman blowing endless loud calls on his horn to encourage his confrères and, he hoped, frighten the defence.

Below the archers and behind a solid screen were gathered the small body of knights who would undertake the initial assault, the screen when dropped acting as a platform on which they could begin a fight designed to push the defenders back onto their own parapet. With the heavily armed knights stood a quartet of lightweight *milities* whose task was to cast grappling irons upon which they would then haul in an effort to ease the task of the whole mass pushing below.

Originally, at ground level and in front of the tower, the *milities* and camp followers had been pulling on ropes, but that was abandoned as soon as the arrows began to fly. Now they were behind and pushing hard, partly screened from harm by the structure, lined up on either side of the supporting knights, ready to aid their confrères by rushing up the internal ladders to join as soon as the fighting began. That had to wait till the tower was stationary: too many bodies on the floors made it impossible to move.

Given they were pushing and the ground was less even, progress slowed until even a snail would have outrun its progress, its four great wheels creaking as it edged forward, the weight of the tower enough on its own to send out wisps of smoke from the greased axels. Waiting along the wall was a frisson of pikes, as well as swordsmen ready to cut those grappling-iron ropes, while as soon as they came within range javelins were cast in a high arc in an attempt to draw first blood by looping over the screen.

There had been yelling from both sides, to go with that relentless horn blowing, since the tower first moved but the closer it got the louder such shouting became as men sought to bolster their courage by exhortation, until the air was filled with the combination, the cursing of both faiths now loud enough to fill the air. If Raymond could be blinded by his pride he was no tyro as a general: an attack with ladders was launched against the northern wall to split the defence. In plain sight the archers atop the tower saw some of the defenders rush off to contain that assault and they were not alone.

Bohemund was watching events with as keen an eye as his rival, just as earlier he had listened to his Armenian interpreter, Firuz, who had been sent to sniff out Raymond's tactics and came to report the surreptitious preparations for the supplementary attack, making an assessment of when to launch his own attempt against the southern ramparts, which if they were not unguarded should have few men in place to repulse him.

'It will not remain thus,' were the words he had

employed when he outlined his thinking to his senior captains, as dawn rose prior to the opening of the battle. 'Raymond's northern attack will draw off strength from his main effort but they will soon see that for what it is, a diversion.'

Canny as ever, Bohemund had held back this conference till it could be delayed no longer, for his men needed time to get into position. Where he would launch his attack – on the east wall or to the south – was a secret he had held close, for the very simple reason that if no one knew it could not be betrayed either by a loose tongue or a needy purse. Also his delay in deploying was designed to make Raymond think he might stand aside to await the outcome of the Provençal effort, only moving when he was sure of its success.

'If our task is to get onto the southern curtain wall, there is to be no attempt to get into the city from there.' That got many a raised eyebrow and quite a few low-voiced comments. 'Once we have cleared the parapet, seek out a tower and take it. Once in our possession it is to be held regardless of who seeks to dislodge us.'

If the first remark had set minds working, those closing words had an even greater effect: that the Muslims of Ma'arrat would seek to dislodge them could be taken as a fact; 'regardless of who' could only mean Raymond's men, which was quickly acknowledged by their commander, but with a sharp caveat.

'Kill as many infidels as you like, but spill a drop of Christian blood and you will answer to me. The task is to take and hold the towers so

210

that even if the Count of Toulouse takes the city he does not hold it without our cooperation.'

Tancred spoke up and it was clear by his tone of voice he was far from happy. 'This is a repeat of Antioch.'

'No, nephew, it is a reverse of Antioch.' Aware of a shifting of feet among his other captains Bohemund was quick to add, 'There are those of you who are bent on Jerusalem, and that is so of many of the men you lead. I say here and swear that nothing I will do will ever keep you from that goal.'

There was temptation to reprise all the things he had said to Tancred: Antioch must be held if the Crusade was to have any prospect of success and it had to be in the hands of a man who could repulse any attempt by the Turks to retake it, while no faith could be placed in Alexius Comnenus and Byzantium to do that for them.

That he, Bohemund, was set upon holding the city even against the Emperor, and if any man saw that as covetousness, it was not something for which he was prepared to seek approval, for if he could gain remission for past sins in the Holy City he would gain little else. Instead, the thought of Alexius – the reasons he had lost to him in Thessaly and Macedonia all those years past – gave him a better way to appeal to these men.

'Antioch is the most vital trading city in Syria, if not the richest between Constantinople and Cairo, so no words of mine are needed to tell any one of you what opportunities exist for a man bent on gaining prosperity in my service. Those

211

of faith who serve with me but wish to fulfil their vow must do so and go on to Jerusalem. But know this, once that task is completed, they will be welcomed back to my banner should they choose to return. Any man who wishes to stay with me in Antioch I will ask to aid me in holding the city and the province in my name.'

The more pious could not look at Bohemund, for he had stated his position with clarity for the first time, not that it had been obscure to anyone with an ounce of sense. Others did hold his eye and it was clear why: Antioch and Northern Syria, which their liege lord now controlled, would require to be administered by the senior men he led.

Castles would have to be built and garrisoned, which meant that the lands around them would be handed out to those who took command of the region, kept it at peace and held their fiefs against invaders. From that came the things of which any landless knight dreamt: titles and wealth.

If it was less than benevolent, Bohemund was challenging their faith, pitting it against their sense of personal yearning. The men who went on to Jerusalem might indeed fulfil their vow – they might also die in the attempt – but if they succeeded in taking the Holy City and survived, by the time they came back to Antioch all the best land would have been parcelled out to those who had stayed. Loyalty to Bohemund would stand higher in their leader's estimation than the depth of their dedication to Christ.

'This day, we have a battle to fight that will

212

decide more than what happens here at Ma'arrat an-Numan. Just as I respect the faith of the true Crusader, I will also not press any of you to participate who think that my actions are blameworthy. But that is a decision you must make right now!'

The last expression being made with a bark had all pulling themselves upright; to decline now would be seen as a lack of courage and that they would never show.

The strip of daylight between the tower and the walls of Ma'arrat had so narrowed as to almost disappear yet that last tiny gap was proving the hardest to overcome. For all their efforts the stone crossing they had built over that dry moat had none of the consistency of the impacted ground they had earlier traversed.

The tower first swayed forward, only to lean back again as it was pushed onto another uneven patch, causing the screen which had protected the knights to first drop slightly then be hauled back up again; without it and not engaged in actual combat they were vulnerable in a situation where long pikes could outdistance their lances, while arrows and javelins launched at such a short range might even penetrate their chain mail.

Bohemund had been determined not to begin his own assault until the Provençals were fully engaged, thus pinning the defenders, but matters were not progressing as he had anticipated; it was all taking too long. Too much time had been wasted before the thing first moved and he could feel the stirrings of frustration not only at its slow progress but the way it was compressing the amount of daylight in which he would have to fight.

Behind him stood his warriors and they would be feeling the same impatience, mail-clad knights ranged in an extended line alongside the climbing frames, those lying on the ground where they had been placed overnight. Constructed in numbers they would allow his men to assault an entire section of the southern wall between two towers, an effort harder to defend against than a series of single-person ladders. They also served to send a message that this was no probing attack but one designed to take the city.

There was also in his calculation the notion that even if the danger of his attack were seen as soon as those frames became visible, there would be a time delay between the realisation of the threat and the moves needed to counter it by a defence already heavily engaged in two places. That it was not working as he had hoped required that he change: for the whole assault to succeed and in the available time he would need to draw off some of those opposing Raymond.

'Blow the horns,' he commanded, moving forward himself under his red banner so that all along the line his men could see it was time to move.

Up from the covering brushwood came the frames; as soon as they were in view they caused a ripple of obvious alarm on the battlements, as the nature of what they portended was assessed. It should have been a time to break into a run, to get to the base of the walls at speed, regardless of the ditch, but those frames, as they had to be, were made of heavy timber and green stuff with it, full of sap and ten times the weight of seasoned wood.

Thus the Apulians shuffled forward, dragging the frames behind them, seeking with their free hand to place their shields in the best place to ward off danger. If they bellowed their bloody intentions, their count in his dignity could do no more than threaten those men on the walls with the fierce nature of his appearance – his massive height added to the mighty axe he carried, the white surcoat he wore, still with its red Crusader cross – for the threat of Christian retribution to a Muslim was more forbidding than any de Hauteville family device.

As he came closer the men on the walls might see the look in his eyes, steady blue orbs on either side of the drooping nose guard of a conical Norman helmet. If they did it should chill their blood, for the promise of the gaze was one of death and mutilation. Naturally because of his stature and the position of leadership he adopted Bohemund became the prime target that had to be stopped, so that every projectile cast or fired from the walls came in his direction.

To protect him, and this was their duty, his familia knights stepped up to surround their lord and used their shields to create an impenetrable barrier off which arrows and javelins bounced, that raised to cover heads the closer they came to the massive rectangular stones, jointed with mortar, that made up the walls. All along the line his men were dropping into the dry moat, before setting down their burdens, a foot set on the base to secure them, while those who came behind rushed to raise them hand over hand until the tops rested on the battlements.

The enemy sought to immediately push the frames away, only to find the very weight that had slowed the Apulians made it impossible for the defenders to budge them and that was rendered even more difficult as soon at the attackers began their slow climb. What came down on them to slow their progress was dangerous – boiling oil, rocks, javelins and heavier spears – but it was widespread and not sufficient in content or concentrated enough to impose a complete check.

That came from the tenacity of the defenders, who, when engaged fought with a fury that surpassed anything the Crusaders had encountered previously and their efforts increased when reinforcements arrived from the western wall to stop this fresh assault. Bohemund, as was required by any warrior chieftain, was well to the fore, his axe swings deadly to anyone caught in their arc, for each blow was not of a weight to merely wound, aware that even with this form of assault only so many of his fighters could engage at any one time.

The frames were full of knights waiting to get into the action, which could only come about if one of their number succumbed to their front, albeit if that person fell with a mortal wound his falling body was as likely to take with him that of his waiting replacement as slip on by. Try as they did, the Apulians could not breast the battlements in numbers enough to gain a foothold.

For all their prowess in battle the Normans began to show signs of weariness. The arms ached, the throats were too dry to properly breathe, the sweat from exertion filled the eyes to make misty that at which they were aiming, and all was being undertaken with a precarious balance. The saving grace was, apart from the latter, the defence suffered likewise, so that it became possible for exhausted fighters to be replaced on both sides in a battle that was making no progress for either; the Turks could not drive back the Crusaders and they could not get onto the parapet where their greater height, weight and reach could be made to count.

It was in a short period of rest that Bohemund was able to observe that Raymond was faring no better than he, and if his admiration for the tenacity of the Crusaders was great, be they Apulians or Provençals, he had nobility enough to extend that to a race he had respected ever since he first fought them, for the Turks were every bit as formidable as any Latin and just as inspired by their faith as the most devout Christian.

If he loved battle Bohemund desired success more, so instead of rejoining the fight he took to trying to direct the efforts of his men from below, looking for areas where resistance seemed to be weakening or a gap began to appear and directing them to that spot. Time might have lost all meaning but it was obvious from the state of the light that the fight had been going on for a long time.

Messengers, Firuz included, had been passing

to and fro throughout to let Bohemund know if Raymond was making any progress and the news was far from encouraging. Having finally got his tower up to and leaning on the curtain wall he could no more get his men over it than could Bohemund.

Several times the defenders had set it alight, which meant all hands went to the buckets of water needed to douse the flames, warring knights included, while his diversionary attack had faltered completely from lack of the men to push it to a point where the defenders were pinned in place and thus unavailable to thwart the main assault.

'He has men sapping at the wall beneath the tower.'

This was information Bohemund passed on to a blood-soaked Tancred, who had likewise been obliged to take a rest from fighting and come to join him. His nephew, who replied through strenuous efforts to get back his breath, suggested that it was a waste of time. How could men, with picks and shovels, in half a day hope to undermine the foundations of such well-constructed walls that had been standing for centuries?

'And if nothing happens to aid us soon,' Tancred gasped, using his sword to indicate a darkening sky, 'we will be obliged to halt the attack.'

'I have sent for torches. We fight on.'

'Even if Raymond withdraws?'

'He had the devil's own task to get his damn tower into place and I doubt he can get it off again, so he will not abandon it.'

That was part of a message he had received: the

front wheels, huge shaped timbers hewn by those English carpenters, had begun to sink into the imperfect ground underneath, its weight dislodging the earth and pebbles, even shifting the rocks that formed a more solid base. Bohemund's informant reckoned there was no force of men nor beasts that would have the strength to get it off, so there were only two alternatives for the Count of Toulouse: to fight on in the dark or to torch the tower and fall back.

'And that is a retreat that will not end back in his lines. There's no time to build another tower with the state of our food.'

'It would be better Raymond knows we intend to fight on, Uncle.'

The reply to Tancred had to wait until Bohemund had finished directing some of his men to a perceived weak spot, or was it that he wanted to think upon the notion – his nephew did not know – but when he did reply it was in the affirmative.

'It has to come from a trusted source and my pride will not allow that it be me, so you must be the messenger.'

'Happily,' Tancred replied, which got him, even if all he could see was his uncle's eyes, a less than kindly look.

'Deliver the message and no more, for I need you here.'

'Am I allowed to ask Raymond to reinforce us? He must have men free from his failed diversion.'

'No.'

There was little temptation to dispute that, even if Tancred thought it short-sighted. The mere movement of Raymond's knights from one wall to another might help to confuse the defence, might cause them to move men best left in place. These thoughts stayed with Tancred as he made his way to where flew Raymond's banner. The ripple of reaction when he was sighted approaching was unmistakable; indeed, a pair of familia knights were detached in the increasing gloom of a cloudy twilight to intercept him.

He was just about to pass to them his message when they halted with startled expressions and looked beyond him, this at the same time as Tancred spun round, the reason for both a sound not unlike a thunderclap, except it did not come from above. He had to peer to see the crack that began to run up the wall to one side of Raymond's tower but what followed was easily visible. The battlements at the top of that crack began to sag and with a rumble that sounded like the end of time the whole wall collapsed, to leave, once the dust cleared and Tancred could see, a high pile of rubble and above that a clear breach.

Despite his scoffing, the sappers had succeeded.

CHAPTER FOURTEEN

It took little time for the news of that collapsed curtain wall to find its way to the ears of those opposing the Apulians, less than it took to reach those of the Count of Taranto himself. If he had heard the rumble of that falling masonry he lacked sight of it so had no idea why those Turks

220

who had held his men at bay for so long suddenly stopped fighting. There was a lapse too before those who had been wielding weapons at enemy heads found them to be swishing through fresh air as their adversaries fled, another before they realised that there was no barrier to their climbing over the battlements and onto the parapet.

By the time the truth dawned Bohemund was alongside his men to remind them of his instructions, to take control of the nearest towers and not to seek to get down into the city, an instruction that was not easy to obey given there was no one to obstruct them, indeed it fell to their leader to curtail their progress; he was happy with a few of the towers of Ma'arrat an-Numan, he did not need them all. Tancred found him on the Apulian side of that collapsed breach, with barely enough light left in the day to see what lay on the other side of the gap.

'Raymond has called on his men to fall back, leaving only the number needed to secure the battlements.'

'In God's name why?'

'It seems he fears to fight in the streets in darkness, against an enemy that seems to consist of the whole Muslim citizenry of Ma'arrat, which means a fighter and perhaps a knife in every doorway. The cost in blood would be too high, though since he would not talk with me there may be another cause.'

'I cannot think what it might be,' came the reply, with a slow shake of the head. 'Perhaps it is wise.'

'What do you intend?'

'Whatever it is will not be served by us standing in the open where we can be seen as soon as someone fetches a torch.'

'Raymond will know that we have succeeded as well.'

That was said to his uncle's back; Bohemund was already heading for the nearest tower, and the chamber within that had provided accommodation for the Turks who had previously occupied it. Entering upon his heels, Tancred was asked to shut the studded wood door that led to the breach, which plunged the tiny space into darkness, until Bohemund called for light and a torch was brought, this allowing him to set the flame to the tallow wads resting in the hollow sconces carved out of the solid stone.

The room, cold with thick stone walls and no fire, had a table and chests that served as seats in daylight, then, when set together, as beds at night, on one of which Bohemund sat, indicating that Tancred should do likewise, before falling into a contemplative silence, his chin resting on the haft of his axe, a position he maintained for some time and held even when his nephew spoke.

'I think it sensible to wait for daylight.' That got a slow nod. 'If the enemy is not truly beaten that means they will still be fired with hope and still numerous enough to spill much blood in the streets.'

'They are bound, on such a night, to be as dark as pitch and narrow.'

'Which is deadly.'

'You are saying it would be equal folly for us to

attempt to do what Raymond has postponed?'

'Possibly, but then there is the notion that we will have a free hand to plunder as well before sunrise.'

'What of our men, Tancred?'

'They have obeyed your orders and will continue to do so unless you change them.'

'Even when tempted by such a rich prize?'

Tancred produced a grim smile. 'That will not be much use to a man hanging from a doorway for disobedience.'

'And how, nephew, do you think Raymond would react to find that his own men had been denied any part of what is rightfully theirs, arrived in Ma'arrat to find it plundered by us?'

'He would have to be incensed, his lances even more so.'

'Which might push him to act against his better nature.' Bohemund looked at his nephew and grinned then. 'Always assuming he has one.'

'You think he might resort to arms?'

'He might have no choice, Tancred. The pressure from those he leads might oblige him to seek bloody redress.' Another silence followed, Bohemund's chin was back on the wooden haft of that axe until he had cleared his thoughts. 'In all my disputes with Raymond, as I have said before to you, I have had a care to never push it to a contest of weapons.'

'You would kill him in such a fight.'

That got a faint nod but there was no pride in the response; Bohemund was the foremost knight of Christendom and well aware of the fact. He knew that Raymond, even given his prowess as a fighter and leader of men, could never defeat him in single combat. Quite apart from his greater age – he was in his fifties and so a good decade older than Bohemund – there was the sheer difference in height and strength, let alone repute. Such a contest would be an uneven one and Raymond of Toulouse was equally aware of that.

'And I would have no choice lest I wish him to kill me.'

'The Crusade,' Tancred responded in what was a statement not a question.

'If blood is to be spilt on this venture it will not be by me, or those I lead. I will hold to my papal vow.'

Tancred had to bite his tongue; where did Antioch come in such a declaration?

'Single combat fills me with no fear, but a battle of factions...'

'And you sense that here?' Tancred asked as his uncle's voice trailed off.

'I see the possibility.'

'You could ensure it is single combat by issuing the challenge?'

'The Provençal knights would not stand to see their leader slain.'

'So you are going to leave Raymond's men a free hand to plunder the city?'

'Never!' Bohemund spat back, before sitting up and smiling, his tone benign. 'But I will wait till his men make their entry before any of ours move a muscle. Then we can happily see to the garrison and plunder in company to our heart's content. No one can gainsay that.'

'He will want the governor's treasury, to com-

224

pensate for the silver he expended on his siege tower.'

'Then he best move with speed, for to lay his hands on it he will need to get to it first. Now oblige me by fetching Firuz.'

Raymond of Toulouse had as much discipline over his knights as did Bohemund, so that his instruction to wait until daylight before entering the city was obeyed, as much because his men were exhausted from fighting most of the day as the fear of disobeying their liege lord and the consequences. They were now sat round their fires earnestly discussing the wealth that would be theirs on the morrow, as well as how the Turkish citizenry would pay for their obstinacy.

Such talk had a deeper resonance than in normal times for these men. Since leaving Constantinople most of the towns and cities taken, faced with a formidable and successful Crusader army, had surrendered and opened their gates, only for possession to be taken as imperial fiefs by the body of troops Alexius Comnenus had sent to accompany them, this before treaties were made respecting the inhabitants, which meant plunder was out of the question.

The first occasion on which this had occurred had been at Nicaea, the primary target of the campaign. That had been a proper siege, yet instead of the expected booty and other pleasures which normally came from the surrender of a place that had refused terms, the fighting men, high and low, got nothing. All had stood by to watch Byzantine troops take ownership.

They had been rewarded by the Emperor's largesse, which if welcome could not compare with the prospect of what might be gained from a man's own efforts in a captured city of some size and wealth. The princes and their senior supporters had received gold and silver, the rest had to be content with copper, albeit in abundant quantities.

In Antioch, with Kerbogha's huge army in the offing, common sense dictated they should not alienate the populace and that debarred the Crusaders from engaging in mass pillage, albeit there had been many individual acts of thievery. Only at Albara had the Provençals been allowed to behave in the time-honoured fashion, that being a proper sack, which whetted an appetite never much hidden.

The mailed knights had, as was commonplace, the best pickings, being first over the walls, able to kill anyone who stood in their way, quick to spot the homes of the wealthier citizens as well as the public buildings, bound to be repositories of high-value items to steal, albeit care had to be taken not to cross the avarice of their liege lord and his senior subordinates. Food and wine was carried off to their own encampments for later consumption and that too applied to any well-born women.

The *milities* coming along behind them, if they often found that the easy pickings were gone, had been able to find booty, if necessary by torturing the ordinary citizens to find out where they had hidden money and provisions their betters had missed, killing those who refused to reveal their secret places while treating their womenfolk of whatever age as chattels to be abused prior to being passed up to their liege lord to be sold into slavery.

By the time the pilgrims got entry to Ma'arrat – those thousands who had followed Raymond and the Holy Lance to Albara and to here – the infidel, from whom they could with a clear conscience steal anything they could find, would have been stripped even down to their naked bodies, and if they had a storeroom it would be long emptied. The only pleasure to be gained in dealing with the enemies of their faith would be from granting them the choice of forced conversions or immediate death.

Thus it had been at Albara, yet there they had not faced near starvation, which is what afflicted them now. In the short time Bohemund and his Apulians had been outside Ma'arrat, their condition, poor to begin with, had shown a marked deterioration. They had been reduced to rutting in the surrounding landscape for weeds and roots with which to make some kind of soup, while any edible berries had been already picked and consumed.

Now these pilgrims were sat outside a city seemingly devoid of defence – the walls were deserted – with the possibility of well-stocked larders, while those who were armed and could stop them were sat round their fires dreaming of plunder, so here lay an opportunity to be first to the trough. It was not a mass affair or in any way organised: people weighed up their situation and acted in small groups, slipping out of their camp at various intervals to bypass, on a night of Stygian darkness, the sentinels set by Raymond.

When it came to discipline the writ of Raymond and Bohemund ran less well within the minds of their poorer soldiery, the *milities*, who collectively had none of the haughty pretensions, nor the dreams of riches, which exercised the knightly cohorts. If they expected to be second to the sack, and would be on the morrow, it was more of a present concern that they had enjoyed less of the food here at Ma'arrat that kept their betters in superior health.

If they were not starving they were hungry, for food distribution naturally favoured the men in chain mail, who undertook the burden of fighting in a siege, the *milities* being required for the base work of making and carrying ladders or pulling and pushing the tower built by the Count of Toulouse into place, before plying their shovels to undermine the walls. Had they not, for all their mean standing, brought about the fall of the city, so why should others have first rights?

The movement of the pilgrims did not go unnoticed either – they were camped closer to the *milities* than the lances – and soon bands of foot soldiers, pikes and daggers in hand, were on their heels. In Ma'arrat they found the streets full of pilgrims but free of any Turkish soldiers, who had retreated to the Governor's Palace to await their fate, while the Muslim citizens who had fought so hard were cowering in their dwellings: nothing stood between them and rich pickings, including the unarmed pilgrims.

Bohemund had sent his interpreter Firuz to seek out the Governor of Ma'arrat with an offer that he should surrender his now untenable city. If he did so and gathered together in a body the leading citizens at his palace, he would provide a strong guard to secure their lives, bound to be forfeit if they did not concur in the frenzy that would follow the entry of the soldiery, regardless of their rank.

Once they were inside the walls there was not a high noble born, however feared he might be, who would be able to control his men in a city that had refused terms. Knights or *milities* it made no difference, each would be determined on what he saw as his just reward, the size of which tended to grow in the imagination the nearer the fall of a city approached, and grew out of all proportion when plunder was to hand.

Not to be cheated of what was theirs by right became the paramount emotion, often fuelled by wine taken to excess – bloodlust apart that was the primary object seized – so that in the unlikely event there was an ounce of compassion contained in a Crusader breast it was soon swamped by avarice. It was a sad commonplace to find those engaged in plunder, comrades in battle but intoxicated with drink and envy, seeking to rob each other.

Raymond had waited till first light to send forward his own herald to demand the surrender of Ma'arrat, only to discover there was no one in authority prepared to answer the ultimatum, which obliged him to lead his lances and the attendant priests over the breach in the walls and into the streets, where he expected to find the Turks ready to sell their lives dearly.

Instead he came across a teeming mass of pilgrims of both sexes, mixed with his own drunken *milities*, as well as bodies littering streets and alleys that ran with victim blood. More to the point, both groups had in their possession items of gold and silver, while their belts were hung with bulging leather purses.

Mindful of his standing as protector and possessor of the Holy Lance, Raymond forbade his men to take from the pilgrims what they had plundered and that, for military reasons, also had to apply to his *milities*, an instruction for which the citizens of Ma'arrat paid dearly. There would have been unbridled savagery whatever had occurred, but seeing themselves robbed of what they presumed as rightfully theirs sent the mailed lances in a passion even greater than that which would have attended their depredations.

As they moved into the city no one was spared, with the Armenians suffering too, and both Raymond and Robert of Flanders were to the fore in the killing and encouragement to do so; man, woman or child, a goodly number of the inhabitants that had so far survived were dragged through their smashed doorways to be executed in the streets, the only delay in instant despatch – there was no offer to convert for the Muslims – the chance to tell where they had hidden whatever they still possessed.

Bohemund had moved into the city at dawn as well, but with more purpose, no less surprised than Raymond of Toulouse to find that his men had been beaten to their pillage by a mass of villeins, drunk with wine and bloodlust, now crowding the streets and squares, his Apulians reacting in a similar fashion to the knights of Provence, for they too felt cheated.

He made no effort to contain them, nor did he even delay to observe; following the guidance of Firuz, he and Tancred, surrounded by familia knights, were led to the Governor's Palace where he found that the arrangements his interpreter had made overnight were in place.

Assembled were all those of wealth and position, the merchants that had in their trade made Ma'arrat an-Numan such a tempting target for a conqueror, along with their possessions. There too were their many wives and even more children, all under the protection of the governor's personal retainers, those Turkish soldiers who had been the backbone of the defence.

'Firuz, tell those men to throw down their weapons,' Bohemund commanded, after the governor had executed a deep bow.

A sharp command from the bent-over official saw that obeyed and Firuz translated his next words, uttered while he stood fully upright once more and pointed to the chests of coin that lay before him, a sweep following to include the objects of value that lay behind them.

'He offers this to you as yours by right of conquest.'

'And what does he seek in return?'

'That which you proposed I offer, My Lord, their lives and the right to depart Ma'arrat with what they can carry.'

About to agree, Bohemund was forced to react to the sudden commotion as a body of knights entered, with Raymond of Toulouse and Robert of Flanders at their head, both blood-coated magnates stopping dead in their forward movement wearing expressions of surprise, or was it fury, to find the Count of Taranto present. That was before their eyes were drawn, as they must be, to the treasure that lay between Bohemund and the richly clad Turks, who had recoiled at the intrusion and were now gathered in a knot.

'The city is surrendered,' Bohemund said.

'It is not,' Raymond spat, 'until it is ceded to me.'

'It matters not, My Lord who has the glory, more who has the walls.' He gestured for his Armenian to approach and spoke softly. 'Firuz, tell the governor who it is that has just entered and that having surrendered to me he must also do so to the Count of Toulouse. Add that a very deep bow, even abasement, would not go amiss.'

There was a degree of terror in the governor's eye as that was translated, but he was quick to throw himself onto the mosaic-tiled floor, an act that was copied by the whole knot of assembled males to his rear. From the floor came the words that asked for mercy, following which Bohemund explained what he had arranged.

'Nothing of yours applies to me,' Raymond barked.

'It would have done so, Count Raymond, if you had climbed off your high horse and deigned to talk with me.'

Raymond's response was to wave his blood-stained sword and order his men to seize both the assembled Turks and their possessions, an act which had Bohemund move forward to block their way, Tancred and the familia knights acting in unison to support him, all the Apulians having unsheathed weapons.

'I have given certain guarantees.'

'Which I had told you–'

'You, My Lord, do not tell me anything.'

'The lives of these infidels, as well as anything they possess, is forfeit.'

'Their possessions, yes, their lives I have granted, as well as that which they can carry.'

Bohemund and Raymond were two sword blades apart now, and glaring at each other, which had Tancred wondering if that restraint which his uncle had stated the previous night was in danger of being broken. He was in a position where his pride would not let him withdraw but so was Raymond, and the younger man could only speculate what was going through the mind of Toulouse.

He had more men with him than his rival, but that would aid him little if it came to a fight, for he was well to the fore and might fall before his superior numbers could save him and such was the prowess of Bohemund that several of them might be despatched in the attempt, which as his familia knights they would be bound to do. Tancred thought he knew what Toulouse did not: his uncle would never strike the first blow, but it was the last one that counted and that would certainly be his.

Robert of Flanders pushed through to get between the two men. 'Is there not enough here for all? No good will come of spilling blood in place of a share of the spoils.'

'I demand their heads on my lances,' Raymond spat, gesturing to the Turks, cowering in a group once more, 'as recompense for the blood and treasure I have spent.'

'Settle for their wealth, Raymond, for I have given them my word on their lives.'

Robert of Flanders put his mouth close to Raymond's ear and spoke in such a low whisper that Bohemund could not hear what he said, words which did nothing to soften the look aimed at his Apulian rival. Bohemund held Raymond's eye, but kept his countenance mild, until either from the words he was hearing or from the uselessness of maintaining it Raymond turned his head slightly and broke the mutual stare.

'You would fight a Christian to save a Turk?' Raymond asked, when Flanders had ceased to whisper.

'I would fight to defend my bounden word.'

That caused the other man to blink, for it flew directly in the face of his low opinion of Bohemund, who to his mind was careless with his vows. It was then obvious that Flanders had suggested a compromise that would save the face of both men. It was equally the case that Toulouse was unhappy in the making of it, for his voice was strained.

'You may have their lives, but they leave this palace with nothing but that in which they need for modesty.'

The time taken by Bohemund to consider that did nothing to lighten the threatening atmosphere, but eventually he called forward Firuz, with instruction being given that the Turks should be stripped of their personal valuables, including their rich garments, while explaining the alternative, which was worse.

'Tell him I will provide an escort to the city gates and beyond, to ensure they are safe.'

'And what of these men we had to fight to get here, Count Bohemund?' Raymond asked. 'Do you intend to protect them too?'

'They are not subject to any promise I made.'

'Then,' Raymond hissed, 'it is fitting that they pay the price for their deeds.'

Receiving no reply, Raymond issued a sharp command and the men who had led the Muslim citizens of Ma'arrat an-Numan and shown them how to fight, now without arms to defend themselves, were slaughtered to the frantic screams of the women present.

CHAPTER FIFTEEN

Ma'arrat had suffered greatly but in truth the majority of the population survived, even some Muslims of both sexes, but more tellingly a high number of Armenians. For every body in the streets or blocking the doorway to a dwelling there were another three citizens still drawing breath, albeit they kept out of sight in their cellars and attics until the murderous instincts of their enemies had run their course and exhaustion added to full bellies brought an end to the killing.

Still, the place smelt of death and it was sound policy to begin to clear away the already rotting cadavers, as well as ensure that any buildings still smouldering were doused to prevent a spreading conflagration that could consume half the city. Corpses were piled on carts by the survivors of Ma'arrat and taken out of the city to be burnt in a huge human bonfire that sent pungent clouds of stinking black smoke into the air, the sticky ash falling to cover the clothing of those who had been engaged in the destruction.

The Crusaders were sated, both by blood and plunder, for they had been given a free hand to take for themselves that which they wished, while their lords and masters had a care to see that they got a share in the spoils that had been haggled over in the Governor's Palace. Raymond had insisted that it was his labours, most notably in expending a great amount of silver on his siege tower, as well as the blood expended in its employment, that had led to the fall of Ma'arrat. That being so, he and his Provençals, as well as the men under Robert of Flanders, should have the lion's share of the booty.

Bohemund was equally adamant that the Apulians, in drawing off men from the main assault, had contributed just as much to success and that both he and his lances deserved an equal share. Besides, it was he who had made the arrangements that had seen such treasure assembled in one place, for had it not been, given the mayhem of the sack of the city, with the pilgrims matching the soldiers in their avarice, the high nobles might have been lucky to see a single coin.

In the end, after much bluster and negotiation, the promises Bohemund had made to the governor and the wealthy citizens of Ma'arrat cost him dear: stripped as they were of everything they possessed, and in terror, these people still had their lives. Raymond made it obvious that unless he was satisfied in his demands they would suffer the same fate as that of the men who had been guarding them – those retainers who were now at best twitching carcasses laid out on a tiled floor swimming in bright red blood. It took a part payment of what Bohemund should have got for the Apulians to get them safely out of the city and on the road to Aleppo.

Such arrangements saw no more favour in the Provençal ranks than it did with their liege lord: to their mind Bohemund's men were latecomers who had done little to deserve even that which they had, which caused their leaders to withdraw their contingents to those areas of the city under their control, the southern towers for Bohemund and the rest of Ma'arrat for Toulouse and Flanders.

'Flanders,' Tancred announced from the doorway, receiving in reply a nod that the man should enter.

He stood aside to let Count Robert of that province enter the small chamber where his uncle

had set up his quarters, the very one he had occupied on the previous night. It was one of eight
held by the Apulians, fully a third of the towers of
Ma'arrat an-Numan and, being the outer
defences, of greater value than any city dwellings.

Standing to greet his visitor, Bohemund noticed
that Robert's eyes, before engaging his, took in at
a glance the chests of treasure that lined the walls,
making cramped what was already a room much
lacking in space. A servant was sent to fetch
refreshments – bread, grapes and dates as well –
while the host indicated that his visitor should
occupy the lid of one of those very chests.

'Will you sit, My Lord?'

'I have come as an emissary of Count Raymond.'

Robert had replied as if such a thing precluded
comfort and he did not move to accept the offer,
which led to a silence that he clearly found awkward. Before responding to what he held to be
obvious – he had been waiting for some kind of
emissary – Bohemund took a short time to
reprise his relationship with this handsome man,
nearer Tancred's age than his own, well built and
with a full head of brown hair, worn long, and
with steady eyes of the same colour.

Brother-in-law to the Duke of Normandy, Robert had come on the Crusade under his banner,
which made him better disposed to the Norman
Apulians than would be the case with the knights
who served Toulouse. In common with most of
his fellow magnates that relationship had fluc-
tuated, sometimes good and on other occasions
fraught with bile and recrimination – it very
much depended on the circumstances of the

crusading endeavour.

Like all the crusading princes Flanders had been wary when they first met, again in common with his noble peers, unwilling to quite believe and accept the reputation for successful soldiering that hung like a corona around the Count of Taranto. Yet as his brother-in-law mellowed towards Bohemund, so it seemed had Flanders until, if they were not quite friends, there was no open antagonism.

The nadir had come when foraging on this very plateau of Jabal as-Summaq in the spring, for it was there they, in joint command, had been obliged to abandon the mass of food they had gathered to take back to Antioch, as well as the bulk of the men who had done the collecting, caught unawares because no piquets had been set overnight to warn of any approaching threat, common practice when camped overnight in strange and enemy territory.

Had it been the responsibility of Robert or Bohemund to set those guards? That had never been established and neither had ever accepted that they were to blame, which had naturally led to their being cold in each other's company. Yet for Bohemund there was much to admire about the man: he was a doughty fighter, the leader who had held off Kerbogha for days at the fort of La Mahomerie, which, given the odds, should not have survived one.

Added to that, in the Battle of Antioch, if there had been any residual resentment, it had never surfaced; he had stoutly obeyed the man and later had shown him, in the glow of such a stun-

239

ning victory, some regard that laid to rest the events in the disaster that befell them both on that foraging fiasco.

Where matters lay now was a mystery, but it was Robert who had whispered to Raymond to get Toulouse to modify his stance. At the moment his features were rigid, so when he did speak, Bohemund's reply was gentle and delivered, if not with a smile, at least with a sympathetic look for a fellow noble on a thankless mission.

'That I guessed, just as I surmised Count Raymond would not see it as fitting to come himself.'

The tone had a definite effect: Robert's face softened and his response had something of a weary air. 'I had to dissuade him from commanding that you attend upon him.'

'Now that he occupies the Governor's Palace our Count of Toulouse no doubt feels he has that right.'

'You can guess, Count Bohemund, why I have come.'

'As an emissary to demand that I surrender the towers I hold?'

'Ma'arrat is Raymond's by right.'

'An opinion he firmly holds to, Count Robert, but one, I suspect, which you know is nonsense.'

'So you reject his demand?'

'As would you, My Lord, were you in the same position. There is, however, one act of his that will persuade me to accede. Let Raymond surrender to me the Bridge Gate and what he holds in Antioch and he can have these towers of Ma'arrat.'

'Which is why you came to this place?'

'Hardly a furtive act, indeed an obvious one, which you guessed when I first arrived, and if what I offer is accepted it still leaves Count Raymond the man best off.'

'He will not agree.'

'And I will not then surrender my towers, which means that as we jointly hold Antioch, so we jointly hold Ma'arrat an-Numan.'

The servant had entered with the sent-for refreshments, but Flanders declined to partake of them. 'Count Raymond will be eager to hear your answer.'

'Please, My Lord, he would have known my answer before he sent you on what is a fool's errand and one that is an insult to your dignity.'

For the first time since arriving, the face of Robert of Flanders showed genuine anger. 'Allow me to be the man to measure my dignity.'

Then he spun round and left, Tancred filling the doorway as he departed.

'You heard?'

'Everything, and I wonder at it,' Tancred replied. 'Giving him Ma'arrat does not entirely secure Antioch.'

'Would you have me offer nothing?'

'You could offer to join in the march on Jerusalem.'

'Tancred, there is no such march.'

'And nor will there be, Uncle, while you continue to dispute with Toulouse.'

The reply was scathing. 'If you are looking for someone to soften their stance, try him, not me!'

'Perhaps I will,' Tancred replied, in an equally intemperate manner, before he too was gone.

Word soon spread of the impasse between the two princes and if the attitude to it was an increase in exasperation it was not for want of land and cities, but for the fact that such a dispute caused even more delay in the Crusade to which all these people, knights, *milities* and pilgrims at Ma'arrat were committed. Men already disgruntled at the lack of progress became even more vocal, their ire not dented by the plunder they had gathered by their own hands or the largesse showered on them by their leaders.

If Bohemund's standing sank in both camps – a goodly number of his Apulians were as angry as any – so did that of Raymond of Toulouse. Demands began to be heard that if he was not going to use the Holy Lance for the purpose to which it was best suited, namely as an icon to lead the faithful to Jerusalem, then he should hand it over to his troops and let them march on without the benefit of his presence.

The relic, from being a massive benefit to Raymond's standing, was now working in the opposite direction: he was being seen as undeserving of possession. Acutely attuned to the mood of the faithful, Raymond sought a way to shift the blame squarely onto the Count of Taranto. He initiated a public assembly, using the pretext of an open-air Mass to celebrate the taking of the city.

This was a setting he knew Bohemund would not be able to avoid. He knew just as well as anyone how he was being perceived, even amongst his own followers. Held in the square before the Governor's Palace, not long after first light, the press of bodies was so great that many were stuck in the adjoining streets and needed to be dealt with by suffragan divines and satellite altars. The sun shone bright in a cloudless sky and if it was cold on the cusp of December, it seemed that the heavens had decided to bless the celebration.

Kneeling at the front of the assembly, Raymond had with him the Holy Lance and he ensured it was highly visible. Not far off from that knelt Bohemund, with Tancred and Flanders in between. That the two leaders did not talk to each other as they took their places was obvious enough to set up a murmur of disapproval, which rippled through the crowd.

That faded as the archdeacon saying Mass began his litany, aided by his clerical supporters as they blessed the body and blood of Christ, the paramount vessels for both brought before the relic in Raymond's hand as if to underline not just its own importance but his.

No one but the archdeacon and his acolytes saw how Raymond reacted to the catcalls that surfaced then from hundreds of throats, few comprehensible. Yet a few transcended the mass of noise by being shouted, questioning why he had the Holy Lance and what he intended to do with it.

A glare from the archdeacon was enough to quell that disturbance, unbecoming at such a time and in such a ceremony, so the giving of Holy Communion went on throughout the square without further interruption, though given the numbers seeking to be shriven, the sun was well past its zenith before the Mass ended, at which point Raymond took up a position to address the crowd.

'I call on the Count of Taranto,' he shouted, holding up his lance, 'in the presence of all and this lance which once pierced the body of Christ, to renounce what he holds here in Ma'arrat and hand it over to those who took it by their brave endeavours.'

The approval of that was far from universal; if the Provençals cheered, many of the Apulians did not, added to which if he had hoped to embarrass his rival it failed utterly as Bohemund gave to the assembly the same reply he had given to Robert of Flanders: Give me Antioch.

'A plague on both, I say.'

Whoever shouted that, and it seemed to echo off the very sky, was, in such a dense crowd, too well hidden to be identified, but he was secure anyway, given the cry was taken up by many, soon to be joined by openly vocal demands to Raymond of what had hitherto been just murmuring. The demand that the lance be surrendered became a cacophony, and with the relic still in his hand, it was a chastened Count of Toulouse who retired to what was now his palace.

Bohemund was no less affected, receiving as much abuse as his rival, and he began to issue his orders to Tancred as soon as the square appeared clear. Try as he did, there was no missing the hateful glares thrown in his direction as the crowds dispersed; he was in the same steep tub of opinion as Toulouse, for if there had been any doubt about his intention to claim Antioch for himself, that had been laid to rest by his declaration.

'We return to Antioch on the morrow.'

'The towers?' Tancred asked.

'Will be garrisoned,' his uncle replied, in what was near to a shout; he wanted them all to know.

The year had turned before the princes gathered at a town called Rugia, in the Ruj Valley south of Antioch, called there by a request from Raymond of Toulouse, who had spent the month of December at Ma'arrat an-Numan, despite the fact that Bohemund's men still held a large section of the walls. The garrison could now worship, like the mass of pilgrims still there, in churches that had once been mosques, as they waited with open impatience for the march on Jerusalem to recommence.

All the magnates complied with Raymond, for what was obviously going to be an attempt to broker some kind of agreement. Bohemund was aware, if the others were in ignorance, that the Count of Toulouse had not just sought to turn Ma'arrat into a Christian enclave. His men had ridden out from there to take a firm grip on the surrounding countryside, he being eager to continue in his quest to isolate Antioch from the regions to the south.

Expecting Raymond to use that to again insist that Antioch should be held for Byzantium, what he did offer, once he had finished boasting of his exploits and laid strongly the case for a march on Jerusalem, came as a surprise.

'My Lords, such an endeavour we cannot undertake in a like manner that has got us this far in our quest.' That had the Duke of Normandy and Godfrey de Bouillon shifting uncomfortably: Raymond was about to openly vie for the leadership and his next words proved such suspicions correct. 'I am, amongst you, the most potent in terms of men, and none, I can assure you, are ahead of me in purpose.'

To pause then was a clever ploy, allowing, as it did, his fellow princes to adopt looks that presaged refusal.

'Yet I am aware also that we have come from Constantinople and succeeded by collective opinion. Therefore I cannot ask of you that you hand to me command of our enterprise merely for the fact that I can put more lances in the field than all of you here assembled.'

'Many of whom you have seduced from our service with promises of silver and the power of your relic.'

The Duke of Normandy was scowling as he said this and if the likes of Godfrey de Bouillon remained silent his expression alone demonstrated that he too shared the same sentiment.

'I have only ever sought that we have the means to fulfil our vow, and in order that we do so I am willing to extend to you, my fellow princes, the same, based on that which you can bring to the campaign, which we must, in all conscience, pursue.'

There was uncertainty then, those he was addressing unsure what it was he was offering and again Raymond used a long pause to heighten the tension.

'To you, My Lords of Normandy and Lower

Lorraine, I offer ten thousand silver *solidi* each, to the Count of Flanders six thousand to serve under my banner.'

'Nothing for me?' Bohemund enquired, a smile playing on his lips.

'To do so would be to waste my breath, Count Bohemund, but I am prepared to offer your nephew five thousand *solidi* to take service with me.'

All eyes turned to Tancred, who was close to a blush, for to a man of his standing it was a lot of silver and he was near to being ranked with the Count of Flanders, so the temptation to grab what was offered was high. Fortunately, Godfrey de Bouillon spoke then, which allowed the young man to remain silent. 'You do not see this, Count Raymond, as flying in the face of the spirit of the Crusade?'

'I see it, Duke Godfrey, as a means to break an impasse that has held us in Syria too long. If we cannot serve for faith, then let those amongst you who are tempted to serve for a less Christian motive come with me, for I intend to march on my own if that is required. What matters is not why we act but that we do so, for at our rear are the men we lead, who cannot understand the delay and that takes no account of the mass of pilgrims, who clamour only to attain the goal for which they have given up everything they possess.'

'Surely you do not seek an answer here and now?'

'No, but I would want it soon for I have made my plans to march south within the week and I will not delay.'

There was a telling response to that: was Raymond speaking truthfully or bluffing? Was this just a ploy to isolate Bohemund or did he genuinely wish to march on to Jerusalem at the head of the Crusade? Judging by the faces of his fellow magnates, and such was the mistrust that had grown up between them, they were ruminating on both possibilities without being able to come to a conclusion.

CHAPTER SIXTEEN

With the conference concluded most of the princes, Toulouse excluded, returned to Antioch, with Tancred uncomfortable and making a poor fist of concealing it. If he looked to his uncle for a way to proceed he was sadly disappointed: Bohemund would not advise him, seeking to avoid the subject and only saying when forced to comment that his nephew should look to the dictates of his own conscience, that even more unsettled on the news that the Duke of Normandy, hitherto one of the most vocal in complaint against Raymond of Toulouse and his habit of bribery, had accepted his offer.

If that came as a real surprise, it had to be recalled that, in order to fund his personal Crusade and assure the adherence of his knights, Duke Robert had mortgaged his Normandy holdings, as well as the income thereof, to his brother the King of England for a hundred thousand crowns, a sum long ago consumed; Robert Curthose was a man with few options when it came to the revenues required to fulfil his vow and in his case plunder had been in short supply.

The news regarding Normandy was followed by an equally surprising defection: Robert of Flanders, who had supported Raymond at both the sieges of Albara and Ma'arrat an-Numan, arrived from Rugia having declined to follow the lead of his brother-in-law and flatly, even insultingly, refused the offer from his erstwhile ally.

'How do you think he feels,' Bohemund enquired, when his nephew questioned the Flanders decision, 'when having given such faithful service and suffered the excess of Raymond's pride for many a month, he is ranked as worth only a thousand *solidi* more than you?'

Tancred's response was mordant. 'I think, in truth, neither of us count for much.'

'Your greater worth lies in your connection to me.'

'Something I am being asked to sunder.'

'Which is of the greater concern to you, nephew,' Bohemund replied, with an enigmatic grin, 'your soul or your bloodline?'

That was said in such a way as to preclude one question, but not another. 'What of Duke Godfrey?'

The reply was emphatic. 'He too will decline.'

'How can you be so sure?'

'To be paid to regain Jerusalem would, in his mind, sully the endeavour, and for Godfrey purity of motive is paramount. Besides, with his brother Baldwin to back him, and through that the revenues of Edessa, he does not want for silver or support.'

'They are not close, Godfrey and Baldwin; indeed, I was of the opinion, more than once, they came close to loathing each other.'

'What heir to a fiefdom loves his lord?'

That, a reference to the fact that Godfrey was childless and his brother next in line to the ducal title of Lower Lorraine, raised another question never addressed and one that would not be raised now: Bohemund, too, lacked an heir and many supposed that Tancred was close enough both in blood and friendship to the Count of Taranto to be next in line to succeed him in Apulia.

'You think Baldwin will support him. If he does I am curious to understand why.'

That got a rousing laugh, loud enough to echo off the battlements of Antioch. 'If you are waiting for me to say to you blood is thicker than water, Tancred, you will wait in vain.'

Raymond's ambitions for Jerusalem did nothing to dent his desire to rein in the ambitions of his rival; he still intended to control the entire supply of food to Antioch from the south by holding an arc of land hinged on Ma'arrat, which abutted Turkish territory, through the Ruj Valley to the coast, with control of the roads to the nearby ports to complete his aim.

There were other ambitions too, based on possession. In Ma'arrat, as he had in Albara, he had installed one of his priests, the one-time archdeacon, Peter of Narbonne, as the bishop of that see. Both would adhere to the Latin rite, albeit they had needed to be consecrated by the only available high divine, the increasingly feeble Armenian Patriarch, John the Oxite, these designed to raise his standing among the pilgrims as well as to curry favour in Rome.

These manoeuvres, and he knew of every step his enemy took, were watched by Bohemund, though it would have been fruitless to seek to observe how much such moves concerned him. All an observer would see was a man going about his business, ensuring the walls of Antioch, where damaged, had been repaired, that his forage parties, albeit obliged to work to the north and east, were bringing in enough to fill more than just the storerooms of the citadel, over which he had total control.

If he had a major concern, it was one he did not spread abroad. When John the Oxite shrugged off his mortal coil, something that seemed increasingly imminent, Bohemund was determined, in the same manner as Raymond, that the person who replaced him should be a Latin bishop. This engendered much correspondence with Rome, a steady stream of letters, his aim to persuade the Pope to accede to his request and to send someone of stature to take the office, not forgetting to add that he, unlike Raymond of Toulouse, did not have the arrogance to assume that he could appoint someone from his own retinue of priests and of his own choosing.

In every communication lay several references to the loyalty to the Holy Church shown by his family, not least Count Roger of Sicily, which conveniently glossed over the several times a reigning

251

pope had been humbled by a de Hauteville over the previous decades. Added to that lay a subtle undercurrent of doubt, in which Bohemund detailed the lack of support the Crusade had received from Alexius Comnenus, not omitting to add that an emperor who had so far taken as much as he could of the spoils of the Crusade without spilling the blood of his own men, would no doubt claim that Jerusalem, like Antioch, should be a fief of Constantinople.

How then, when Byzantium ruled in the birthplace of Christ as well as the mighty city of Antioch, the site of St Peter's first church, could the Bishop of Rome lay claim to be the universal head of the faith? How then, with Byzantium in such a powerful position and entrenched, could His Holiness hope to persuade the Orthodox Church to heal the divisions of the forty-year schism?

When it came to the unity of the faith, a matter of vital concern to Rome and the future of the Christian mission, who was the true enemy, Byzantium or Islam?

'I know a great deal of your grandsire's family, Tancred,' Robert of Normandy said. 'They were much talked about when I was growing to manhood, he most of all.'

'Not with much affection, I suppose.'

That was a remark that made both men smile, though it did not last long with the Duke. The de Hautevilles – if successful, they were at least distant – were typical of his own subjects, men whose loyalty was to their own success and well-being, not that of their liege lord. Norman knights were able to shift allegiances with an alacrity that made the task of ruling Normandy, indeed anywhere the heirs of the Vikings had planted their feet, near impossible, as the *Guiscard* too had found to his cost.

His own father, William, had taken years between his succession at seven years of age and the great Battle of Val-es-Dunes to exert control over his subjects and in that he had required the support of the King of France, his titular suzerain, who did not supply such aid to the nineteen-year-old Duke William without extracting a territorial price, one redeemed when the young man, a decade older and finally secure in his domains, turned on his one-time ally and defeated him in battle.

Robert himself, succeeding to Normandy on the death of William, now called the Conqueror, had been forced to fight his brother, who ruled England, to maintain the title bequeathed to him; in that contest the ability of his subjects to change sides, and to do so at the drop of a gage, made a successful defence near impossible.

The two men talked on – Robert had been kind and indulgent to Tancred ever since they had marched in company with Bohemund from Nicaea – each recalling the feats of their forbears. Robert was able to range with pride all the way back to Rollo, the Viking raider who, to keep him and his ferocious raiders quiet, had been given Normandy as a fief. If Tancred's lineage was, in terms of nobility, a shorter one, their deeds were just as remarkable, so a happy period was passed in talk of Norman success.

'You have accepted the offer made to you by Raymond of Toulouse?' Tancred said, in what seemed an abrupt change of subject and one that fractured the pleasant mood.

'I have,' Robert replied, with a look indicating that any enquiry into motive would be unwelcome.

'Who can doubt your faith?' Tancred responded, neatly sidestepping the issue of Raymond's silver. 'For myself...'

The ploy, leaving any conclusion to his words hanging in the air, was obvious and intended to be. Robert was sharp enough to pick up on what was required.

'You are here to seek my advice?'

'Some would be welcome, My Lord, since I can extract none from my uncle.'

'You have asked?'

A nod accompanied by a gloomy look. 'And been told to follow the dictates of my own conscience. Were it anyone but Toulouse I would not hesitate, like you I am all committed to Jerusalem, but...'

Robert, with his saturnine complexion and dark eyes, gave Tancred a look that seemed to enquire if he was ever going to finish a sentence, yet he declined to be drawn once more and remained silent, forcing the younger man to continue.

'If it were Godfrey de Bouillon seeking my sword arm I would not hesitate, yet if I join with Raymond, Bohemund will surely see it as a betrayal.'

'That is not necessarily the case.'

There was an air of real artificiality in the way

that Tancred brightened then, made more apparent by his eagerness to hear anything encouraging.

'We have just been talking about our ancestors, have we not? Ask yourself, Tancred, what the *Guiscard* would do in the same circumstance, indeed what your uncle would do if matters were reversed? What is here for you in Antioch but continued service under his shadow? What waits for you if you do as I have done, and you follow the dictates of your crusading vow?'

'Bohemund is fond of saying he cannot see into the future. I am no better than he.'

When Robert responded, it was with an emphatic tone and a sharp chop of his hand.

'That was a vow taken by Bohemund too, to march on Jerusalem and bring it back to Christianity, yet you and I know he will not progress one step beyond Antioch, for he sees no advantage to himself in doing so. Think like your uncle and that will give you the answer you seek.'

'I have spoken with the men we lead, both lances and the foot soldiers, as you said before that I could.' That got a gesture from a seated Bohemund, a twitch on the enjoined hands under his chin; it implied such a thing was hardly a secret. 'Fifty of our lances are set on Jerusalem, nearly all the *milites*.'

'They are more pious, the *milites*.'

'And I am determined on Jerusalem myself, but I will go without Raymond's silver if acceptance of that offends you.'

'Take his money, for not to do so would be

foolish,' Bohemund snapped, but it was not said in anger. 'But this I advise, trust Raymond in nothing, stay close to Robert of Normandy and even more to Duke Godfrey when he decides to march.'

'For someone who claims not to be a seer you seem to know a great deal of what de Bouillon will do.'

'What he must do, proceed to Jerusalem, but it will not be under the banner of Toulouse.'

'How fractured this effort has become.'

'The miracle is that there was accord for so long. I doubt if even Adémar, had he lived, could have kept it in harmony.'

'If I am to take Raymond's silver that means I must join him at Rugia.'

'Then do so with my blessing, Tancred.'

'If you are keen to give it now, why has it been so withheld?'

Bohemund stood and approached his nephew, taking his shoulders in his hands, his smile that of an indulgent parent.

'It is not my place to make such decisions for you, regardless of what feelings I have for you – and those you know, so I will not reprise them. The time has been long in coming when you must strike out on your own, and I esteem you for the considerations you demonstrated in not wishing to do so in the service of a man who is my enemy.'

'It is still an uneasy choice to make.'

'Enough that it is done,' Bohemund insisted. 'I know you will fight well when the time comes, as you have done with me and perhaps, when men talk of the fall of Jerusalem, it will be of Tancred they speak, not the Duke of Normandy or the Count of Toulouse.'

'With your permission I will leave on the morrow and I ask for the supplies of food I need to get to Rugia, enough for two days' march.'

The benign expression on Bohemund's face disappeared and his tone matched the look that replaced it. 'You are in Raymond's service now. If you want food, ask his men holding the Bridge Gate to provide it for you.'

With Tancred and his men barely gone, the news that arrived from Ma'arrat shocked even those inured to brutality; as had been observed by Bohemund, the land close to the city had been ravaged by the passing of armies, the good red earth lying fallow till the spring planting. Even with the city in Crusader hands the feeding of the masses that waited there, wondering when the march on Jerusalem would finally take place, imposed a burden on the countryside that could not be met.

Each time a traveller or messenger arrived in Antioch, they spoke of the increasing dearth of supply in the territory of Jabal as-Summaq, a high plateau, in the grip of winter. Supplies sent from other places, to the Apulians by Bohemund, to the rest by Raymond from Rugia, did not even begin to meet the needs of such a mass of mouths, and with nothing in the fields – even the barely edible roots were gone – the people there, pilgrims especially, were bordering on starvation.

The likes of Bishop Peter of Narbonne and his

attendant priests lacked for little, churchmen never did, while the soldiers, following the sack and distribution of the spoils, had coin enough to buy from the traders who ventured into the city and set up a market as soon as matters settled. Likewise those pilgrims who, in the plundering of Ma'arrat, had sought valuables rather than food, yet even they were getting hungry in a situation so perilous it was balanced on an edge.

News came that dearth was rapidly descending into crisis and predictions of an impending catastrophe. The tale arrived at both Antioch and to Raymond at Rugia and told of a riot in which the sparse market had been pillaged by hungry pilgrims, the traders, those who were not killed, being driven off in terror, yet so numerous were the needy that only a few gained enough sustenance to stave off hunger from their depredations.

It was what followed next that caused many to cross themselves, for with even the limited trade cut off by fear, no food was to be had in Ma'arrat at all and the entire polity, it seemed, had begun to resort to eating the human remains of the Turks so recently slaughtered when the city had fallen.

The bodies of the infidels had been dragged out of the streets to be dumped in a nearby swamp. Now, after weeks of both water and weather, their rotting cadavers were being dredged out for the softer parts to be cut up then cooked. If it had been only one or two at first, the last reports told of an entire mass of people engaged in the same heinous crime, which had those still at Antioch –

there were vessels arriving daily bringing yet more pilgrims from Europe – loud in their lamentations.

With a quickly gathered oxen train, Raymond rushed food to the city, there, when he followed in person, to be received with less of the acclaim to which he had become so accustomed. The faithful were loud in their condemnation of the lack of crusading progress, and if Bohemund was equally damned he was not present to have it assail his ears. Holding aloft the Holy Lance no longer brought genuflection, more a furious growl and that turned to open dissent when he stated his intention to march only once the walls of Ma'arrat had been rebuilt.

That such an aim acted as a red rag to the already discontented pilgrims could not be foreseen; to them such an intention spoke of territorial ambition not zeal in the cause of Christ. Led by their angry preachers the lay folk attacked the walls of Ma'arrat intent on tearing them to the ground, for such a place was of no account against their devotion and, if such a task was beyond them, the message was plain to Raymond of Toulouse.

To regain his place in their hearts, it was he who ordered that the said walls be destroyed, the stones being smashed by hammers then thrown down to fill that dry moat, the news of which flew back to Antioch. That was sent by Tancred who had so recently joined Raymond and found his men required to aid the Provençals in Ma'arrat's destruction – the remaining Apulians declined to do so, but were happy, on Tancred's orders, to rejoin Bohemund.

The day came to depart, and so that their endeavour should be reconsecrated, it was decided that the whole host – clerical, military and pilgrim – in order that there should be no doubt as to their devotion to their Christian God, that no hint of pride should sully their enterprise, must march out of the city walking and barefoot. Raymond, shoeless like the meanest servant, was at the front holding aloft the Holy Lance, alongside Peter of Narbonne, his so recently appointed bishop, who with his priests, intoned prayers seeking the blessing of Christ and the intercession of the saints.

At the rear came Tancred and his Apulians, no less loud in their devotions but with torches in their hands, these used to set light to every structure they passed, be it the splendid residences of the one-time city merchants, a tradesman's shop, hovels lived in by the poor, a sty or a stable. The Crusade marched south, vigour renewed, and behind them the city they had just left turned to a smoking inferno which would, very quickly, consume everything that could burn. Ma'arrat an-Numan would be no more.

From the citadel of Antioch, Bohemund observed the Occitan banners of the Count of Toulouse that still flew from the Governor's Palace and the Bridge Gate, a sign that whatever else he was willing to surrender it was not these. Yet he was content: they were few and he was many, while their liege lord was marching further and further away.

Antioch was his to control, though not without

concerns: Toulouse had left Albara strongly garrisoned, which meant he still held the strategic key to the plateau of Jabal as-Summaq and the harvest it would produce in the coming year. Then there was the Emperor, Alexius Comnenus, whose intentions were as yet a mystery.

CHAPTER SEVENTEEN

It was clear that in his slow march to the south, Raymond of Toulouse was looking in two directions at once, that in which he was headed and the difficulties that lay before him, another over his shoulder to the actions of Godfrey de Bouillon and Robert of Flanders, without whose aid he could not hope to succeed in even marching to and investing Jerusalem – he could discount any help from Bohemund.

Tancred was not alone in suspecting he was torn, loath to leave behind the territory he had captured and controlled: what he possessed was unlikely to be respected while he was not there to defend it, hence the unhurried progress. That being so, he also had an excuse, which was the parlous fitness of those he led, especially his fighting men, still not recovered from the lack of victuals that had troubled them at Ma'arrat.

At first they passed through country that had been extensively foraged to sustain that siege, so there was little surplus to fill strained bellies, but there was hope too, for the land that lay ahead and into which he would soon lead his host was extremely fertile and dotted with wealthy cities. It was also, and this was a deep concern, densely populated with Arabs who yielded nothing in the depth of their Islamic faith to the Turk, while the final destination was a place as well defended and formidably walled as Antioch.

News of what the Count of Toulouse had done previously proved his most telling aid: reports of the massacres at Albara and Ma'arrat sped before him, so that the first obstacle to progress, the city of Shaizar straddling the lower Orontes, sent envoys from the Emir to talk peace long before the Crusaders caught sight of their walls. Along with their supplications came gifts for the expedition leaders, a trio of fine horses, caparisoned in gorgeous harness. To Raymond went vessels of gold, for his senior captains elaborate sweetmeats as well as offers of ample food to eat for the entire host as they made their way through the Emir's territory.

The Arab rulers of Shaizar had, it transpired, no love for the Turks and had manoeuvred successfully over decades to stay independent of their control by the payment of a large annual tribute. They had no desire to either fight their battles or to see their city razed to the ground, their lands ravaged and their subjects slain or sold into slavery by fighting an army that had defeated a mighty general like Kerbogha.

The best way to avoid that was to divert the Turkish tribute to this new power in the land and to make their passage as agreeable as possible, as well as speeding on to the lands of the next satrap. Let others do battle for the Prophet; they would be content to pay the price necessary to avoid conflict.

'All My Emir asks, Great Lord, is that none of those you lead are left free to take more than we are prepared to openly give.'

Tancred observed the way Raymond's chest swelled to be so addressed by the Latin-speaking envoy sent from Shaizar, added to the way he looked around the assembly of his captains, his confessors and his fellow peers to ensure it had been noted. That reprised the feelings that had surfaced in his mind over the past week: how different it was to be under the orders of such a man.

That the Count of Toulouse was excessively proud meant little; that he had been aware of for over a year. Yet previously it had been a distant impression, whereas now it was before him as a constant as well as an irritant, and as a way of behaving it did not stand comparison with his uncle, who if he would not surrender an inch in pride to Toulouse, was not a man to allow syco-phancy to affect his judgement or even to show that he was moved by it.

'As a ruler himself, My Emir knows that con-trol of such a host is something only a man of true eminence can achieve. Yet he knows you to be that, has heard of your deeds, Count Ray-mond, which have sped to the four corners of the earth to make mere mortals wonder at them. Mighty Kerbogha fell before your sword, did he not?'

There was a moment when Raymond was

slightly flustered and had a chance to indicate the other men present who had actually fought the Atabeg, though there was no chance he would deny the praise he was receiving for something he was singular in not doing; he could hardly say he had taken to his bed in a fit of pique.

'He's going to flatter Raymond till he bursts,' whispered an irritated Normandy.

Tancred replied by leaning to talk softly into the Duke's ear. 'Is there such an amount?'

Raymond noted the exchange, if not the words they employed, and irritation flashed in his eyes. Toulouse was seated on a chair while they were obliged to stand and observe, this to underline that regardless of rank he was the leader. In his hand, as always, he held the shard of the Holy Lance, to which the eye of the envoy had flicked more than once, for news of that discovery, as well as the power it exerted, had been disseminated throughout the land as quickly as the deeds of the Crusade.

'If all the needs of my people are met, what need have they to disturb the country?'

The envoy used the flat palm of his hand, in a slow and unthreatening gesture, to indicate the Holy Lance. 'Perhaps if they saw what you hold as a divine requirement, Great Lord, they would see the need to obey Allah as well as their leader.'

Peter Bartholomew, stood to Raymond's left, cut in without seeking permission, so much had he grown in arrogance. 'There are many who would demand you and your kind pray to the same God and acknowledge his disciples.'

'There is but one God,' the envoy replied, in a soft, non-threatening voice. 'Allah is his name and Muhammad is his prophet.'

'We are not here to dispute the path to salvation,' Raymond snapped, in French and in a clear rebuke to his personal prophet, one that would not be understood by the Emir's envoy. His eyes then swivelled to Tancred and Robert of Normandy, who were speaking in hushed tones again, and his voice was firm. 'And no good is served by whispered conversations in the offing, either.'

'I had a tutor who addressed me so once,' Normandy replied, also in French, his tone, Tancred thought, deliberately even and non-threatening. 'When I was old enough to do so I boxed his ears.'

If the envoy and his attendants were confused, they were alone in that; everyone else present understood perfectly that Raymond had overstepped the mark of respect due to a man who held a noble rank greater than his own. If they had harboured any doubts about the effect of his being checked that would have been dispelled by the way the florid face of the Count went a deeper shade of red.

'We are engaged upon important matters here,' he protested, 'and I know you would agree that any sign of dissension will not aid our progress. We are being offered free passage through the Emir's lands, are we not, but that is because we are united. If this fellow returns to tell him we are divided, what then?'

'You have the command, My Lord,' Normandy replied, 'but if my father was here he would tell you, mighty warrior that he was, that dissension comes very easily from a lack of respect.'

Raymond clearly thought no response was possible without a loss of face so he turned his attention back to the envoy, who had made strenuous efforts to keep his mask of diplomatic indifference in place throughout an exchange, which if he did not understand in words, was plainly fractious in mood.

'I will let it be known that it would be seen as a sin against God to take from your people anything that is theirs, as long as we are, on our march, not in want.'

With those words spoken, the Holy Lance was raised slightly, which caused the envoy to bow low, while the priests present, led by Narbonne, and joined by the ever-present Peter Bartholomew, crossed themselves.

The Emir of Shaizar was as good as his word: wherever the Crusade set up camp there was food in abundance, fresh-baked bread, roasting meats and fruit, enough for pilgrims and soldiers alike. Disseminated through his priests Raymond had made it known that any depredations against the Emir's subjects would be severely punished, the truth of that driven home by a couple of his own *milities* being burnt at the stake in full view of the men sent by the local ruler as escorts, this for the rape of a Muslim woman.

If the Emir wished to speed his passage he found that Raymond was in no rush to clear his lands, for, with such provisions, daily the effect on the army was visible and remarkable. Men who had struggled along head down when they set out from Ma'arrat now marched with heads lifted, the horses they still had likewise filling out until their rib bones no longer showed with alarming prominence.

How obvious it was when they passed into the territory of another ruler. There was no food awaiting them as they camped, although that mattered less now, for they were reduced in need and also in a terrain as yet untouched by warfare. If there was no food in the fields or fruit on the trees there were peasant storerooms full of the harvest of the previous year and, now that the promise Raymond had made no longer constrained them, those he led could indulge in all the acts that had previously been denied to them.

Never had the reputation of the Crusade been so forcibly established as when they came to the city of Raphania, the next on their line of march, set on a slight elevation overlooking a wide plain full of productive fields and orchards that ran close to the defences, with distant hills to feed the streams that irrigated the soil.

At long sight the high walls, bright cream stone shining bright in the sun, looked formidable enough to promise a siege of some duration. Raymond, Robert of Normandy and Tancred donned their mail and rode forward with their personal retainers, having ordered that camp be set up, anticipating perhaps that emissaries would emerge from the gate towards which they were headed to meet them in the open and discuss the same kind of peace they had just had from the Emir of Shaizar. They even halted well short of that gate to

267

allow such messengers to make their way, but none appeared, so Raymond spun his own horse to talk to his fellow leaders.

'I would hope that they accept terms.'

'Can we bypass them?' asked Normandy. 'A siege could mightily weaken us.'

That sent Raymond's head onto his chest, for it was not a ridiculous suggestion. Besieging both Albara and Ma'arrat had taken time, led to losses in men, and at the latter resulted in an even more telling wound to morale, and if there was food now in peasant holdings, to stay in the area would soon see it stripped as bare as any terrain supporting a winter siege.

Nothing they had heard indicated that the Emir of Raphania was a warlike individual, indeed he was akin to his compatriot in Shaizar, a tribute-paying Turkish satrap whose main desire, it was likely, was to be left in peace. To have such a ruler on the line of communication with Antioch and the other contingents might not pose too much of a threat.

Tancred spoke up, as was his right. 'We would have to leave behind some men to mask the city, which would perhaps weaken us more than fighting. If they are not inclined to a stubborn resistance we may overcome the walls with a quick assault.'

'That is so,' Raymond said, more to himself than to Tancred. 'But my Lord of Normandy is nearer to being right, I think: better we progress on our way, perhaps, than linger here.'

Aware that the younger man did not whole-heartedly agree, Raymond added, 'We will give

268

them terms and then judge from their response. If it is pure defiance, then we must overcome them, for that means they will seek to raid our rear once we pass. If they seek naught but to be left untroubled then...'

There was no finishing that, for it was unnecessary. Raymond spun his mount once more and led the way to a point close enough to the walls where his voice could carry, and there he demanded to speak with someone who would both understand him and pass on his words to the ruler of the city. The call floated upwards, but no head appeared at the battlements to even acknowledge their presence and that was repeated on the second call.

'Go forward,' Raymond said, to a pair of his familia knights, 'and see if your being close tempts them to react.'

Up till now the whole party had been bareheaded; the men ordered to move were quick to don their hauberks and helmets, as well as ensure they had a good grip on the shields they would need to raise quickly should any arrows, the first line of any defence, come their way. They advanced one step at a time, their mounts under stern control, in an eerie silence, waiting for the yell that would bring up the Arabs from behind their walls to rain missiles in their direction.

No bolts came their way, nor when they moved closer did a single lance fly over the walls, even when they were in easy range. It was with due trepidation that they approached the gate, heads stretched back to keep a sharp eye on the high twin towers that enclosed it, and still there was

269

nothing. One knight spun his lance and used the haft to bang upon the wood of the high door, the thuds echoing back to his confused leaders.

When that too got no response he spurred his horse slightly forward until both it and he were up against the gate and pressing. Even if it was heavy and studded with iron bolts, it swung a fraction, which had both knights pushing in a blink. The gate swung open enough to create a gap, which had both men immediately spur their mounts away, for there had to be danger behind that.

'If it is a trap to ensnare us, it is a cunning one,' Normandy said.

'Every one of you forward,' Raymond ordered.

He did not mean the leaders, so the knights led by Normandy and Tancred looked to their own masters for permission to obey, which was quickly forthcoming. It was now a strong party of thirty mailed and helmeted men that went for the gate, there to join the pair already present. With still no reaction, two of Tancred's Apulians dismounted and put their shoulders to the wood and with a creak of unoiled hinges it swung wide open until it hit the interior walls.

'Plague,' Duke Robert hissed, crossing himself.

'Do you see any dead?' Raymond shouted, getting a negative response.

Now the knights had both gates open and before the leaders, once their men had stood aside so they could see, lay a deserted and long cobbled avenue, lined with buildings, of the kind that formed a main route into many a city they had seen on the Crusade. Raymond spurred his own mount, followed in a blink by his confrères, and they rode through their own knights, under the gate barbican, their hooves echoing on the stones of the pavé.

Still with proper caution they advanced into the dark gully formed by the high buildings that enclosed the roadway, past open doorways, fearful that a screaming mob of armed men might at any second appear from the side alleys to assault them, in their breasts still recalling the terror in Normandy's voice when he mentioned that the city might be ravaged by disease.

'Nothing,' Tancred said. 'Not a soul.'

Then he shouted, which coming without warning spooked not only his own horse but also those of Normandy and Toulouse, which got him an angry growl from the latter. All he could do in response to that was laugh, first a chuckle, then louder and louder until the sound echoed through the streets, that fading when they entered an equally deserted square hemmed in by more imposing buildings that spoke of the centre of authority. Raphania was abandoned; fearing massacre, it was now obvious: the population high and low had fled.

'I suggest, Lord Raymond, that we have no need to camp when we have a whole city in which we might contentedly spend the night.'

'Lances first, Tancred, let us see if when they fled they took with them everything of value.'

The pickings proved to be meagre in terms of plunder, the flight of the population having clearly been well organised, but there were storerooms full of food too heavy or bulky to bear away, so it was a comfortable place to rest for a short period while some of that was consumed, with care taken that enough was brought to a central point so as to provide the supplies needed for the onward march.

There was some discontent: without seeking permission, parties of lances set out to search the nearby countryside, the distant hills especially, in a search for the Emir of Raphania and the chests of gold they were sure he had taken with him, even to find the more lowly, the traders who might have about them money or possessions to steal. It proved fruitless: no firelit encampment was visible and the caves they found were as empty as the land around them. It was as if the inhabitants of the city had been spirited away by some divine power.

Still, it was an optimistic host that departed Raphania, that too set alight like Ma'arrat, this to avoid the need to detach a garrison, for Raymond was very aware that his numbers did not permit that he leave a line of fortified towns to his rear. Let those who came after him, if they came after him, make their own way. Even now, with their bellies full and the pilgrims singing as they plodded along, the Count of Toulouse was in no hurry, partly hoping to be reinforced by de Bouillon and Flanders, partly eager for news as to what Bohemund was up to. Information was scant in all respects.

The feeling of well-being and easy passage was shattered when a party of Arabs, possibly from Raphania, raided the rear of the column and inflicted heavy casualties on the pilgrims and camp

272

followers; worse they stole back a goodly quantity of the food the Crusaders had gathered from the storerooms of their city. The people the lances had hoped to find and rob had not been spirited away, and now they were intent on exacting revenge for the torching of their city.

Stung, Raymond took personal control of the rearguard, forming a strong screen of knights to protect the vulnerable. Yet progress, remaining slow – he would not be rushed by mere brigands – allowed those raiding to get ahead of the host so that the next attack came in the centre of the line of march, which obliged Tancred to wheel his Apulians in order to drive them off. This was achieved but not without further losses and the raids continued sporadically until distance intervened.

Since leaving Shaizar and that part of the River Orontes they had ascended and traversed a lengthy plateau. Now they were coming to the end of those uplands, yet Raymond's hopes that his fellow magnates might come to join with him showed no sign of happening. If he did not understand why, others did; de Bouillon and Flanders would not march with him for to do so would be to acknowledge his leadership.

Would they ever do so, or would they abandon the Crusade altogether? There was no way of telling and that uncertainty increased the further the distance he put between himself and Antioch. The thought that he might be alone was troubling but one he would not discuss with those who had taken his silver – indeed, he rarely sought to include them in his thinking regarding any future plan, but that could not be maintained; the time had come when alternatives to how they would progress from this point on needed to be examined and that had to be done in the light that they might, indeed, be alone.

CHAPTER EIGHTEEN

The direct route to Jerusalem through Nablus was tempting, yet even if Raymond had enjoyed the full strength of the Crusade he and his noble supporters would have hesitated to follow it. First it was flanked by the major city of Homs, before it then took them perilously close to the huge and even more dangerous Muslim metropolis of Damascus.

Being only a fraction of the Latin force made such a course doubly hazardous, it being too much to expect that a city with such a numerous population, as well as one able to draw in strength from the surrounding countryside, would be cowed into submission by stories of Crusader bestiality.

It was not necessary to see Damascus to know that, unlike Homs, they lacked the power to invest such a city – there were enough local voices to relate its size as well as to boast of the defences – added to which such a route increased rather than diminished their seeming isolation, for once committed they must proceed all the way to Jerusalem.

No news had come from Antioch since they departed Ma'arrat, so Raymond had no real notion of how he stood in relation to the final goal and the further he marched south the greater that lack of knowledge affected their chances of achieving the ultimate objective.

'The other route is by the coast,' Raymond said. 'Supplies we can purchase, we will be in contact with Europe as well as the sailing fleets of Genoa and Pisa, and we can also get news from Antioch of what progress is being made by our confrères.'

The Count drew a line, with the point of his dagger, on one of the ancient maps by which, in a series, the whole Crusade had progressed from Constantinople. What the Roman surveyors had drawn to ease the passage of the legions had not physically changed in the thousand years since. It was not necessary to add that by taking the latter course he was both eschewing haste as well as avoiding the notion of closing in on Jerusalem by himself.

The air of confidence by which this alternative was advanced did not fool Normandy or Tancred; it was a tacit admission that Raymond was taking a detour because he was obliged to wait upon de Bouillon and Flanders to reinforce their expedition before he could even think of entering Northern Palestine. Mingled with a certain sense that the Count of Toulouse was getting what he deserved for his hubris was another emotion: neither man was here to parade around Syria posturing as Crusaders.

They as much as anyone in the host wished to get to Jerusalem and, either peacefully or by siege, take possession of it for their religion and their vows. If their leader was frustrated by the actions of the men they had left encamped at Antioch so were they, though such thoughts they kept to themselves so as not to feed Raymond's temper.

'There are many obstacles to overcome in a march down that coast,' Normandy insisted, pointing with a finger to such ancient ports as Tripoli and Sidon, which had Raymond drawing in a deep breath of air in preparation to make his case more vehemently, that dissipated when the Duke added, 'But it is the better course by far.'

'And for you?' Raymond asked, looking at Tancred.

Well aware of his relative strength and thus his position in this triple hierarchy, the young man replied tactfully, 'I have no choice but to bow to your superior judgement, Count Raymond, for in truth, I do not know for certain which is best.'

Normandy reached up a hand and slapped him on the back. 'None of us know that – it is a guess, no more.'

There was pleasure to be had for the way Raymond looked affronted at such an opinion of his abilities.

As they passed through the abundant al-Bouqia Valley, still marching at a leisurely pace, events contrived to underline what they might have faced had they chosen the route through Nablus: the Crusaders were subjected to the first coordinated proper military attacks since setting out from Ma'arrat. The inland side of the valley was overlooked by the mountains of Lebanon, in particular a fortress called Hisn al-Akrad, stuck on the end of a pointed and rocky promontory, which gave those who possessed it a view of the whole region for dozens of leagues in each direction. Small and reputedly somewhat dilapidated as a stronghold, Hisn al-Akrad was still reckoned by repute to be impregnable, being unassailable on three sides due to the sheer near-endless drop from the walls on the remaining three, nothing but sheer escarpments impossible to climb.

The garrison held it for the Emir of Homs, a potential Arab enemy and that, added to the feeling of security the location generated, led them to descend from their eyrie to raid the marching and overextended Crusader columns as they crossed the plain. In doing so they inflicted much more damage, in terms of killing as well as the stealing and destruction of food and livestock, than the pinpricks they had suffered after leaving Raphania in a raid that left Raymond incandescent with rage.

'I say we ignore it,' suggested the Duke of Normandy.

His opinion was based on the difficulty of assaulting such a location, one that was now being examined from below by all three contingent leaders. It would involve a long climb through wooded hillsides and over barren open slopes, then an assault on the one assailable wall, which would have to be carried out with whatever they could hastily construct in the way of ladders once they got there.

'Tancred?' asked Raymond.

'The damage they can do is limited and will lessen as we march on.' With Raymond quick to frown, he was equally quick to qualify and add what to him was the paramount consideration. 'The trouble lies in the message it sends to those we must face up ahead.'

It was Normandy who responded, not Raymond. 'You see it as encouraging them to resist?'

'Look at Raphania. Fear has been our friend so far and it is an invaluable asset that has kept the likes of the Emir of Homs within his walls. To let pass what happened here will surely dent Muslim caution.'

'It is your command to give,' Duke Robert concluded, unwilling to make a stand on his own opinion.

Raymond, his fury unabated, did not hesitate. 'Then we will attack on the morrow.'

It was not an assault carried out at the customary time of dawn; it took all of the morning just to climb high enough to even get onto the massif at the end of which the fortress sat. It was fortunate that Raymond now led a force well fed and fully restored to vigour, for to navigate the narrow paths through the lower woods, followed by the traverse of the screed and bush-covered slopes, was exhausting.

Their arrival before the walls was no surprise either, not least because it was necessary to recover breath and organisation on what was close to flat ground. Besides, progress had been easily marked at first light, from the moment the lances set out from their camp. Now when actually facing that one exposed wall the Crusaders were sub-

278

jected to a massive outpouring of jeers and insults to both their manhood and the manner of their birth.

These were ignored and they immediately set about lashing together, to form rough ladders, the lengths of wood cut from the lower trees and brought up with them, this being carried out with such energy that it silenced any catcalls from defenders who now realised this was no mere demonstration. As was the custom, Raymond, through an interpreter, invited them to surrender and march out unmolested, an offer that was refused.

'Convey to them how happy their refusal makes me,' he said to his Arab-Latin speaker, 'for I look forward to their pleas for mercy as they slow-roast over open fires.'

Raymond, determined to personally lead the assault, called his lances up to join him, the men of Tancred and Normandy held back in reserve. With a loud cry the Provençals rushed forward, ladders at hand, those swiftly laid upon the wall despite a hail of arrows and lances, with the knights climbing at pace, their own weapons out to engage.

Raymond was to the fore, his anger carrying him forward, so much so that he nearly became utterly isolated from his personal knights. Such was his prominence – he had made it plain he led the attackers – that the defenders rushed in numbers to the spot at which he was attacking in an effort to kill him and they nearly succeeded, only a furious assault by his own men driving them back.

None of these efforts broke the defence and nor was it expected that they would, the Provençals, Raymond included, soon being withdrawn so that the Apulians and Normans could take their turn to fight. If this occasioned losses to the Crusaders, it inflicted a greater number of casualties on the defenders. These men had never faced the like of these determined and mailed European warriors.

Fading light forced Raymond to call off the assault, but not before he had promised that he would return on the morrow and the day after that, with the added rider that these scabrous dogs had wounded his pride so grievously that nothing would assuage it but their heads on pikes. With torches lit to guide their way, his force of knights made their way back to the camp on the plain below, from where the defenders could watch them enjoy food and rest around their numerous fires.

The lances were marching again at dawn, following the same route and with no diminution in determination. Before they entered the trees they could just see the heads of the defenders as they marked their progress, the view soon cut off by the thick upper branches of the woods. Above the treeline, they scrabbled across that screed once more, then debouched onto the gentle slope before the fortress, with Raymond again lining up his Provençals for the initial assault. He was exhorting them to a supreme effort, until one of his knights pointed out that there seemed to be no one manning the walls and prepared to offer a defence; within a blink they found out the garrison had fled and the place was wide open.

The rest of the day was spent casting down as much of the walls as could be achieved while the light held, not enough to completely destroy Hisn al-Akrad as a position that could act as an outpost, but enough to render it vulnerable to anyone determined to press home an attack. Apart from that there was nothing to celebrate: when they left, the Emir's men had taken with them everything, which the Crusaders surmised did not amount to much.

Two days later, with the host still moving slowly and eating heartily, the leaders were alerted to a body of mounted men approaching from the east in a cloud of dust. With evening approaching and close to water, Raymond called for the host to camp and for his pavilion to be hastily erected, orders also relayed that allowed those riders to approach, they being in numbers insufficient to present any threat.

What they did proffer, once they were allowed into the tent, were the gifts sent by a chastened Emir of Homs who had quickly been appraised of the defeat of his garrison: more fine horses and more gold, as well as a statement of his peaceful intentions.

'How shocked he must be at the loss of Hisn al-Akrad,' Raymond preened, speaking in French to Tancred and Normandy, 'to be so alarmed that he sends all this while we are marching away from his lands.'

'How good it would be,' Duke Robert replied, 'to retrace our steps and show him what Homs would look like after we have finished with him.'

'Translate that,' Raymond ordered his interpreter, 'and make it sound like a threat.'

Spoken in Arabic, those words saw the blood drain from the face of the Emir's messenger. It also produced an immediate flood of pleas to discover what it would take to satisfy the Lord of the Host for the insult made to him by those fools at Hisn al-Akrad, men who had acted against his master's wishes and whose heads, he wished to assure him were, at this very moment, adorning the gates of Homs as a message to his subjects.

'Probably a lie,' Tancred opined, 'and one we cannot verify.'

The interruption made Raymond tetchy, which lent verisimilitude to his next words, harshly delivered in both Latin and translation.

'Then let the Emir stay within his city boundaries, for should I hear that he has left them I will turn back and set the walls of his city about his ears.'

The emissary looked at the other two Latin leaders, as if seeking a more pacific intercession, both with stone-like expressions on their faces, not easy to maintain given they were inwardly amused at Raymond's bluff: Homs would be a hard nut to crack with the forces at their disposal and was now in the wrong direction. That they knew it to be so mattered not; it was only of concern that such a message as had been outlined went back to Homs and was believed.

'And tell him,' Raymond added, his voice loud and overdramatically terrifying now, 'to send out riders to the other cities that they too will face the same fate if they insult us, for our God will smite you through our swords.'

Tancred moved closer and spoke softly, using French, in Raymond's ear. 'Can I suggest, My Lord, that they be camped well away from our lines, for in the morning, when they can see our true strength, they might assess that you have issued an idle threat.'

Silence was a clear indication that the Count did not want to accede to that, he was too full of his own joy at the success of his attack on that supposedly impregnable fortress. Yet the sense of what he was being advised was too great to counter: he had set out from Ma'arrat with barely five thousand lances, and even with a relatively easy passage men had fallen by the wayside, while that recent fight had cost him more.

If this emissary had a sharp eye and any military knowledge he would soon see how small was the actual crusading army and how much of what looked formidable was in fact made up of thousands of useless pilgrims.

'Make it so,' he finally replied, leaving Tancred to pass on a message: his pride would not allow him to do so himself.

So the instructions were issued: their camp was to be set up well beyond the crusading perimeter and they should depart eastward as soon as the first hint of light coloured the morning sky and be not visible to any western eye at full daylight.

Progress to the coast was not only peaceful, it became like a victory parade as the inhabitants of every settlement passed came out to line their route and prostate themselves, with food as gifts and even sometimes a path strewn with leaves of palm. When another embassy arrived, this time ahead of their line of march and from the Emir of Tripoli, it underlined how much alarm was caused by their approach.

Again, the usual gifts of gold and horses were proffered, as well as an offer of amity that would allow the host and the pilgrims to make camp north of the ancient port city. Their soldiers would be allowed to use the markets in constrained numbers, while the men of rank would be treated as the Emir's honoured guests should they choose to reside within.

'I will do so only with an army around me and holding the walls,' Normandy proclaimed, when this was relayed to him. 'I would no more trust an Arab than I would my own blood brother.'

This time the embassy from Tripoli marched onwards with the host, a multitude that saw, a few days later, in the blue water of the Mediterranean, something to be savoured. Soon the shallow waters and wavelets were full of splashing Latins, knights – some mounted – and pilgrims alike, with Raymond of Toulouse on his knees.

Peter Bartholomew was at his side, something he tried to be often, the Holy Lance held up as he prayed for thanks to God. Those who followed Raymond, Bartholomew and the relic were only brought to more moderation by the call to prayer and Mass, a temporary altar having been set up on the beach by Narbonne.

That was soon followed by the construction of a proper camp and one that had about it an air of permanence, so unlike those set up since Ma'-arrat. Expecting a conference, both Normandy and Tancred were confused and a little put out when Raymond retired to his tent and showed no indication of wanting to include them in what his thoughts were for the next act.

From the seafaring traders of Tripoli came confirmation of what Tancred had suspected: his uncle had chased Raymond's Provençal knights out of the Bridge Gate, though he had left them the Governor's Palace, which had no tactical value. Subjected to Provençal rage at this news, all he could do was listen to it in stoical silence; what had Raymond expected?

Of more importance was the fact that instead of marching south, Godfrey de Bouillon and Robert Flanders were more intent on making secure the whole of Northern Syria. The effect of this on Raymond, the utter repudiation of his claims to any kind of leadership, was equally a cause of rage.

Better news arrived with an embassy from the Fatimid ruler of Cairo, the Vizier al-Afdal, which finally had Raymond call upon Tancred and Normandy to join him in facing them. Hearing of the fate of Kerbogha and knowing how such a defeat had thrown their Abbasid rivals into disarray, they had marched on Jerusalem, which was now in their possession.

If this apparently meant a more friendly ruling polity in that city, any enthusiasm was soon damp-ened: the Sultan in Cairo was no more willing to surrender the city to the Christians than their reli-gious adversaries in Baghdad. Yes, pilgrims were welcome in certain numbers – knights too, if unarmed – and would be respected, but no one should approach Jerusalem carrying weapons as that would be seen as an act of war.

Raymond was in no position to issue threats to counter such a sanction, though he did try. He hinted that when he was joined by his noble confrères, who at this very moment were making the move from Antioch to join him, and when the Emperor Alexius, the ally of the Crusaders, brought his full forces to join with the Crusade, the Fatimids might see it as better for themselves to hand over the Holy City, lest risk the fate of Kerbogha.

His words had no effect on these emissaries from Cairo: somehow they knew them to be hollow. There was no concession offered, just a repetition that they held Jerusalem and that the wishes of their ruler should be not only respected but obeyed, a word which had the Count of Toulouse spluttering with indignation when they departed, loudly declaring that from the Holy City to Cairo was a distance Moses had covered and perhaps his footsteps might be followed by the sword and warriors of Rome.

Relations with the Emir of Tripoli were much more fruitful; now with the Crusade on his doorstep he was determined to avoid any kind of confrontation which would see his personal rule and his city destroyed. He offered to pay Raymond a regular tribute in gold to be left in peace and to that was added another success achieved at no cost.

Raymond, ignoring the Apulians and Normans,

had sent a small part of his army under the Count of Turenne north to the next port of Tortosa, which they found strongly held and in no mood to negotiate; the demand to open the gates was refused. This led Turenne to employ the overnight tactic of lighting increasing numbers of fires, as if he was in receipt of constant reinforcements, indeed that the whole host might be outside the walls come dawn.

Even Turenne was surprised by the extent of success his bluff achieved; like the high fortress of Hisn al-Akrad, dawn showed open gates and supplicant emissaries, the entire contingent of armed citizenry having decamped, which allowed Raymond's men to occupy a town with full storerooms and a fine harbour.

Even better, the emir of the next port up the coast, in terror, for his neighbours in flight had descended on him, sent an offer of abject surrender. There was gold, a herd of horses, as well as a willingness to accept a Crusader garrison. Soon the Occitan banner of Raymond of Toulouse was flying above the walls of both.

CHAPTER NINETEEN

News travelled swiftly in both directions by sea and the arrival of Raymond on the coast was known to Bohemund and his fellow nobles within days, soon followed by the successes he had enjoyed in subduing the nearby enclaves, which

287

seemed to them remarkably similar in territorial ambition to that which he had previously sought to achieve at Albara and Ma'arrat, as well as on the Jabal as-Summaq.

This was especially deduced since no word came from the Count of Toulouse himself seeking that they rejoin the march on Jerusalem, not that they would have obliged him, being busy themselves in securing Northern Syria and still, as they had been at the turn of the year, unwilling to accede a claim to leadership yet to be set aside.

Nor did it seem, in Raymond's camp, that there was any urgent intention to do that either, for he had found a way of filling his coffers, always with Toulouse a pressing concern, by squeezing tribute out of the towns north and south of Tripoli to add to that which he was receiving from that city and its emir.

If there was avarice in this there was an absence of greed in the host: what monies came in were placed in a central fund prior to distribution, Normandy and Tancred naturally receiving the shares due to their standing, money going to every lance and foot soldier, with even enough spent to feed the pilgrims.

If such delay in the Crusade frustrated the Duke of Normandy, he was mollified by the amounts of money he received, so great as to promise he could acquire enough over time to pay off his mortgage to his brother, King William, and recover his territories.

It was less so for Tancred, who felt he had sacrificed much in the way of family loyalty to get to

288

Palestine. He chafed at the lack of progress but was aware that his status as the most junior of the lords left him little room to challenge the policy adopted. He too reckoned Raymond to be on a quest for territory, an attempt to set up, not unlike his uncle, a fiefdom for himself that would rival Antioch.

The strands of what happened next were hard to fix. Partly it was the desire of the Emir of Tripoli to divert the Crusaders away from his city; partly that Raymond had no immediate goal in sight and an army at danger of being idle, always dangerous to its long-term capability and morale. The Emir hinted at a great payment to be made if the Count subdued the rival inland city of Arqa, ruled, much to his chagrin, by an assembly of its citizens and a commercial rival to dent Tripoli's income.

This played upon Raymond's greedy territorial instincts, given it was an important trading centre full of fat merchants, a link to the north that might hamper communications and a fortress of some strength which, if held, would allow him increasing dominance of the region; the fall of such a city would also bring in more tribute from those who feared the same fate.

What tipped the balance was not the pleas of the Emir, but the refusal of the citizens of Arqa to not only surrender their city but also to pay heavily for the privilege of having Raymond's garrison lord it over them. Always at risk of allowing his pride to override his judgement, such a refusal, coming on the back of so many others having acquiesced, sent the overly conceited Count into one of those passions from which actions sprung regardless of wisdom.

Arqa would feel his wrath, he insisted, this justified to his confrères by the intimation that to allow such an insult to pass would embolden others, even perhaps Tripoli, to do likewise, thus drying up the stream of gold filling their coffers.

So the horns blew and northward marched the best part of the host – a good number had been left behind to keep Tripoli in check – buoyant in the mass as was their leader in his breast until they came upon Arqa, white-walled and sat atop a slight atoll, every bit as formidable to the eye as it had been reported to the ear.

Fully expecting the sight of his army to bring about that which verbal thunderbolts had failed to achieve, he was even more deeply offended when the leading citizens of Arqa, with utter disdain for his rank and his fame, made him aware of their determination to resist by laughing in his face.

'This is fruitless,' Tancred snapped to Normandy when the result of the parley became known. 'Arqa lies in the opposite direction to that which we should be travelling.'

For once the Duke was not placatory, a habit he had formed since Ma'arrat to meet the passions of his younger confrère, who was often irritated by Raymond's pretensions as well as his actions, while being unable to be too open about it with the man himself.

Normandy normally suffered from this too, but not now, which, to Tancred's mind, showed just how much that stream of gold had affected his thinking. 'Then march on north and tell your Uncle Bohemund and those who support him to join us.'

'Would such a move detach Toulouse from this foolish diversion?'

'Nothing other than that will.'

'Well, if Raymond commands an Apulian attack on those walls I will hesitate to obey. I will not set my lances forward as an offering to his pride and see them bleed for it.'

'What makes you think he will ask?' Normandy snapped. 'This is a fortress on which he will want to stamp his own name.'

It was an expansive Raymond who dined with them that night, his talk full with boasts of the speed with which he would subdue Arqa. Such comments were received with little in the way of challenge, for even if Tancred thought the enterprise imprudent he expected that as a siege it would not be one of long duration; with luck he and his Apulians would have no participation at all.

Easy conquests had clouded the judgement for them all: a look at Arqa should have alerted them to some of its advantages, the first of which came on the primary assault, in which they discovered that the defenders had several huge catapults, mounted on platforms set well behind the parapet, that could bombard them with a spray of large rocks before they ever got close to the walls, deadly missiles that no shield or mail could withstand.

Even if he had had the presence of the English carpenters to build a siege tower – and Raymond did not, for they had returned to Antioch – he would have been unable to employ one. Sitting as it did on an all-round incline, Arqa made such a weapon flawed, for to get it up the slope with such weight was beyond the strength of man, and even if it were not, the likelihood of it toppling backwards was too high to be risked.

Moving away from the area covered by the catapults offered the best chance of a successful assault, albeit that with nothing but ladders it would be difficult. Leading that assault himself Raymond once more came close to death – he lost two of his own familia knights – as rocks rained down on them well short of their goal. The suspicion that the defenders had endless catapults proved to be false; what they had were machines easy to break up and reassemble, as well as sighting positions on all four sides of the city to employ them.

The next option chosen, a bombardment screen, took time to construct, though sporadic attacks were maintained to keep the defenders occupied and tire them out, the concomitant of that being the same effect on the Crusaders and to that was added an unusual level of casualties. Worse still, the men suffering the most were the influential captains who led from the very front by example. To see their leaders struck down and killed by those flying rocks was enough to annul the attempt to even raise a ladder.

When the bombardment screen was ready, hopes rose that sapping could bring down the walls. Cheers greeted the assembly as it moved forward, more when catapulted rocks bounced off its sloped roof, for it had been made extra strong with those in mind. Slowly, for it was heavy, it inched towards those white walls until it was firmly placed against them and the diggers could get to work with their picks and shovels.

The contraption that appeared above the screen excited comment but no fear, a thick wooden frame with what seemed like pulleys attached to the top of it, the curiosity aroused doubled by the way the defenders began to knock away some of their own battlement crenellations to create a gap. Next, there were men lined up on either side and even at a distance the Crusaders could hear the shouts that indicated the calls needed to move a heavy object.

When what those men were lifting appeared it caused gasps, for its purpose was obvious. Eased up to the level of the gap in the wall, it was a massive round rock in a cradle of ropes that was soon being pushed outwards; indeed the whole pulley structure was now leaning towards the attackers at an angle that increased with agonising slowness. Eyes were on Raymond of Toulouse now, wondering what he would do, let his diggers continue or call off both them and the screen; he chose the former.

When the huge rock was finally pitched over, more by its own weight than any pressure from those pushing, it seemed to roll downwards at no pace at all in the minds of those watching. But when it struck the wails were loud, for it smashed through the roof of the screen as if it were mere bark, sending great splinters of wood in all directions, worse still carrying on to crush those sappers, who of necessity were right up against the base carrying out the task.

Few of them survived, for the place from which it had been pitched lay right above their heads, the foremost point of the screen roof. Many of those who had helped to get it into place, the men who had built it, perished too from being felled by their own handiwork, those that did not subjected to a hail of lances then arrows as they fled.

If the news of the Latins being held up outside Arqa was not helpful, the stories of such stunning reversals as the destruction of the bombardment screen began to act upon the minds of those who were feeding their coffers. Tripoli in particular, according to Raymond Pilet, the man Toulouse had left to mask it, was showing signs of unrest, with soldiers being hissed at in the streets when they ventured into the markets to buy food and a couple even suffering an assault.

'Such things would not happen, My Lord,' Pilet insisted, 'without the Emir being aware of it.'

'Then perhaps it is time to remind him what he might have faced if he had not offered us treaty.'

'Perhaps you should command he attend upon you?' Normandy suggested.

'I think, My Lord Duke, that the Emir will pay more attention to a touch of bloodletting, perhaps even some of his own.'

'The threat of that should suffice,' Tancred added, 'for if there is resistance we will find ourselves fighting in two places simultaneously.'

'I will decide the merits of that,' Raymond barked, with a startling lack of courtesy.

'Do not allow our reverses here to cloud your judgement, My Lord.'

Raymond's reaction proved that what Tancred surmised was correct – that he was losing his grip – for he lost his temper completely then. 'Do not presume to cast your opinion on my judgement. Remember who leads here.'

Tancred had to work to keep his response calm. 'If I did not fear to ask questions of Count Bohemund I will not fear to do so of you.'

It was the wrong name to use; if Tancred had harboured any hope of diverting Raymond from his bloodletting it went with the mention of his sworn enemy. In an insult that was all the greater for being silent, he turned his back on Tancred and ordered Pilet to take his men into Tripoli and show these infidels the wrath a Christian God could mete out to them.

'And remember you are not Apulians, act like the men you are, of Provence!'

The reason for the Emir's early offer of peace soon became apparent; he ruled in a place not much threatened for many a long year, this under the umbrella of light Turkish rule, which had existed on the same payments as he was now making towards the Latins. He had few men trained to fight and added to that his gates were open to these devils, who entered in small groups to allay suspicion before setting about their task.

Any armed defenders were quickly despatched, which allowed Pilet and his men to go on a bloody rampage unhindered by any threat to themselves, this watched from his fortified palace overlooking the Mediterranean by the ruler who knew that to step outside his walls would probably result in death. Not that the heavy palace gates he had were enough of a defence even if he stayed inside; for that reason a boat was sitting by the watergate to carry him away if he was threatened.

What saved him from flight was a combination of weariness on the part of the attackers and an emissary prepared to sacrifice his life. He found Pilet and persuaded him to desist in lieu of a gift of a chest of gold coins. Raymond's man knew his master; while accepting the bribe for himself and his men, he also insisted on increased tribute to the Count of Toulouse, a dilemma the Emir resolved by demanding payments from the merchants of the port. Thus the message went out to the other towns that paid a levy, all of whom immediately sent more gifts to ensure their continued safety.

If that solved one problem it did not address the real issue, which was Jerusalem, for Raymond was once more coming under pressure from the pilgrims to act, a desire he could not meet while locked into a siege he could not abandon for the loss of face that would ensue. Nagging most vociferously and using his position as the man who found the Holy Lance, was Peter Bartholomew, who to Raymond's mind was growing more arrogant by the day.

'He has the heart of the rabble, which you used to own.'

Peter of Narbonne had been given the See of Albara in place of destroyed Ma'arrat an-

Numan. Divine he might be but still he got a jaundiced look, though Raymond said nothing in reply, for there was no gainsaying the truth of it. If he could sometimes ignore the views of his equals, he found it hard to do so with the pilgrims, for he craved their good opinion as a bolster against the low esteem in which he was held by his fellow princes; it rankled that he could only get support, and that partial, by the buying of it.

'You know why I cannot leave here.'

Narbonne knew he did not mean Arqa but the region itself, without he had the support of the rest of the Crusaders, and even with that he would be loath to move on. To do so, against the unbroken force of Vizier al-Afdal holding Jerusalem, would be to risk annihilation for his fighters and his pilgrims.

'I have a notion of how to get the support you need.'

There was little need to ask for permission to proceed, the eagerness to hear anything that would break the deadlock was obviously welcome.

'I fear that to detach Bohemund from Antioch is a lost cause.' That got a glare for stating the very obvious, which Narbonne ignored. 'But I see in Duke Godfrey a man of different motives.'

'He is no better than his brother Baldwin.'

It was an indication of the state to which the morale of Toulouse had shrunk that Narbonne felt able to question that statement and in doing so he reprised the opinion all had held of Godfrey de Bouillon, that he was a good man whose only concern was that the Crusade should get to and capture Jerusalem.

'Then tell me, clever Peter, why is he not here?'

To say 'because of your pride and past behaviour' was possible, but unsafe for a man who, bishop or not, owed all he had to the Count. Instead he managed, with a careful shrug, to let the reasons be set aside.

'I think if he felt the whole endeavour to be at risk he would drop his reservations...'

The last word was enough for Raymond to shout to the heavens, and ask his God to give him strength.

'What united us more than any other event, My Lord?' Peter did not wait for a response but hurried on. 'Was it not the prospect of losing everything, our lives as well as our cause?'

Narbonne had to be careful then; he could not allude to the Battle of Antioch without reminding Toulouse of the way he had behaved in taking to his bed, which was far from glorious. 'What if the likes of Duke Godfrey felt that such a threat existed once more?'

'But it does not.'

'Godfrey does not know that. If he fears it to be true, I would suggest that he, and the Count of Flanders, will hurry to aid you lest by the loss of the army you lead they lose the chance of Jerusalem too. No more than you, My Lord, can they contemplate a move on the Holy City with only their own lances. My notion is to relay to them that there is another Turkish host preparing to descend on you and relieve Arqa, that without they come to your aid all their own hopes for

Jerusalem will be dashed.'

Toulouse sighed, evidence that he was far from convinced. 'Trust a man of the church to think with such a devious mind.'

'I think only of what might reignite the Holy Crusade, which surely must be foremost in the mind of a cleric.'

'Who would you send?'

Narbonne allowed himself a sly smile. 'A churchman, who else, My Lord?'

Narbonne found Godfrey de Bouillon and Flanders besieging a town called Jabala, well to the south of Antioch, where they had been joined by a new Crusader prince and a long and seasoned campaigner, Gaston of Béarn, though they had lost the support of Bohemund who had returned to Antioch.

That was a city still with a future undecided, given there was no sign of the Emperor Alexius and his army, just a written demand that it be respected as a Byzantine fief, a message Bohemund could safely ignore; nothing short of a main force would shift him.

Given the news that Narbonne brought, it was far from surprising that these princes were alarmed and to that he added, even if it had not been discussed with the Count of Toulouse, that his master was no longer seeking leadership of the whole Crusade, so great was the threat from eastern Syria.

If they were as proud as Toulouse, Godfrey and Flanders perhaps had more sense. With what they were being told the reasons for delay had been removed; an immediate truce was agreed with their adversary in Jabala and they prepared to march south. Of the entire host Godfrey was the happiest, never having been comfortable with the rupture.

Only when they arrived at Arqa did they discover the threat to be at best a chimera, at worst a downright invention, the latter notion doing nothing for Raymond's standing and one which destroyed for ever his leadership ambitions, this time not among the princes but in the hearts of the whole non-Provençal fighting element of the host.

What did elevate him, even in the eyes of pious Godfrey de Bouillon, was the sheer amount of money pouring into the Crusaders' coffers from all over the land, not to mention horses, mules and endless amphorae of wine. Every one-time satrap of the Turk was keen to be on good terms with the reunited Crusade, the new power in the land.

Only Tancred had a jaundiced view of their motives. 'They wish us gone, and there is no amount of gold, food and horses they will not part with to see our backs.'

CHAPTER TWENTY

The coming together of the crusading princes at Arqa did not put an end to disputes – if anything it intensified them, for Raymond flatly refused to give up on his siege, the purpose of which, when laid against the ultimate aim, made no sense to anyone but him. Godfrey de Bouillon was eager for an immediate departure, Flanders backing his view, but Toulouse would not be shifted and that position was made more intractable when messengers arrived from Constantinople carrying a communication from Alexius Comnenus that made uncomfortable reading.

First he wanted to know by what right the Count of Taranto held on to Antioch when specific undertakings had been made and vows sworn that any possession taken back from the Turks must be handed over to Byzantium? Next he issued what amounted, however diplomatically it was couched, to a demand that the Crusade wait upon him in their present location, prior to his arrival with both an army and a fleet, at which point he would take personal command of the march on Jerusalem.

'Therefore,' Raymond insisted, 'we must do as the Emperor desires and await his arrival.'

'Just as we waited at Antioch?' Tancred enquired.

'This time he will keep his word.'

'By what divine knowledge do you see this?'

Raymond waved the scroll on which this commitment was inscribed. 'We have it here.'

'You have a promise, My Lord, and we all have had near two years to observe the value of an imperial pledge.'

That florid face went a brighter hue, as it always did when Raymond's anger ran ahead of his tact. 'How much you sound like your uncle. Might I remind you, Lord Tancred, that your voice in these councils is a courtesy, not merited by your following. You took my silver, are obligate to my banner and for that I expect your loyalty.'

Normandy was quick to react. 'Am I too obligated?'

'Less so than Tancred, given your rank and your many lances, My Lord, but for the same reasons, yes.'

'Would this have anything to do with the siege of Arqa?' Flanders asked. 'If we wait for Alexius, that can be maintained.'

'The two meld, I will not deny it. The siege can be pressed to a success before Alexius gets to us.'

'He will not come,' Tancred insisted, 'and even if he does, are we to bow the knee to a ruler who has so far failed us?'

Godfrey de Bouillon, hitherto silent, but clearly by his expression less than content, finally spoke up before Raymond could reply. 'Such a delay permits the Fatimids to take a strong grip on Jerusalem. They may make it a city harder than Arqa to capture.'

'Who is to say it is not that already?'

'Count Raymond, you of all people know that when al-Afdal's men took the city from the Turks

302

– and by all the accounts we have he did so with ease – their first task would have been to make it safe from anyone else. It would be reasonable to judge the defences were in poor repair when the Fatimids arrived, which will not be the case the longer we leave them in possession.'

Everyone but Toulouse was in agreement with Godfrey, but as a discussion it went on to be circular, as the two sides covered the same ground time and again with slight variations in their arguments. What was missing, and this was plain to Tancred, was the overarching voice that would draw matters to a conclusion, an authority that had been missing since the death of Bishop Adémar of Puy. Without the consent of all, neither side could safely move so the siege went on, pressed home by Raymond's men over several weeks, with no more success now than previously: Arqa refused to fall.

The time spent in that allowed for messages to pass back to Antioch, not least the imperial displeasure at it being held by not only a Latin, but by Bohemund of Taranto. Along with that was the news of Alexius's intention to join the Crusade in the Lebanon, obviously by sea, and then march on Jerusalem, which at least relieved the anxiety that he would come to Antioch first and soon. Not that such a course, even if it was followed, provided security; with the Holy City captured what would Alexius do next?

The answer was obvious and, coming from the south, Bohemund would have a much reduced chance of blocking his way in order to negotiate terms advantageous to him – there were no natural obstacles, narrow easily defended passes like the Cilician Gates, as there were if he came from the north. Whatever, if he had to fight for the city he would.

At the very least Bohemund had decided he would hold Antioch as a subject of Alexius if he had to and could negotiate such a grant in lieu of a costly Byzantine siege. But his ambition raised higher than that: to be, in person and in fact, Prince of Antioch. Yet to achieve that elevated aim he required two things: a reason to hold it that would be admired and some protection.

Ever since he had first written to Rome, his letters had been aimed at getting papal authority to turn it into a Latin bishopric, that eased when John the Oxite finally expired and he blocked the appointment of an Orthodox successor. To achieve his aim, the appointment of a bishop both sanctioned and sent by Rome, he had to create in the mind of the Pontiff and those who advised him a distrust of the motives of Byzantium. Were they truly committed to the Crusade or was it mere territorial expansion gained by the swords and on the backs of those faithful to Rome. Were they dealing in good faith over the matter of the schism or merely leading the donkey of Rome with a carrot on a stick?

The tone of the replies tended to show that doubts were creeping into the papal policy and its attitude to Byzantium. Additional news of the imperial intentions provided another thrust to the impression Bohemund was seeking to create: that of an utterly untrustworthy supposed ally

who would never acquiesce in any of the inter-faith disputes and, indeed, would grow as a rival to Rome rather than act to create a universal and undivided church.

'It has to be asked, Your Holiness,' he dictated to the monk who acted as his scribe, as well as an advisor, 'why the Emperor, now so keen to march on Jerusalem, was prepared to leave us to our fate at Antioch?'

'My Lord, every letter I write on your behalf talks of that very same failure.'

'It cannot be said often enough,' Bohemund in-sisted, which was understood to mean leave it in. 'Now he says that he will march on the Holy City. First, is such a thing to be believed, or will he as he has in the past hang back to let the blood of Christian Europe be spilt, as at Nicaea, only to appear when the spoils are secured?'

'It might be wise to expand on that, My Lord, and tell Rome again of the way Byzantium has failed to act in the entire march.'

Bohemund nodded. 'But add this: what are the intentions of Alexius when it comes to Jerusalem? Is it to secure the Holy City for Christendom or for Byzantium? Will the lot of Latin pilgrims be any easier if it is controlled by a Greek emperor, and who is to say what will be the nature of the successors of Alexius, for he must die, as must we all?'

'The last communication from Rome told us the Pope is unwell. Such a reference to the death of rulers may be unwelcome.'

'Then find the words to say it better. What we must plant in the mind of the Pope – and if he

305

does die whoever succeeds him – that the enemy of Rome is no longer the Turk. They we have beaten so effectively they are spent and the Curia will know from the communications from Lebanon that the Arabs are likewise cowed. But there is still an adversary and in time it may be a greater one than either.'

The monk smiled. 'And to counter that enemy it is necessary to hold Antioch?'

The reply was emphatic. 'More than that, the rival we must keep in check is Byzantium, and not just in Syria. Alexius must be kept from the Holy City itself, for if it is controlled from Constantinople what hope can Rome have that its voice will carry weight in how it is governed or what access will be granted to pilgrims? Jerusalem in imperial hands will become a bargaining counter that may see the power of our faith move from the Tiber to the Bosphorus.'

'You are saying if Rome believes such a prospect exists it will terrify them?'

The doubt in the monk's voice was unmistakable, which did not anger Bohemund; the man was paid to be awkward and question every act of his master.

'We must aid them to see it as a possibility, that is all, which we will do by repetition of the risks. Even if they only perceive a slight danger it is one the papacy must guard against and that can best be achieved by turning the lands over which the Crusade has marched into bishoprics and lay holdings that owe allegiance to the Latin rite.'

Since the march from Ma'arrat, Peter Bartho-

lomew, who had joined his lord from Albara, had shown increasing signs of self-belief and arrogance, indeed that had been growing ever since he personally dug the Holy Lance from the ground. If there were those who doubted the veracity of that act, indeed had reservations about Bartholomew himself but were not elevated in rank enough to avoid repercussions, they were careful not to state them, so strong was the belief that Antioch had been won by it being present among the multitude.

Bartholomew rarely strayed far from Raymond's side now he had gone from humble preacher to where he saw himself, as the soul of the Provençal enterprise, feeling free to speak when not required to do so, as he had done with the envoys from Homs. Now he was having visions once more – to the cynical, these manifested by the failure to take Arqa, which by rights should have fallen long before and so were designed to aid Raymond of Toulouse.

These revelations, unlike those centred on Antioch, were of a more brutal nature. He claimed to have been revisited by his celestial interlocutors, who had castigated him for allowing the host, especially the armed members, to fall into sin and debauchery. Thus he was instructed to weed out the unworthy so that the Crusade could be purified.

Few of the other preachers, and they were still numerous, had been prepared to openly challenge Bartholomew – Peter the Hermit, who alone might have had the prestige to do so, wearied as well as disillusioned had long ago sailed back to

Europe – and neither had the other princes. But that changed when he proposed his solution, which was alarming.

The soldiers, lances and *milities* should be lined up in five equal ranks, they themselves choosing which file to join without being told why. The vision told Bartholomew that those in the front three ranks would be the men true to the faith and Jesus Christ; those in the two to the rear were such endemic sinners that no hope of salvation could exist for them and in being present they were risking the souls of the whole host, pilgrims included.

'And what are we to do with these sinners?' asked Godfrey de Bouillon, when Peter Bartholomew was called upon to explain his vision to the Council of Princes.

'Kill them!' That produced a shocked silence, into which Peter added, 'Then all that remain, from the highest to the lowest, are to do what has been bidden, which is to scourge themselves to remove the taint of transgression.'

'The high to the low?' asked Normandy, disbelieving.

'No noble is a power enough to stand against the word of God.'

'And you see yourself as passing on the word of God?'

'I do.'

'No army,' Tancred said, with deep irony, 'can stand to lose two-fifths of its strength on a questionable apparition.'

'How dare you call it questionable,' Peter replied, his tone cold. 'I see you, Lord Tancred, in

308

the rear rank, and if your uncle was here he would be alongside you, for if ever there was a sinner it is he.'

'While I see you in a jester's cap and, peasant, if Bohemund was here and you spoke thus your head would be on the carpet and several body lengths from your trunk.'

'Will you allow me to be so traduced, My Lord?'

This demand was directed at Raymond of Toulouse and in a manner that he would have struggled to accept from an equal. From a one-time ragged supplicant here was a man who had elevated himself to near divinity, such a mode of address was, in front of his peers, like a slap to Toulouse, yet such was his reliance on Peter, who was ever loud amongst the pilgrims in his praise that the Count was a man of true faith, he did not dare check him as he should.

'This must be told to the host,' he responded weakly.

'Tell them and the sinners will avoid their just fate.'

'Perhaps,' Normandy interjected, 'we should put your faith, or maybe your visions, to the test.'

'You dare to question the word of those who come to me in the night?'

'I dare to question the sanity of any man who claims to speak for the Almighty.'

'There are many of those,' Robert of Flanders reminded the assembly. 'I wonder how they would take to this vision, indeed take to such a massacre?'

'Let us assemble them and ask them,' Raymond said, in a tone of voice and with an expression on his face of a man looking for a way out of damning his own seer.

When the word was spread, albeit in a controlled way, the reaction of those who saw themselves as at least Bartholomew's equals in the strength of their mission was absolute and negative. No deity, whom they worshipped, one who had allowed his son to die on the Cross so that sinners could be saved, would contemplate such an act. Their refusal to accept what Peter said sent him into a towering rage in which he dammed them to perdition and the fires of hell.

'Let it be an ordeal by fire,' he shouted finally, after every argument in seeking to persuade them of the truth of his vision had been exhausted. 'I speak the words of God through messengers he has sent to me. And I will have in my hand the Holy Lance that won for us the Battle of Antioch. If I am a deceiver, he will burn me, if I am not I will emerge not even singed by the flames.'

That silenced those who were disputing with him, for to talk of such trials was a commonplace; holy men were ever quick to propose such an ordeal, less willing ever to follow it through and take the actual risk. Peter's declaration was of a different order, for having made it and in such an assembly it was not one from which he could, without utterly losing face, withdraw, even when Raymond, fretful of the consequences, sought to dissuade him. Peter fasted for four days, praying to God all the while, the Holy Lance, which he claimed would protect him, taken from Raymond so that it could prove his visions were real and it truly was the point of the weapon that had pierced the side of Christ.

A pile of olive saplings was set up as a long walkway and soaked with pitch so that it would burn fiercely. Now that word of such a happening was abroad all action in the siege was suspended on the day of the ordeal and the slope that ran up to the walls of Arqa was crowded with fighting men and pilgrims; no one wanted to miss this and that incline gave many a good view.

Peter appeared dressed in simple white robes, the Holy Lance in his hand, and indicated that the faggots should be ignited, he, like the whole assembly watching as the flames took hold and were transferred from the slivers of wood to the main timbers, the orange and red flickers quickly rising to well above the height of a man, a pillar of black smoke rising from the top of those into the blue sky.

Bartholomew was now in deep and silent prayer, a state in which he stayed until murmuring indicated that it was time to walk, that if he delayed much longer the inferno would die down and not be enough to maintain his claim. Gathering the crucifix he wore on his chest into his one free hand he stepped forward and walked with slow deliberation into the fire, now with flames so thick he disappeared from view.

The creature that emerged did so with his hair on fire, as were his garments. All over the exposed flesh there were blisters while on his face there was clear sight of the agony caused by such a scorching. The hand that held the Holy Lance had strips of flesh hanging from it, the wooden crucifix in the other hand actually burning as he

311

held it. Forward he staggered, until the pain was too great and he collapsed to a groan from the many who had put faith in his prophecies and still believed in his enchantment.

If a goodly number sought to give Peter succour, to stamp out the singeing of his clothes and hair before lifting him to carry him to one of the tents where the mendicants plied their trade, more were now looking at the Count of Toulouse, while in response he was gazing at the sky. One of the men who had assisted Peter Bartholomew just as he collapsed pushed through to Raymond, the shard of the Holy Lance in his hand, this proffered to a man who had ever valued the holding of it.

Now he was reluctant to take it, for it had proved to be false, proved that it could not offer Peter a carapace of faith that would protect him from his now obvious fate, for without divine intervention, and that now seemed unlikely, he would surely die from such wounds as he had sustained.

But Raymond had little choice; if Peter Bartholomew had placed much of his reputation in that relic, so had the Count of Toulouse. Had he not used it to advance his claim to lead the Crusade, and now it was seen for what it was, nothing but a piece of rusted metal? All around him there was loud wailing, for if the lance had failed the Count there were thousands amongst the host who had resided as much faith in the relic as he.

'What now, My Lord?' asked Narbonne, the Bishop of Albara; he had come, like many, to witness a miracle.

Raymond was very obviously aware that within earshot were his fellow princes, who if they had thoughts, and they would not be flattering ones, were keeping them to themselves.

'We have a siege to pursue,' Toulouse replied, his voice strong, 'so let us be about it.'

Raymond knew as well as any of his peers that his standing was blown. Despite what had happened with Bartholomew, who lingered in deep agony twelve whole days before he expired, he sought to replace the power of the lance with a new relic that would bind the faithful to his side. The late Bishop Adémar had purchased, in Constantinople and from the Emperor, a piece of the True Cross, a sliver of near black wood that, it was claimed, formed part of the crucifix on which Christ had been nailed.

Highly respected as Adémar had been – many would call him a saint – such a shift from one relic to another was seen for what it was, an attempt by Raymond to maintain his authority among the deeply religious and numerous pilgrims. By regaining that, he felt he could continue to impose his thinking on the fighting elements of the Crusade. Try as he might, and word was spread of miracles being wrought by that sliver of wood, it failed to convince anyone; if anything, such perceived desperation weakened him more than the exposure of the Holy Lance as a fraud.

After a talk with Godfrey of Bouillon Tancred was able to meet with the Count of Toulouse and

vent his own frustrations by telling him the unvarnished nature of his opinion of both his past
and present behaviour, not least the folly of
besieging Arqa.

'And I will have you know, My Lord, that from
henceforth I have pledged my banner and those
men I lead to the Duke of Lower Lorraine.'

The response was a sneer. 'So your loyalty can
only be bought with silver?'

'To a man like you, Count Raymond, yes! To
Godfrey de Bouillon, as with my uncle, I give it
freely.'

With any hope of outright leadership entirely gone
and with no sign that the promised expedition of
Alexius was even on its way, which laid Raymond
open to the silent sneers of his confrères for being
doubly gullible, he had no choice but to raise the
siege of Arqa and agree that the Crusade should
finally set off for Jerusalem.

CHAPTER TWENTY-ONE

For an army with a divided command, and the
man leading the strongest element of that
sulking, the Crusade when it did move managed
it with surprising speed. Raymond of Toulouse
had faced a difficult choice of route when marching south and had turned for Tripoli; now the
whole faced a similar dilemma, one direction to
Palestine fraught with risk, the other involving

the subjugation, either by treaty or battle, of strongly held and ancient cities on the way.

The decision, that haste was the more vital requirement – that the longer the Fatimids were left in peace the harder Jerusalem would be to capture – when discussed in the Council of Princes, only saw unanimity because Count Raymond declined to put forward an opinion. That rendered the voice of Godfrey de Bouillon the most potent and in Tancred, who aided him, he had an adherent raised in war by an uncle famed for boldness.

'I have talked with our Maronite Christian brethren,' Godfrey explained, his mode of speech suffused with enthusiasm, 'and we will save much time by marching along the coast. It is narrow in places, it is true, hemmed by mountains and the sea, but it favours us and allows for naval support.'

The Duke of Lower Lorraine looked at Raymond then, altering his tone to speak softly and slowly, as if seeking to mollify his fellow magnate's obvious pique. 'Should the Emperor come, then all he has to do is sail further south to unite with us, which would not be possible if we take the inland route.'

'I too have spoken with the Maronites,' interjected the newcomer, Gaston of Béarn, a slack jawed man with a protruding lower lip and sad eyes in a large head that made him seem more gloomy than he was by nature. 'The coast road is, we are told, so narrow in some places that we can only make our way in single file.'

'Think of how it will confound our enemies.'

'As long as it does not confound us.'

Béarn saw no need to explain the risks of that to the whole assembly: the vulnerability of rounding the rocky promontories that enclosed every bay along the Mediterranean, in places reducing the so-called road to a track for halter-led donkeys, was obvious. Godfrey, albeit there was acknowledgement, barrelled on in his usual way, his confidence based on the notion that the God to whom he was so passionately devoted would bless his endeavours.

'But what enemy would think a man so foolish as to come that way?'

'The Fatimids will know of it before we are passed Sidon,' Béarn insisted.

'Will they?' Godfrey replied. 'The Arabs of the Lebanon and Palestine have no love for the rulers of Baghdad, why would they have any more for the Sultan in Cairo?'

Tancred spoke up, having gestured to Godfrey to seek permission, eager to back up the man to whom he had so recently transferred his allegiance. 'And, if we move with speed, we may well get ahead of any news of our movements.'

That roused Raymond from his seeming torpor. 'What host can move at such a pace?'

'The one we command, My Lord.'

Godfrey took up his argument again as Tancred got a cold glare.

'I have studied the maps, as have you all. Every obstacle we must get round leads to a fertile region, a river-fed plain between one set of hills and the next.'

That truth silently acknowledged, he gestured

towards Tancred.

'My young friend here has made a most telling suggestion, that we cannot march as we would in open country, always looking for the next place to set up a camp. It has been put to me that if we march hard without anything in the way of a halt, bar the need to drink and quickly eat, we can cover the ground so fast that we will confound any news that can get ahead of us.'

'Not camp?' asked Normandy, though more from curiosity than objection.

'That we do every third or fourth day and for the whole of it, to allow our men to recover from their exertions and to eat well before the next stage.'

'As well as scout well ahead,' Tancred added, 'which will give us good intelligence of what we might face.'

'The pilgrims?' Raymond asked, implying that if they had not been forgotten they were being ignored.

'Our rest day will give them time to catch us up.'

'And at what risk will they run coming in our wake?' Flanders said. 'For we face no threat from the interior, and if we did we would know of it well in advance of any danger.'

'I will not deny there is risk,' Godfrey concluded, aware that Raymond remained unconvinced, 'but within the two evils of that or a long march I see this as the lesser way. So now, My Lords, I ask for your vote, for the more time we waste talking the stouter will be the defences of Jerusalem that we will, with God's help, face.'

That was hyperbole and all present knew it: a day or two of rumination would make no difference, but Godfrey, frustrated for so long in his aim of freeing the Holy Places – to which he was committed to do or die in the attempt – gave the impression that even the seconds it took between the posing of the question and receiving the assent of the majority were too long. His eager look forced a response and only Raymond dissented from his proposal.

To talk of risk was one thing, to face it quite another and Tancred, tasked to ride ahead of the host and warn of any danger, knew that should such a thing be manifest, turning round and reversing the march of twelve thousand fighting men, not to mention the equipment and camp followers in their train, would be impossible without the fighting elements getting mixed up with the rest and the whole descending into useless confusion.

That was true where they had a strip of land and beach to traverse; on the really narrow passes, like the first true obstacle south of Tripoli, a rocky promontory known to the Arabs as 'the Face of God', the crags ran right to the shoreline. Such a reverse there could not be achieved without massive loss of life to the men and animals edging along a single-man track with a precipitous drop on their right hand. With a mere glance they could look to the foaming ocean below, or the sharp rocks upon which the waves were breaking and too easily imagine a terrible fate.

To counter that Godfrey's promise of fertile valleys was borne out. Given the time of year, full spring blessed with abundant sunshine, in a land full of good red earth that was favoured by several harvests of a huge variety of crops every year, there was no shortage of food for everyone to eat. What horses they still mustered, as well as the livestock on the hoof, were fattened with ample pasture and if there was caution from the inhabitants regarding such a warlike body in their midst there was no trouble, not least because of the way they quickly moved on.

In the sections of open country, moving in normal marching order, the leaders knew the whole army was at just as much risk, for if they did face danger in their manoeuvres on the narrower strips of territory, they at least knew, thanks to those scouting ahead, there were no enemies waiting for them in numbers. On an open plain in extended formation any military host was vulnerable; experience had told the Crusaders that their enemies could gather and move with speed enough to spring a surprise.

No sign of the Fatimids was observed and that did come as a shock; even resting at Sidon, like all the other coastal cities with an emir happy to pay for peace with gold and horses, there was no indication of any enemy ahead seeking to block their way. Any problems they encountered came from nature, most notably a type of venomous snake, numerous in quantity, that killed a number of men by its bite, they dying in an agony that had a near panic ripple through the ranks. Not many slept in the face of such a threat and those that did had to do so through the sound of others banging swords on shields to frighten the creatures off.

Such good fortune, no sight of an enemy, held as they passed through names that were scarred into their Christian understanding, Old Testament places such as Tyre and Acre, the Roman city of Caesarea, where they rested and celebrated Pentecost. On the entire march so far so few men had been lost it was thought to be a miracle, only one foraging party having set out failing to return; some jested they had found a fertile spot on the nearby Sea of Galilee full of wine and women, more sober minds sure they had fallen to some unknown force of Muslims, which had them warning others to avoid overconfidence.

The last place they would encounter if they carried on down the coast was Jaffa, known from pilgrim tales to be formidable; it was the port which led to the Holy City and surely the route by which Cairo fed men into Palestine and therefore bound to be well garrisoned. In order to avoid being held up by both fortifications and the defenders Godfrey got agreement that they should head inland from Arsuif and make for Ramleh.

This was the last city before their goal and, expecting to have to fight for what was a vital strategic centre protecting Jerusalem, they were both surprised and delighted to find it abandoned, and obviously that had been carried out in a headlong panic, for the inhabitants had taken only what they could carry. Ramleh's storerooms were stacked to the rafters with grain, and resting there they had both time and food enough to reorder their lines prior to the final thrust.

Lying just outside the city was the famous Basilica of St George, said to hold buried in its vaults the saint's bones. Eager to send a message ahead regarding the nature of the Crusade, Godfrey de Bouillon put forward the notion that once the basilica had been rededicated to Christ, Ramleh should become the first Latin bishopric in Palestine. This had all the contingents vying that one of their number should fill the office.

Raymond of Toulouse, being so insistent that one of his divines must have preference, united everyone else to agree to a priestly candidate drawn from the remnants of the French forces once led by Hugh of Vermandois – he being known as Robert of Rouen no doubt swayed Normandy and Flanders – and the man was duly consecrated in the office with word sent to Rome so that they could approve his elevation.

They departed Ramleh with every man-sack bulging and every animal laden with grain, moving on to the town of Qubeiba, a mere three leagues from the walls of the Holy City, buoyed by the feeling that the Fatimid garrison they would face had to be lacking in numbers and purpose, or surely, if they had either, they would have come out to fight rather than hide behind their defences.

In a final council Godfrey sought to reach a consensus as to how Jerusalem should be assaulted, only to stumble on what was, as ever, the intransigence of the Count of Toulouse.

'Would you have me fight under your instruction?' he demanded of Godfrey.

'Not instruction, My Lord, but in cooperation so that we act as an aid to each other, not a hindrance.'

'No one will hinder my sword,' Raymond barked, 'lest they seek martyrdom.'

'This is insufferable,' Normandy responded, in a voice very close to a shout.

'Yet suffer it we must,' added his brother-in-law with a grin as he sought by a hand to calm Normandy.

The way he had expressed it made Tancred look at Flanders hard. He had the sense that the Count was not truly distressed by Raymond's attitude, that reinforced when he whispered urgently in Duke Robert's ear. To that was added silence from the Count of Béarn, which gave another indication of the impression forming in the younger man's mind.

The only person present who was lacking in ambition was Godfrey, whereas the others present were thinking of their own reputation, none wishing to be tied to a plan that might see another achieve a glory after which any man would hanker, namely to be the first to overcome the defences of Jerusalem, the first knight who could claim to have conquered the city.

The fame that would accrue to that would be massive. Throughout Europe, in every parish church and cathedral the faithful were praying for success. It was a sobering reflection that perhaps what they were about to attempt, and in pursuit of that glory, was likely to be a free-for-all in which individual desire would trump common purpose.

A messenger entering the pavilion interrupted that train of thought. 'My Lord Godfrey, outside there is a delegation from Bethlehem, seeking audience.'

The name of that place, the birthplace of the Saviour, had even these high-born men crossing themselves and Godfrey quickly ordered that they should be allowed to enter. The trio who did so, elderly men and venerable, made Tancred think of the three kings who had followed the star to the lowly manger where Mary had borne the Son of God.

The request they conveyed, the hope of shucking off Muslim rule before the attack on Jerusalem, was one that could not be refused, yet it was strange how no one present vied to meet their desire that an armed party should be sent to Bethlehem to chase out a body of Muslim soldiers who garrisoned the barracks and manned the watchtower.

'Tancred,' Godfrey finally spoke so as to fill an embarrassing silence. 'Take a party of your Apulians to Bethlehem and bring it back to the true faith, as these good people so crave. It is not fitting that it should remain in the possession of the infidel any more than the Holy City itself.'

Had anyone else suggested such an act, Tancred would have refused, for if it led to a hard fight he might be kept from the assault on Jerusalem. Godfrey obviously sensed this and added reassurance.

'No one will set foot from here until Bethlehem is secured.' Then he seemed to reconsider his first

323

instruction. 'Take some of my lances too, those captained by Baldwin of le Bourg will serve.'

Night was falling by the time the party set out, not that it mattered much in a sky so filled with stars as to provide clear sight of the ground over which they rode. In order to reach Bethlehem he was required to lead his men in an arc round Jerusalem. As evidence of how numerous was the population of that great conurbation, and how nervous were the defenders, their combined oil lamps and wall torches seemed to add a distant orange glow to the sky above the city.

Bethlehem had no walls, only the small Muslim garrison, set there previously by the Abbasids to milk the pilgrims who came to pray, indeed abase themselves, at the shrine of such a holy site. The Fatimids who had chased their religious rivals away were no less keen on extracting money from visitors, for if the Christian pilgrims of Europe were with the Crusade, there were plenty of co-religionists to feed infidel greed: Copts, Armenians, Maronites, indeed all the fragmented branches of the faith Pope Urban was so keen to unite under the canopy of Rome.

Tancred made no attempt to negotiate that the garrison should peacefully depart. He rode right into the hamlet and, advised by those who had come to plead with the princes, made straight for the barracks in which his enemies resided. The noise of the mounted approach had awakened these men and, well aware that escape was impossible, they elected to fight from behind walls that were no more than half again of the height of a normal man; Tancred was so tall he could practically engage them on the tip of his toes.

Like nearly every infidel the Crusaders had fought in the last two years they were not inclined to easily succumb. Either their faith was equal to that of any Christian or, knowing death awaited them, or a forcible conversion, they were left with little choice but to engage in an uneven contest. By the time the first hint of light touched the eastern sky, the men Tancred led were over those flimsy walls and doing terrible execution, their swords swinging until no one was left to stand in their way.

The crowd that appeared when the fighting stopped, bearing beakers of wine for their champions to drink, were close to ecstatic; how many generations had lived under the Muslim yoke, how many times had they hankered after this deliverance in discreet prayer? Impatience did not permit the fighters to leave, the people of Bethlehem leading them to the Church of the Nativity, there to say a Mass of thanksgiving on the exact spot that saw the birth of Jesus.

Tancred, still covered in Muslim blood, was moved and he was not alone. Most of his men were moist of eye and possibly thinking how they would tell, once they got home, how they had liberated this venerable spot. Added to that they sensed that salvation was sure to be theirs: surely God would see that Bethlehem was as much a source of remission as Jerusalem; surely, when the time came for them to join him, it would be in his celestial paradise.

Mass over, the locals asked for men to protect them, after all there could still be Muslims close by who would come to take revenge for their fallen comrades. Tancred had to agree yet it was not just to assuage their fears: that conference from which he had been sent away left in him an impression of ambition so unbridled that there was no way of knowing how matters would conclude.

Thus, much to the annoyance of Walter of le Bourg, he raised his de Hauteville banner above the Church of the Nativity before detaching some of his Apulian lances to occupy the barracks and provide protection. Whatever happened in the following days, for success would lead to a parcelling out of the domain of Palestine, he would claim Bethlehem and the lands surrounding as his own fief.

On the return to Qubeiba it was obvious that no host was encamped there, indeed when they entered the town it was close to being deserted, with no sign even of Godfrey de Bouillon. Calm interrogation of the few people he found informed him that the men of Provence had moved out in the hours of darkness, with Raymond at their head, seeking to steal a march on his noble rivals.

With the Count of Toulouse being obviously determined to be first outside the walls of Jerusalem, this had quite naturally led to the rest hastily following to seek to thwart him, including the Lotharingians. His initial anger at Godfrey's broken promise had to be set aside; he would have had little option but to do likewise, with his lances champing at the bit lest others take the city by a *coup de main*.

There was no time to rest his tired mounts and

for the same reason: Tancred was just as keen on the potential glory as any count or duke, so the food and drink he and his men took on was hastily consumed, the horses fed with oats given they would be walking not galloping, and off they set in the wake of their confrères, the route easily marked by the passage of a whole army.

They found the host outside the walls of the Holy City, not making camp, indeed many were on their knees in less than silent prayer, soon joined by the remaining Apulians and those of le Bourg's. There was no shame in the tears they shed; how many months had they prayed to see this sight? For most it was three years since the day they first came together under their lords and priests to dedicate themselves to the cause of Crusade.

From that day their journey had been filled with as many doubts as elations, added to which were the numbers, friends and comrades, who had perished on the way and were not here to witness this stirring sight. There, lit by the rising sun, was the Temple Mount on which sat the Dome of the Rock and when he climbed the Mount of Olives, Tancred could look upon the epicentre of his religion, the Church of the Holy Sepulchre. All that was now required was to take it back for his faith.

CHAPTER TWENTY-TWO

The headlong rush to Jerusalem had masked many dangers that quickly became apparent, not least that the Crusade was isolated; they had nothing but enemies behind them as well as to their front. If cities like Acre and Beirut had paid tribute to be left in peace they were Muslim in faith and not well disposed towards Christians. Having bypassed Jaffa, the princes had no hope of the kind of naval support that required a port in which to land reinforcements, so even if Alexius kept his word and sailed to their aid, which was still considered unlikely by everyone but Raymond, he would have to fight to get his host ashore.

Added to that, the army was nothing like the force that had set out from their homelands, indeed it was seriously more diminished now than it had been outside Antioch. To set against that was the fact that those who had finally made it to Jerusalem were amongst the hardiest of their breed; there were no doubters now, everyone had suffered much privation to get here, so within them lay the kind of spirit, as well as a depth of belief, that could overcome obstacles the size of mountains.

The Holy City well fitted that description; it was formidable and its dimensions were no secret, for like Antioch every returning pilgrim described them with awe. Forming a fairly rectangular shape, the massive walls of Jerusalem extended a whole league in length, were the width of three knightly lances and the height of four fair-sized men standing on each other's shoulders.

Accessed by five gates, each one of those had a set of twin towers to protect it and, at the sections deemed most vulnerable, stood two great fortresses able to maintain themselves independently of the city; they had their own storerooms and water supply. The larger bastion was known as the Quadrangular Tower, the other the legendary Tower of David, this constructed of great stone blocks fixed to each other with molten lead to well over half its total height.

Jerusalem was near impervious to assault on two sides due to the valleys of Josaphat and Qidron that protected it. To the north and east the rest of the defence was rendered equally difficult by man-made additions such as a secondary outer wall as well as dry ditches. Given the dimensions of the whole, set against the number who had finally made it to their goal, the notion of surrounding the city and cutting it off from support and resupply was unachievable.

The garrison, under the command of one Iftikhar ad-Daulah, was strong and had recently been reinforced by a large body of elite cavalry. If ad-Daulah had foolishly failed to impede the Crusade reaching Jerusalem he had shown some sense in poisoning or collapsing the outside water wells before they arrived. Added to that, suspecting the Christian inhabitants would aid their allies in faith, he had chased them out of the city to prevent them rising in rebellion.

Food was not a problem for the besiegers: they still had possession of the granaries of Ramleh, but the lack of water was crippling in the full throbbing heat of a Palestine summer, where the very ground shimmered. The only uncontaminated source, a small spring-fed puddle called the Pool of Siloam, at the foot of Mount Zion, was within bow shot of the southern wall and the Fatimid archers gathered there in numbers for sport.

Each time it was drained the Pool of Siloam took three long days to refill and that was diminished, as it occurred, by thirsty animals, though not enough to prevent it becoming near full eventually, at which point it was rushed by every man made brave enough by desperation to risk death.

A hail of arrows greeted them, yet it was a harsh choice: expire from want of water or from a piercing bolt that might strike some vital spot. With so many seeking relief, that which was consumable soon became churned with mud, making it less than quenching, it being already rendered vile by the rotting carcasses of dead beasts. Each time the lack of remaining fluid persuaded the men to retreat they left behind them the bodies of their comrades, some of whom had been so trampled as to drown in what was now no more than deep sludge.

The two main divisions of the host, the leaders barely on speaking terms, moved to take up separate positions. Godfrey de Bouillon, supported by Tancred and Flanders, lined up to the north-west of the city between the Quadrangular Tower and the St Stephen's Gate. Raymond having arrived first, and supported by the Duke of Normandy, had originally set up his camp opposite the Tower of David, but that being an obstacle too difficult to easily overcome he had moved south to a more exposed position opposite the Zion Gate.

If the split was brought about by continued dispute it nevertheless had the advantage of forcing ad-Daulah to do the same. This divided the defence for it was moot how much the Fatimid governor knew about the mood in the Crusaders' lines. Since Arqa, both because of the failed siege but more from the exposure of the Holy Lance, the position of Raymond of Toulouse had steadily diminished. He was no longer considered a spiritual leader as well as a military one, not that anyone meeting him would have realised this to be the case – his arrogance was fully intact.

Hopes in that area had shifted to the much more pious Godfrey de Bouillon, and men, even many Provençals who owed allegiance to Raymond, looked to him to lead them to their ultimate goal for the obvious sincerity of his faith as well as his undoubted ability as a fighter and leader. Seeing the need for a symbol, one of de Bouillon's confessors had had made a cross of solid gold, this fashioned from the tribute the marching host had gathered on the way, to be displayed outside Godfrey's pavilion.

If it was not of the one-time stature of the Holy Lance – not being a relic – it was nevertheless an object to which men could attach some meaning and the effect was soon demonstrated when, perhaps under pressure from his troubled knights, the Duke of Normandy detached himself from Raymond and moved his men to the north of the city to take up position alongside Godfrey de Bouillon.

'Bohemund predicted Godfrey would end up as the leader of the Crusade,' Tancred said, as the Norman lances rode up to form their new lines.

'When?' asked Flanders, watching with him, the implication that it was easy to see that as true, quite forgetting that the man mentioned by his nephew was many leagues to the north and could have no notion of the fall from grace of Toulouse.

'After the fall of Nicaea.'

The doubt on the Count's face was very noticeable, for he made no attempt to hide it, which brought a smile of superior knowledge from Tancred. 'I asked him about the leadership of the Crusade, which I thought should have been gifted to him from the outset.'

'You would, being of his blood.'

'No, it was that I have seen him fight many battles, much more than any of his peers and he has a gift for leading men to feats to which they would not normally aspire. I think you too saw the sense of that at Antioch.'

'He never so much as hinted or put himself forward.'

'Bohemund was certain he would never be acknowledged as leader, just as he was sure that if we ever got to Jerusalem the man the Crusade would choose to rule the Holy City would be

Godfrey, as being the only one deserving of the title, though he was equally certain Raymond would seek to be gifted it by acclaim.'

'There might have been a rival other than Toulouse.' Flanders spluttered as he said that, not, Tancred thought, because he believed it to be so, but merely to underline that he too might have laid claim to the prize. 'Even you must acknowledge, Tancred, that your uncle forsook the Crusade.'

'I cannot deny it, but let those who wonder at his claim to Antioch, and the zeal with which he pursued it, think on what he saw well before any of us: that if he wished to profit from our endeavours and his ability it was not going to be where we now stand.'

'Think what troubles we would have if he was here,' Flanders replied.

This induced a hoot of laughter from his companion; if relationships were troubled now, the addition of a pugnacious Bohemund, sure of the rightness of his view, would have plunged them to new depths.

'Our God moves in strange ways, his wonders to perform.'

The response was caustic. 'And do we not need those wonders now?'

Even if they had been united, neither time nor the tactical means to overcome the walls were on their side. Yet after only six days the first assault was launched, a bid to take the city by sheer force of their passion. A lack of growing timber around Jerusalem obviated the ability to make ladders and the only one existing, a rickety frame, had been made by Tancred's men, that from a stack of well-hidden wood found only by the pressing need to evacuate a set of loose noble bowels in private.

The mass of the host sought to drive back the defenders from the walls with lances and arrows, fired from ground level at men well above their heads, which was soon seen as ineffectual. The Apulians had at least a chance to fight on more equal terms, albeit if being perched on a strand of wood, your shield used as much as a hook to keep you from falling as it was for defence, with either sword or axe being swung from a position which diminished the weight behind it, could be called anything like parity. Yet that was enough to get them over the secondary wall and then, with the ladder shifted, onto the main defences.

It got harder from there: one giant fellow on the battlements was wielding a two-handed executioner's blade, so heavy and weighty it sliced through the mail and took off the arm of one of the Apulian knights in a single blow. Then he was threatening to repeat the act until Tancred, at the next victim's side, thrust his sword up into the ribs beneath the executioner's upraised arm, twisting it to catch the bones and drag the fellow forward so that both he and his weapon fell to the ground below.

Despite that small victory the attack was close to fiasco on all fronts and the Crusaders were forced to withdraw; Jerusalem was not going to fall with ease and no one with an ounce of vision could doubt the difficulties ahead. Godfrey, with some subtlety, let it be known that his pride would not stand in the way of a conference and Raymond, really with no choice once that had been covered to him, sent a message to imply that he was willing to arrange one, only insisting it took place in his pavilion.

'Make him come to you,' Tancred insisted.

That got a sigh. 'To what purpose?'

Flanders and Normandy spoke in unison, suggesting it would dent his conceit.

That brought forth a smile from burly de Bouillon. 'No weapon is that potent, my friends. We must speak to each other or our endeavour has no hope of progress and never let it be said that I was the cause of the failure by my intransigence. I will, however, hold no grudge against anyone who declines to join me.'

'Of course we will support you,' Tancred said.

'Has anyone ever told you what a cunning old fox you are?' Flanders asked, for it had been a loaded offer.

That got a bellow at the jibe, which was, to be fair, delivered with a grin. 'With such rascals around me do I not need to be?'

'These walls will not be overcome without siege towers, Duke Godfrey,' Toulouse said, adding, in a tone he might have used with a dunce, 'I take leave to suggest even you will agree.'

The reply came with suppressed irritation. 'Count Raymond, my agreement does not make it practicable. We lack timber and we lack also the tools to build a device that will not fall to pieces the moment we seek to move it.'

Flanders cut in, his voice as bitter as his expression. 'And we will die of thirst in the time it takes to construct one.'

A party of his men had, the previous day, been ambushed while seeking to fetch in water from wells further afield, cut down by one of the now numerous Muslim bands that roamed the countryside, able to cut off small groups of Crusaders. Not that he had suffered alone; every lord present had lost men to such snares.

That many succeeded in bringing in water, often fighting off attacks, was a positive, even if that commodity, carried in animal skins that had been given no time to cure, tasted foul when consumed. Another hazard existed to match the arrows fired at the Pool of Siloam; the skins sometimes came with leeches inside, which if ingested by men drinking greedily led to a painful death.

Talk was unlikely to bring about a solution, but that did not debar the employment of it, with Raymond coming close to suggesting they were wasting their time, which annoyed de Bouillon.

'I am sure not one of us here has any notion other than to press home our attack?' asked Godfrey, in a confrontational tone and a sweeping glare. 'If so, I state now I will remain on my own and find a way to overcome these walls.'

Tancred replied, he hoped for all bar Toulouse. Godfrey, and it was well known, had a soft spot for the younger man, for both his nature and the fact that he had been party to the saving of his life when he had been attacked by that bear.

'No one suggests such a thing, My Lord.'

'What no one is suggesting,' Raymond barked, 'is a solution to our dilemma. Without we have the means to meet those Fatimids on equal terms we are pissing into the wind.'

If there had been bells in the siege lines they would have rung out to the news that a Genoese flotilla, laden with supplies, not least amphorae of wine, had anchored at Jaffa, this being brought to them in person by one of the ships' captains. Added to his welcome, the princes were brought to the realisation that what they had been told about the port by their informers had been lies bordering on wild exaggeration: it was not a formidable city at all, for the sailors had found only a weakly manned and dilapidated tower from which the tiny garrison had fled before they could set foot ashore.

An expedition was despatched immediately to escort the cargo to Jerusalem, or to put it more truthfully, several separate expeditions, since it seemed that noble mistrust extended to any faith that a princely confrère could be relied upon to undertake such a task properly. In the end, if their God had smiled upon them by the arrival of that fleet, he had also done so by the fact that the forces that went to Jaffa, when confronted, were, once combined, strong enough to fight off the enemy they faced.

Godfrey's men were to the fore, a dozen knights and fifty men under a captain called Geldemar Carpinel, this party shocked to find themselves barred from any progress by a force of Muslims

larger than they thought possible to assemble; the whole plain before them was covered in the enemy, a good proportion of them cavalry. Carpinel had no notion to back off from a fight, however outnumbered he might be, and immediately engaged – he assumed his enemies to be a scratch force – only to find that they were disciplined warriors that soon had him in some difficulty.

It was Raymond Pilet, leading sixty of Toulouse's knights on what remained of the Provençal mounts, who came to his rescue. Instituting a charge, the mailed lances sliced into the Muslim lines and, with their weight and brio, scattered them like chaff. Soon the field was strewn with enemy bodies, the horizon dotted with those fleeing from the fight.

If there was enmity between the contingent leaders, that did not always extend to their followers and success in battle easily cemented over any resentment, so it was a jolly band combined that entered Jaffa to see the cheering sight of half a dozen Genoese vessels riding high at anchor, even more heartening to see the quayside and jetty lined with their discharged cargo, an order going out to immediately gather to that place all the carts and donkeys in Jaffa.

It was agreed, by all, that such a success as their recent battle demanded a proper feast and one washed down with a goodly quantity of wine. One of the Genoese sailors owned a set of pipes so they had music too and, with abandon and under torchlight, they took to singing and dancing, until, one by one, overcome by excessive con-

sumption, they fell into a deep slumber.

The first to open an eye – daylight had touched his eyelids – having scratched himself and yawned, not forgetting to run a hand over a throbbing head, peered out into the haze-filled harbour and that induced a cry of alarm, albeit croaked, that wakened the rest. Seeing what had so alarmed him had all of the men scrabbling to their feet for in the offing, outside the bay, was a fleet of Fatimid warships, seeking to beat their way into the harbour against an offshore wind.

'Can you get your vessels clear?' demanded a hung-over Raymond Pilet.

'Never,' replied the senior Genoese captain, 'lest you get your fighting men aboard and drive them infidels off.'

It was Godfrey's man Geldemar who responded to that idea. 'We don't have any notion of their numbers and they are likely to be well manned being vessels of war, friend. That is not a set of odds I would seek to challenge.'

'None of the men I lead are accustomed to fighting at sea,' Pilet added.

'Then what do we do?'

'Get back to Jerusalem and take along with us that which you have brought us.'

'And what of me and my crews?'

'Seems you must become Crusaders, friend.'

'Damnation!'

'That you will surely achieve if you seek to fight alone, that or a Muslim oubliette.'

That brought on a face of near despair, until Pilet added, 'You might get remission for your many sins if you come with us.'

Still peering out to sea and nodding, for really there was no choice, the Genoese captain called to his men to man the boats.

'You are going to seek to get past them?' asked Geldemar, confused.

That got an emphatic shake of the head. 'Never manage it, and even if we were lucky, them ships can outsail us all day. But judging by the time they are taking to tack and wear it will be an age before they get alongside, time enough to fetch our chattels.'

'It would serve you to bring along any tools you have,' Pilet suggested.

'Whatever for?'

'Because you are skilled in using them, friend, as are some of our own fellows, and we are in need.'

The soldiers set to loading every conveyance they had gathered, from dog carts added to one or two drawn by oxen and even sacks tied to single donkeys, a job completed by the time the sailors had recovered their possessions, clothing, personal chests as well as their tools, setting light to their ships before they abandoned them. The whole combined number had cleared the port and city long before the Fatimid fleet thought of launching boats to chase them.

The arrival of the sailors allowed for the calling of another Council of Princes, first to rejoice in the cargo that had been fetched from Jaffa, but more to decide how to employ a much more precious asset, the woodworking skills of the men of the sea, who knew how to cut and shape timber and had brought with them the means to do so. With their help they could begin to contemplate the building of the necessary siege towers.

'Now all we need,' Godfrey exclaimed, 'is the material to do so.'

CHAPTER TWENTY-THREE

It was easy to see the attraction of the County of Edessa as a possession: sat on a huge and fruitful plain between two of the great rivers of Asia Minor, and thus with well-watered soil perfect for the growing of crops, anyone who controlled it would have revenues sufficient to allow for regal magnificence. Passing fields full of toiling folk working that soil, Bohemund was aware that the sight of his forces caused a ripple of alarm to interrupt their labours; armed men, especially those with the crusading cross emblazoned on their surcoats and their reputation as bloody invaders, would always do that.

The road ahead was long and straight, evidence that the force of knights he was leading were still in country that had at one time been Roman. Thus it was possible to see far into the distance and observe the dot that was a rider closing with him and his conroys. The fellow did so with no haste; there was no danger in what Robert of Salerno later imparted to his liege lord.

'It seems we are to be met before we even see the city.'

'Baldwin himself?'

'By his standard yes, and with an escort of several hundred knights, most certainly.'

Bohemund looked around him, at fields of good pasture on either side of the road. 'How long before they get to where we are?'

'I did not ride hard when I spotted them and neither did they seek to close with me. A glass of sand perhaps, certainly half that.'

'Give the order to make camp, Robert, and with haste erect my pavilion. I would want to meet Baldwin out of the heat of the sun.'

The large tent was quickly set up and furnished by the minimum amount of furniture that the master of the household had fetched along in a cart. All was in place before the thud of hooves began to reverberate through the ground, the sound of an approaching host. Bohemund was bareheaded, unarmed and outside his tent, with his familia knights close by and tense, as the one-time Baldwin of Boulogne, who now called himself Count of Edessa, rode close enough to remove his helmet and speak without the need to shout.

'I am bound to ask what brings you and your men into my territory?'

'Since the Battle of Antioch, Baldwin, I have felt free to go where I please.'

The lack of a title was deliberate and it hit home judging by the reaction on Baldwin's face. He might style himself Count of Edessa, his brother and other magnates may oblige him in that; the acknowledged Count of Taranto was not one of them. His given name would suffice.

'How do I address you, as Prince of Antioch?' Baldwin sneered. 'I have heard you lust for the title.'

'My Apulian entitlement will do, given it is not in question by anyone.'

'You are on my land, without my invitation, which displeases me.'

'I did not come to offer you comfort, Baldwin, but to remind you of a duty you owe to the Crusade.'

That got a scoff. 'A rich reminder coming from you.'

'Ah! Baldwin,' Bohemund sighed, 'I had quite forgotten your gift for making enemies.'

That had the other man looking over his shoulder, then, quite dramatically casting an eye to the encampment behind Bohemund, the point obvious: he had arrived at the unarranged meeting with more men.

'At a quick glance I would say that is something you should fear more than me.'

'There may be in the future a time when I may call you to account for past deeds, but this is not one of them. If you have not already heard the reports, your brother Godfrey and his confrères have reached Jerusalem.'

For a man said to be impious, Baldwin was quick to cross himself. 'When?'

'It matters not, they are there and my information is that the Holy City is under siege. But what is troubling is this, they are far away from any succour should that siege take time, though they may be reinforced by sea.'

'The Emperor?' Baldwin exclaimed. 'I would

have thought you would trouble him more.'

'Let us put Alexius aside, and as well we must put aside any opinions we have of each other, as well as any matters that need to be examined. I invite you to dismount, enter my pavilion and talk of what we must do to aid them, not least your own elder brother.'

'I will only do so armed.'

'So be it,' Bohemund replied, with a full smile and his huge hands held out, which made Baldwin flush; this giant was telling him that he had weapons enough to deal with an assault from a man he thought a short-arse.

Any meeting between the Count of Taranto and Baldwin of Edessa was bound to be fraught. No satisfying explanation had ever been given to Bohemund for the way a hundred and fifty of his Apulian knights had been massacred by the Turks outside Tarsus, this following on from Baldwin – with a bit of low cunning that seemed, along with his brutal manner, to be his defining characteristic – having cheated Tancred out of possession of the famous city.

This was the first time they had clapped eyes on each other since the Crusade split up after the victory at Dorylaeum, but that type of behaviour had manifested itself in Baldwin from the very first days since the Crusade had crossed the Bosphorus. He was rude and openly disputatious with his own brother, to whom he owed both filial and bounden service, and was heartily disliked for his brusque manner by all Godfrey's equals, constantly implying that he had a better brain and superior military ability to any of an assembly of men very experienced in war.

Unknown to his brother Godfrey, and certainly a mystery of which the majority of the princes were ignorant, Baldwin secretly supplied the Emperor with information that should have been kept within the confines of the Latin forces, with greed at the root of his duplicity, for while the childless Godfrey de Bouillon was both a duke and well-endowed with land, Baldwin, his heir, was strapped in both; anything he did own he had pledged to fund his Crusade.

If Edessa had not been his initial aim when he parted from the Crusade, Bohemund had no doubt that he had something of the kind in his mind when he and Tancred were detached from the main body. Both, with a hundred knights each, were tasked to scout the fast route to Antioch through the Cilician Gates and the Belen Pass, two tight bottlenecks that were thought too dangerous for the host to pass through safely. That either could and should claim as a fief any place of value they could capture, subject to approval from and in line with vows made in Constantinople, was taken as only their right.

Secretly – even his brother did not know until he found them gone – Baldwin had added another one hundred and fifty Lotharingian lances to his contingent, meeting them at a secret rendezvous, which ensured that he would outnumber Tancred should they ever be in dispute about who owned a capture. When this became known Bohemund, having no trust whatsoever in Godfrey's brother, sent the same number to reinforce his nephew.

Tancred got to the first major prize, the ancient city of Tarsus, without Baldwin being anywhere in sight. He had first fought a skirmish with the Turks and, having won that, he set about negotiating the surrender of the city by bluff, intimating the whole crusading host was close behind him. That engendered an agreement that would see the garrison march out unmolested the following morning, though without anything of value bar their weapons. In addition there was an agreement that Tancred's de Hauteville banner should be immediately hoisted above the battlements.

When Baldwin arrived, having been delayed by his need to combine his forces, the first thing he noted was that red flag with the chequered bar of white and blue streaming out above the city. With stunning audacity – he had taken no part in anything to do with the forthcoming surrender – he immediately claimed half the spoils as his due, a demand Tancred was quick to deny.

That he had underestimated his adversary was later seen as being to Tancred's credit, he being upright where Baldwin was sly and dishonest. That was not the way the young Lord of Lecce saw things, for he felt like a fool when he awoke the following morning to find his banner gone and Baldwin's in its place. Worse, the man himself, as well as his two hundred and fifty lances, were inside a set of walls now too potent and well manned to consider attacking; numbers alone were telling, but in addition to that he would be fighting not Turks, but knights of his own calibre.

Baldwin informed Tancred he was now negotiating his own terms with the Turkish governor
and these did not include any reward for the
Apulians, which led to the first instance of Latins,
in strict contravention of their vows, taking up
arms against each other on Crusade. It was not,
however, driven to a fatal conclusion, being no
more than a brawl, albeit with weapons, resulting
in slight wounds and a few taken prisoners on
each side.

Nothing more could be achieved by Tancred
than an exchange of the latter, his Apulians for
Baldwin's Lotharingians, with the man himself
refusing him even entry to Tarsus. Baldwin insultingly threw down his banner from the walls
and told him to be on his way. It was a bitter pill
to swallow but one that left Tancred with no
choice.

He was obliged to lead his disgruntled lances on
to the south-east, for there was still the mission to
consider. It was only later, when he had, with
Armenian aid, taken the town of Mamistra as his
own, that he found out what had happened at
Tarsus to those reinforcements sent by his uncle,
of which up to that point he had been entirely
unaware.

They had arrived at Tarsus within half a day of
his own departure, tired from hard riding and in
need of both rest and food, neither of which were
forthcoming from an obdurate Baldwin. He even
denied them the dubious comfort of accommodation within the city, obliging them to make
camp outside by the nearby riverbank. What
occurred next was clear in only one respect: the

Turks, still armed since negotiations were un-concluded, sneaked out of the city in darkness and slaughtered the Apulian knights, not one of whom survived, despite a desperate fight.

Had Baldwin, in league with the Turks, engin-eered the massacre? Even some of his own lances had initially thought so, aroused by the cries of the last Apulians to die. The Lotharingians then set about securing their own safety by mass blood-shed within the city, yet such was the depth of suspicion that Baldwin was obliged to lock himself in a tower until his pleas of innocence could calm his accusers enough for him to resume command of his forces.

That achieved and his banner claiming Tarsus as his own fief, with all his lances sharing in the ravages he had inflicted on the survivors, Baldwin abandoned the Crusade completely, riding due east in search of conquests by which he could enrich himself, ending up at the massively affluent and important trading centre of Edessa, which he also not only took for his own, but one he then turned into a bastion of Frankish power that controlled the whole region.

Baldwin was never again seen anywhere near the Council of Princes, where he had once acted as a tendentious supporter to Godfrey, and because of that absence he had never been challenged by men who were either his superiors in noble rank, or even his peers, to provide an explanation of what had occurred at Tarsus, and the man who wanted to know most was with him now.

Much as Bohemund wanted to challenge him, indeed push him to the point of trial by combat,

such desires had to be set aside in the name of
the greater good.

'You sitting in Edessa and my doing likewise in
Antioch will not do anything to aid the safety of
the Crusade.'

'Is their security any real concern of yours?'
Baldwin demanded. 'You have your principality,
what more do you need?'

'I think my conscience demands that I do
more, as should your own.'

'I have no qualms to trouble my conscience.'

Was the swine challenging him to refer to Tarsus?
Bohemund did not know. What he was aware of
was the pressing need to do something to ensure
that the siege of Jerusalem could proceed without
any threat of relief from the east and he took
refuge from his suppressed anger in an explanation of the strategic problems that to a warrior
like Baldwin, and despite his manifest shortcom-
ings he was a good one, that were probably
unnecessary.

'If the Fatimids attack from the west there is
nothing you or I can do to relieve them.'

'But a force of Turks—'

'Yes, but would such a host move if they felt
threatened on the flank?'

'The Turks are cowed, and much as it pains me
to admit it, you are the one who achieved that.'

'They have been beaten before yet still raised
new armies.'

'Do you have any proof they are doing that
now?'

'No, but I see the need to let them know that

such a thing would be unwise. In order that such a thing should happen and be taken as serious, it requires that both you and I make moves to threaten the possessions they still value.'

Baldwin dropped his head to his barrel chest. 'They would fear for Baghdad.'

'Only against you and I combined.'

That produced a laugh. 'What is this – the mighty Bohemund seeking aid from the cursed Baldwin of Edessa?'

'Who would not be so cursed,' Bohemund said softly, 'if he was seen at home, and especially in the duchy you hope one day to inherit, to have abandoned his vows? Yet what if that same man had done something to make the capture of Jerusalem possible and quite possibly be reputed to have saved the endeavours of the Crusade, and most tellingly those of his brother and liege lord?'

In the silence that followed, Bohemund recalled his talk with Robert of Salerno regarding what he had proposed to say to Baldwin, very much what he had just expounded, the younger man convinced that all his lord would get was an insulting refusal. Yet no man likes to be seen as a pariah and no knight would ever want to carry to his grave the reputation now attached to Baldwin's name, one that could so easily be tarnished further.

The whole of Christendom knew that he had deserted the Crusade and that meant he had repudiated those most solemn vows which, should he return home, would see him brayed at in the street as an apostate and a traitor. Even if he never departed from Edessa, that was not a stain to easily carry, and on top of that what had happened at Tarsus would be a subject of discussion in all territories from which the Crusaders had come, something Bohemund could easily foster.

What Bohemund had not said to Robert was that in some senses the same opprobrium might be attached to him for there were many who saw his attachment to Antioch as a less than faithful adherence to those same undertakings. If he was dangling redemption of reputation before Baldwin, there was an element of the same for him in the approach.

'Do you foresee battle?' Baldwin asked finally.

'Would such a thing trouble you?'

'Not if it was the Turk battering himself against my walls.'

'More than that is required, you must make a demonstration towards the lands of our enemies. I think them cowed but if they do rise up to dispute with you...'

'And you, Bohemund, and you!' Baldwin insisted. 'It is we both or nothing.'

'Why am I here if that is not so? If they do attack you, then you have the walls to retire to, as have I, but in doing that they are not attacking Jerusalem and we will have done what is needed to give our confrères a fair wind. Let the news run back to Rome that you have acted to aid your brother and the others. The priests will see it is spread through all of Europe, that Baldwin, Count of Edessa, was and still is a Crusader.'

The light in Baldwin's eyes then was proof

351

enough that the prospect was to him an alluring one, a chance for redemption in the eyes of people he probably despised, yet whose good opinion he wished to have. Then those eyes narrowed and the glow he had manifested faded, to be replaced, Bohemund thought, with a way of behaviour and a mode of speech more akin to his true nature.

'Do not ever again address me,' he growled, 'without you favour me with the title of Count of Edessa.'

Bohemund just nodded, for that was as good as a yes to that for which he was asking. Then he called for wine to be fetched, so that the two could toast to the success of the siege of Jerusalem, before calling for one of the priests he had brought along – no large body of crusading knights rode anywhere without the addition of a divine – to both say a Mass for Baldwin's men and his own and publicly state by vow that they would act as had been agreed for the greater glory of God.

Bohemund might have been smiling throughout all this, but as he said to Robert when Baldwin had departed, 'I nearly choked sharing wine with that viper and, God willing, I will slice the throat by which he gobbled it down if I find he had any hand in the killing of my men.'

'And you think he will keep to that which he just swore?'

'Yes. Even Lucifer himself likes to be seen as a fallen saint, capable of redemption.'

Baldwin was true to his vow. He, like Bohemund,

sought no great battle, nor did he take possession of any of the strongholds, those that lay close to his borders, still in Turkish hands. But by their joint manoeuvres the two magnates kept those Turks who might have been tempted to make for Jerusalem within their walls. Such lords were fearful that, at any moment, a combined force from Edessa and Antioch might appear before their walls to invest their own cities. Even Baghdad and the Abbasid Sultan remained cautious and inactive.

CHAPTER TWENTY-FOUR

Having those Genoese sailors and their nautical tools – short saws, adzes, chisels and mallets – provided only a partial solution and was, on its own, insufficient to progress the siege of Jerusalem. They could work with planking as well as being able to turn short lengths of timber into the dowels necessary to secure heavily pressured joints. But siege towers required them to also fashion great baulks of wood for both the base and the platform supports. Added to that was a fair amount of metalwork, the latter less of an obstacle given the army marched with armourers and blacksmiths.

Long lengths of tree trunk, and also of the required thickness, were at the heart of the process and these had to be cut down, then formed to the required dimensions, which entailed the use of two-man saws, with one cutter required to work from above, the other below in a pit dug for the purpose and that process would have to wait; these were the same instruments needed to gather the material in the first place.

It proved yet another indication of how split was the Crusade that the princes could not combine to construct the apparatus needed to carry out the task before them, even to the point of gathering the required timber. Not that acquiring that was easy; the kind of wood needed, from a long-matured and untouched forest, lay several leagues distant and that necessitated a major detachment of mounted fighting men to escort the *milities* designated as woodcutters.

Flanders and Normandy went forth on behalf of Godfrey de Bouillon, Toulouse trusting to Bishop Peter of Narbonne who, if he was a cleric, was also a good administrator and fighter. More grist to the mill of argument came from the man Raymond chose as his master builder, William Embriaco, for in doing so he offended Gaston of Béarn, hitherto a strong supporter of the Provençal faction and a man famed for his ability in the craft of building weapons of war – Gaston immediately transferred both his allegiance and skills to Godfrey de Bouillon.

If such endeavours put an end to assaults on the walls, the teeming and visible activity before the twin encampments sent a clear message to the city of the determination of the Crusaders to eventually press home their attack. The air was filled with the sound of woodworking, the clang of blacksmiths' hammers as well as the smell of the pitch and glue being used to coat the timbers and to secure the various joints.

In addition, men more accustomed to war, working alongside the many thousands of pilgrims who toiled for their love of God, put their hands to cutting and plaiting brushwood with which to protect the triple platforms on which they would later want to fight, those covered with animal skins that did not easily catch fire, for the standard first defence against such a weapon, in the hope of stopping it before it could be set against the walls, was to set it alight with flaming arrows.

The next form of defence was toppling, using grappling irons to fix on and pull over an inherently unstable construct. To avert this, each tower would be provided with detachable outriggers – long lengths of timber that set into the ground on either side and locked into a position on the whole from which they could only be manually removed. These outriggers rendered the towers both stable and immovable, yet there was always a time before they could be secured in place where the construct was vulnerable.

Such precautions did not obviate the inherent problems that came with the employment of siege towers: it was obvious that, with their huge fixed wheels, they could only be rolled to the point of contact in a straight line, this along a path cleared of any stones and depressions that required to be filled in. Thus the defenders knew to the width of a couple of pikes where the attack would come, allowing them to strengthen their own defences in anticipation.

Raymond was building his before and slightly to the north of the Zion Gate, which left the Fatimid defenders in no doubt where it would strike, while added to that there was the dry ditch over which it had to be pushed. That needed to be filled in, a problem Raymond of Toulouse solved by the offer of a copper penny to any man who was willing to rush forward, mostly in the dark of night when the only light came from battlement torches, to cast a stone into the void. It was a task eagerly taken up by the pilgrims, who still, when it came to sustenance, were obliged to purchase it where they could.

That was not the only expense Raymond was obliged to undertake – so unpopular had he become that he was having to pay even his own men, as well as pilgrims, to work on his weaponry and also use dragooned Muslim slaves, in a situation where Godfrey was happily employing willing volunteers.

On his behalf and before the Quadrangular Tower, Gaston of Béarn was supervising the building of Godfrey's tower, and those working on it could see the men they would later face placing long wooden barbs through the ramparts, no doubt well anchored behind them, which they hoped would keep Gaston's tower from contact with the walls until it could be destroyed.

Neither Embriaco or Béarn was willing to rely solely on their towers; mangonels were also constructed to fire both rocks and balls of flaming cloth and rope soaked with pitch, which would be employed to keep the defenders away from the primary points of assault. Prior to that, heavier weapons would batter the walls in the hope of creating a breach.

To further split the defence there was a fearsome battering ram – a huge baulk of timber with dozens of handholds drilled right through and tipped with a metal barb – that would move forward under a bombardment screen and seek to drive in one of the gates. There were endless ladders and climbing frames, as well as wattle panels behind which armed men could advance with some degree of safety prior to climbing to engage.

The noise of construction was not the only sound to fill the air outside the Holy City; it was almost as if, having got to Jerusalem in rancour, the princes needed a new dispute to keep alive their spirits and this one was Antioch all over again. Who, when the city fell and the hallowed places were in Christian hands, should be the person tasked with defending what would become a prime target for recovery by the Muslims?

Pious protestations of holding the city for the faith did little to hide another reason for seeking guardianship; there was also the usual one of greed, carefully concealed under more openly expressed and pious concerns. Revenues from the flood of pilgrims that would flock to the Holy City once it was in Christian hands would be enough to dwarf the income of Rome itself, and whoever had title to Jerusalem would also have its coffers.

Naturally Raymond favoured himself as the

prime candidate, seemingly, due to his arrogance, unaware, even if the evidence of it was staring him in the face, that he would never get the role by acclamation. Lords with more sense did not openly aspire, even if they held secret hopes that a stalemate between Godfrey de Bouillon, the only other viable candidate, and Toulouse would entail an agreement on a compromise nominee.

Thus the two Roberts, Normandy and Flanders, refused to come down on one side or the other while Tancred used his position of being a junior magnate to claim he lacked the position to even take part in any decision; Gaston of Béarn was too busy with construction to even consider attending. Yet opposition to the very idea of a layperson being given the role of guardian was vociferously challenged from the churchmen; even Peter of Narbonne went against his liege lord on the matter, though he chose another target to make his point.

'Is it not an indication of how unbecoming such a notion is that we have within our councils a man who does not fear to hoist his standard over one of the most, if not *the* most holy place in Christendom? I refer to the Church of the Nativity in Bethlehem. By what right does a man not consecrated place a temporal banner on a religious site?'

'Bishop Peter,' Tancred replied, for the accusation was levelled at him, 'you have clearly not yet visited Bethlehem.'

'What does it matter that I have not?'

'If you had,' came the response, 'you would see

that there are few buildings of any size other than the church. How else can it be signalled to any Muslim seeking to recapture it that Bethlehem is defended, without they see a Crusader banner?'

Raymond's personal confessor, a namesake cleric who hailed from Aguilers, spoke up and with scant courtesy, a manner obviously approved of by his nodding master. Toulouse was a man strong in grievances who made little secret that he now saw Tancred as both greedy, treacherous and still, even if it was not openly made obvious, a liegeman of Bohemund.

'That, Lord Tancred, is a piece of sheer sophistry. Had you hoisted a Crusader cross above the church your argument might carry some merit, as it is any thinking man can only see the avarice of possession.'

The reply was icy. 'Your cloth protects you from the consequences of such an accusation, Aguilers, but I would not wish to hear it from any lips not consecrated.'

'I am sure you acted without wickedness,' insisted Godfrey, before anyone else could be foolish enough to speak.

There was no one in the room who could fight Tancred and be sure that they would emerge from the encounter in one piece; if he was not quite Bohemund, there was not a great difference in either his regard for his reputation or his ability with weapons.

'Our cleric does not understand war and the needs that press upon us in such situations.'

'On the contrary, Duke Godfrey,' Aguilers replied. 'We understand only too well.'

Peter of Narbonne took up the argument. 'My colleague refers to that of which there seems a reluctance to speak, namely the spoils that will accrue from Jerusalem if it falls.'

'*When* it falls,' growled his master, who was obviously far from pleased that a man he had elevated to a bishopric was taking what he saw as sides against his claims.

'That, My Lord, is in God's hands,' Peter replied sonorously, but he had a sharp rejoinder to add. 'As should be the monies that will accrue to the holder of the city. I say that should be a man of the cloth, for, without that, ambition will ever triumph over the needs of our faith.'

'Is this discussion not premature?' asked Godfrey, with a sigh.

'As it was at Antioch, perhaps?' Raymond snapped. 'I have no mind to have my rights trampled here as they were there.'

'Trampled, Lord Raymond,' Tancred replied. 'I think you agreed, in a council no different to this one, that whosoever opened the city to capture should have title to it.'

Robert of Normandy, hitherto silent, spoke up, cutting off any response from Toulouse, who was no doubt about to reprise what was now a redundant discussion.

'Which tells me that what we decide here may well not hold once the city is ours. Should we not convene to decide such a weighty matter at a time when our deliberations will have a true and pressing purpose, namely when Jerusalem is ours?'

'I can think of a very good reason why delay might suit Normandy,' Raymond snapped.

'While I can see no purpose in you, My Lord, pressing your case for a position that you cannot now aspire to.'

That was like a slap and Toulouse took it in that fashion, almost physically recoiling to have his lack of support so publicly stated. But the Duke was not finished and proved that he was also capable of showing he had a good understanding of the needs of diplomacy.

'Perhaps by your deeds you may stand head and shoulders above us all when Jerusalem is overcome; I should add that will be an opportunity that falls to us all. Let us then wait to see if an act of outstanding valour elevates one of our number higher than the rest, for surely that would be by God's divine intervention.'

Invoking the Almighty was enough to terminate any further argument from nobles and clerics alike, but only for the moment; it was necessary that they meet often to discuss how the assault was to be pressed home and no such gathering could convene without at some point the vexed subject of guardianship being raised.

If the Crusaders were working to perfect the weapons of assault, the defenders were just as occupied in counter-measures. Sure of the places at which the towers would make contact they moved their own mangonels to batter them with rocks in the hope of killing the attacking knights.

Noting that some of the Crusaders' heavier

ballistae were of a size to batter their walls, that was countered by the hanging of skeins of thick knotted rope from the battlements, as well as sacks filled with wheat chaff, both to deaden the impact.

Added to that, if there was a lack of actual attacks to keep the whole in a state of nervousness, there was no shortage of attempts at terrorisation. One of Godfrey's cousins, le Bourg, on a foraging expedition captured a venerable Muslim, a noble-looking fellow of advanced years and some eminence, for when he was paraded before the garrison of Jerusalem it was clear he was recognised. Not that such recognition altered his fate; to show them the destiny that awaited those watching, given he had refused to convert to Christianity he was summarily beheaded.

A Fatimid spy caught trying to slip into Jerusalem was crudely tortured for information, not that anything he provided would affect his ultimate fate. He was tied to one of the heavier mangonels that was hauled to full torsion, then released, to send his body, it was hoped, over the battlements. As an experiment it was not a complete failure: if he did not overreach the walls it was moot if the result was any more comforting, for he crashed into the stone face, then fell onto the rocks below, his neck broken and his body shattered.

The Fatimids were short on the means to reply in kind, but they were just as keen to trouble their enemies, who – and to their mind this was blasphemy – used symbols in their religion. Thus crucifixes were hung upside down from the ramparts, onto which, in full view of the Crusaders, the Muslims spat and urinated, acts that aroused, at least to them, a pleasing amount of loud fury.

In the midst of continuing mutual antagonism, there was no shortage of preachers willing to see in their dreams and visions portents that warned of either disaster or glorious victory. One, yet another Peter, this time called Desiderius, claimed to have been granted a revelation by none other than the late and sainted Adémar, Bishop of Puy. Given he was close to Raymond of Toulouse, who had sought to use the memory of the papal legate to replace the failure to inspire by the discredited Holy Lance, his prophetic messages were greeted with some scepticism.

'I see us plagued with too many Peters,' Tancred opined, on his way to the pavilion in which the council met, well aware of what was to be discussed. 'There must be some pile of ordure out of which they do not crawl.'

Flanders, who felt the same way, laughed. 'Perhaps, one day, we will truly be granted a miracle.'

'If there was one thing my Uncle Bohemund taught me it was that it was folly to even think the Lord might actually intervene in a battle. He saw it as the stuff of the deluded.'

'Even after Antioch?'

Tancred patted his right arm. 'That was won with these, Robert – it was not due to some flaming vision that we triumphed, regardless of what our divines say.'

Yet for all their doubts regarding that to which

they were about to be exposed, both men knew that lip service had to be paid to such notions when they came from such preaching sources. They believed with all their hearts in the divine oversight of God the Almighty and were sure he did play a part in their endeavours. When they celebrated Mass it was in the sure knowledge that he could see into their hearts and judge their motives, and if at times they were less than pure, then all they could do was seek his all-encompassing forgiveness.

To kill was a sin, yet they did it as a vocation, sure that the slaying of God's enemies would be seen not with condemnation, but as a route to salvation. It was in the manifestation of that forgiveness and insight that they held doubts: the Holy Trinity, the Blessed Virgin and all the saints would bless their sword arm as they used them to press home the true faith, but did such messages as might be sent to them come as a flaming horseman riding to their support on the field of battle, as had been claimed so many times, or through the certainties of preachers like Desiderius or Bartholomew?

'The meaning of my dream was obvious,' Desiderius insisted. 'Adémar demands that we find harmony in our endeavour and he seeks this in death just as he did in life.'

'Amen,' intoned Narbonne, crossing himself, an act and expression dutifully followed by all present. 'Therefore he insists we must fast, we must look into our inner souls and see what is there. Is it truly that we are here before Jerusalem in the service of our Lord God, or are you great lords here merely to add lustre to your names and riches to your strongbox? Alms must be donated to show that is a false accusation, yet some of the host are so sinful, as are the pilgrims who look to me for guidance, that nothing short of scourging by whipping will cleanse them.'

'Harmony we need,' Godfrey exclaimed, his eyes alight with a genuine fervour that aroused nothing but admiration in those observing. 'Tell us, Peter Desiderius, how it is to be found.'

The solution, according to the preacher, was a procession in which all would participate regardless of rank. This would be carried out barefoot and in solemn and continuous prayer, each man examining his own soul for the sins that resided there, for no man was without it. Trumpets and horns would blow and perhaps, as at Jericho, the walls would crack and tumble.

'Will it be so,' cried Godfrey, with such passion he seemed about to go into a frenzy.

Desiderius seemed to realise he had gone too far and the offer of crumbling walls was withdrawn on the grounds that Jerusalem was not Jericho and he was not Joshua. But there would be feet washing, with noble dukes and counts, as well as high church divines emulating Jesus Christ, who did not so fear to humble himself with the lowly.

Such supplications agreed, the procession set out on a sunlit morning to march round the walls to the Mount of Olives, threatening the jeering garrison with what weapons they bore, there to watch Godfrey very willingly, Raymond reluctantly and the rest of the lords with manufactured zeal, wash the feet of the meanest pilgrim peasants Desiderius could identify. Mass was said on the spot of Christ's resurrection and the nobles were called forward to make peace with each other in the sight of his grace.

To much rejoicing Godfrey, expression alight, embraced Raymond who then shook arms with Tancred, both men vowing to aid the other to the point of death if need be, an undertaking repeated to Normandy, Flanders and Gaston of Béarn. All around, anything that smacked of enmity was being put aside, Apulians swearing loyalty to Provence and vice versa, the pledging of their souls and their blood by both to the knights of Lotharingia.

Shriven and feeling bolstered by the obvious grace of God, the procession made its way back to their lines. The Fatimids showed how much they cared for what had taken place and how much such obvious faith affected them by showering the march with arrows and catapulted rocks, killing several of the worshippers, including several priests.

'Two days hence,' Godfrey swore, 'you will pay for that insult to us and to God.'

'We will strip the skin off their bones,' Raymond added, his arm clasped in that of his so recent rival. 'They cannot see into our souls, but we will see into theirs.'

CHAPTER TWENTY-FIVE

The Fatimids knew the Crusaders were coming long before dawn, just from the noise of their preparations, added to the amount of darting torchlight that had illuminated their night-time activity. They were at their places while it was still dark, sweating on what was a hot and humid mid-July night, nervously awaiting the final sound that would bring on the assault – the sound of the battle horns blowing the advance.

First the sky took on a hint of grey, which failed to provide enough light to show the ground before the walls or the great hulking silhouettes of the towers before the Quadrangular Tower and the Zion Gate. The gradual increase in the level of daylight did begin to touch the upper frame of the siege engine built by Raymond of Toulouse.

But the men facing the expected attack from the contingents led by Godfrey de Bouillon were confounded by the absence of what they expected to see, until it became obvious that before the Quadrangular Tower the ground was completely clear – Godfrey's siege engine had disappeared and so had his entire encampment; all that was now visible was the clear pathway along which the defenders had anticipated the siege tower would advance.

News was swift to arrive that the very construct was now being hurriedly assembled before the St

Stephen's Gate, a story initially disbelieved by every Fatimid commander from Iftikhar ad-Daulah down, for what they were being told was that the impossible had occurred. Only the man on the spot knew it to be the undoubted truth for he could see the very same lengths of timber being put together by a positive army of willing hands furiously wielding hammers.

In employing Gaston of Béarn, the Lotharingian Duke Godfrey had been gifted a craftsman of genius, a man who had built siege towers many times before in his life and thought long and hard on ways to improve their efficiency. The better axles he had designed made it possible to move it more quickly – not that it was ever swift – giving the defence less time to interdict its progress, but that did not obviate the major tactical flaw, the need to move it in a straight line from its start position to its final deployment.

Try as he might Gaston had never been able to come up with what he so keenly sought, a way of turning off a true course an engine that weighed several tons, for the leverage to change direction was beyond human endeavour. But in Godfrey he had found a magnate willing to experiment and had been given leave to put together a tower that, in the space of a dark night, could be dismantled to its very base, the last part of which was of a weight that men were able to man-oeuvre.

Since it was put back together with like speed it was now taking proper shape opposite a section of the walls of Jerusalem ill-prepared to receive it, and at the same time, protected by framed wattle bombardment screens, men, women and children, no doubt the pilgrims so eager to see the Holy City fall, were progressing forward, levelling out, by clearing and filling, the new ground over which the tower must now pass, which led directly to the easternmost tower that framed the St Stephen's Gate.

Before the sun was far above the rim of the horizon the engine itself was on the move, the great wheels grinding across the earth to send forth a terrifying sound, yet it was halted well before it came within range of the defences, the hope being that by seeing it so close it would instil greater fear, this while the mangonels, also moved from before the Quadrangular Tower, moved well forward of the tower and began to fire their deadly missiles to subdue what was a scratch defence, given Iftikhar ad-Daulah had yet to sanction the movement of the men needed to meet this shocking development.

The only part-protection they had, set to either side of the St Stephen's Gate, was a low curtain wall that made any approach to the main fortifications impossible and to counter that Godfrey was about to employ the great battering ram. The Fatimids would have assumed it to be used to pummel against one of the wooden gates, to the mind of such men as Gaston uselessly, given gates had been buttressed since time immemorial to withstand such a weapon.

Now its purpose was clear, if not its progress, for it was a beast of an edifice to move; where the huge wheels of a siege tower could, by their sheer dimensions and the numbers employed in moving

369

it, overcome obstacles, the smaller orbs on the battering ram meant even the most minor impediment, even a small stone, was a problem. Yet as the men on that struggled forward, the inner walls and undermanned ramparts were peppered with missiles – rocks and balls of burning sulphur and pitch bound with wax, designed to make any counterstroke hazardous.

With a supreme effort, and this by heavily muscled knights more accustomed to wielding personal weapons, the ram was brought close enough to the outer curtain to be employed. Eschewing protection the men pushing got it up to the speed of a fast walk, so that when the metal tip hit the stonework, secured only by mortar, it went crashing straight through, filling the intervening space with rubble into which the defence, fearful of being immediately overcome, poured their own incendiaries, that wasted as an effort at killing since none of the Crusaders could cross the area due to the fallen stonework.

What it did do was set the ram alight: the great single block of timber would have needed a great deal of time and inflammables to cause it to catch fire, but it was full of staves driven through from one side to the other, this the means by which it had been pushed forward. Those lighter pieces of timber went up quickly and threatened to carry the fire to the inner part of the ram, which had the alarmed Crusaders rushing to douse the whole with water before the massive tree trunk could ignite, this being carried out under a constant rain of arrows.

The Crusader effort proved fruitless even if

the flames were doused. The aim was to repeat the battering exercise against the main wall and likewise drive that in to make a breach, which would, when the siege tower was employed, further divide the defence, given men would have to man both the upper parapet and breach in a situation that would make mutual support impossible.

Yet not only was the head of the ram buried by masonry, the very success of the initial effort had made any further forward movement impossible. Try as they might, and most of the rest of the day was thus employed, there was no amount of force which could get those small wheels over the mound of debris and it was clear that if it was left there it would be right in the path of the siege tower when that was employed.

Orders were sent forward to set alight a weapon the flames of which the men who had been pushing it had only just managed to extinguish, which led to what many saw as a farce. With Crusaders seeking to set it alight, the Fatimids, who wished it, for obvious reasons, to remain an obstacle, sought by throwing great tubs of water over it to snuff out the flames. So it became a battle to keep it burning, this finally achieved when the whole was so much ablaze that no amount of drowning could put out the conflagration.

That accomplished, Godfrey's men withdrew, the fight being over for the day. If there was disappointment, the employment of the ram had been a positive, for the under-resourced defence had used against it weapons that would have been better employed against the real and soon-to-be-employed threat, Gaston of Béarn's siege tower.

Raymond of Toulouse had, unbeknown to him or his knights, always had the harder task, given that the Fatimids had assumed his attack to be the main effort, while that on the formidable and easily defended Quadrangular Tower was seen as a diversion, which proved that if they had got wind of Crusader dissension, they had failed to make sense of it. These leading magnates were men who were barely talking to each other with civility, never mind leaders coordinating a winning strategy.

Godfrey's surprise had thrown that notion to the winds, yet on the previous assumption the Provençals were attacking the best and most comprehensively organised resistance, with the walls well protected by ropes and filled sacks against the rock-throwing ballistae and sharpened baulks of timber protruding from the fortifications at the point at which they knew for certain Raymond's siege tower must come upon the ramparts.

Here also the Fatimids had concentrated the mass of their mangonels and the majority of their archers and they were targeted on what was a very narrow field of battle, the known line by which Raymond's siege tower would progress. That he had a clear run to the main defence – there was no outer curtain wall to impede him here – proved a small positive against such a ferocious attempt to counter his advance.

High-fired stones rained down on the heads of

those pushing the tower as well as the men following behind it, the engine itself, once within range, being hit by flaming arrows and burning bolts, soon added to this wooden hammers wrapped in pitch-soaked straw and studded with nails so that they would adhere to whatever they struck. Those fighting men not on the tower were advancing under an endless bombardment but it was the siege engine, and those at the very top, that would decide the fate of the attack.

Raymond's main weapon was placed under such relentless bombardment that following several hours of pushing it had still not reached the wall alongside the Zion Gate and, despite all the precautions to avoid it happening, it was alight in many places, so much so that Raymond ordered his men to pull it back out of danger so the fires could be dealt with – without the presence of their main assault weapon that meant a withdrawal of the whole of his forces.

That night it was hard to find anyone not too exhausted to stand guard, this being a must lest the Fatimids sortie out in a surprise raid, even harder to find those willing to risk their lives by going forward in torchlight to clear as much as possible of the larger pieces of rubble that had fallen into the path of the siege tower from that destroyed curtain wall.

Every captain and fighting man, as well as those who were mere labourers, was weary from the efforts of a day of combat and, even if it was kept to mumbles of disgruntlement around their cooking fires, alarmed at the ferocity of the defence they had faced. It was the task of leaders like Tancred, despite his own fatigue, to move amongst his men and point out that if they were dispirited, so must be their enemies, well aware that the coming dawn would see the attack renewed.

In Godfrey's camp there was no gratification to hear that their Provençal confrères had fared worse than they, suffering more casualties and an even more spectacular reverse. For the men before the St Stephen's Gate it was to be hoped they would succeed if for no other reason than to make easier their own assault. Yet there was true fellow feeling to add to that – the whole could not enjoy any triumph if one part failed.

Before dawn they were awakened to eat a breakfast of gruel and to say their prayers, many seeking out a priest to bless them as a habit before battle. Then, as the light again touched the eastern horizon, the horns blew and Godfrey's men took their places around Gaston's great siege tower, which would, this day, either prove its worth or, like Raymond's, miserably fail.

In its favour, Gaston's tower was a much more formidable construct, three storeys in height and with a few more of his innovations, which would only prove their worth when tested. Godfrey de Bouillon would not hear that any other man should take the lead, so he was on the top level, under the golden cross banner so beloved by the faithful, when the tower began to slowly grind forward again, before them, again under bombardment screens, a mass of people clearing the last of the rubble as well as the ashes and charred remains of their battering ram.

In choosing to move to the St Stephen's Gate there had been several considerations much discussed by Godfrey and his fellow magnates, the two Roberts and Tancred. First it was a relative weak spot in an otherwise stout defence, but it was also, on the reverse side of the walls, a place much crowded with buildings and one in which the streets were really alleyways, too narrow to allow the Fatimids to deploy their mangonels.

This meant these weapons could only be employed on the actual ramparts and right below the fighting parapet, which entailed them sending most of what they discharged in a high arc, which of necessity reduced their range. More important to the advance of the siege tower, that range was fixed, so that once it covered a certain amount of the intervening ground it would be impossible for the defence to employ large objects to impede its progress.

Raymond of Toulouse attacked again at dawn, just like Godfrey, for the second day pushing forward his tower and in receipt of the same response; in fact, if anything the defence was even more ferocious, an indication that the Fatimids knew that the slightest breach could lead to destruction. Every man that Iftikhar had, it was expected, would be on the walls and now in both places they would be required to engage in a test of will as much as warfare; the Crusaders could not fight without respite and another day of reverses might kill off their fervour for the battle.

The same anticipation lay within the besiegers; these were the men who had defended the walls of Antioch against Kerbogha and they knew only too well how debilitating that could be, a constant daily effort that sapped both the will to fight and the degree of faith they reposed in the spirituality of their cause. What they had once experienced would apply to those defending Jerusalem; all that was needed was that the Crusade impose its will.

For Raymond the second day was an even greater debacle than the first; again he and his men advanced into a hail of stones and arrows, the rocks from the Muslim mangonels large enough to crush any shield as well as the man holding it up as protection. Drop the shield a fraction to see what was coming and there were sharp-eyed archers skilled enough to choose a now exposed target, a task made easier the closer the attack came.

But again it was Raymond's siege tower that bore the brunt of the retaliation, the same methods employed as the day before to set it alight in so many places that it see-sawed back and forth, dragged just out of range of more fire so that those already alight could be doused. That achieved it was pushed forward once more, but another difficulty began to manifest itself.

Regardless of what carpentry skills were employed, such a construct, built in such a place, had to be flawed. No amount of effort could take all the potential hazards out of the ground over which it must travel, and to the men at the top, not only in the most danger, it seemed to sway alarmingly and that put a heavy strain on joints that were secured by no more than glued and hammered-in wooden dowels. Fire also led to structural weakness and the tower before the Zion Gate had been set ablaze several times.

In the end it was the combination that caused the tower to partially collapse, leading to a hurried exodus by those manning the top levels, few because the greater the number the higher the weight that had to be moved. Slowly, with much creaking, Raymond's tower began to sag and if it was still capable of being employed, no exhortations of his or even offers of gold could get his men to trust to it, for the very simple reason that if it fell apart completely, and it looked as if it might, then those fighters manning it would be doomed to die in the wreckage.

In the fog of war the failure of Raymond's attack looked like a setback too far; there was no point in the construction of a replacement tower, never mind the time it would take to build, given the way the first one had so spectacularly failed. Added to that, such a fiasco could only embolden the defenders, given the part morale played in battle.

Yet through that thick mist, if only the Count of Toulouse could have gazed, he would have seen that the two-pronged attack, albeit brought about by discord rather than strategy, had achieved more than was obviously visible.

Godfrey de Bouillon nearly died well before his tower got anywhere near the northern wall, where it adjoined the gate tower, the top of that set at a slightly higher elevation than the ramparts. The man standing beside him on the top platform, employed by archers to suppress the defence, was killed instantly by a huge rock that crushed his head and cracked his neck like an eggshell.

The Duke was holding a crossbow and was quick to retaliate and kill one of his opponents, but even he could see the sense that for him to be in such an exposed position, loading a weapon that took time, was folly: if he fell, such was the regard in which he was held, the whole endeavour might do so as well.

For all that he had to be dragged to the steps that went down to the next level, where he joined Tancred and Robert of Flanders, as well as the party of the twenty knights who would commence the initial assault if the tower could get into the right position. On this platform he was blind, before him a stout wooden screen, riddled with metal spikes on the face that would drop onto the ramparts at the right moment and hopefully pinion some of the defenders. From there he was unable to see if Gaston of Béarn's other innovations were aiding the assault.

The usual practice was to line the exterior of the tower with wattle screens and animal skins, which Gaston had done, but, and this was different, he had made them with stout frames and created angles so that they protruded out from the siege engine on all sides. This rendered useless most of the inflammables hurled at his construct for they glanced off instead of sticking and fell to the ground.

Yet it was nip and tuck as the rocks rained down, for they were harder by far to deflect and some crashed through his defences. Added to that, however well built was Gaston's tower it still had the inherent defects of all such weapons of war. Heavy stones and the movement over uneven ground were likely to put excessive pressure on the joints and cause them to fail.

The fighting men knew when they had reached an arc of relative safety, merely by the diminution of the noise, the lack of thundering cracks as the mangonel rocks fired by the Fatimids battered their crawling conveyance. Yet that also told them they were close, which had knights tensing muscles and taking practice sweeps with their swords, thudding them on the screen before their faces. Tancred, holding his axe in one hand, a lance in the other, remained stationary and in prayer.

'Greek fire!'

That shout had him open his eyes, for there was good reason to be fearful of such a weapon, a fluid that once ignited could not be doused by water. It was a piece of good fortune that had given them information that it might be employed as a last line of defence, this from the Christians Iftikhar had expelled from the city. That made possible for them to have ready the one substance that could counter it: impervious to water it might be but vinegar, which they had in tubs on each floor, was able to quench Greek fire.

An increase in the swaying motion, though it had never been still and was exaggerated by the height at which they stood, told Godfrey and Tancred that they were passing through the gap cleared of rubble where had once stood the curtain wall and the charred remains of their battering ram. Soon it would be time to let go their screen and begin to fight against massively unfavourable odds until behind them more knights would rush up the internal ladders to their aid.

The cry came from those who could see and the men tasked to drop the screen released the ropes that held it in place. Down it crashed onto heads and bodies that could not get clear of its spikes for the numbers crowding onto the parapet eager to engage, their screams of pain the first thing to register. The second thing to register was more sobering, for to their front as they advanced onto that platform stood a mass of screaming Fatimids, who had only one aim: to kill as many of these Latins as they could.

CHAPTER TWENTY-SIX

The first task was to advance to near the leading edge then to hold the platform, which was resting on the very top of the crenellated battlements, not easy as the defenders quickly employed long pikes kept on the parapet to prevent that very manoeuvre, the points of these countered by both broadswords and swinging axes lopping off spikes aimed at taking away their legs. At the same time shields had to be held high to protect against arrows, loosed over Fatimid heads, potentially dangerous given they were being fired at short range.

That meant a tight line in which advance, once

the primary moves had been completed, was secondary; let the enemy die as they sought to clamber up to make contact at a level much higher than their fighting parapet, leaving them vulnerable at a time when their weapons could not be properly employed. That they did so, despite the risks, was either testimony to their zeal or the same quality of those to their rear, so eager to get into battle that they pushed their own men onto the Crusader weapons.

Those initially pierced by a lance, or in a second wave taken by sword and axe, presented a barrier to the mass of their fellows, who solved this problem by seeking to shift them out of their path, regardless of the fact that to do so was to heave them off the platform edge into thin air, the screams of those still living adding to the cacophony of noise, that silenced as they hit the pile of rubble below.

Once fully supported from below, Godfrey, Robert, Tancred and their confrères, the most puissant knights from each of their contingents, could seek to advance, which was carried out in the standard tactic of one pace at a time and that only possible when the whole line could move as one; a dog-leg here was more dangerous now than the same predicament on an open field, until they got to the very edge and from there sought to clear enough space to get onto the walls themselves.

To aid the whole endeavour, Gaston of Béarn had fashioned another innovation, the ability to cast off the wattle screens on the next floor down, deliberately made wider than the top storey, and from there, using extension planks and ladders, to get men onto the flanks in order to stretch a defence that was short on numbers, it being forced to do battle on two fronts so far apart that mutual support was not possible.

That was about to become more telling in a wider sense too: with the siege tower fully employed and sucking in the enemy defenders, the mass of the attackers, hitherto idle, could assault the walls using stout ladders with which to clamber up to the level of the ramparts, the situation and stretched defence giving them a good chance of getting over the battlements and onto the wooden parapet.

Once there in sufficient numbers, complete success became a real possibility, not that it was ever guaranteed, for it was an axiom of such an action that the defence would always outnumber the attackers, and if the Muslims held their nerve and fought with brio, to drive the Latins back off again was achievable. Perception was all: if men thought they were losing, whichever side they were on, they would slacken off their efforts, half concerned with escape rather than wholly committed to victory.

Tancred's height played a part as it always did, his reach being that much greater than those who lined up beside him, which meant he had to show restraint so as not to advance too quickly. But right now it was the billowing smoke blowing across the platform, stinging his eyes and affecting his vision, that seemed the greater problem. Right before him a gap appeared, he having chopped the lower arm of his immediate opponent, who was so immobilised by the loss that he temporarily blocked the way to those at his rear. That allowed for the briefest glance to right and then left, which engendered an immediate shout.

'My Lord Godfrey, look to our left.'

Having made that call Tancred was forced to once more fully engage with the enemy, and with Godfrey likewise fighting hard there was a gap before circumstances allowed him to comply with the cry from the younger man. Yet when he did, what he saw had a similar effect on him: the top of the eastern tower that framed the St Stephen's Gate was emitting a great mass of smoke, which, caught by the wind was blowing across to envelop the combatants.

'Close up!' Godfrey shouted, immediately pulling back, a command obeyed by both Tancred and the knight on de Bouillon's left, Ludolf of Tournai.

Able to retire to a point from which he could assess the situation, the gap the Duke left was quickly filled by a supporting knight from the reserve. This was Ludolf's brother Engelbert, who moved up and called to be allowed to act as a replacement, entering the line with his vigour fresh and his passion for the fight at full stretch.

Godfrey, to get a better view, dropped down one level and, cutting through what remained of the wattle screen, peered out of the side of the siege engine. What he saw lifted his already bubbling spirits: if the gate tower was on fire that meant the interior wooden frame that formed the support for the stonework was ablaze. Such a conflagration, being embedded, would be impossible to extinguish.

If weakened enough, and it would be as the fire progressed, it was only a matter of time before the whole edifice collapsed, which would take with it the supporting pillars of the gate itself, causing that to sag open, thus fully opening the way into the city for the whole mass of Godfrey's fighters. An added danger lay on the wooden parapet on which the defenders fought: that too could catch fire, and being constructed the way it was, with open slats, it would burn quickly and ferociously.

The panicked cries from above, albeit they were in Arabic, indicated to the Duke of Lower Lorraine that he was not alone in seeing the danger and drawing the requisite conclusion. To seek to hold a section of the walls when the means to outflank you were imminent, and the ground beneath your feet could disappear, was madness. A call from one of his knights, telling him that the Fatimids were weakening, posed the possibility for Godfrey that he would not be in action at the most vital moment.

Slashing at the wattle and knocking one of his own men out of the way, he was on a ladder and climbing at a furious scrabble, able to catch sight of his men, now standing on the very top of the ramparts. By the time he joined them they were on the parapet, now doing combat with an enemy that seemed more intent on disengagement than continued resistance.

All along the battlements the men led by Godfrey, Robert of Flanders and Tancred were pushing over the crest of the walls and occupying a

wooden fighting platform on which only tho
trapped by the inability to get clear were still cor
testing the ground. Massively outnumbered, the
were to die for that, while it soon became appar
ent that the remainder of their comrades had
fled.

Before the Zion Gate, Raymond of Toulouse was
seeking by personal example to inspire an attack
rapidly running out of energy. His voice was
hoarse from shouting that his men should continue to advance in the face of a defence that had
not lost one iota of its power since the previous
day. If anything it seemed more potent. There
was no weakening of Raymond's sword arm for it
had yet to be employed; no one, him included,
could get close enough to the walls.

With his siege tower unusable – his men refused
to enter it and climb – there were only ladders
with which to seek to overcome the Egyptians,
that and the rocks fired by his lighter mangonels
and they were as nothing compared to what the
Fatimids were raining down in response on his
stuttering advance.

Much as he hated to contemplate retirement
there seemed little choice, and in doing so he
knew he would be faced with a complete rethink
of the ways needed to take the city, which was
complicated by the fact that time must be short.
The Vizier al-Afdal must be aware that the city
was besieged and that would force him to leave
Cairo and come to its rescue. The Crusade, still
without the walls of Jerusalem, faced possibly a
worse dilemma than they had at Antioch.

Suddenly the air, which had been full of rocks and arrows, was clear of both. Looking up at the battlements there were no heads peering over, bows at the ready and eyes roving to pick a target. It took time to register, time before the advance broke from a stumbling walk into a run, men amazed, none more so than Raymond himself, that they could raise their ladders without interference, even more so when that applied to their ascent and the crossing of the ramparts themselves.

The parapet, when they occupied it, was empty, which induced an amazed pause as the likes of Raymond sought to glean some meaning from what had just occurred. It did not take too long to realise that the defence had collapsed because it was breached elsewhere, which meant Godfrey and his men were inside Jerusalem, and with a head start on the sack of the city. From the fervour of battle, it soon became the Provençal purpose to be equally dedicated to the pursuit of plunder.

Jerusalem paid a high price for its resistance, with later chroniclers, such as Aguilers, seeking to exalt the success, claiming that ten thousand Muslims gave up their lives to appease God. That this was an untruth was not allowed to interfere with the glory of the capture of the Holy City, yet there were those who later spoke the truth: if that number died, to be eventually burnt in great mounds outside the walls, the frames of the siege engines used as kindling, there were as many Christian victims as Muslims.

The sack was brutal as every Crusader sought personal enrichment, many succeeding given Jerusalem was a place full of the means to do so: rich in gold, even more so than in metal, as well as silver, fashioned into objects designed to venerate the memory of Jesus Christ, a massive number given as gifts by pilgrims that had preceded the Crusade in more peaceful times.

Following the frenzy of acquisition men would later gather to pray and hear Mass in the Church of the Holy Sepulchre, a church from which they were quick to eject any who adhered to another branch of the Christian faith – Armenians, Copts, Nestorians and Maronites. They did not ask for forgiveness for the acts of barbarity which they had just carried out: houses invaded and left wrecked, women ravaged, babies dashed against pillars and young children slain, bodies of both sexes sliced open to seek any wealth that might have been consumed to hide it from view.

The Crusaders did not see the need: what they had done had been carried out for the greater glory of the god they worshipped and one who had shown them divine favour, not a single worshipper present doubting this to be an absolute truth. Three years had passed since they took their crusading vows and left their homes, hearths and wives to fulfil that pledge, three years in which they travelled a thousand leagues, conquered disease, hunger, battle, despair and the elements. How else could they have overcome such obstacles without that their God had strengthened their resolve as well as the arms with which they wielded their blessed weapons?

Conquest did not end dispute, for there still existed the vexed question of to whom control of Jerusalem should devolve. The churchmen demanded it be a divine, yet that faltered on the fact that there was no one of sufficient stature to fill the office of bishop, a man who could command the necessary respect.

In a break with previous intentions, and at the instance of both Godfrey de Bouillon and Raymond, one cleric called Arnulf was appointed to the See of Jerusalem. He being bound to take Mass in the Roman rite, that was a message to Byzantium and the Emperor Alexius Comnenus that whatever vows had been taken in Constantinople were now void.

Secular dissension was unabated: Raymond of Toulouse, always with an eye on how to exert pressure on his confrères, had quickly occupied the Tower of David, into which Iftikhar ad-Daulah had fled with his best troops, a detachment of Egyptian cavalry. In order to secure it peacefully, Raymond had given Iftikhar and his men safe passage to the west, which was seen as folly, given any attempt at recapture must come from that direction.

Not that Raymond was bothered: the Tower of David acted as the citadel of Jerusalem as much as that which Bohemund had held fast did for Antioch. Without it the Holy City was not secure and when called upon to give it up, Toulouse refused, still hoping that by his action he could claim title to the whole. In this he was thwarted by his own unpopularity set against that of the man who could claim to have engineered the capture.

Godfrey de Bouillon was the choice of the host for his personal piety. A degree of political wisdom had him listen to the priests who insisted that no man should allow himself to be called 'King' in the city of which God was the only sovereign. Accepting the title of Advocate of the Holy Sepulchre, he knew that what he had taken on was a fief in all but name, a wealthy one and one that would require to be defended: it was a prize of incalculable importance to three faiths.

In a huff Raymond decamped to an encampment in Jericho, leaving the Tower of David to be held by Bishop Peter of Narbonne; he promptly betrayed the man who had favoured him with the See of Albara and handed it over to Godfrey. Yet Jerusalem was not secure: scouting to the west, Tancred had caught wind of a huge army landing and gathering around the port of Ascalon. It was under the personal command of the Vizier of Cairo and further enquiry produced the alarming proportion that the Crusade, even combined, was outnumbered by a measure of four to one.

'Here I can invoke the name of Bohemund,' Tancred insisted, once more back in the Holy City and able to alert the new advocate to the looming threat. 'If we stay inside the walls of Jerusalem it will be a repeat of what we faced with Kerbogha.'

'Even if the gate of St Stephen is fully repaired?' asked Normandy.

'We overcame it, My Lord, and therefore we

389

must accept that others might follow our example.'

'Do they have our spirit,' Godfrey mused, '... or our ability?'

'What they have is numbers and I would say what my uncle always advocated, if there is to be a battle let us choose the ground on which it is to be fought.'

'And I say let them batter themselves against the walls.'

Nonplussed that Normandy should advocate such a course, Tancred pressed on.

'One of the factors that sustained us during our siege was the sure knowledge that the Fatimids were no more loved than their Turkish predecessors. We expected to hold this city with the good opinion of the inhabitants, but can that be said to be so after the actions of our newly consecrated bishop and his priests?'

Arnulf was present and offended, even more so when Tancred pointed out how, by barring other Christians, who made up the bulk of the population, from the holy sites, he had mightily alienated them. In order to counter his own folly he had 'miraculously' discovered a piece of the True Cross, which to Tancred, his own piety much dented, looked very suspiciously like a repeat of the Holy Lance. Clearly the Jerusalemites felt a similar suspicion, for they had failed to rally to Arnulf's relic.

'We can only adopt the course you advocate, Tancred, if we are joined by Raymond.'

Normandy responded to Godfrey in a manner that, if he shocked him, he did well to disguise. 'I will not march on the news Tancred has brought to us.'

'You do not see the threat?' Godfrey asked.

'I see an army disembarking but I do not see one marching towards us. Unless they do and their intention is clear, why should we countenance the threat as real?'

'I cannot think you believe that,' Flanders exclaimed.

Normally friendly to his brother-in-law, Normandy snapped back. 'Being related to me by matrimony does not give you leave to question my judgement.'

Flanders was not to be put down; his response was just as forceful. 'If I observe any judgement within you, perhaps I would question it, as it is I see nothing but foolishness.'

'I could make you eat those words.'

'You could try.'

'My Lords, I beg of you,' Godfrey cried. 'Let us not bicker.'

'No, let us not,' Normandy replied, 'and to ensure there is no more of such I will withdraw.'

The advocate was left looking at his fellow nobleman's back and Tancred surmised he was thinking that now Godfrey was close to understanding the depth of the task that had so troubled Bishop Adémar of Puy, this as Flanders spoke.

'I agree with Tancred. If we are to meet this vizier let us do so in open battle, where our tactics have always favoured us.'

'You wish to march out and face the Egyptians,' asked Godfrey softly, 'without Toulouse or your kinsman of Normandy?'

'I do. If God's grace got us to where we now stand, I have faith that he will continue to bless us with his favour.'

'I agree,' Tancred said.

'Then let it be so, and may God protect and preserve us.'

Led by the nobles and Bishop Arnulf, parading his piece of the True Cross, barefoot and in prayer, the half-host under Godfrey left Jerusalem to take on the might of Egypt. Such was the shame heaped upon both Robert of Normandy and Raymond of Toulouse by their own followers that both men were obliged, only days later, to lead their forces to join with them at Ramleh, the Provençals still using as a totem the Holy Lance. Jerusalem was stripped of fighting men, left to be held by prayer alone and once more, as on so many occasions, the Crusade was facing either triumph or death.

Luck or divine intervention gave them details of al-Afdal's intentions, this tortured out of a group of captured Egyptian scouts. The Vizier had completed his landings, bringing from his domains a massive force made up of heavy Egyptian cavalry, Berbers, Bedouins and giant Ethiopians. His intention was to march on Jerusalem on the very next day. In the discussion of how to respond, Tancred once more invoked the name of Bohemund, advocating that boldness would outweigh Fatimid numbers.

'We know where they are camped and we know they think themselves invincible,' he insisted, 'and therein lies our best weapon, their own arrogance.'

'Trust a de Hauteville to know all about arrogance,' Raymond of Toulouse cawed.

That got him a jaundiced look from Godfrey de Bouillon, now, even to Raymond's own knights, the undisputed commander of the host. So telling was that glance that the Count of Toulouse had no more to contribute.

'Let us attack him, instead of waiting for him to attack us.'

Flanders demurred. 'Defensive battle suits us.'

'Which al-Afdal well knows. He will anticipate that we will pick a good field on which to fight him and dispose his troops accordingly.'

'And we should do what?' Godfrey asked, his eyes ranging around the pavilion; no one but Tancred responded.

'Attack him at first light.'

It took an age for Godfrey to make a decision, but when he did the words were prophetic. 'May the Good Lord preserve and protect us.'

Marching out in darkness, the host found that in al-Afdal they had an adversary so full of confidence that he had not thought to set out piquets on the outskirts of Ascalon to warn of any hostile approach. Unhindered, the Crusaders fell upon his encampment while many of his men were barely aroused from their night's slumber, their arms stacked still by their campfires and slow to be employed. In a situation where mercy, never in good supply, would have been folly, the slaughter was immense.

Raymond of Toulouse on the right flank, for all his faults a good general, having ridden right through the camp, in the process stealing the Vizier's personal standard, drove the only troops that held their formation, the Egyptian cavalry, into the sea, where men and horses drowned. Godfrey attacking on the left drove his enemies towards the gates of Ascalon, too narrow to permit mass entry and soon closed so that those inside could save themselves. The remainder were butchered on the outside.

Tancred and Robert of Flanders, attacking in the centre, routed the men they faced, many of whom sought to hide in trees and bushes to escape their fate, which was useless: all they became was sport for lance and bow, while those who prostrated themselves and begged were slaughtered like beasts. When the Crusade departed the field they left only corpses on which the carrion could feed. In their train they carried immeasurable wealth, the treasures and possessions of one of the richest rulers in the world.

Under their banner and their holy relics, Godfrey de Bouillon led them in triumph back through the gates of Jerusalem, at his right hand Tancred de Hauteville under his own red flag with its blue and white chequer, now truly, to all who spoke of him, the martial equal of his blood relative Bohemund. To Godfrey's other side rode Raymond of Toulouse, Robert of Normandy and his namesake of Flanders. In their wake came carts laden with such treasure it would not have disgraced a Roman triumph of old.

The Crusade called by Pope Urban at Clermont had fought its last battle and they had won: Jerusalem, the holiest city in the Christian world, was in the hands of men who could now claim, without being challenged, to be the most puissant warriors in the world.

The publishers hope that this book has given you enjoyable reading. Large Print Books are especially designed to be as easy to see and hold as possible. If you wish a complete list of our books please ask at your local library or write directly to:

Magna Large Print Books
Magna House, Long Preston,
Skipton, North Yorkshire.
BD23 4ND

This Large Print Book for the partially sighted, who cannot read normal print, is published under the auspices of

THE ULVERSCROFT FOUNDATION

THE ULVERSCROFT FOUNDATION

... we hope that you have enjoyed this Large Print Book. Please think for a moment about those people who have worse eyesight problems than you ... and are unable to even read or enjoy Large Print, without great difficulty.

You can help them by sending a donation, large or small to:

**The Ulverscroft Foundation,
1, The Green, Bradgate Road,
Anstey, Leicestershire, LE7 7FU,
England.**
or request a copy of our brochure for more details.

The Foundation will use all your help to assist those people who are handicapped by various sight problems and need special attention.

Thank you very much for your help.